FILE 13

by Elizabeth Leavens

I hope
you really enjoy
the book !
Elizabeth Leavens

Dedication

To my parents Jack and Betty Leavens, you are my strength and inspiration.

PROLOGUE

ON NOVEMBER 9, 1989, THE Berlin Wall fell and communism died. On November sixth of the following year, espionage, the cold war, and the KGB passed into oblivion, and became simply another chapter in the history books - or did they?

Waging war between communism and capitalism isn't always a matter of choosing sides. Sometimes, it becomes a global struggle between good and evil. It is almost always a desperate attempt to save lives. The struggle begins with a man who had become comfortable with the old ways, when everyone knew who the enemy was, and the lines between the virtuous and the corrupt were clearly defined. He would do anything, no matter how heinous, to bring about a rebirth of communism, featuring the United States and NATO as the decadent western enemy.

The nightmare begins when this man's seemingly unlimited power and corruption are mixed with an obsession for the past - and a touch of insanity.

Chapter 1

SOME SAY IT'S like the end of the world: desolate, lonely and barren. The arctic Russian wind could chill the thickest skinned polar bear to the bone, and the three Americans, wearing only black knit caps, thermal turtleneck sweaters, and slacks were poorly prepared for the freezing gusts outside the Russian Protectorate building, which constantly whipped them without mercy. Inside, light musical refrains, witty conversation, and expensive champagne flowed freely. The elegantly clad guests were unaware of the constant patrol of the Soviet Guard in the halls outside the offices on the second floor of the Protectorate, and no one suspected that espionage was about to take place in the courtyard below.

Tia Johnson, a beautiful blonde with sapphire eyes and ivory skin, masqueraded as a wealthy American debutante. She was among only three Americans invited to the reception for the new head of the Protectorate, the ruling Soviet Party. Every country in the Eastern Block had sent a representative to the capitol for the swearing-in ceremonies and the week-long round of parties to follow.

Tonight was the last and the most lavish of the parties. The palace ballroom was trimmed in winter greenery tied with gilded, ornamental festooning. The scented pillar candles gave off a gentle light that moved as though swaying in time with the tempo of the orchestra, and lent a warm glow to the shining faces of the guests. The iridescent, hand-cut panes of leaded glass twinkling between the ruby velvet drapes made the bitter Russian winter outside look like diamonds peeking out from beneath a woman's long holiday gown.

Tia had taken extra time to ensure she looked her best for the occasion. She had chosen a glistening ruby gown that complimented her coloring and her eyes, and fit her slender figure like a second skin. The strapless dress bared her shoulders, which were adorned with clear sequins and strands of white pearls. The jeweled strands hung gracefully over the shear, flesh-toned bodice and were attached to strategically placed jeweled appliqués. The clinging silk material licked her breasts like flames, covering just the tips, and cascaded in beams of sparkling brilliance all the way to the floor. The thigh-high slits in front and back exposed Tia's long, shapely thighs when she strolled across the room. Her gown and her coy flirtations had had the desired response from the male guests, as was evident from her ever-increasing circle of distinguished admirers. Tia had worked hard, dressing and acting as she had, to establish a solid cover as a charming, flirtatious, and somewhat uninhibited heiress from the United States. She danced, chatted, and smiled at their bad jokes. She even succeeded in convincing the Soviet Guard and the Protectorate's Secret Service that she was in Russia only to attend the parties.

The men surrounding her were debating among themselves how each could best maneuver to be her escort home after the party. The Ambassadors of several countries were among those in active competition for Tia's attention. They filled and re-filled her glass with champagne, and brought over their native delicacies for her to sample. These, like the champagne, were left untouched on a nearby table.

Glancing at her watch casually, Tia excused herself from the little group and stated sweetly that she must "powder her nose." She made her way up the sweeping staircase to the ladies' lounge. She smiled at the older, more stoutly proportioned women who passed her on the stairs, trying to appear calm. Her nerves were on edge, thinking of what could happen if she were discovered. Tia's cover had to be perfect. The lives of a dozen people relied on it.

Tia made her way down the dimly lit, lavishly furnished hallway, past the ladies' lounge. She had three minutes before the guards would make their rounds again on this hallway. Once out of earshot, she examined first one lock and then the next on the west side of the building. Tia knew that all of the doors to the General's office would be locked except one. She crept down the hall until she found what she had been looking for. The fifth gold door latch she tried was unlocked. Glancing quickly up and down the hallway to make sure she was alone, Tia quietly slipped into the darkened room and locked the door behind her.

The doors leading to the hallway and the next room didn't fit the moldings tightly, and a cold draft whispered under the door, across her ankles and up her calves. Tia removed a small pen light from her jeweled purse and, lighting it for only an instant, found the chain for the overhead light. The dark, musty room smelled of cleaning supplies and was lit by a single bulb directly over her head. Tia had turned on the overhead light long enough to get her bearings. She looked around at what was obviously a storage room with office supplies lining the shelves and a bucket and mop pushed into the corner. Tia couldn't risk someone in the hall seeing the light and becoming suspicious, so she worked quickly. Tia pulled a pick out of the design on her shoe and quickly worked the lock on the connecting door. Tia remembered the diagram of the offices in the West Wing, and she knew that this door led to the General's office. She didn't have much time to get inside and open the office window before the men waiting in the shrubs below froze to death or were caught.

As soon as Tia gained entry to the office, she slipped on surgical gloves, turned on the small pen light and extinguished the overhead fixture in the cleaning room. Gently, she shut the storage room door behind her. Tia moved quickly to the window and carefully pulled the drape aside. She looked down through the foggy window to see if the guard had left the side of the building to make his rounds. He had. Everything was going according to plan. The three black figures were almost invisible in the moonlit darkness. Quickly, Tia opened the lock on the window and then signaled the three men waiting below. She flashed the pen light twice down at them, and in response, one of the three tossed a rubber-coated grappling hook up to the window where Tia waited in silence. The hook made a dull thud as it hit the windowsill and stuck. She secured the hook and rope and then tiptoed back to the office's hall door to check for any unusual noises. She listened intently as two maids walked briskly down the hall outside, gossiping about the guests in Russian. Much to Tia's relief, they continued on without stopping. Obviously, they were too caught up in their own conversation to notice any noise that she or the grappling hook might have made.

Tia crossed back to the window quickly and helped the three men inside. Robert was the first through the window. At six feet even, he was about the same height as the other two men, but he had a thinner build. His pitch black hair was touched by just a smattering of gray at the temples, but his devilish grin made him look much younger than his years. Joe was the second man through the window. He had all-American good looks, with blond hair and sparkling blue eyes. When he smiled at a woman, his whole face would light up and she would be putty in his hands. Peter, the tallest of the three and the last to climb through the window, had dark, brooding good looks, and women were frequently willing to do just about anything he asked them to do. There was just a magical *something* about him. His eyes told you he was always planning and knew considerably more than he was telling.

Robert and Joe gave Tia a quick, friendly hug as they entered the room. Peter kissed Tia briefly on the lips and held her close once he was inside. All three men quickly shed their winter gloves and put on surgical gloves so that they would leave no trace in the room. Without uttering a sound, he smiled at her and then walked briskly over to the portrait of the aging General hanging on the paneled wall across from the desk. He ran his hand along the wall behind the antique gilt frame, looking for the micro switch that would activate the alarm system. He'd studied its location on their smuggled copy of the building's schematics. The diagram indicated that the pressure of the guilt frame against the crown of the switch had completed the circuit and the slightest movement would trigger the alarm. Peter found what he was looking for and snapped his fingers, signaling to Joe.

Peter stepped back from the portrait, providing Joe with plenty of room to work. As Joe started to work, Peter walked over to the desk with Tia and they stood very still, his arm possessively around her waist. Robert, the fourth member of the team, kept watch at the door for any unusual noises. Joe removed a small, high-speed silent drill from his bag and attached a circular bit. He cut a four-inch hole slightly above and to the right of the micro switch, taking care not to make contact with the alarm wiring. He knew that if the drill severed the wire, the alarm would sound automatically. Joe carefully tugged the wires through the opening in the wall and used strippers to remove a quarter-inch of the insulation. He carefully pulled a wire jumper from his bag and attached one alligator clip to each wire, completing the electrical circuit, preventing the alarm from sounding. Then, Joe carefully pushed the wires back inside the wall so that a casual observer wouldn't notice his handy work.

Moving the picture and opening the safe with ease, Joe had spent less than two minutes on the whole operation. Robert signaled the group to be quiet and pointed to his watch. It was time for the guards to make their rounds. All four of them froze when they heard the footsteps approaching the door. They heard muffled conversation between two men and then there was the cursory jiggling of the door handle. Satisfied, the guards' conversation had not even skipped a beat as they continued on down the hall to the next office.

Once they were confident that the guards were gone, Tia disengaged herself from Peter's strong arms and walked with him over to the safe. They removed and opened each envelope, verifying the contents, and then replaced the official documents with identically shaped blank slips of paper. Peter was careful to replace the envelopes in the exact order they'd been removed, and then he softly closed the safe. While Peter was working, Joe carefully replaced the circle of plaster board and sealed the seam with a fast-drying, clear liquid adhesive, so there was no need to match the hue of the surrounding paint.

Peter stepped back and tucked the black silk bag containing the official documents into the front of his shirt. Joe cautiously approached the safe, reset the combination to the beginning number, and returned the picture frame to its original position. He replaced the drill into his tool belt and, using a hand vacuum, removed any traces of plaster. Collecting their tools, Tia and the three men crossed to the window, leaving as they had come.

Tia quietly wished them all luck, giving them each a peck on the cheek as they climbed out the window. Peter, the last to leave, reminded her that they would be waiting for her in the cold outside and that she'd better leave the party quickly. He kissed her passionately and told her to be careful. The three men silently lowered themselves to the ground and then waited for Tia to release the rope and grappling hook. Tia closed the window, but she didn't have time to draw the drapes before the doorknob was turned from the outside and two men, speaking loudly, entered the office. Tia dove under the desk and prayed they hadn't seen her. Discovery would mean a slow, painful death for all of them.

Grouchev, the rotund, newly self-appointed General, and his pale, thin, cringing aide entered the office. Grouchev was doing most of the talking, complaining about the inconvenience of all the parties and the security problems they were having because the Americans were present at the Protectorate.

If only he knew, Tia thought as she hid just inches from his booted, oversized feet. The aide turned on the lights in the office, and respectfully agreed with everything Grouchev said. Grouchev stopped in the middle of the room, signaled his aide to be silent, and then sniffed the air like a bulldog who has detected an unfamiliar scent.

Frowning, he stalked over to the phone on the desk and lifted the receiver. He didn't dial out, only punching three numbers on the keypad, so the person on the other end of the line had to be in the building. Grouchev mentioned something to his aid and then spoke quickly into the phone. "The line is clear

Lieutenant. We can talk." Grouchev listened to the details for stealing the microfilm from the American Agency, which contained the names of all the NATO imbedded agents in Europe, including those working inside the Russian Mafia. He decided that the name of the document containing the information would be *FILE 13,* the next in a series of secret files on NATO counter-intelligence.

Grouchev was discussing the time and place of the pick-up when he stopped speaking abruptly and listened. "What was that clicking noise?" he demanded. "I don't know" must have been the response on the other end of the line, because Grouchev ordered the lieutenant to find its source immediately.

He slammed the receiver into the cradle and then turned viciously on his aid. "The security of the complex has been compromised and the leak must be plugged at once!" After he completed the list of instructions, which he demanded that his aide follow immediately, Grouchev stormed out of the office and slammed the door shut behind him. After Grouchev left the room, his aide mumbled something intelligible to himself and then turned to leave. The aide was poised with one hand on the door, ready to extinguish the light, when he froze and listened. Tia's dress had shifted and she attempted to right it, and the aide had apparently heard her. Tia froze. After a few moments of listening intently to the silence, the aide was obviously convinced it had been his imagination. He shrugged and turned out the light before he left. Tia heard him lock the door behind him.

As soon as he was out of earshot, Tia crawled quickly out from under the desk and drew the drapes. *Hopefully Grouchev was too distracted to notice that they had been open,* she thought. Tia checked her watch. She'd been gone almost fifteen minutes. She didn't have much time to make her way back to the party before she was missed.

Throughout the week Tia had worked hard to get close to several of the most influential Ambassadors. While this familiarity afforded protection from the lesser security people and a certain amount of added freedom, it also had its drawbacks. Now, when she most needed anonymity, her popularity could prove fatal. Tia left the office quickly through the adjourning dark cleaning room, rather than through the office door, in case she was seen leaving.

Tia cracked open the door to the dimly lit hallway, permitting her eyes a moment to adjust to the light before continuing. She looked both ways before venturing out of the tiny room. Seeing no one, she closed the door quietly behind her and crept cautiously back to the wide stairway. She hiked her gown up to her thighs so that it wouldn't swish around her ankles and attract any attention.

As Tia reached the door to the ladies' lounge, she

lowered her dress cautiously to preserve her only undergarment, her silk stockings. She smoothed the dress over her slender hips and continued to the stairs as if she'd just left the lounge. The noise of the reception below increased as Tia neared the wide, sweeping landing. The boisterous commotion was strangely comforting after the extreme closeness of the office she'd just left. Gracefully, Tia smoothed her gown once again for effect and descended the length of the staircase. She was constantly alert for a sign that she'd been missed. Halfway down the stairs, Tia paused to look over the guests in the room. She was looking for Grouchev and her contact. She spotted them both, each on opposite sides of the room. She patted her long, golden tresses in a purely feminine, vain manner in order to conceal her preoccupation with the two men. *So far, so good,* she thought. No one gave any signs of missing her – that was, until she reached the bottom of the stairs.

As Tia's foot touched the last step, Grouchev and two guards approached her. Tia froze and smiled confidently. He sneered condescendingly at Tia's apparent poise and then grunted his interest in her. "Miss Johnson," Grouchev said as he nodded in her direction, addressing Tia with a sarcastic tone, in broken English. Then, speaking to his confederates, he commented on her decadent, revealing outfit in Russian. Tia spoke fluent Russian, but right now it was to her advantage to deceive him. Trying to maintain her cover, she acted as if she didn't understand his insinuations and excused herself politely, pleading extreme thirst. Hoping to distract the guards with her obvious sexuality, she deliberately swayed her hips to the music as she walked to the refreshment table. This movement caused the sequined material to flash in the candlelight and flare out along her long legs as she walked, baring her thighs. Grouchev made a comment to one of his aids about Tia's supple body, loudly detailing his plan to debauch her. Tia smiled to herself, thinking of the pain she'd like to inflict on Grouchev if she ever got him alone. She didn't think he'd ever be able to subject another woman to his fantasies again once she was through with him.

Ignoring Grouchev's comments, Tia smiled warmly at the Yugoslavian Ambassador when she reached the refreshment table and accepted a tall glass of champagne from the waiter. While she sipped the cool sparkling liquid, she turned slowly, sweeping the room casually while keeping an eye on Grouchev over the rim of the glass. Next to Tia, the intoxicated ambassador was holding a large prawn in one hand and a glass of champagne in the other. He leaned in toward Tia sloppily and was just about to become a little too familiar with the appliqués on the bodice of her gown, nearly snapping one of the strands of pearls, when something diverted his attention. Without noticing his actions, the

Ambassador dropped his shrimp into his champagne and stared, open-mouthed, as the guests parted like the Red Sea when Grouchev and his men walked as a group across the room to where Tia was standing. Following him like the wake of a large ship, a hush fell over the crowd. The waiters stopped serving and everyone turned in Grouchev's direction, curious and a little fearful. The room was silent until Grouchev spoke.

It was unusual for Grouchev to appear at social events, even when they were in his honor. When he did attend, he usually left early and didn't attempt to talk to anyone in particular. Never before had he publicly approached a woman at a social event in such a bold manner. Silent wagers were already being placed on the possible outcome of his conversation with the beautiful American.

The guards stood a few feet behind Grouchev, weapons at the ready while he took advantage of his political position and considerable girth to force himself between the Ambassador and Tia, pressing his rotund torso against Tia's slender body. Grouchev calmly asked her in broken English, "Did you find anyting interestink in my office?"

"Mr. General, I don't understand your question," she said sweetly, forcing her voice to be level.

"You use most unusual fragrance, Miss Johnson," Grouchev said, lifting the inside of her left wrist to his nostrils. He sniffed loudly and then, forcing her hand open with his chin, he slobbered a wet kiss onto her palm. Tia tried to pull her hand away, but he only clutched her wrist tighter and continued, "I smelled same scent in my office not too long ago. Can you explain?" His self-satisfied smirk caused his jowls to wobble as if he was anticipating a particularly tantalizing meal.

"No, General Grouchev, I cannot explain it," Tia said smiling sincerely up at him. Grouchev released her wrist as Tia continued calmly. "Perhaps someone wearing the same scent happened to be using your office to meet someone *privately,"* she added with a wink. As she spoke, Tia tried to hide her trembling hands behind her back. Straightening her spine to conceal her fear, she was unaware of the pressure this movement had put on the bodice of her gown. Tia's answer sent a murmur through the shocked crowd. No one had dared ever answer the General in such a bold fashion. However, Tia had responded to him with such a sweet, innocent expression on her face that the General didn't take offense. Instead, he smiled at her apparent composure and poise.

"Perhaps, my dear," the General countered, "you vould care to visit me, *privately?* Den, you could tell me more of dis interesting tale of yours." He suggested, "You could tell me about da mystery woman who vares the same scent as you." His smile faded and his bushy eyebrows rose in hungry

anticipation. He signaled his guards without waiting
for a reply from Tia, and they took a step forward,
prepared to take her away. Grouchev grabbed the
upper part of her arm and held onto her tightly. The
Turkish Ambassador, who had been enamored with
Tia all evening, was hoping to be her escort when she
left the party and, perhaps, continue their relationship
at her hotel. The Ambassador became distraught at
seeing his carefully cultivated prize being snatched
away from him and rose to Tia's defense. Protesting
loudly in his native tongue, he initiated a tug-of-war
between himself and one of the guards, with Tia as
the rope. Tia's gown was pulled from one side to the
other as her body was jerked first in one direction and
then the next, exposing more of her milky white
breasts than good taste and decency permitted. With a
loud shredding sound, the front of her gown was
ripped vertically from her abundant cleavage down to
her navel. Finally releasing her arm, Grouchev
chuckled at Tia's attempts to cover herself. Soon, he
was laughing so hard that he had to hold onto one of
his guards for balance. Tia didn't find the situation
amusing however, and jerked her other hand from the
Ambassador's grasp in order to gain a better hold on
the material of her dress.

Tia glared at Grouchev and the Turkish
Ambassador with smoldering anger while she tried to
cover her breasts with the shreds that had been the
bodice of her dress. The joke was over for Grouchev

too. He told the Ambassador that he was no longer needed at the ball. Without worrying about the political consequences, Grouchev signaled to one of his guards, who had been standing beside the Ambassador. The guard calmly drew his revolver and silenced the Ambassador's objections with a single bullet between the eyes. The bullet made a clean exit from a small hole in the back of his head, and a surprised look accompanied a single drop of blood, which trickled down from the hole, across the bridge of his nose, and dripped onto the carpet. The Ambassador fell into the arms of those guests standing directly in back of him as a loud crack echoed through the hushed room. The bullet had gone all the way through his skull and had lodged in the ornately decorated entrance way, causing small splinters from the exit hole in the Ambassador's head to splatter those nearest to him.

With one collective gasp, the crowd pulled back from the violent scene, horrified. The guard who still held onto Tia's arm gave her a firm push toward the open door. As they proceeded, they encountered an older man. He was one of the agents who had been watching Tia from the stairs. She tried to warn him off with her eyes, but he didn't notice. He tried to rescue her by overpowering her guard. Before he could make any headway, a second guard, the one who had killed the Ambassador, grabbed the older man. The guard took the older man's right hand, twisted it behind his back, and caused a loud popping sound as he dislocated his shoulder.

The elderly man's 19 year-old son, dressed as a waiter, couldn't stand watching his father being treated this way. He yelled to the guard to leave his father alone and cursed at him violently as he dropped his tray and ran toward them. The guard holding Tia released her to grab the young man. He dragged the youth screaming from the door over to the serving table. He calmly took the boy's hand, laid it alongside the roasted pig on the serving table, and removed the carving knife from the dead carcass. The stunned young man suddenly realized what was about to happen and began screaming even louder as he struggled to pull away his hand. Tia couldn't watch as the guard easily held the terrified man by the forearm and severed his hand from his wrist with one swift blow.

The victim's screams were joined by those of the stunned, horrified crowd in the hall. The sobbing, butchered man was left writhing on the floor, moaning into the bloody stump he cradled next to his chest. The guard dropped the quivering hand to the floor and skidded in the growing puddle of blood as he walked briskly toward the front door, gun drawn. Tia was gone.

Tia didn't bother to pick up the coat she'd dropped in the entrance way, and ran out into the snow wearing only what was left of her gown. She was so frightened that she didn't even notice the sub-zero temperature. The three men who'd been waiting outside the Protectorate, hidden in the bushes, had heard the commotion through the open doors, and they quickly formulated a plan. When they saw that Grouchev and his guards were preparing to take Tia into custody, they realized that her cover had been blown and that she'd be killed. They immediately began working to prevent Grouchev from executing his plans.

By the time Tia ran outside, the trio had set a trap for the guards just past the gate. In her haste, she never saw the net barely concealed by the falling snow, and fell right into it. The three were poised by the stanchions, guns aimed at the person in the net, ready to open fire. Luckily for Tia, she'd not worn any outer garments, and there was no way that she could've been mistaken for one of the guards. They helped her out of the net and the group ran for a delivery truck that Peter had *borrowed* earlier. They jumped into the truck and Robert tried to hot-wire the engine. It wouldn't start.

Inside the Protectorate, the guards were unsure what to do when they realized that Tia had escaped, so they paused and waited for Grouchev to provide them with instructions. He shouted and cursed at them for their stupidity and sent them in the direction of the truck. He also ordered that the soldiers from the nearby barracks be summoned to help in the pursuit. As the alert alarm rang out in the cold night air, the snow began falling heavily. The drifts were deep and the snow was so heavy that the soldiers who were running from their barracks were forced to slow their pace as they tried to get to their Jeeps. The embassy guards ran to the outside gate and began firing at the truck from a crouching position just outside the Protectorate gate. One bullet whizzed past Peter's ear, drawing blood. Just as they were about to say their final prayers, the engine caught and the delivery truck jerked into gear. The soldiers who had been running from the barracks were now approaching the truck in their vehicles. Rapid machine gun fire followed the truck through the cold, desolate streets as the armed soldiers pursued them in their Jeeps. Robert, however, was a better driver than his Soviet counterparts and, through a succession of sharp turns and subterfuge, outran them.

Once safely away from the pursuing soldiers, Robert headed for a small farm about thirty kilometers from the Protectorate. There was no heat in the truck, so Joe gave Tia his coat and the small group huddled together trying in vain to stay warm. The jerking and bouncing of the truck, as it hit every rut and pothole in the road on the way to the farm, succeeded in bruising the team and leaving them in a very poor disposition. They pulled behind the barn into a secluded hangar where a decrepit twin-engine plane was waiting for them, the engine choking and the exhaust coughing out black smoke. Exchanging looks of horror at the prospect of making their escape in this winged coffin, the group trudged slowly through the deep snowdrifts from the truck to the plane.

Robert, the pilot of the group, took over for the mechanic, who had warmed the engines in preparation for their flight. Once safely in the air, Robert flew below the Russian radar so they couldn't be followed. During the flight, Tia told the rest of the team about the microfilm called *FILE 13*, and when and where it could be found. They planned to tell the Agency, so the microfilm could be recovered. After an exchange of planes in Germany, they landed at Agency headquarters just outside of the NATO offices in London. They brought with them the papers they'd taken from the General's safe and perhaps a more important, more deadly secret.

When the Agency debriefing was complete, the team was congratulated. Their mission had been considered a success by their supervisors, despite the fact that Tia had watched her uncle beaten and her cousin butchered. Tia had had enough. She told the team on the flight home that this would be her last mission for the Agency, regardless of the risk *FILE 13* posed to the free world. She would resolve what she'd do about her career after a leave of absence. Tia decided to go to New York and spend some time with her cousin Orlando Corogan.

Chapter 2

AS THE YELLOW cab slowed to a stop outside one of New York's largest office buildings, Orlando smoothed her sleek auburn tresses and checked her makeup. "How much do I owe you?" she asked the cab driver as she gracefully stepped out of the taxi.

"Twenty-six twenty-five," the cabby replied, giving her a friendly smile. She paid him the fair, plus a substantial tip. "Thanks, lady. A looker like you has a place in my cab anytime. Name's Tom. You just ask for me," he added with a wink. Orlando smiled politely at him and assured him that she would. She turned, glad to be home, and climbed the steps to the entrance of the Panama Building. The elderly doorman was ready to open the door for her as her foot touched the top step. "Good morning, Miss Corogan. Welcome back."

"Thank you, Richard. How are you feeling?" Orlando asked, pausing.

"Fine, thanks. And did you enjoy your trip?" he asked politely.

"Yes, it was very good, for a business trip. But I'm really glad to be back."

Richard smiled in response as he opened the door for Orlando. She took an elevator directly to the penthouse office suite. She knew most of the employees personally, and greeted each by name as she walked briskly through the reception and executive office areas. The constant movement and noise in the office would convey a lack of order to the casual observer, but Orlando's company was consistently rated one of the top five best-run companies on the New York Stock Exchange. Opening the door labeled "President," Orlando announced lightheartedly to Sally, her assistant and confidant: "Hello, I'm back!"

"Hello, Orlando. Did you have a good trip?" Sally asked, smiling at Orlando's enthusiasm and boundless energy.

"Sally, the trip was great! The merger looks like it's going to go through, which means there will be a substantial increase in profits for this quarter. Have I missed anything here while I've been gone?"

"No, not really. It's been pretty much business as usual. Coffee?"

"Yes, please. I could drink an entire pot. Bring me the mail too, please. I might as well jump into it before the jet lag catches up with me," she said, walking into her office.

"Okay, Orlando, but please take a minute to catch your breath," Sally answered as she picked up the mail from her desk and followed Orlando into her office. Orlando smiled at Sally's concern and took off her jacket. She sighed and stretched like a languid feline and then inhaled deeply as her senses captured all of the familiar scents surrounding her.

Orlando sank slowly down into the warm embrace of her burgundy Italian leather chair. It enveloped her like a warm embrace. She smiled, remembering Sally's insistence that Orlando needed a richly appointed office because it was in keeping with the image of a large international investments firm. Orlando didn't like extravagance in any form and had only compromised with Sally to end the argument. Sally had said that any prospective clients would judge Orlando and Investments Internationale by their first impressions of Orlando and her office, and as usual, she had been right.

Leaning back and closing her eyes, Orlando reflected on how lucky she was to have Sally. She wasn't only a valued employee; she was a close personal friend. Sally and Orlando's father, Sam Corogan, had worked together from the time he had founded Investments Internationale. Sally had watched Orlando grow up and had worried about her just as if she were Sally's own daughter. Mrs. Corogan had died when Orlando was only three years old, and Sally had spent many nights sitting with Orlando, holding the tiny, trembling girl until she cried herself to sleep over some childhood catastrophe. Sally and Sam had grown very close over the years, and Orlando often asked her father why they didn't marry. Each time he'd give a different reason, but Orlando surmised that her father had never gotten over her mother's death. However, even though Sam was unable to reciprocate, Orlando was sure that Sally was deeply in love with her father.

As an only child, Orlando had benefitted from certain advantages. She had had the opportunity to grow even closer to her father and Sally, and because of this close association, she had developed a keen interest in the corporate world by the time she had reached high school. Orlando worked at Investments Internationale while attending college and completing the MBA program at Stanford University with honors. After graduation, she worked full time, learning the daily operations of the company, specializing in marketing. Orlando had moved up quickly because of her knowledge and enthusiasm for the business. Within four years from the date she joined the company full time, Orlando became the Marketing Vice President and increased corporate sales by 35 percent. Then, Sam Corogan was suddenly and brutally murdered, almost three years ago. Orlando stepped in as interim-President and ran the company as she'd been groomed to do. After eighteen months on the job, Orlando was voted President and Chief Executive Officer by unanimous vote from the Board of Directors. She prided herself on the fact that she'd earned the respect of her peers by achieving her position through hard work, not through nepotism, and she was quickly becoming a shrewd businesswoman.

During her tenure as the President and CEO, Orlando had run the company at a substantial profit, as the quarterly reports demonstrated, but it was common knowledge that there were many projects that her father had chosen to keep to himself, and for this reason some of Orlando's strongest competitors predicted that disaster could strike at any time. Daniel Hartt, Sam Corogan's strongest adversary and Orlando's most vocal critic, publicly predicted financial ruin for Investments Internationale within five years. He attributed the company's impending downfall to Orlando's gender and inexperience. He quite often proclaimed that "any woman, especially such a young woman, was incapable of making intelligent business decisions." Hartt made Orlando's skin crawl and his words made her blood boil. She was determined that, with hard work, shrewd investments, and a little luck, she would prove Daniel Hartt wrong.

Orlando relaxed for a moment in her chair, gazing absently around her office before attacking the mountain of paperwork on her desk. Orlando's office was the heart and soul of the business. It had been designed by her father, and in his memory, Orlando had changed very little. The plush sculptured carpeting was a shade lighter than the furniture. It covered the expanse of the office, including the area under the wide mahogany desk. To the right of the desk was a panoramic view of the city, magnificent from the forty-seventh floor. The three beige leather captain's chairs placed directly in front of the desk contrasted perfectly with the mahogany paneling across the room. A wet bar and a beige love seat in front of the paneling were at Orlando's disposal for more *informal* negotiations.

Sally sat down quietly in one of the captain's chairs across from the desk. Orlando stood slowly and began pacing as she read her mail silently. Sally handled most of the correspondence, but Orlando preferred to handle the more important or interesting letters herself. Abruptly, Orlando turned and said, "Sally, take a letter."

"Mr. Sloan of Sloan Enterprises:

Regarding your letter of the fifth, I have no desire to sell any of our real estate holdings in Los Angeles, which are managed by your firm. However, as the majority stockholder in your company, I have to question the current management's handling of our investment. The quarterly report you enclosed only serves as a further example of your maladministration of our investment. Furthermore, I will be present at the September board meeting to recommend a management change in your organization, beginning with the position of Board Chairman. You need to go back to Rutgers and take a refresher course in Accounting and Economics. You obviously missed the point the first time. Our auditor will be calling you soon for an update on the situation. Orlando Corogan, etc., etc."

Orlando reached unconsciously for the next unopened letter. She read the return address and then turned the envelope over in her hand. Smiling to herself, Orlando quietly read the contents inside. In response she said, "Sally, send this one to Isabel Sanderson:

'I would love to come to Rudi's birthday party on the tenth, but something's come up. I'm terribly sorry that I can't make it.

Tell Rudi to visit the marina on the ninth for his birthday present. In slot thirteen you will find that quaint thirty-footer he was admiring the last time we went boating. Love, Orlando.'"

Orlando absently sipped her coffee and then reached for the next unopened letter, stopping when she saw the return address. It looked strangely familiar but the name was foreign to her. "Sally, who is Robert Taylor?"

"I don't know. I thought you knew him. The front of the envelope said *'PERSONAL AND CONFIDENTIAL,'* so I left it for you."

"Okay, let's see what Mr. Taylor has to say." Orlando opened the envelope and frowned as she read the letter.

She stopped halfway down the page and walked around the desk to where Sally was sitting and sat down beside her. Smirking, she said, "Sally, you've got to hear this:

'*Dear Miss Corogan,*

I've been an admirer of yours for some time. You are perhaps the most attractive executive I've ever met. It's been several years since we last saw each other, so you probably don't remember me. Your father and I were good friends and we did quite a lot of business together. He asked me to deliver a message to you, should anything happen to him, and since I don't trust the mail or the Internet to keep this important message confidential, I am asking you to call me at your earliest convenience to set a time and place to meet face to face. Please take me seriously, Orlando. It could be a matter of life and death -- YOURS!

With my fondest regards, Robert Taylor'

"Can you believe this guy?" Orlando asked looking up at Sally.

Sally replied, eyes wide, "He sounds like some kind of a nut! Are you going to call him?"

"No. Not right away. I want time to check him out first. I don't remember my father mentioning him to me. He could be on the level, but then again, he could be just like all of the other nuts who sent me threatening letters when my father was killed. You know," she said, pausing and tapping the envelope against the table, "it's been a long time since I've received any letters this ominous." Orlando sat still in thought for a couple of minutes. Sally was becoming more anxious by the moment and watched her closely. Orlando abruptly broke the silence, saying, "Take this letter over to security and see what they can find out about Mr. Taylor. Then call our contact at the FBI and see if he has a record with them. I want to know who this guy is and if he really has some connection with my father. Maybe he can lead us to my dad's killer."

"Okay," Sally said quietly. She was worried about Orlando because she was taking on the same determined expression she had worn when Sam was murdered. The same killer who murdered Sam had tried to kill Orlando, and had succeeded in putting her into the hospital. Sally prayed that things weren't going to end up that way again, or maybe even worse. She decided to change the subject. "What do you want me to do with the rest of the mail?"

"I'll answer it on the digital voice recorder and you can take care of it later. This is more important. I want to know what Mr. Taylor's connection was with my father."

Without another word, Sally left to carry out her instructions. Orlando was deep in thought, and didn't even hear her close the door. Sally knew that trying to reason with Orlando when she became obsessed with something like this was useless, so she decided not to try. *Maybe Orlando would be more reasonable in a little while,* Sally thought.

Alone now, Orlando walked back around the desk and flipped through the rest of the mail, not

really looking at it. She was anxious to find out what
the computer had to say about Mr. Taylor. Orlando
was unable to concentrate and allowed her mind to
drift back into the past. She walked over to the wet
bar, her mind in a misty haze. Here, for her
convenience, was a fully stocked refrigerator, a
microwave, and a Keurig coffee pot that was always
stocked with her favorite blends. Orlando refilled her
cup without really thinking about what she was
doing, and then reached for an apple in the
refrigerator. She returned to her desk, trying to
remember everything her father had told her about
his *other* business. She couldn't remember him ever
mentioning a Robert Taylor. Wondering about Mr.
Taylor and all the possible implications of his
involvement with her father only gave Orlando a
headache. She turned her attention back to the mail,
resolved to wait until she had more information
before making any decisions about him. After about
ten minutes of dictation, however, Orlando couldn't
concentrate. "Sally, have you heard anything yet?"

"No, I haven't. I'll check on it again, but they said
it would be at least ten more minutes. Do you want
me to buzz you when it arrives?"

"No, just bring it in. I'm going in back to get
changed for the board meeting at two. When I'm
finished, I'll need you to help me polish up the
presentation on the merger. Meet me back in my
office in twenty-five minutes. That should give them

enough time to have a runner bring the information back to you. In the meantime, can you get started on the dictation? Oh, and Sally... thanks!"

"You're welcome," Sally said with a smile in her voice.

Orlando pushed a small black button underneath the desktop, just to the right side of the middle drawer, and a panel in the bookcase behind her clicked and swung open. This private door to her apartment opened silently into the room as the apartment's intercom began playing soft jazz and the lights offered a muted ambiance automatically. This apartment wasn't Orlando's home. Her primary residence was the family estate in the Hamptons, on Long Island. This apartment was just for the times when she didn't have the opportunity to go home and change, or had returned after a long trip and wanted a retreat. Once Orlando walked past the electric eye, the bookcase and apartment door slid silently back into place. Orlando looked around the comfortable hideaway. On her left was the fully stocked wet bar and kitchen area with a panoramic view of the city and the horizon beyond. Across from her were the closet and the vanity, and her one extravagance: a round bed dressed in cream-colored Mulberry silk sheets and a chocolate and cream-colored Kumi Kookoon Mulberry silk comforter. The bathroom was on the right, completing the compact but comfortable apartment. Orlando poured herself her favorite chilled drink, which was waiting for her in the refrigerator. She had developed a passion for the Coladina, a pineapple-and-coconut liqueur, when she vacationed in the Caribbean last summer. She smiled remembering the liquor company's slogan: *"A tropical moon, a sleepy lagoon, and two Coladiñas between ya."* As she sipped her drink, the handsome man who had brought Orlando to such passionate heights during those steamy, seductive tropical nights came rushing back into her memory as well. Orlando took another long, slow sip of the drink, savoring the sensation and the memory, and then, sighing, set the glass on the counter top. She looked out at the unobstructed view, drew the heavy drapes, and then unbuttoned her blouse and slipped out of her travel clothes quickly as she walked toward the shower. She was wearing only a towel, checking the water temperature, when the phone rang. The second before she picked up the receiver, Orlando realized that she hadn't told anyone she was returning early from her trip. This was her private, unlisted line, which didn't go through the switchboard. As these two ideas collided in her brain, a cold chill ran down her spine. The phone rang a third time as she slowly lifted the receiver.

Before she could say anything, Orlando heard an inviting male voice ask her, "Did you have a good trip?"

His tone held a hint of mischief. "Who is this?" Orlando demanded. "How did you get this number?"

"I'm Robert Taylor, Orlando, and it's very important that I see you as soon as possible to discuss an urgent matter with you. I can't go into it over the phone." He was strictly business now.

"Mr. Taylor, I just received your letter today. Now, if you'll kindly tell me what this is all about, we can save some time and avoid all of the mystery." Orlando was quickly becoming annoyed.

"Miss Corogan, if you received my letter, then you know that I can't discuss this with you over the phone. It is very important that I see you in person. I've made reservations for seven at Michael's."

"Mr. Taylor, I read your letter, and for all I know, you're some kind of nut that gets off on threatening people. I will not be meeting you at Michael's or anywhere else, so if you feel it is absolutely necessary to meet with me in person, I suggest you call my assistant and make an appointment. Then we can sit down to discuss this calmly in my office, like rational people." Orlando was about to hang up on him when his next statement stopped her cold.

"Miss Corogan, you *will* meet me tonight at seven at Michael's if you want to stay alive!"

His tone clearly indicated that he wouldn't take no for an answer. "And," he added, "you will wear that red dress that's hanging in your closet." Then, he playfully added, "You may want to shed that towel you're wearing and get into the shower before you're late for your board meeting."

"What?!" Orlando exclaimed.

But before she could utter another word, he replied quickly, "I'll be seeing you tonight, Miss Corogan," and hung up. There was no question in his voice, no compromise. He had given Orlando an order, and he expected it to be obeyed.

For a long moment she just stood and stared at the receiver, trying to comprehend what had just happened. No one but her father had ever dared talk to Orlando like that. As she slowly realized that this man seemed to know everything she was doing, even before she did it, Orlando became furious and more than a little frightened. She quickly checked the apartment for any type of electronic audio or video recording devices and then checked the heavy drapes that were closed across the full-length windows behind the bar. She couldn't find any indication that there were cameras in the apartment, but she didn't take any chances. Orlando took her clothes with her into the bathroom, where she showered and dressed quickly. As soon as she'd returned to her desk, she buzzed Sally. "Any news yet?"

"Yes. It just came in."

"Good. Bring it in!" Orlando couldn't hide the tension that was building in her. She didn't have the time or the inclination to play games with a sick prankster, and if that is what Mr. Taylor was, he was going to pay dearly. On the other hand, if this guy was on the level, he could even be her father's murderer coming back to finish what he'd started. Sally brought in the folder and handed it to Orlando. She sat in silence and watched Orlando as she read the material carefully.

Sally finally couldn't contain herself anymore and said, "I've noticed it's rather lengthy, but it looks complete."

"You've already read it, haven't you?" Orlando asked, not really surprised.

"Well, I skimmed it." Sally hesitated, shrugging.

Smiling at Sally's maternal instincts, Orlando discussed the information. "It says that Robert Taylor is the son of Sherman Taylor, an import-export dealer who specializes in liquors and wines. The business has offices in New York and Los Angeles. It goes on to say that Robert Taylor is currently maintaining a residence in New York and a ranch in Florida. The Florida ranch is just outside Orlando, near Walt Disney World, in a town called Buena Vista. His penthouse apartment in New York is in on Park Avenue. He has taken over the important business from his father, after he suffered a heart attack two years ago. Evidently, the business was losing money while Sherman Taylor was running it, probably because of his poor health. Robert Taylor, according to this report, put more than two million dollars of his own money into the business to improve cash flow, and the last two quarterly reports show that revenue projections look better than they have in the past five years. The report continues with information about the business and Robert Taylor's education, but there's no mention of any connection with my father. There is also suspiciously little information about his personal life. Sally, I want you to see what else you can find out about him and let me know as soon as you have some word from our contact at the FBI."

"Orlando, why are you so worried about this guy? Why don't you just let the FBI and security handle it? You don't think this guy really has a connection to Sam, do you?"

"I don't know, but that's not what's giving me the creeps about him. Sally, he just called me on my private line," Orlando said, tapping her pencil on the desktop. She was rereading the information about Robert Taylor.

"He *what*? How did he get that number? What did he say?" Sally whispered.

"I don't know how he got my number, but I'm going to find out." Orlando walked over to the window and looked out over the city. "I want to know if Robert Taylor had anything to do with my father's death. The police talked to all of my father's business associates when it happened, but not one of them could shed any light on who was behind his murder,"

Orlando said, thinking out loud. "Nothing in these twenty pages on Robert Taylor indicates that he and dad were even acquaintances. Perhaps he knew dad from his *other* business activities," Orlando suggested, raising her eyebrow and looking intently at Sally before continuing. "He said in the letter, and again on the phone, that I am in danger. I wonder if he's on the level, or if he's amassed his significant fortune from blackmail and death threats instead of the import-export business." A look of defiance and challenge glowed from behind her dark eyes.

"What are you going to do? Do you want me to call the police?" Sally asked, becoming more and more concerned.

"No. I want to find out for myself what he's up to. I'm going to accept his invitation to meet him for dinner tonight," Orlando said confidently as she smiled at Sally.

"You're going to do what? Have you completely lost your mind?"

Ignoring Sally's response, Orlando continued. "When he called, he gave me specific instructions, saying I had to meet him, and that it was a matter of life and death: mine. He also told me not to discuss it with anyone."

Orlando stood up as she continued speaking. "I'm going to meet him at Michael's at seven. He has made dinner reservations in his name. It's a public place, and it should be relatively safe with the dinner crowd there, but all the same, I want to make some precautions."

"Such as?" Sally asked sarcastically. "I mean, really, Orlando. What happened to that common sense you're known for? I can't believe you're even considering meeting him!"

Ignoring Sally's objections, Orlando continued, "If something should happen to me tonight, you won't know until tomorrow. If you don't hear from me by tomorrow night, call my personal attorney, Mr. Casey. Tell him he should deliver *FILE 13* to the head of national security at the White House. Tell him to follow the instructions in the accompanying envelope *to the letter*! It will tell him exactly who to contact." Orlando stopped pacing and sat down across from Sally. She took both of Sally's hands in hers in an effort to make her understand.

"Sally, this is very important," she said in a hushed tone. "Don't let anyone know what you're doing until it's been done, and don't tell anyone about *FILE 13*, or you and Mr. Casey will both be in danger."

"What do you expect to happen to you?" Sally's concern was evident in her voice.

"I don't expect anything to happen, Sally, but we have to be prepared just in case. This might be the break we've been waiting for, the chance to find my father's killer. If it is, I'm going to follow it through." Orlando put her hands flat on the desk and looked for acceptance from Sally. Her decision was made, and the subject was closed. "Now, let's get ready for the board meeting."

Sally recognized that stubborn streak. She knew it from her long relationship with Sam, and from watching Orlando grow up. Orlando was much more like her father than she would ever know, Sally thought. "Be careful," Sally said, picking up her notepad.

"I will."

"Are you sure you don't want me to call the police?" Sally added, trying one last time to get Orlando to act rationally.

"Absolutely not! If the police get involved, it may scare him away. No. We'll just go on with business as usual, and I'll handle it. I'm a big girl and I can take care of myself. If something happens and you don't hear from me, then call the police... but only after you've called Mr. Casey. Now, could you please send out for Chinese for lunch? I'm starving. And while we're waiting for the food to get here, we can get started on the outline for the meeting."

"Just like that?" Sally threw her hands up in the air in disgust. "How can you be so calm about this, Orlando?" Sally inhaled deeply before continuing. "You tell me that you've been contacted by someone who could be connected with your father's death and that he knows your private number..."

"He knows more than that, Sally," Orlando said

calmly.

"What do you mean?" Sally asked, taken aback.

"He knew what dresses I had hanging in my closet, and he also knew that I was only wearing a towel and that I was on my way to the shower."

"What? He's been spying on you and you still don't want me to call the police?" Sally asked, incredulous.

"No, I don't. The matter is settled," stated Orlando. "I'm doing this my way. *I* will find out who killed my father. Do you understand? The police had their chance and they came up empty. Now, can we please stop discussing this and have lunch? I'm starved."

"Fine," Sally replied angrily. "If the fact that this guy could be your father's killer doesn't bother you, far be it from me to object. Would you like egg rolls with your lunch?" Sally asked sarcastically as she stood poised with her hand on the telephone and one eyebrow raised in stern defiance.

"Yes, please," Orlando said, smiling without looking up. Sally shook her head, but said nothing. Then, in silence, they started outlining the agenda for the meeting. While they worked and ate, Orlando forced herself not to think about Robert Taylor and the impending dinner engagement. She tried to concentrate on the notes in front of her, but Sally's words kept creeping into her consciousness. *"This man could be your father's killer."*

Sally and Orlando outlined the presentation for the two o'clock meeting. Orlando had cautiously arranged the facts of the merger so that the older members of the board wouldn't get too upset, as it would mean their voting rights would be diminished quite a bit. However, the merger meant substantial increase in the company's projected annual profits. A 15 percent growth in the value of the stock was guaranteed within minutes of a public announcement of the merger.

The merger would mean acquiring oil wells in the Gulf of Mexico, off the Louisiana coast and a new diamond mine in South Africa, as well as a trade agreement with OPEC for all shipments abroad of crude waste and by-products. All in all, Investments Internationale would stand to gain about 20 billion dollars in cash and assets when the agreements were finalized, and an additional $500,000 per month in commissions after that for the next 10 years. Orlando knew that she had to stress the good points to the board to get them to accept the merger. As per the terms of the agreement with the Kroger conglomerate, if the vote wasn't unanimously in favor of the merger, or if the vote was delayed for any reason, the contract would be canceled.

They finished the outline and agenda in plenty of time. Orlando walked quickly from her office, through the underground tunnel to the conference center across the street, and arrived in the board room about 20 minutes before anyone else. She wanted to get a feel of the place where she would wage her campaign. Two o'clock came and went, and two of the board members were still missing. They had fifteen minutes more in which to send a proxy vote or lose their rights to vote at the meeting. There was a quorum, so there was no problem with that actual vote, but Orlando felt uncomfortable about their unexpected absence. Orlando knew the two elderly men who were missing. They had helped her father to found the company and build it to the success it was today, and they had both been instrumental in her education and training to take over as CEO. Orlando checked her watch again, pacing nervously in the room. Neither man had ever missed a meeting without notifying Orlando first. She became concerned about their health, primarily because both of the men still worked hard and lived alone, even though they were in their eighties.

The board members started arriving at 2:15 p.m. for the 2:30 meeting, and at 2:35 p.m., all of the people in the room turned in unison to welcome the late arrivals. Daniel Hartt, a small, round, greasy, middle-aged man and one of his huge, uneducated, bulked-out bodyguards strolled into the board room. As the bodyguard took his position next to the only exit, Hartt arrogantly surveyed the room. He walked to one of the only empty chairs at the board room table and sat down. As luck would have it, Daniel

Hartt was directly across from Orlando. Before she could speak, Hartt announced loudly, "I hold in my hand the proxy votes for Mr. Tandy Mr. Mead." As he spoke, he held up the slips of paper in his hand. The muscleman at the door shifted back and forth from one foot to the other, as if he was anticipating a fight. Hartt grinned broadly at Orlando's concerned expression, mocking her.

"Excuse me, Mr. Hartt," Orlando said flatly. "We have had no notification that Mr. Tandy and Mr. Mead would not be attending. Please explain how you got their proxy votes." Fear for the safety of her two old friends was choking the air out of her, but she was determined to hide it behind indignation.

Looking around the table, Hartt replied casually, as if he was discussing the weather, "Oh, they decided, after a bit of gentle persuasion, that they wouldn't be attending the meeting." He looked pointedly at Orlando and added, "Let's just say they weren't feeling up to it."

Leaning forward, Orlando spoke quietly to Hartt, in tones barely above a stage whisper, "If you've done anything to hurt those two kind old men, you'll answer to me, Hartt!" Orlando sat back stiffly in her chair, fists clenched in front of her on the table. She made no effort to conceal her hatred for him.

Mocking her, Hartt replied musically, "Miss Corogan, I'm crushed. You know me better than that. I would *never* resort to physical violence to get what

I want." Then, Hartt leaned forward and added in a hushed, threatening tone only Orlando could hear, "Now, drop those accusations, or you'll hurt my feelings, and believe me, Miss Corogan, you *don't* want to do that!"

Not intimidated in the least, Orlando also leaned forward to meet Hartt face to face, replying in the same hushed tone, "I don't scare that easily, Hartt. I don't know what you expect to gain here, so you can just save your threats. The only thing you're going to get from me today is trouble!"

"We'll see, Miss Corogan," he said, smiling broadly as he regained his composure and leaned back in his chair. "In short order, you'll give me exactly what I want, and you'll *enjoy* it," he said smugly.

With one final warning glance, Orlando let the matter drop and regained her composure. Then, as if the entire exchange had never taken place, she addressed the board members and started the meeting. "I apologize for the *rude* interruption," she began, glancing pointedly at Hartt, and then continued. "Let's get started," she said, smiling reassuringly while making eye contact with the other board members. "As you know, this is not a scheduled meeting. Because we are working under a very tight time constraint, we are going to dispense with the formalities and move directly to the presentation. You all have a copy of the financial report, which I sent to you last week before leaving for Paris to meet with the Kroger Consolidated management team. Mr. Hartt, I regret to say that I don't have an extra copy for you. You may share with one of the gentleman sitting next to you, or you can vote your proxy on the basis of the presentation alone." Orlando was finding it difficult to keep her tone civil when addressing him, so she looked away quickly and continued. "This meeting is for the sole purpose of voting on the merger between Kroger Consolidated and Investments Internationale. If the vote is in favor of the merger, the terms of the agreement will go into effect on the twenty-second. You all know the voting rights of each member, and the rules governing the proxy votes. But for the benefit of our *guest,* I will review the voting procedure." Without looking at Hartt, Orlando opened the portfolio in front of her and read from the by-laws. "Each member may vote once, and all votes being equal, excluding proxies, are counted as one vote per member. In the normal course of business, there only has to be a simple majority vote to pass a motion on the floor. In cases of a merger, such as this one, the terms of the merger will prevail. In this case, the board must have a two-thirds majority vote in favor of the merger for it to pass. This means there may not be any abstentions. Unfortunately, Mr. Hartt, you hold proxy votes. Therefore, you may only vote in case of a tie by the regular board members. Are there any questions?"

Orlando looked around the room and noticed nervous expression on the faces of the older board members. Each of them had learned through business dealings with Hartt that he had no ethics. They also knew that Orlando had inherited the hot-headed temperament of the Corogan family, and that she blamed Hartt for her father's death, even though she couldn't prove it. Hatred and resentment sparked between the two principles in the room suggested that almost anything could happen. Although the tension was thick in the air, no more threatening comments were made by Orlando or Hartt, and no response was made to Orlando's query. If Hartt so chose, and if he was given the opportunity, his mere presence could intimidate the other board members and sabotage the merger. Orlando was convinced that that was why he had chosen to attend this particular meeting. If the board were to tie, Hartt would have his chance. She could only hope for a unanimous vote in favor of the merger the first time through. Knowing the possible consequences, Orlando said a silent prayer for some kind of divine intervention and continued, "Since there are no questions, I will begin the presentation. Bill, if you would lower the lights, please..." Her assistant lowered the lights and Orlando opened the presentation with a brief background on the company. She showed a short film of the properties that Kroger Consolidated owned and made a brief yet effective presentation in favor of the merger. As she spoke, Orlando rearranged her facts so as not to tell Hartt too much about the financial disclosures made available to Investments Internationale. This information had been detailed in the board members' packets, but her presentation clouded the real financial structure of Investments Internationale enough to conceal the total amount the company would gain from the merger. Orlando closed the presentation, stating, "I am recommending that the board vote in favor of the merger, based on the financials you have already received in your board packages. Due to *present circumstances,* I will not be presenting them again at this time." The board members looked at each other and then at her, knowingly nodding but saying nothing. Orlando completed the presentation, stating that it was imperative that the vote be taken today, as time for a decision on the merger was running out. The board members trusted her judgment and aptitude implicitly, primarily because they had watched Orlando grow up, acting as her mentors. They also saw in Orlando the same insight into business and the same ruthlessness in dealing with adversaries that they had experienced with Sam.

After the presentation, a brief discussion period was requested. The questions about the merger mainly revolved around the acquisition of the properties in Europe. When all of the questions had been answered, the vote was taken. Orlando voted first because she was the newest board member, as was customary, and as predicted, the other board members followed Orlando's lead and voted in favor of the merger. The vote progressed until the senior members were called by name. Hartt held the proxy votes for the two most senior members, who would have voted last, but since the vote was unanimous, the proxy votes were not needed. Orlando met Hartt's smug smile with a level expression. "Mr. Hartt, I *regret* that you will not be able cast your proxy votes, as there is a unanimous vote in favor of the merger." Silence filled the room as each of the people at the table waited for his reply. He, however, just continued grinning at Orlando and remained silent. The meeting was called to a close quickly, just after the vote was taken, and silence reigned.

Each of the board members looked anxiously at each other and then at Orlando, uncomfortable with the heavy silence in the room. After the meeting was adjourned, the board filed past Orlando on their way out of the room, shaking her hand and whispering to her as if they were in church. Hartt noticed the silent communication, but said nothing as he stood up from his seat. When he finally walked around to where Orlando stood, he stood silently and stared at her and waited to speak until the room was cleared. Hartt, his muscleman, and Orlando were alone in the room, and the two men were between her and the door. Hartt moved threateningly close to Orlando, pinning her between the board room table and her chair, his sour breath filling her nostrils even before he spoke. "Well, my dear," he said, running a dirty, calloused finger along her cheek. I trust everything turned out like you wanted it to." He grinned hungrily at Orlando as he used his physically intimate position to intimidate her.

"Just tell me what you want, Hartt," Orlando replied, pushing him back and taking a step away from him. "I have a business to run, and I don't have time to play your games. Why are you here? You didn't accomplish anything by being here today, so why did you attend the meeting?"

"My dear," he said, sitting on the edge of the table and faking a pout, "you *still* don't trust me. Didn't the vote on the merger turn out the way you wanted?"

"Yes, but that's not the point. Why did you go through such an elaborate charade if you weren't able to vote anyway? Why didn't you let the board members come for themselves? I don't really see where you accomplished anything." She met his devilish grin with an icy stare. Her anger was just about to surface, and it was taking extreme control to keep it in check.

"Now, Orlando, if I had let those two old fools come to the meeting, you wouldn't have your merger.

They planned to vote against it and they planned to talk everyone else into voting against it too. I know because I asked them. So, by coming in their place, you got what you wanted, and now you owe me. Besides, I wouldn't have had the chance to talk to you alone like this, like I am now, just the two of us." Hartt grinned as he spoke, taking another step closer to her.

"Why don't you just cut the crap and tell me why you're here?" Orlando asked through clenched teeth. "You could've made an appointment like anyone else."

"That's true, but if I'd simply made an appointment, I couldn't have done this." He grabbed the back of her head with his enormous hand and pulled her close to him. He forced her head still as he bent his bulk toward her and pinned her against the table again. Sheer will kept Orlando from crying out in pain and fear. She had one hand pinned behind her, holding her body off the table while she pushed at his shoulder with the other. She wouldn't allow him to enjoy this. She wouldn't give him the satisfaction of frightening her. He roughly tilted her head up so that he could attack her mouth. She knew she couldn't push him away, so as his tongue penetrated her taught lips, she bit down hard, and the next sound she heard was his anguished cry. He pulled back immediately, releasing her unceremoniously as he jumped up, applying pressure to his swollen tongue with his hand. "You bitch!" he screamed at her as he reached for his handkerchief. It was already turning blue, and the blood was seeping through the layers of handkerchief that he held against it. His cold stare and curses implied physical superiority and even danger, but Orlando was beyond fear.

Orlando had stepped back from Hartt with the intent of fleeing the room while he was distracted, and she hadn't noticed his bodyguard's movements during this exchange. The armed man had moved into position behind Orlando and had placed his hand on the butt of his gun, ready to use it if Hartt gave the signal. Hartt, ever so faintly, shook his head *no* and the armed man relaxed. Orlando noticed Hartt's movement but didn't acknowledge it, as she realized that she was in a precarious position between an armed guard and Hartt. She quickly regained her composure, and the only outward signs of her anger and fear were the slight quivering of her lower lip and the clenched fists at her sides. "Don't you *ever* try that again, Hartt. I promise you, the next time you'll get more than a swollen tongue."

Hartt stopped dabbing at his tongue, and in response, he started chuckling. Then he laughed harder and harder until he was fighting for control. He dabbed one final time at his tongue and put the handkerchief back into his pocket. "Now don't get excited, *sweetheart,*" he said with a mockingly affectionate drawl. "You got spunk. I'll give you that.

I'm glad. You're gonna need it."

"What is that supposed to mean?" Orlando asked, crossing her hands protectively around her waist. She looked cautiously at the armed man behind her.

"What I'm talking about is what I want you to do for me. And don't worry about it," he responded, seeing her disgusted expression. "It has nothing to do with what just happened. I just wondered what it'd be like to kiss you. Not bad, but not as good as I'd imagined, either. You need to work on your passion a bit," he finished, grinning at her horrified look. Suddenly all business, Hartt snapped his fingers, and the armed man behind Orlando removed a small leather pouch from his pocket, leaned across her, and handed it to Hartt. "When you see Mr. Taylor tonight, I want you to give him *this.*" Hartt handed Orlando the pouch. She accepted it reluctantly as he continued speaking. "Tell him this one didn't contain the right information, and he'd better get the right one to me soon if he values his life. He made a deal with me, and I don't like welchers. And one more thing…" he said, running a finger along her cheek. Orlando recoiled instinctively from his touch. Hartt dropped his hand and, shrugging, continued, "Tell Mr. Taylor that my patience is running short."

Orlando stared at Hartt, speechless. His request was totally unexpected. When he turned to leave, she was brought back to reality. "Wait a minute! How did you know I was supposed to meet him tonight, and why should I do anything for you, especially after this?" Orlando asked, incredulous.

Hartt turned slowly and looked directly at her for a long moment before answering her. "You could give it to Mr. Taylor because I asked you nicely, after I saw to it that your merger went through, or you could give it to him because if you don't, the same thing that happened to your father could happen to *you.*" Without missing a beat he added, "And as far as knowing that you're seeing Taylor tonight, I know things. I also have a lot of friends," he added, smiling like the reptile he was. He turned to walk toward the door and continued confidently, "My friends would be happy to see to it that you do as you are told. You'll be watched, Miss Corogan… so for your own sake, don't disappoint me." Hartt turned one last time to meet her shocked expression with a smirk. "I'm expecting you to get the right information from Mr. Taylor for me. We'll be seeing each other again, very soon. It's late, and I believe you have a dinner engagement. Don't dawdle, Orlando. I wouldn't want you to be late."

He turned and walked briskly out of the room followed by his brooding bodyguard. Orlando left alone, holding the pouch that he'd given her. Still shaking, she sat down at the table and opened the pouch slowly, dumping its contents on the hard surface. When the single stone fell out of the pouch,

Orlando gasped. It was the largest emerald she'd ever seen. It had to be at least fifty carats.

Hartt had said it was the wrong one. She held it up to the light, moving it ever so slightly so that the light reflected through the stone. The color was right, but there were only two small, round inclusions. It was too perfect. It had to be man-made. It was definitely beautiful; the cut and clarity were excellent. Now, more than ever, she was anxious to meet Mr. Taylor.

Walking quickly out of the conference center where the meeting had been held, Orlando looked at her watch. It was almost five o'clock and Orlando had to get changed before she met Mr. Taylor. She needed to know what was between Hartt and Taylor, and she wanted to find out what Taylor's connection was with her father. She decided that it might be more interesting to go along with the charade and see what developed than to approach this problem head on. She walked back to her office through the tunnel under the street that divided the Investments Internationale offices. It was a fifteen-minute walk from the conference center to the executive suite, and she took advantage of the time to weigh the events of the day against what she already knew. She decided that she didn't have enough information about Mr. Taylor, and it seemed that she wouldn't get anymore information before she met him. Everyone except Sally had left the offices by the time Orlando had returned. Sally was setting everything in order on her desk when she saw Orlando walk in and started to welcome her with questions about the meeting. But, before even one word passed Sally's lips, Orlando quickly held up her hand to stop her. He said, "Sally, I need to talk to you right away!"

Without waiting for a reply, she walked quickly past Sally and walked quickly into her office. She pushed the panel button on the underside of her desk and went into the apartment. Sally followed her in, wondering what had happened. "What happened? Didn't the merger go through?" she asked anxiously as she paused by the bed.

"Yes, it went through. It was unanimous," Orlando replied abruptly, not looking up. She quickly stripped off her work clothes, taking out her frustrations on each button and zipper.

"If the merger went through, then what's wrong?" Sally asked, puzzled. "You're not acting like yourself."

"This," Orlando said deliberately, as she dropped her blouse walked over to the bed, wearing only her bra and skirt, to pick up the pouch. Ignoring the chill that the air conditioning was creating on her bare skin, she opened the pouch and allowed the stone to fall onto the silk comforter.

Sally's eyes and mouth grew wide in unison as she gasped, "What in the world? Where did you get this?"

"From Daniel Hartt. He showed up and acted as one of our proxy voters at the board meeting. He gave it to me," she said pointedly, watching the expression on Sally's face change from surprise to confusion with devilish enjoyment.

"I don't understand," Sally replied, reaching for the pouch. "What proxy voters? And what was Hartt doing at the meeting?"

As Orlando answered Sally's questions, she unmercifully brushed her long auburn hair, each stroke a slap in Hartt's face. "Daniel Hartt and one of his over-muscled body guards showed up at the meeting and took the places of Mr. Tandy and Mr. Mead. According to Hartt, Tandy and Mead were going to vote against the merger, and by taking their places at the meeting, he prevented them from voting down the merger. He seems to think that puts me in his debt. Anyway, after everyone left, he gave me that." Orlando excluded her exchange with Hartt.

She didn't really feel comfortable telling Sally because she'd only worry more than she already did. "He wants me to give that to Robert Taylor tonight when I meet him for dinner. He implied that it has something to do with my dad's death."

Orlando ignored the soft lights and music, and concentrated on getting dressed. The plush surroundings and expensive decor were taken for granted and overlooked by the two women preoccupied by the large stone glittering on the hand embroidered satin comforter. The salmon-colored carpeting and earth-toned appointments gave the room a peaceful, almost tranquil tone. Sally broke that peaceful spell when she broached the next question.

"What does this stone have to do with Robert Taylor and Sam's death?"

"I don't know, Sally. I guess I'll just have to ask him tonight."

"I can't believe you're still planning to go to dinner with that man after what Hartt said today. For all you know, he could be the one who killed Sam."

"That's precisely why I am going to dinner with him," Orlando said stepping into her dress. She lifted the hem of her cocktail-length dress to adjust her pantyhose. The designer had made the skin-tight dress so that no other undergarments were necessary. "Would you zip me up, please?"

"Orlando," Sally began as she worked the zipper, "do you remember what you said about Hartt when Sam was killed?"

"Yes, that I held him responsible—and I still do. Hartt told me that I would be followed tonight, and that I was to do exactly as I was told. Then he threatened me saying that if I didn't, the same thing that happened to dad could happen to me."

"Orlando, I'm calling the cops! Now you can't meet Taylor tonight. Hartt or Taylor, or maybe both of them, could be responsible for Sam's murder, and you're just putting yourself in danger for nothing!"

"I disagree, Sally," Orlando said, walking back over to the bed from the dressing table and picked up the emerald. "You know Hartt. He's always had a flair for the melodramatic, and he is known for his gross exaggeration. Besides," she continued as she carried the emerald over to the dressing table, where she looked at it again under the light and then set it down and continued touching up her makeup as she spoke, "if he were dad's killer, the police would've had no trouble convicting him. Hartt definitely isn't smart enough to have committed the murder and successfully covered it up."

Sally walked over to the dressing table and picked up the emerald. She examined it closely under the makeup lights, just as Orlando had, and then asked, "How much do you think this thing is worth?"

"A couple of hundred. Maybe a thousand," Orlando said nonchalantly. "It's a fake. Man- made."

Orlando turned and took the emerald from Sally. She held it up to the light and motioned to Sally to come closer, saying, "Look here and here. There aren't any flaws. There are only these two round dots. A real emerald, even the most perfect stone would have at least one flaw... wait. What's that?"

"What?"

"That spot. See it? That little round, black spot

right there, on the left. It's different from the other one. This one is perfectly round."

"Yeah. What is it, a carbon spot?"

"I don't know." Orlando moved the stone slowly under the light to get a better look at the spot.

"But why would Hartt give you a fake?" Sally asked, standing up.

"I don't know. He said he wanted me to deliver it to Taylor tonight and tell him it was the wrong one. Maybe he was expecting a real emerald and Taylor tried to slip him a paste one. If that's the case, then Mr. Taylor can add con man to his other attributes."

"Orlando, I really think you should notify the police. This whole thing could blow up in your face. Even if you don't think Hartt killed Sam, I don't like any of this. It could be very dangerous."

"You could be right, Sally, but I can't go to the police yet. I don't have anything substantial to tell them. They'll want facts. Besides, the police might scare Taylor away, and then where will I be? I want to find out what's really going on."

"Okay, but what if Taylor doesn't have anything to do with your father's death? What if he only wants to kidnap you... or worse? Considering your position, it's not an unreal possibility. You've had kidnapping and death threats before, especially right after Sam's murder."

"Don't worry. I can take care of myself," Orlando replied, smiling reassuringly. "Besides, I'll check in with you from the restaurant. If you wouldn't mind, could you stay here tonight and I'll call you on the back line?"

"Sure, I can do that, but if I don't hear from you within two hours, I'm calling the police and Mr. Casey."

"Okay, but… there's something I have to ask you before I leave. Do you remember my father ever mentioning *FILE 13?"* Orlando asked. Sally nodded. "Well, did he ever tell you exactly what *FILE 13* is?"

"No, he never told me what it was, only that I'd be better off not knowing," Sally replied. "He said that when the time was right, you'd tell me about it. I never pushed because it never seemed right. Sam only mentioned *FILE 13* once, just before he was killed. He said something about how dangerous it was and that if anyone came after you I should take it to Mr. Casey and follow his instructions."

"Well, that's not exactly right. You see, Dad died to keep a national secret. It's probably the most dangerous collection of information the United States ever lost."

"I don't understand. What is it?"

"I know that the Cold War is officially over, but there are still those in power throughout the world that would like to see the United States involved in an embarrassing and potentially compromising international incident. My father was working with the Agency when they discovered that several ex-

KGB agents had gone into business for themselves and formed a rather vicious branch of the Russian mafia. These ex-KGB agents had been using their international contacts to sell arms to emerging third-world countries who are eager to enter the nuclear arms race. Just about the time the U.S. started reducing the number of war heads, these guys were building up arsenals of them and then selling the weapons to some of our worst enemies, and the American public doesn't even know it. We started working with our NATO allies to stop these guys before another terrorist attack or war started, this time with nuclear weapons. *FILE 13* is the code name for a list of all of the NATO agents in Eastern Europe who have infiltrated the Russian mafia's black market arms operations. If that list were to fall into the wrong hands, those men and women would be killed within 48 hours."

"Where in heaven's name did Sam get a hold of something like that?"

"Evidently, he had been using the company and his overseas trips as a cover to carry information on the Russian mafia back and forth to Europe for the Agency. I'm not sure exactly what happened. *FILE 13* was originally on microfilm because it was easier to transport than a typed list. Then, as technology improved, the updated information was move to a microdot. There also a double agent who was trying to get a hold of *FILE 13* so that he could sell it to the ex-KGB agents who are now running the Russian mafia, or back to the Agency-- whoever would pay more. Anyway, Dad found out about it, and he was on his way to deliver *FILE 13* to a *safe* agent--one who both he and the Agency could trust-- when he was killed. The microdot was on him when the car exploded and everyone assumed it was destroyed. When Dad died, I found a letter and an explanation of what *FILE 13* was in his personal papers in the safe. He said he'd left the only existing hard copy of *FILE 13,* one that he had created as a backup, with Mr. Casey for safe-keeping. Mr. Casey was told that the envelope he was keeping for me was a letter from Daddy to me, to be read only by me, and only upon his death. When Mr. Casey gave it to me at the reading of the will, I decided to hide *FILE 13* the same way. So far, it's worked pretty well. Now, I'm starting to think that the copy Dad had wasn't actually destroyed after all."

"Now everything is starting to make some sense," Sally said, nodding. "When Sam was killed, everyone just assumed it was an attempt to take over the company, or that some rival or enemy was just getting even."

"That's why the police never found his murderer, and didn't have a solid motive, either." Sally looked up at Orlando, comprehension filling her eyes. "Is that why you worked so hard to stop the investigation by the local police?"

"Yes. I had to work with the FBI to convince them. If they'd uncovered the real reason why Daddy was killed, we'd have all been in danger. I figured that whoever killed him didn't know about the hard copy, or we'd have been contacted by now. Now I'm wondering if they didn't come after us because they thought they had *FILE 13* all along."

"Okay. I understand why you stopped the investigation, but why did you offer the $100,000 reward?" Sally asked.

"I was hoping to draw out the killer and find out the truth for myself."

"So what now? Did Sam ever tell you who his contact was?"

"No. He felt that I'd be safer if I didn't know."

"Then Robert Taylor must somehow be involved with this list. He could be the contact your father was going to meet."

"That's what I'm hoping to find out," Orlando said softly. "And if I don't hurry," she added, standing up, "I'm going to be late."

"Be careful, Orlando. I mean it. Two hours, and I'm calling the cops." Then, in a softer voice, Sally added, "Don't worry. You can count on me to carry out your instructions." She stood up and gave Orlando a solid hug.

"I'm not worried, Sally, except for your safety. If for some reason someone does try to contact you and you don't know them, you don't know anything. You understand? You're the obedient, uninformed employee. Okay?"

Sally nodded tentatively, smiling.

"I'm serious, Sally. Don't put yourself in danger," Orlando instructed. "If you're told they'll kill me to get *FILE 13,* you're not to even let on that you know what it is. If you do, they'll kill you once they get it just to shut you up, and then they'll kill everyone on that list."

Sally didn't say anything, but she looked hard at the girl who she loved like a daughter. She knew that Orlando had made up her mind to go through with this insanity, and there was nothing she could do or say to discourage her.

"I can't believe how you've grown, Orlando. You're the embodiment of Sam," she said, smiling at her.

"I'll be careful," Orlando replied, smiling, reading her mind. She gave Sally a peck on the cheek and picked up her purse and jacket as she headed for the door.

"Don't forget this," Sally said quickly as she tossed the emerald to Orlando.

"Right. Thanks!" Orlando said, smiling as she tucked the pouch into her purse. "See you soon." Orlando waved to Sally, without turning around, as she walked quickly to the elevator and then through the lobby to the waiting cab. Orlando thought about what the evening might hold for her. She was anxious to determine Robert Taylor's real interest in hers and Hartt's part involvement in this whole intrigue. She pushed all of the dark memories out of her mind and climbed into a waiting taxi.

Thinking positively, she hoped to return early from dinner because she had a big day planned for tomorrow. It was her first weekend back in the States in a long time and she wanted to take full advantage of it. Orlando was sure that all of this was just a case of two women with over-active imaginations and that when she returned home from dinner, she'd have nothing interesting to tell Sally. She was wrong.

Chapter 3

"JEWEL THIEF ABSCONDS With Millions in Jewels! Covington Mansion in Uproar!"

The Friday morning edition of the *Times* carried a full-page story on the Covington robbery, complete with pictures and interviews with the police. The article cited "an unnamed close friend" of the Covingtons who "happened to be in the neighborhood when this awful tragedy took place" as the source for all of the most scandalous details. The Covingtons, one of New York's richest and most infamous families, had once again made the front-page headlines. Usually, the unnamed close friend supplied the press with the names of the Covington girls' latest conquests. Today, however, that unnamed friend was providing the press with the details of the family's large party the night before the robbery.

Tia Johnson sat quietly at her kitchen table reading the story. Several months had passed since Tia had ended her leave of absence and formally resigned from the Agency. While with the Agency, Tia had taken almost no vacation time and didn't have extravagant tastes, so she had banked almost her entire paycheck for more years than she wanted to count. Her coworkers frequently told her that she had no life because of all of the extra assignments she took and the long hours she worked. Ironically, she now had plenty of savings, so money wasn't an issue, and she decided to use this break to spend some quality alone time before making her next career move. Still undecided about her future, Tia's only plans for the day were to get ready for a long weekend in the Hamptons with her cousin Orlando. While Tia read the article, toast popped out of the toaster and the coffeemaker brewed a steaming pot of freshly ground espresso roast coffee. The aroma of warm bread and roasted coffee beans filled the room, but they went unnoticed as Tia reread the details of the robbery. Something was familiar about the burglar's technique. Her mind was intrigued by the story, trying to sort out the reported facts, like pieces of a puzzle that refused to fall into place. "I'll have to call Orlando and cancel," Tia said softly to herself as she became more absorbed by the mystery.

The Covingtons, one of the most scandalous families in New York, had just become the third family victimized by what the media was calling a "world-renowned, master cat burglar." Tia noticed that while there was a lot of speculation about how the burglar gained entry, there were few solid facts. The burglar was suspected to have had advance knowledge of the family's routine and where the most valuable, negotiable possessions were hidden. The burglar was also thought to be an electronics expert, because the Covington's state-of-the-art alarm system had been bypassed completely. Experts quoted in the story stated, "The soldering and splicing of the external sensor systems was obviously done by a professional. Internal motion and heat sensors were also bypassed, but detectives on the scene would not explain the method used." The story concluded with the statement, "Police do not currently have any leads, but they are actively investigating the common elements between the robberies. The most significant of these is that there were no witnesses and no fingerprints." Police Chief McDermott stated, "So far, we're considering all possibilities. We have set up a task force specifically to investigate these robberies. The Covington's insurance company will be sending over their own team of investigators, and we will be collaborating with their investigators, just as we have been working with the other two victims' investigators."

Setting down the paper with a frown, Tia poured herself a cup of scalding black coffee, buttered her cold toast, and returned with them to the table. She pulled her thick honey blonde hair away from her face while sipping the steaming liquid. As she analyzed the description of the robbery scene, fragments of her past started flashing through her mind. The images were out of focus, blurred faces just on the edge of her vision, but the voices were familiar. Slowly, the pieces of the puzzle were falling into place, but the pattern was still out of reach. Tia glanced at the paper again. Something just didn't add up. The early morning sunshine rose over the neighboring buildings and brightened the quiet kitchen. It bounced off the Venetian plaster walls, and the clock on the wall ticked the seconds softly away, but Tia didn't notice any of this. She lifted the cup to her lips again, deep in thought. Suddenly her hand froze in mid-air as the puzzle pieces in her mind melded into a singular, familiar image. "Of course!" she said out loud. Tia knew who the burglar was.

Tia set down her cup and rested her face in her hands. Suddenly the pictures running through her head were very, very clear. She forced herself to re-open that portion of her memory that had been sealed off for what felt like a lifetime. She remembered the work they had done for the Agency in Russia and immediately knew that there was only one man who could handle a burglary of this magnitude without getting caught. It had to be Joe Cramer. He had had a flawless record when he was with the Agency. Joe left the Agency shortly after she had, but Tia had kept track of him through mutual friends. While he didn't want to deal with the bureaucracy as a full-time agent, he couldn't turn his back on people in trouble. His compromise with the agency was that he would be "on call" and continue to freelance for the Agency in trouble spots around the world, almost magically acquiring sensitive documents before they could be used against the

United States. When Joe finally left for good, the Agency circulated a story that he had become disenchanted with the politics and had gone into business for himself. In the months following his departure from the Agency, Interpol attributed more than a hundred robberies to Joe Cramer and his associates. However, none of the crime scenes provided enough evidence to result in a conviction. Tia sat back in her chair and smiled as she remembered the fun they'd had working together. Then, like a knife cutting through her brain, the memory of that tragic last day at the Moscow Embassy overpowered all of the pleasant feelings she was experiencing.

The doorbell rang and Tia jumped. She was relieved, as the sound interrupted her reflections and abruptly brought her back to the present. Tia wiped the moistness from her eyes with the back of her hand, stood up, and straightened her robe as she walked into the living room. She strolled toward the door, calling out, "Just a minute. I'm coming." As she approached the door, Tia pulled her robe even tighter around her slender frame, placed her hands automatically on the door locks to confirm that they were secure, and leaned toward the peephole. Glancing down at her watch, she wondered out loud, "Who could that be at this hour?" She stood on her toes and tried to focus on the figure she saw through the glass.

Stepping back, Tia whispered as she exhaled in astonishment, "Peter Dixon!" Then, louder, she repeated, "Just a minute!" Tia glanced at her reflection in the foyer mirror and smoothed her rumpled hair, and then brushed imaginary lint nervously off the shoulders and arms of her robe. She glanced around quickly to see if the apartment was in order. Satisfied, she opened the door. For a moment, they each stood silently, staring at each other. After their long separation, Tia was so stunned by Peter's sheer physical presence that she just stood and stared. She had almost forgotten his rugged handsomeness, his dark curly hair, and his searing gaze. Her eyes ran down his figure, remembering how his clothes always seemed to fit as if they'd been custom-tailored in order to emphasize his most attractive masculine attributes. As her eyes slowly returned to his face, Peter's slightly sarcastic smile made Tia realize just how long she'd been staring at him. Blushing a deep red from her neck to her forehead, she said in a hushed tone, "Peter, I... I'm sorry. Please come in." He stepped over the threshold without saying a word, but his eyes never left hers. Tia closed the door and reset each of the locks before she took him by the hand and led him down the foyer into the living room.

"Thank you," he said easily as he followed her. He watched her walk in front of him, assessing her figure with a long, confident gaze. As she turned, she caught him assessing her from head to toe before returning to her face. He feigned a casual air when he asked, "So, how have you been?"

"I'm fine," Tia said just as casually, trying to cover her pounding pulse with feigned composure. "How about you? I mean, it's been what,... 13, 14 months?"

"Yes, about that," he responded casually as his gaze washed over her. "I needed to see you," he said, smiling at her. He was obviously aware that his presence was unnerving her. Peter walked over to the couch and sat down, smoothing a crease in his pant leg. He watched as Tia walked confidently into the kitchen.

Once she was out of sight behind the kitchen door, she regained her composure and decided to act as if she hadn't missed him over the last 14 months. Taking a deep breath, Tia let the air out slowly and tried to slow her pulse as she remarked casually over her shoulder, "I'm drinking coffee. Would you like some?"

"I'd love some," he called back to her, before he checked his watch. Peter was experiencing the same exhilaration from seeing Tia after their long separation, but he forced himself to suppress his feelings. It had been one year, two months, and twelve days since he'd last seen her, and while he could hardly believe that it was possible, Tia appeared even more beautiful and more confident than when they had separated. She was perhaps the most physically beautiful woman he'd ever known, and her spirit was indomitable. Tia had always given freely of her time and herself to those who genuinely needed her. But their careers always seemed to interfere with their personal lives. The only argument they ever had was that although he loved her more than he thought he could love anyone, he couldn't bring himself to propose. Tia didn't want to wait in limbo forever, and she had given him an ultimatum: either commit or leave. Peter chose to leave. After they had broken up, he tried to forget her by becoming involved with a myriad of beautiful women, but none of them could erase her memory.

"What's the real reason you're here?" she asked, emerging from the kitchen with a tray holding two cups of coffee and fresh fruit. She set the tray on the table, and then added cream and sugar to each cup as she spoke. "After all, it's been a while since we last saw each other."

He smiled at her gracefulness as she leaned over to hand him his coffee. He'd missed their daily routine and he deeply regretted their separation. After their last mission together, Tia had despised the Agency and asked Peter to quit too. When he wouldn't, she told him that she didn't want anything to do with him either. They had tried a reconciliation, but it was too soon. Too many words had been spoken in the heat of anger to forgive and forget. Eventually, they both agreed that the only way they could remain friends was if they didn't see each other for a while. Their temporary separation had lasted more than a year. Each had put off contacting the other until too much time had passed to make an attempt. Now he had a reason to see her, and Peter promised himself that when this mission was over, he would win her back.

Tia sat down across from him on the matching loveseat. As she eased back from the edge of the seat, balancing her coffee, her robe parted slightly, revealing her lean, tanned thighs. She self-consciously adjusted the robe until she was completely covered. She didn't realize that the clinging terrycloth material clearly revealed her lack of attire underneath.

Peter noticed all of this in a single glance over his cup and smiled to himself. A strange longing possessed him all at once. He'd have to ignore it, at least for the moment. The feelings provoked by seeing Tia after these long, lonely months were strong ones, and they could seriously interfere with his job. He had come here to ask Tia for help, and for that reason, he couldn't allow himself to give into his feelings--at least not now.

"Peter, I'm waiting for an answer," Tia repeated, slightly agitated.

"Hm? Oh, I'm sorry. What were you saying?" he asked nonchalantly.

"I asked you why you've come to see me after all this time."

"I need your help," he said simply. Tia started to respond, but he held up his hand to silence her.

"I know we haven't seen each other for quite a while, but you're the only one I can turn to. Just hear me out."

"Okay, fine. But you're not making any sense. Help you with what? I'm not doing anything with the Agency ever again." Her tone was absolute and left no room for discussion.

"I'll explain while you're getting dressed. There isn't any time to lose. You're not safe here." Peter stood up abruptly, placing his cup on the table as he arose. Tia stood up to meet him, placing her coffee cup on the table next to Peter's. She glared at Peter with building frustration, while Peter's expression was one of loving concern.

"You're doing it to me again, Peter. I told you I won't be part of this nonsense with the Agency!" Peter reached for her arm and she pulled it away. "I'm not budging until you tell me what this is all about," she said through tightly clenched teeth. "What do you mean I'm not safe *here* anymore? Why is there no time to lose?"

"If you'll just get dressed, I'll explain," Peter said, trying to calm her. Then, looking at his watch, both his expression and his tone became anxious. Peter implored, "Please, Tia. I know I've put you through a lot in the past, but you have to know that I'd never intentionally hurt you." He reached out and grabbed Tia's upper arms with both of his hands, and through the sheer power of his will, forced her to meet his eyes. "I've never lied to you, and I'm not going to start now. After everything we've been to each other, you have to trust me now." Tia didn't respond. She just searched his eyes for the truth. "Tia, your life is in danger, and the longer we delay, the worse your chances are! Tia, please, hurry!"

"Okay, okay," she responded, shaking off his grasp. Still irritated and more than a little frightened, she added, "I'll get dressed, but you'd better tell me what this is all about." Tia walked briskly into the bedroom and Peter followed her closely, glancing at his watch again.

"I will if you'll just give me a chance," he responded as he paced the floor in front of the chair across from her bed. His impatience and concern were obvious, and because it was, her voice softened a bit.

"The last time you asked me for help, Peter, it cost me ten thousand dollars to get you out of a Pakistani prison. I'm sure this time your story will be just as good," she said, smiling sarcastically as she stepped into the bathroom. "Go ahead. I can hear you."

"Okay. I'll give you the cliff notes version," he said as he sat down and looked at his watch again. "Have you heard about the robbery at the Covingtons' compound?"

Tia popped her head out of the bathroom with her toothbrush in her mouth and sputtered, "Uh-huh."

Peter continued as he stood and paced the room. "Well, we tried to keep it quiet. But the newspapers got a hold of it and now the story is all across the front page, and the networks are using it as their opening story." He looked in Tia's direction expectantly before continuing.

"What do you mean by 'we tried to keep it quiet'? Who is *we?*" Tia asked suspiciously, as she emerged from the bathroom.

"I'm sure deep down you know who *we* is, Tia," he answered with irritation. "It's the Agency. I'm trying to tell you that the robbery was orchestrated by the Agency. I'm working with them again."

"You're what?" Tia asked, shocked and angry at the same time. "You promised you were going to leave the Agency. After all this time, when you showed up here, I just assumed..."

"They recruited me again shortly after you left. I figured I'd already lost you, so I didn't see a reason not to go back. But when they asked me to try to get you back, I told them, 'No dice.' I knew how you felt about the Agency... and about me, and I knew that you'd washed your hands of both of us. Besides," he added, meeting her eyes, "there wasn't much of a market for someone with my skills in the private sector, so my best chance for employment was to go back to the Agency."

"I see," Tia said, looking at him closely. She saw the hurt in his eyes and her tone softened a bit as she continued. "I understand why you went back, but I don't understand what this robbery has to do with me. What can I possibly do to help you? You have all of the Agency's resources at your disposal. Why do you need me?"

"It's rather complicated, and I'd rather not discuss it here," he said. "It's not safe. Let's just say that I'm not the only one who knows how to find you." Peter stood and approached her, saying, "Tia, I have reason to believe that the Russian Mafia has men on their way over here right now. Every minute we stand here talking puts us in more danger."

"The Russian Mafia! Peter, you're not making any sense. I haven't had anything to do with them since I left the Agency. Why would they be coming here?"

"I'll explain, I promise. But can we please get out of here first?" His eyes met hers and then drifted lower until his gaze reached the spot where her robe had opened slightly and the milky whiteness of her upper breasts were exposed. His eyes traveled up the smooth column of her neck and back to her flushed face, where his gaze met hers and told Tia in no uncertain terms exactly what he wanted to do with her. He stepped closer and held her shoulders firmly in his strong hands, his lips only inches from hers.

Their eyes met and locked. "Peter," she whispered, inhaling sharply, "you said we had to leave."

"I know, and we do," he said, watching her closely and breathing heavily. "But we can't leave before I do this." He pulled her roughly into his arms and kissed her. He pressed his lips against her yielding, soft mouth. He could feel their mutual longing build as their desire for each other exploded between them. His right hand slid slowly down under the top of her robe. He inched his fingers lower and lower as his hot breath moved across her cheek to her earlobe and neck. "I need you, Tia," he whispered against her cheek. "Nothing has changed. I still love you and I only want to keep you safe," he added in a husky voice.

"Peter, I want to believe you. I still love you too," Tia murmured breathlessly. "But… I can't," she said softly, refusing his advances. "This business with the Russian Mafia is even wilder than the story you told me about the gorillas stealing your car from the U.S. embassy in Iraq while you slept in the back seat." She couldn't stop herself from smiling when she remembered how she'd disguised herself as an Iraqi soldier and Peter as an old woman in a burqa to get him out of the compound. Pulling away from his embrace so that she could look into his eyes, Tia added, "Besides, haven't you heard? The Cold War is long over. We're all friends now, right?"

"Wrong. The Russian government may have changed, but Mafia is still alive and well. The politicians may think the Cold War is over, but there are still a lot of fanatics out there that would like to see the United States fall flat on its face over some sort of international incident." Peter stepped back from her, sliding his hands down her slender arms until he held her soft hands in his. He looked deeply into her eyes and added, "We don't have much time. Please get dressed and we'll go someplace where we can talk. I promise I'll explain everything."

"Okay," she said, giving him a peck on the lips. She slipped out of his grasp and walked quickly toward her closet. She threw several pieces of clothing and a small bag onto the bed and then headed for the nightstand. "If I'm not coming back here for a while, I will need to take a few things. Can you throw these into the bag while I dress?"

"Fine. Just hurry," he answered as he threw her clothes into the duffel bag and then walked quickly toward the bathroom. Peter started to knock as he reached the door, but stopped short in the doorway and grinned at her. The door was cracked and Tia had just dropped the robe in order to dress. Clearing his throat, he asked quickly, "How much longer are you going to be?"

When she heard Peter enter, Tia turned quickly, her back to the full-length mirror, and pulled the robe up in front of her in an effort to hide her nude body. "Not long if you'll leave so I can get dressed," she said, more embarrassed than annoyed.

"Okay, okay. But I can't believe you're getting modest now, especially in front of me!" His mischievous grin spoke volumes while his eyes pursued her curvaceous figure barely concealed by the robe and the curve of her bare back and thighs reflected in the mirror.

"No smart remarks. Just leave so I can get dressed," Tia said, laughing at him. "I'm not used to dressing in front of strange men, and you're the strangest I know!" she declared, smiling. "Now get out," she told him as she pointed to the door.

He headed for the door and then stopped and looked at her seriously. "Tia, all kidding aside, we'd better be out of here before they arrive." He turned to leave, and then changed his mind. As if in response to her last comment, he turned and hooked her robe with his index finger and took it with him, without a backward glance.

"Hey!" Tia yelled after him.

"Get dressed," he said, laughing, without turning around. He knew that she'd be blushing from her slender ankles all the way up to her golden hairline. Dropping the robe on the floor, he walked over to the bedroom window. "Hey, Tia," he called to her from the window. "Do you know anyone who drives a big black SUV?"

"No. Why?" Tia was dressing as she walked over to where he was standing.

"One just pulled up in front of your building." He stepped back from the window and looked directly into her eyes.

Tia joined him at the window as she finished buttoning the front of her blouse. "Who are they?" she asked, slipping on her flats.

"I don't know, but I don't think we should wait to find out. Let's get out of here," he said, crossing the room and picking up her bag.

"Wait a second," Tia said quickly. She parted the drapes just enough to watch without being seen from below. "There are two guys in suits getting out and they're helping an older, heavy-set man get out of the back. He looks like he's having trouble walking. He's got a cane."

Peter turned quickly and stared at her. "Does he have an ivory cane with a handle carved in the shape of a bear?"

"I can't tell from here, but he looks vaguely familiar. Why?" she asked as she glanced out the window again while continuing to fill her purse. She set her purse on the chair and then grabbed a jacket.

"Because if he does," Peter answered, walking quickly back to the window, "that's Grouchev. I'm sure you remember him. He's the current 'big boss' of the Russian Mafia. He's got gout. At least he did the last time I last saw him in Moscow." Tia looked up sharply at Peter and then stared even harder out the window. "Come on, let's get out of here!" Peter said as he turned quickly. He grabbed her wrist and headed for the front door. Then Peter stopped at the front door long enough to ask: "Is there any other way out of here besides the main entrance?"

"The stairwell. It exits near the dumpster in the back of the building, but they probably have it covered. There is one *other* option," Tia added, hesitating.

"What?"

"The laundry shoot."

"Show me where it is," Peter said, opening the door cautiously. They left her apartment quickly and quietly, locking the door behind them. Tia showed Peter where the laundry room was and they ducked inside the door just as the elevator bell rang. Once inside, Tia told Peter that the other end of the laundry shoot ended up in the laundry room three floors below at the service entrance on the side of the building. Peter cracked the door and looked quickly toward Tia's apartment. Grouchev and his two bodyguards had been joined by two more armed men in front of Tia's door. Peter didn't wait to hear them kick in the door. He opened the shoot, holding Tia's duffel bag tightly, and jumped feet-first into the gaping black hole. Tia followed as quickly and quietly as she could, swallowing the scream building in her throat. She held on tightly to her purse and jacket as she sped down the narrow vertical tube. Peter landed first in the half-empty laundry basket and Tia tumbled on top of him only seconds later. "Ugh!" Peter moaned as her purse hit him squarely in the eye. "What have you got in that thing? Rocks?"

"No," she replied, smiling. "Just these." She showed a Magnum 357, a box of shells, and a tube of lipstick that doubled as an acid dispenser-- leftovers from her days with the Agency.

"Oh," Peter groaned. "All the essentials," he added as he struggled to stand. He was holding his head as he climbed out of the basket, massaging the tender spot on his face. He helped Tia out of the basket and she thanked him softly. Tia leaned in to check out the goose egg forming just over his right eye. "It's okay," he said, waving her hand away. "We have to get moving. Come on," he added, grabbing her free hand. He pulled her to the door and then motioned her to stop. Peter peeked out the door and looked toward the back of the building. There was a man watching the back stairwell. The bulge under his left arm told Peter he was armed.

"Where's your car parked?" Tia whispered to Peter when he ducked back inside the building.

"In the parking garage around the back. We'll have to get past the guy by the stairs."

"Great!" she responded quietly. "Do you think he

knows what we look like?"

"I don't know. But even if he has *your* description, he's looking for a single woman, not a couple in love." Peter grinned at her. "Come on, I've got an idea." He put his arm around her waist and they walked boldly toward the back of the building. The man guarding the stairs turned when he heard their footsteps. He instinctively reached inside his jacket for his revolver, and the paused confused by Peter's friendly wave. Once he had the guard's full attention, Peter kissed Tia passionately, full on the mouth, without stopping. Then, moving his mouth slowly away from Tia's, he whispered in her ear, "It's working. Keep moving."

Tia looked quickly over Peter's head and agreed just as quietly, "I know."

When they heard the man chuckle, Peter knew they'd succeeded and whispered, "He bought it. Let's go." The guard turned back toward the door he was watching and they resumed their walk arm-in-arm toward the parking garage, increasing their speed as they approached the building.

Tia inhaled sharply as they neared his car. She could feel the adrenaline rushing through her veins just like it had in her days with the Agency. "Get in," Peter said quietly, unlocking the doors. The black calf-skin bucket seat of his red Porsche molded itself to Tia's slender frame. "We're not out of this yet, so let's make it look good," Peter said as they pulled out of the garage and approached the apartment building where the guard was watching them.

"Okay," she said seriously back at him. Tia snuggled closer to Peter and nuzzled his ear and cheek. Peter met the guard's eyes as they passed him slowly, and the man gave Peter a wide smile and a "thumbs up" sign. They had passed the test. The Russian obviously thought that Peter was just a lucky guy who was about to get even luckier with his favorite girl.

Once they'd cleared the building and headed down the street, Tia moved back over to her own side of the seat and Peter increased his speed. "You didn't have to do that for my benefit," he said to her, grinning.

"I didn't," she replied, not smiling this time. "I did it for my own." She looked back at him for a moment, not engaged by his smile. "Now, tell me why the Grouchev and the Russian Mafia would want to come visit me."

"Let's just say that you made a good impression on Grouchev the last time you two met, and he wanted to see you again."

"Very funny. Now, tell me the real reason why Grouchev would want to see me," Tia said firmly. Then, looking around, she added, "And where are we going anyway?"

"We're going to a safe house. We can hide there for a while and talk. Grouchev doesn't move as fast as he used to so he bought us some time. We're almost there and I'd like to wait until we get inside before we get into his motives."

Peter gave her a weak, pleading smile. The strain Tia had noticed on his face earlier at her apartment had returned. Concern for Peter replaced the animosity she was feeling. So, she gave him a nod and said softly, "Okay."

After driving in silence for a few more minutes, they pulled into an underground parking garage just off Central Park West, beneath the prestigious co-op at 2 West 67th Street. Peter slid his Porsche between two Cadillacs and they walked quickly toward the elevator. They rode silently to the penthouse, but once inside, Tia couldn't keep quiet any longer. "Okay, Peter, we're here. Now, why would Grouchev want to see me after all this time? He must know that I'm no longer with the Agency. He could've contacted me at any time over the past -15 plus years, and he didn't. So, this must have something to do with you, right?" She turned sharply and faced him. Her expression told him that she wouldn't accept anything but the truth.

"Tia, sweetheart," Peter began slowly, trying to buy time. He wanted to choose his words carefully.

"Don't 'Tia, sweetheart' me!" she interrupted. "I told you I didn't want anything to do with the Agency and I meant it. Tell me what Grouchev wants, and no more stalling!" Her anger was evident in her tone and the expression on her face. Her eyes were sparking off his, with anger--and something else. The passion was beginning to build between them again, just as it had in the past.

"I guess if you feel that way, Tia, I have no choice." He shrugged his shoulders and, taking her hand, led her to the couch. "Sit down here and I'll tell you everything. Remember the work we did for the Agency in Russia? Your last job?"

"How could I forget?" she asked, her eyes reflecting the pain those memories still conveyed. She looked quickly down at her hands in order to compose herself.

"I know, the memories are still painful," Peter said gently as he took her hands in his. "I wouldn't even bring it up, but I need your help. Do you remember *FILE 13?"*

Tia quickly met his gaze with confusion. "File *13?* Wasn't that the microfilm list containing the double agents' names?" Peter nodded, so Tia continued. "I thought that list was ancient history. We reported it to the Agency when we returned to headquarters, and I assumed they took it from there."

"After we turned it into the Agency in London, a double agent stole it. Evidently, she had been a deep plant because she was the assistant to the Security Director. She had been successfully passing information to the Russian Mafia for years, but this time she got caught. When we found the microfilm missing, we launched an investigation. We went to arrest her and two of her operatives. There was gunfire and she was killed. The two men with her took some type of cyanide pill and they died before we could get them to the hospital. We never recovered the film."

"Then the Russians have it?"

"No. If they did, they wouldn't be coming here. We tracked the film halfway across Europe, but then we lost track of it. *FILE 13* surfaced again just before your uncle Sam Corogan was killed."

"Uncle Sam? What does he have to do with this?"

"Your uncle was using his company as a cover to carry important information back and forth to Europe for the Agency. One of our NATO agents in Europe recovered the microfilm, and Sam was going to bring it back to us. He was on his way to meet one of our agents when he was killed. Someone had planted a bomb in his car and it went off just after Sam had taken possession of *FILE 13."*

"I wonder if that's why Orlando publicized such a high reward for her father's killer. Did she know about this? Does she know about *FILE 13?"*

"We're not sure. You see, until recently, we-- that is, the Agency--thought that the only copy had been destroyed. Then, when we heard rumblings that the Russian Mafia had started getting interested in it again, we figured there must be another copy."

"Well, is there?"

"We're not sure, but we think so. We have information that indicates that Krosky, Grouchev's right-hand man, has made a copy. We think he was hoping to use it for his own personal gain. Daniel Hartt, a mercenary, thought that he had found it in with some confiscated Russian intelligence information when the Communists were overthrown, and decided to sell it to the highest bidder. By this time, the information that was on the microfilm had been reduced and placed on a microdot, which was hidden inside a synthetic emerald made to look just like the real thing. To the naked eye, the dot simply looks like a natural inclusion in the stone. The jeweler had replaced the real stone with the man-made stone, and then set it as the center stone in what would become a very expensive necklace–published to cost more than one million." Tia sat quietly and listened, nodding occasionally to indicate her understanding.

"Well," Peter continued, "Hartt got greedy and thought that if both sides were willing to pay a million dollars for the information, then maybe they would be willing to pay 20 or 30. The Russian Mafia decided they didn't want to pay another dime, so they set a trap for him. Robert Taylor was the agent who was supposed to pick up *FILE 13* from your uncle, so he was the logical choice to meet Hartt. We replaced the necklace with another paste copy, hoping to keep *FILE 13* safe, while at the same time, use it to flush out the thief and trick Hartt into confessing. We thought that we could use an indictment for treason as leverage to get him to roll over on his comrades."

"Now, while everyone thinks the necklace was recovered, Hartt used his contacts to find out what really happened. He thinks Robert double-crossed him and has kept the stone containing *FILE 13,* and he wants it back," Peter explained. "You see, Hartt is in a bit of a spot with the Russian Mafia. Everyone was looking for the stone when all of a sudden, the necklace showed up again--this time around the neck of a New York socialite. She bought it at a private auction. We checked her out, and she doesn't seem to have any connections with the Agency or the Russian Mafia. We were ready to set up a buy when the necklace was stolen again. You read the story in the papers this morning about the Covington robbery?"

"Yes," Tia answered quickly, nodding her head as she examined her fingers. "So that necklace was part of the robbery?" she asked without looking up.

"Uh-huh," Peter confirmed, and then added, "and I'm sure you know who did the job." Peter looked at her expectantly.

Tia looked up at Peter, recognition in her eyes, and said, "It had to be Joe. But he can't be working for the Agency again, not after Russia."

"No way," Peter said emphatically, standing up.

"After what the Agency put you through, he wouldn't give them or me the time of day, and he holds me personally responsible for everything that happened to you and your family. Joe left the Agency shortly after you did, and from what I heard, he went into business for himself. I checked with the feds here and with Interpol. He has a rap sheet a mile long, but no convictions. He's under suspicion for about thirty robberies across the U.S. and Europe, but all their *evidence* is conjecture. The cops haven't been able to make anything stick. When Joe robbed the Covington house, he not only walked away with several million in jewelry, he picked up one of the hottest pieces of counter-intelligence on the market, and he doesn't even know what he has."

"Okay, I get all that," Tia said, looking at Peter, "but I don't understand what this has to do with me. What are you expecting me to do to help?"

"Tia," he began slowly, "we think Joe is coming to see you. He's been seen around town, and that's why we think Grouchev came to your apartment. He wants to be there when Joe arrives, and possibly use you as leverage, so he can get the stone back." Peter started pacing and continued, "You see, there have already been two attempts on Joe's life, and I guess he's not planning to wait around for a third. We know Joe feels he can trust you and we think he may be ready to come in. He's going to need some help if he's going to stay alive."

"So what do we do now? How do we help Joe?" Tia asked, genuinely scared.

"Joe was on his way to your apartment, and he could have arrived there at any time. Hopefully, we've drawn Grouchev away from your apartment so they won't run into each other. We also intercepted a letter from Joe to you. Since we intercepted it from several sources, it's obvious that he's been purposely circulating it." At this, Tia raised an irritated eyebrow, but remained silent, so Peter continued. "In the letter, Joe says that he now has enough money for the two of you to get married and you two can now go on that extended honeymoon you have talked about so much."

Tia frowned and stared at him with her mouth open. "Honeymoon?" she asked. "What the heck is he talking about? That doesn't make any sense. He's like a brother to me. I never had a romantic relationship with him!"

"Then you mean it isn't true?" Peter asked slowly, teasing her. He had been pretty sure it was an invention, but he was happy to hear the words directly from Tia's lips.

"Of course it isn't true! I mean, Joe and I are close, but we've never had any romantic inclinations," Tia exclaimed. Then, a little embarrassed, she added, "I mean, we just don't see each other that way, especially when there was... I mean, well, you know what I mean!"

Peter laughed at her discomfort and then hugged her impulsively. "You have no idea how happy I am to hear that!" he said with a soft chuckle.

Tia groaned in reply, but she didn't shrug off his touch this time. She simply closed her eyes and concentrated on the warmth and security she received from his strong arms, and breathed in his uniquely male scent. It had been a long time and she had missed this. Without moving, she asked softly, "Peter, this is a ruse, right? I mean, you don't really think he's serious, do you? You don't really think he wants to marry me?"

"No, I don't think he really wants to marry you," Peter reassured her. "I think he wrote to you that he was coming here to marry you assuming that the letter would be intercepted. Like I told you, he's been out in the cold so long, he doesn't know who to trust. He does know, however, that you wouldn't have anything to do with the Agency or me, so you're a safe bet." Peter added, "In the letter, Joe said he'd be arriving the day after tomorrow. He's made his movements in the city so obvious that Grouchev's agent wouldn't have any trouble tracking him. If I know Joe, he would've convinced the agent watching the hotel that he hasn't left his room. That way he could sneak out and see you without them getting wind of it."

"But if Joe's in danger and trying to dodge these people, why would he make his movements so obvious? Why wouldn't he lay low for a while?" asked Tia.

"Because that's Joe's M.O." answered Peter. "When he goes into a new city and suspects he may be watched, he makes a big splash about where he's going to be. He'll send false correspondence, leak details to people he knows will gossip... and he does it all to establish a false itinerary. Then, he sneaks out, does whatever it is he came there to do, and sneaks back--all without anyone being the wiser. When the job's done, he makes as big a splash of leaving as he did when he arrived. That's why they haven't been able to pin anything on him. Without knowing it, the very cops assigned to watch him have provided his alibi. It's a perfect set-up."

"Oh, I could slap him! He's so used to this routine that he won't even be considering that anyone could outsmart him. He doesn't have any idea how much danger he's in," worried Tia. Looking at Peter, she added, "When he goes to my apartment to meet me, I won't be the one waiting for him! We have to get back there as fast as we can and stop Grouchev before he kills Joe!" Without waiting for a reply, Tia picked up her bag and started for the door.

"No!" Peter said, blocking Tia's path. "Joe will have to take care of himself. I can't run the risk of letting them get a hold of you too. You don't know all the details, and if they started questioning you, then you'd have nothing to bargain with." Tia didn't answer him, but stopped and looked deeply into his eyes. She could see that he was keeping something from her. Peter continued, "There's a mole working in the Agency, and we've suspected for a long time that he was the one responsible for your uncle's death. Robert's been on his tail for quite a while, but every time he gets close to learning his identity, he gives Robert the slip. We need you to help us find out who he is and recover *FILE 13*. Tia, that information is just as dangerous as it was when we first found out about it. If it should fall into the wrong hands, there are at least 250 men and women in Europe and eastern Asia who will die within the first forty-eight hours! We need to put the old team back together. The only people I feel I can trust right now are Robert, you, and Joe." Peter paused a minute and waited for a response. Tia's silence urged him on, so he continued, "And without you, he won't work." Peter paused again and looked deeply into her eyes. He was trying to decide if he should tell Tia the rest of the story. He decided against it for now.

"Okay, Peter. I'll do whatever I can to help. Where do we start?"

"For now, we wait here. Since Grouchev missed you at the apartment, he'll probably leave a couple of men there and start following our trail. I'm sure by now he's heard about the 'loving couple' leaving the building right after he arrived, and has put two and two together."

"But, what about Joe?" Tia asked. "He'll run right into those guys waiting at my apartment."

"It's okay," Peter replied, assuring her. "I apprised the Agency of my plan, and they know where we are. They are also on the lookout for Joe, so if he runs into Grouchev's men at your apartment, there will be one or two of our guys close by to help him out. They will contact me here within the next 15 minutes with an update."

"Okay, that sounds good," Tia responded, dropping her bag on the chair. "But… are we safe here?" she asked, looking around anxiously. "I'm sure Grouchev must know about this place, and I'm sure he's going to send someone here to look for us when they find my place empty."

"First of all," he said, moving closer to her, "Grouchev came here first, so we have some time before he'll come back. Second, I'm sure he'll assume it's unlikely I'll come back here because the building's being watched. There's been an agent stationed out front all day watching for my car. That's why I parked it across town in a public parking lot and borrowed a friend's Porsche. If they had any inkling we were here, they would've already been up here. By the time they get around to checking this apartment again, we'll be gone," Peter stated confidently. Tia looked at him, flabbergasted, trying to decide if he was being serious or if he was trying to be funny. Peter noticed her look and added quickly, "That's why this is the perfect place for us to hide."

"Besides," he added softly as he folded her smoothly into his arms, "you have me to protect you!"

"That may be true," she said, releasing herself from his grasp and looking tersely back at him. "But who's going to protect you from me?"

"Ah," he said, taking her in his arms again. "I guess I'll have to take my chances!" Before she could utter the sharp retort on the tip of her tongue, he covered her mouth with his own, and her words were lost in their passion. They stayed there together, wrapped tightly in each other's arms, for several minutes. Finally, the loud, continuous ringing of the telephone interrupted them.

"Excuse me," Peter said, releasing her quickly and walking over to the telephone. He flicked a switch at the base of the cradle and then picked up the receiver. Peter had installed a jamming device in case anyone decided to tap his line. "Hello," he said quickly. "Yes, it's clear." Tia could only hear Peter's end of the conversation, but clearly they had a plan in mind.

Peter continued answering questions. "Yes, she's here with me now. Yeah, they were at her apartment, just as we expected. They arrived just after I did, but we managed to give them the slip. No, I don't think so, but it doesn't matter. We won't be here that long."

Tia walked over to the window trying to give him some privacy, but it was impossible to miss what he was saying. "He's ready? Okay. I'll tell her. Yeah, we'll be there. Just give us enough time to make sure there's no one tailing us. Do you have any word on his identity? Uh-huh. Okay, I'll talk to you at the next check-in time." Peter hung up the phone and turned off the jamming device.

Tia turned to face him and asked, "The Agency, I presume?" It was a rhetorical question. She knew it couldn't be anyone else.

"Yeah. They said Joe contacted them. He must *really* be scared! Joe said he would contact them again after he saw you. They wanted to make sure that you were safe and that I'd gotten to you before Grouchev. Our plan worked exactly as we expected. One of our agents is tailing Grouchev right now and he's on his way over here. Now, it's time to leave. We're going to double back before they find us. Joe said he'd meet us at your apartment and I want to be there when he arrives." Peter took Tia's arm and started to lead her to the door.

"But wait!" Tia said, pulling her arm out of Peter's grasp. "Grouchev must have stationed men there in case I came back. How are we going to get rid of them? And how is Joe going to meet us there without them seeing him?"

"Don't worry," he said, taking her firmly by the shoulders. "Joe knows what he's doing. Besides, there's something else you need to be concerned about--something that's more dangerous than Grouchev."

"What do you mean, Peter? What haven't you told me?" Tia asked with more than a little annoyance.

"Hartt's working in New York, trying to find *FILE 13* before we do. He's contacted your cousin Orlando. He thinks she knows what *FILE 13* is, and that she can locate it for him. Unfortunately for her, she probably doesn't have the foggiest idea what he's talking about."

"Peter, she could be in real danger! You need to do something about this right now!" Tia broke his hold on her and paced the room as she spoke. "She has no idea what kind of danger she's in! She's very hot-tempered and tends to act before she thinks. She could very easily end up dead!" Tia breathed in sharply and then continued, as if she was talking to herself: "Sam probably tried to keep her in the dark to protect her. She can't tell them about *FILE 13* if she doesn't know what it is. Hartt's probably going to take her somewhere where he can work on her slowly, carefully, without interruption."

Then, abruptly, Tia stopped talking and turned to Peter. She demanded, "What are you going to do about this? What is the Agency doing about this? From the way you described him, Hartt is desperate, and that makes him *very* dangerous!"

"I know how dangerous he is," Peter conceded. "Like I told you, he used to be one of ours, but now we're pretty sure he's gone over to the other side. He met with Orlando at her office, and then he left. We've got Robert on the job. He's already contacted Orlando and he's acting as her bodyguard and at the same time trying to locate any information which might lead us to *FILE 13*. She should be safe enough for now."

"For now?" Tia asked, stunned. "Peter, we've got to find her fast! I'm sure she can't possibly realize the magnitude of the mess that she's mixed up in, and if anything happens to her, I'll never forgive myself!" A loud buzzer interrupted her.

"Don't worry about Orlando right now, Tia. Grouchev's SUV just pulled up out front. That buzzer was a signal from one of my men. We've got to get out of here now!" He walked to the end table and, pulling out the top drawer, removed two objects that Tia couldn't see. Turning, Peter grabbed her hands and turned them palm up. "Here," he said hurriedly as he forced a box of ammunition and a revolver into her open hand. He pulled the side of his jacket back and tucked his ammunition into his pockets. He checked his revolver and put it back in the shoulder harness. "Come on," he said, taking Tia by the arm. "We don't have any time to lose." They took the elevator to the lobby and then walked quickly to the back stairs that led to the parking garage where Peter's car was parked. Before they stepped out of the stairwell, Peter sneaked a peak at the parking garage elevator. As he'd suspected, there was a man waiting just out of sight of the elevator, watching it with his hand resting on his revolver. He had his back to the stairwell, so he didn't see Peter lead Tia through the maze of cars, doubled over, hugging the wall. They paused briefly between the cars and looked back at the stairwell they'd just exited. There were two men approaching the door, guns ready. Just as they were going to make a run for it, Tia and Peter spotted the black sedan parked across from their car in the garage. There were three more men standing at the back of the car, trying to look casual. "See them?" Peter whispered. Tia nodded. "We'll wait until someone comes out to their car and then we'll make a run for it. They won't start shooting in front of witnesses."

As soon as a group of people emerged from the stairwell--three couples walking arm in arm and talking loudly--Tia and Peter made a run for the car. The armed man at the elevator and the men at the stairs started to remove their guns, but as soon as they realized it wasn't Tia and Peter, they replaced their revolvers. The laughing men and women were followed by a group of three other couples, who emerged from the stairwell. The men by the elevator, the stairwell, and in back of the sedan were forced to wait and watch helplessly as Tia and Peter joined the group and walked quickly to his car. As the armed men followed Tia and Peter across the parking garage, Tia and Peter quickly entered the car and started the engine. The men behind the sedan did the same, and they were joined by the men at the elevator and stairwell. Once inside, Tia asked anxiously, "What do we do now?"

"We're going to have to lose them. Hold on," he said, grinning. "This may get tricky!" Peter loved high-speed chases. He looked like a little boy who'd just gotten his Christmas wish fulfilled. The next fifteen minutes for Tia were like the wildest roller coaster ride she'd ever been on. Peter had raced all over Europe and was an expert driver. It was one of his favorite covers, and while on the racing circuit, he had learned all of the tricks of the trade.

The parking garage was under the hotel and several floors had to be traveled before reaching the street. Peter started the car's engine and eased out quickly from between the two Cadillacs. The black sedan's driver also started his engine, but his car was facing the wrong way. He tried to follow Peter by shifting his car into reverse.

They both headed for the first turn, Peter in first gear and the sedan in reverse. When Peter was clear of the other cars, he pushed the gas pedal to the floor and jammed the Porsche into second gear. He approached the turn to the next level at thirty miles per hour, slammed on the brakes, shifted into neutral, and slid around the turn. The turn was so violent that Tia slammed into him even though she was wearing her seatbelt. He grinned down at her as he navigated the turn without taking his eyes off of the roadway in front of him, and shifted back into second. The black sedan had, by this time, turned the car around and was in active pursuit of Tia and Peter. The sedan swung around the corner and skidded to a stop, as the driver shouted obscenities and blew his horn. Unaware of the scene unfolding right in front of them, one of the couples coming out of the stairwell decided to get romantic in the path of the car. The couple was locked in such a passionate embrace that it took a full five seconds of steady horn blowing and shouting before they noticed the driver of the car. The amorous couple finally looked up, the male gestured and shouted profanities back at the Russians as they continued on to their own car.

The Russian driver cursed under his breath in his native tongue, and tried to make up for lost time. The sounds of screeching tires and metal against concrete could be heard as he tried to negotiate the turns at top speed in order to catch Peter's car. The sedan didn't have the same turning radius, and the driver didn't have the same level of expertise as Peter. So when he tried to match Peter's speed, he smashed into other cars and concrete pillars, again and again, on every turn.

Out on 67th Street, Peter took one quick look down Columbus Avenue at the on-coming traffic and, turning right, jumped into the intersection. He expertly judged their speed and the capacity of his own car, and although the screech of horns and thunder of human feet dodging his onslaught was overpowering to Tia's senses, no one was hurt. Peter had missed all of his possible targets. A city bus, however, was determined to make a left turn in front of Peter at the next corner, and he was forced to slam on the brakes. He automatically extended his right arm and put his hand across Tia's chest to keep her from going through the windshield, while keeping his eyes on the road, as he spun the car around. Once the car was righted again, Tia said, "You can remove your hand from my chest now!" Grinning, he complied.

Peter stomped on the gas pedal again and spun the car 180 degrees in the middle of the intersection, heading back the way he had come. Grouchev's driver stared out the driver's window at Peter and Tia, mouth open, as they passed him going in the opposite direction. Peter turned right at 65th Street and drove north on Broadway, trying to lose the Russian in the traffic. Grouchev's driver, however, was cleverer than Peter had anticipated, and he intercepted their car at 72nd Street. Just as they entered the intersection, Peter saw the sedan and spun the car left into the middle of the intersection, just missing the large group of people crossing the street on their way to Verdi Square. Peter took another sharp left and joined the heavy traffic heading south on Broadway. The sedan was right behind him, and followed Peter as he swerved in and out of each lane, barely missing the slower cars as they passed them. The driver followed them through the intersection at 71st Street, then 70th Street, and then 69th Street, gaining speed with each block they passed. He was so focused on his pursuit of Peter and Tia that he wasn't paying attention to the traffic ahead of them, and he didn't see the city bus pull out in front of him, in the right lane, heading for the bus stop at 68th Street. The sedan driver was now going too fast to stop, and so he swerved to the right in order to miss the bus, sending the car in the right lane, skidding sideways to avoid a collision. When the sedan driver tried to correct his trajectory, he overcompensated, driving toward a second city bus stopped in traffic in front of the Apple Store. Screams from the stopped city bus passengers brought the driver's attention to the scene at the rear of his bus, where pedestrians were running for their lives and the sedan was bearing down on the bus out of control. The sedan driver realized that there was no possibility of him stopping in time, so he tried to turn the car in order to minimize the damage to the bus. He was going too fast to alter his trajectory and, realizing that he was going to hit the bus, the driver slammed on the brakes with both feet, and screamed and cursed loudly as he covered his face with his hands. The unconstrained wheel, now turning freely, spun the car back into the direction of the back of the bus. As the front left fender of the Sedan hit the back right corner of the bus and the front right wheel hit the curb, the Sedan briefly became airborne, and careened directly toward the glass walls of the Apple Store. The customers standing at the demonstration counters looked up just in time to run out of the way of the car as it crashed through the scaffolding outside the building and the 30 foot-tall plate glass windows. The explosive impact sent pedestrians, street vendors, and customers running in every direction, while tourists across the street snapped photos and recorded video with their phones. Pieces of scaffolding, awning, glass, smartphones, and tablets rained down on the car as it came to a stop up against one of the demonstration tables in the store lobby. The driver was unconscious, his bloody face resting at an angle on a very loud, annoying horn. His passengers were also bloody and moaning, as they tried to right themselves in the back seat. Peter and Tia were two blocks away from the accident when they heard the explosive sound of breaking glass and falling metal. Peter looked briefly in his rearview mirror and Tia turned around, but neither of them could see anything beyond the traffic and the rushing crowds. They slowed and momentarily breathed a sigh of relief, convinced they'd lost the Russian Mafia, when Peter spotted another sedan behind them. "Now who's following us?" Tia asked him.

"I think it's Krosky. He's number two, right under Grouchev," said Peter.

"How can you tell?" Tia asked, looking over her shoulder.

"I know him," he replied, depressing the accelerator even further. "I can tell by his driving. We've crossed paths before."

"How good is he?" The concern was evident in her voice.

"He's one of their best. He won't be as easy to lose."

"What are you going to do?"

"Watch!" Peter said, almost smiling. Tia swore that he was enjoying this. He always did love a good car chase, and somehow, he had always managed to involve her. Peter turned left on 63rd street and drove east, heading toward Central Park. Krosky was only a few car-lengths behind him and closing fast. Peter turned left again onto Central Park West, and drove north, parallel with central Park, checking his rearview mirror every few seconds. Peter decided that a slight detour might be a good move and turned abruptly right into the park, onto the walking path, squeezing between the brick wall and the lightpost, scaring the people who had sat down on the adjoining bench to rest. Steadying the car, Peter took the first left turn in the path, and continued down the well-trod trail, negotiating the curves easily. Krosky had been following too closely to negotiate the turn and, slamming on the brakes, turned into the next available entrance to the park. Unfortunately for Krosky, it was the 65th street Transverse. He slammed on the brakes and turned into the first break in the wall on his right, which happened to be a paved walking path. Mothers with strollers and teenage street performers populated the area and surrounding grass. Krosky turned onto the sidewalk at forty miles per hour, and as the car skidded toward them, the people started running, jumping, and rolling away in terror. Krosky slammed on his brakes, trying to avoid the stunned pedestrians, and almost succeeded in scaring one old woman into an early grave. She ran screaming to the saints above her, waving her hands over her head, her purse and umbrella forgotten. One teenager, leaning against a nearby tree, continued playing his guitar, oblivious to the confusion around him. Krosky turned left off of the paved walking path, onto the gravel trail through the trees, heading directly toward the young man. When he refused to move as the car approached, Krosky stuck his head out of the driver's window and yelled at him in Russian. Krosky, fuming, his face crimson, pulled out his gun and ordered him to move. The musician saw the gun, eyes wide, and stopped playing. He stepped back so that the car could pass him, and then flipped off Krosky as he sped off around the curve. Cursing the musician as a typical, lazy, ignorant American, in a mixture of Russian and broken English, Krosky yelled that he would come back for the singer after he'd finished his business. The teen only repeated the gesture and continued playing.

Peter was having problems of his own. Just after he rounded the third turn on the nature path, he came head-on into a group of horseback riders. Two of the horses were just as startled as the riders and reared, throwing the riders. Three more horses bolted in the direction of the walking path where Krosky had entered the park. They arrived at the sidewalk just in time to scatter the people who were picking up their belongings after their run-in with Krosky's car. The horses were running at full gallop with their riders holding on for dear life. One of the riders was holding on tightly to his mount's belly. Thinking back, Peter couldn't help but wonder what the stable hands would think when they saw the massive woman charge into the stable, bouncing against the underside of her horse, hands tangled in the reins, knuckles and face white as flour, her feet still firmly in the stirrups.

Once he was sure that the horseback riders were

clear, Peter drove off in the direction of the heavily wooded portion of the park, trying to reach West Drive. He looked behind him and occasionally saw Krosky's car trying to keep up. Peter turned left onto West Drive and then took the next left onto another walking path. A wide opening on his right flew past and Peter slammed on the brakes, skidding to a stop. He again stretched out his right arm across Tia's chest, preventing her from being harmed. He waited a moment before removing his hand, grinning at her. Tia glanced over at him and, grinning back at him, raised one eyebrow and remarked, "I think you're making this a habit."

"I wouldn't mind," he said, smiling. He put the car into reverse and sped back down the walking trail until he reached the opening. The wide, paved path in front of him was blocked by a chained gate and a sign that read: "RESTRICTED! MAINTENANCE VEHICLES ONLY!" Peter looked behind him and couldn't see Krosky's car, but he could hear him gunning the motor and wheels spinning in the dirt. "Time to go," he said to Tia before turning into the path and smashing through the chain on the gate.

"Watch out!" Tia yelled just as they rounded the first bend. Heading toward them was an electric golf cart, painted in the city maintenance vehicle colors. The driver of the golf cart was just as surprised to see their car as they were to see him. The man behind the wheel quickly recognized the difference in size between his vehicle and Peter's and swerved to miss him. The cart ran off the path and onto the grass, overturning and dumping its passenger unceremoniously into the drainage ditch.

"I think we've lost Krosky," Peter said, looking into the rearview mirror. Tia didn't reply, but gave him a cold stare and shook her head. One more curve in the path and they were out onto Terrace Drive. Peter checked traffic and jumped out into the midday rush, turning left onto Central Park West. He kept his speed within limits, driving past the place where they'd entered the park. Peter made his way back to Broadway and when they arrived at the place where the black sedan had encountered the bus, they saw a crowd of photographers, television cameras, and onlookers surrounding police cars and ambulances. The bus driver was standing near the broken storefront window, picking glass out of his hands as he answered questions from the police and news reporters.

Peter and Tia continued past the scene with the rest of the midday traffic. When they had traveled in silence for a few more blocks, Tia asked, "Where are we going now?"

"Back to your apartment to meet Joe."

"But they'll be waiting for us to return."

"I doubt it. By now they know that you're with me, and for all they know, we could be on our way out of the state or out of the country by now."

"Do you think Joe arrived safely at my apartment?" Tia asked.

"We'll find out when we get there. Did you bring your pistol with you, or did you leave it at the apartment?"

"I never leave home without it," she said, smiling as she patted her purse. He smiled too. If there was one thing he could depend on where Tia was concerned, it was that she was always prepared. She meant it when she said she never left home without her "baby," as she called it--cleaned, loaded, and with the safety on.

They arrived at Tia's apartment building just in time to see Joe Cramer entering the front door, dressed as an old man. His long grey beard touched his chest and his equally long white hair protruded from under his hat. He leaned gingerly on a cane as he limped up the steps and through the door, and if Tia and Peter didn't know better, they would've been convinced that the old man had crippling arthritis. Peter parked his car between two delivery trucks across the street, and then they quickly and quietly followed Joe into the building. The door to Tia's apartment was closed, but the lock was broken, and she could see light between the door and the molding. She and Peter each drew their guns before approaching the door. There were no sounds emitting from the apartment. Peter pushed the door open slowly while Tia covered him. They had no way of knowing if Joe had made it to the apartment safely, or if Grouchev's men had intercepted him on his way upstairs. If they hadn't, they could've gotten him when he entered the apartment, and he could still be waiting to ambush them.

Peter and Tia entered the apartment according to procedure. Peter went high and Tia went low, searching every possible hiding place as they went. No one was behind the door or in the bedroom. Suddenly, Peter noticed the curtain between the sofa and the window move. "Come out with your hands up! Slowly now." Nothing moved. Just then, Peter felt the butt of a gun in his back.

"You're losing your touch, old boy," Joe said, chuckling.

"So are you," Tia said calmly behind Joe. She had the business end, not the butt of her gun in Joe's back.

"Hey you," he said, feigning offense. "At least I had the decency to point the civilized end of that thing at Peter. You could at least do the same for me. I mean, after all, I am one of the good guys."

"What do you think, Peter? Should I?" She couldn't help smiling over Joe's shoulder.

"Should you what?" Joe asked with a hurt expression, turning around to face her.

"Sure, he's harmless enough," Peter said, laughing at the offended look Joe was wearing. Tia was smiling broadly at Joe too, as she handed her gun over to him. He looked at her, puzzled, and then took the gun from her outstretched hand. He examined it closely and smiled warmly at Tia.

"The safety's on! I should've known. Well, you certainly haven't lost your touch." He handed back her gun, butt first, before continuing. "Now that you two have had your fun, can we get down to business?"

"Fun!" Tia exclaimed. "You nearly scared us to death. We figured one of Grouchev's men was waiting for us to come back and we thought you were him."

"I know. I saw two of them downstairs and I had to wait for them to walk around the back of the building before I came in the front. I assumed that was why your door was unlocked. I'd just gotten here when I heard footsteps on the stairs. I didn't know if they'd come back or not, so I decided to make myself scarce."

"Well," Peter said walking over to the front door and shutting it carefully, "now that we've got that straight, can we please get this over with?"

"Okay, Peter," Tia said calmly. She took Joe's strong arm and sat with him on the couch. Peter was forced to sit across from them in order to carry on a conversation and he wasn't happy about the cozy picture they presented.

"Tia," Joe began. "First I would like to explain my marriage proposal."

"Oh, Joe, you don't need to explain. My answer is yes, Joe," Tia responded coyly. "I accept. I accept!" she said quickly, trying to be serious.

Joe looked at Peter and then back at her, puzzled. He attempted a weak smile before he continued uncomfortably, "No, Tia, I think you misunderstood. You see, it was just a story I put out about my coming here to see you. It's not entirely true. That is, I mean, it's not that I wouldn't like to… I mean, I'd be proud to… I mean, it's not that I don't think you're beautiful..." He was becoming more flustered by the minute and Tia's giggle didn't help.

"It's okay, Joe," Tia said, looking quickly at Peter. They both burst out laughing at Joe, who just stared at the two of them, puzzled. When they stopped laughing, Tia placed her hand on Joe's shoulder and said kindly, "Peter explained to me why you sent me the letters saying that you were going to marry me. What I don't understand is why I never received any of those letters."

"Because," answered Joe, now recovering his composure, "exactly what I was afraid would happen *did* happen. Grouchev and his men were trying to track me. They knew that I didn't want anything to do with him," Joe said, motioning toward Peter. "He also remembered that you'd worked with me in Moscow. He figured that if I was going to contact anyone, it would be you. So, to cover my tracks, I concocted a story that he'd buy. Getting married was the best I could do on short notice."

"But we haven't seen each other in so long. How did you expect to convince them we were even friends, let alone in love?"

"That was the easy part. I called several numbers in your area code, and of course they traced the calls. Once I made reservations for us at several hotels and restaurants, it was easy to establish a front for a long-distance romance. I even arranged for them to find love letters you had written to me, and for them to intercept the ones I'd written to you." He held up his hand to stop Tia from commenting on his story. "Before you say anything, I want to apologize for getting you involved. There wasn't any other way, or believe me, I never would've put you in the middle of this situation."

"That's okay, Joe," she said, smiling. "I'm getting used to being involved in things without being asked," Tia said, looking pointedly at Peter. Peter ignored her comment and simply sat silently, giving her a weak smile.

"But Joe, if you robbed the Covington mansion, then you have *FILE 13*. Why can't you just give it to Peter now and be done with this whole mess?"

"Wait, wait," Joe responded, holding up his hand. "You mean *FILE 13* was in the jewelry I took last night? How did it get there? What does it look like?"

"It's more complicated than that," Peter said, speaking up for the first time. "I started to tell Tia earlier, and we were interrupted. Orlando, Tia's cousin, had been contacted by two agents. One guy is one of Grouchev's operatives, and the other is Robert Taylor. The problem is that we haven't been able to contact Robert for the last forty-eight hours, and we don't know where he is. Furthermore, we don't know where Orlando went when she left her office. She could be with Robert or she could be with Grouchev's men. So, even if you had the jewelry you stole last night with you, Joe, it would really only solve half our problem."

"Peter, if anything happens to my cousin, you won't have to worry about the Russian Mafia," Tia said quickly. "I'll take care of you myself."

But before either man could reply to Tia's threat, a cylinder crashed through the window and landed with thud on the carpet, sending the three of them diving for cover. The glass door suddenly exploded into millions of flying razorblades. This was followed by an explosion only a few feet from where they lay under the furniture. Rapid machine gun fire from a hovering helicopter followed the explosion. Then, there was nothing but silence. When the smoke cleared, not one of the three moved. The helicopter flew away from the building and slowly approached the horizon. Inside the apartment, silence covered the living room like a warm, dark blanket.

Chapter 4

THE BRASS WALL clock in the foyer of Michael's Bistro chimed seven as Orlando Corogan walked through the front door. Michael was so happy to see Orlando, he greeted her with a fatherly hug and a peck on the cheek. "Cara, you look beautiful tonight! But... are you alone?" Michael asked, looking over her shoulder.

"No, Michael. I'm waiting for someone," she said, smiling. "It's strictly business," she added quickly, noting his broad grin.

"So sorry to hear that, Cara," he uttered compassionately. "Maybe next time."

"Excuse me, Miss Corogan," the maître d' said, clearing his throat softly. "Mr. Taylor is waiting for you at your table. May I show you the way?" Paulo indicated that she should follow.

Orlando nodded and said, "Thank you, Paulo." Orlando squeezed her old friend's hand and smiled. "Take care of yourself, Michael. I'll see you later." As Orlando followed Paulo to her table, she lingered several steps behind him, trying to see who her mysterious dinner companion was. As she strolled slowly between the crowded tables, her eyes were frozen on the man standing to greet her. She didn't see the silver candelabra, the Picasso paintings, or the original Louis XVI furniture. Before she realized it, Paulo had stopped and Orlando had almost walked into him. "Miss Corogan? Excuse me, but we are at your table."

"Thank you, Paulo. I'm sorry I didn't see you. I was… uh… distracted." Orlando smiled weakly at him and avoided Robert Taylor's eyes as she took her seat. Robert held her chair and Paulo waited patiently for them to settle themselves before handing them their napkins. Orlando glanced covertly at Robert Taylor and noted that he was even more attractive up close. She quickly looked away so that he wouldn't catch her watching him.

Robert Taylor was secretively scrutinizing everything about Orlando. His eyes followed the delicate lines of her cheek and long slender neck down to the place where her red sequined dress barely covered the creamy whiteness of her full breasts. Suddenly, he was acutely aware that she was watching him watch her. He could feel his cheeks warming and he was certain the entire restaurant could hear his pounding pulse as his eyes met hers. Without lowering her eyes or breaking eye contact, Orlando adopted an air of professionalism and slowly smoothed the napkin in her lap. After a moment, she said softly, "Good evening, Mr. Taylor. How are you?"

"I'm fine, thank you. And you, Miss Corogan?" he replied, matching her expression.

"Good, thank you. Now that we've dispensed with the pleasantries, perhaps you could explain why it was so urgent for me to meet you here," Orlando said, raising one eyebrow in irritation.

Robert smiled warmly in answer to her question, purposely meeting her cool stare with a warm, lingering gaze. "I would love to answer all of your questions, Miss Corogan, but as you can see, our drinks are here." The waiter, as if on cue, served their drinks quickly and discreetly. When he left the table, Robert raised his glass in Orlando's honor and said, "I took the liberty of ordering our drinks ahead of time. To you, Miss Corogan--a most attractive companion."

"It's in poor taste to drink a toast to oneself, Mr. Taylor," interrupted Orlando, "so let's just drink to the truth." Watching him closely, she raised her glass to meet his, and sipped her drink. Her eyes grew wide, much to his amusement. The Coladiña was perfect. But how had he known? She quickly regained her composure, but one look at Robert told her that he wasn't buying it. "Thank you for the drink," she stated bluntly. "Perhaps now you'll tell me what was so urgent."

"I'd be delighted. As you know from our previous conversation and my letter, I used to work with your father. In fact, we were good friends." He paused to sip his drink. Orlando watched him carefully for any signs of deception, and stubbornly resisted the temptation to continue her interrogation.

"Mr. Taylor, I'm afraid my records don't agree with your story," she replied calmly. "In fact, my records don't indicate any relationship between you and my father at all." Orlando folded her hands on the table in front of her and continued, her stare becoming more intense by the minute. "Now, Mr. Taylor, would you care to start at the beginning and tell me the truth? And if you're after the $100,000 reward I've offered, your story had better be good."

Robert looked at Orlando with new respect. Her manner was direct without being impudent, and her tone masked any apprehension that she may have been experiencing. She obviously had given no thought to the danger in which she had placed herself. If he were indeed her father's killer, he certainly wouldn't admit it for the reward money-- unless he could also eliminate Orlando as a witness. When he realized how naive she was, despite her apparent professionalism, he smiled to himself and then answered her. "Orlando, I'm not interested in your money. Although if you're feeling generous, I'd be a fool to turn it down." He hoped her response to his jab would reveal a little more about herself because he was becoming intrigued by this complex woman seated across from him. However, he was disappointed. Orlando met his gaze evenly and her reaction was as composed as if they were discussing the weather.

Taking another sip of her drink, Orlando ignored his sarcasm and replied, "If it's not my money you're after, then what do you want?"

"*File 13,*" he replied in a hushed, sober tone.

Her face paled noticeably, revealing more than she had wanted, as she avoided his eyes. Forcing her voice to remain calm, she asked innocently, "What is *File 13?*"

"The microdot your father was trying to deliver to me when he died." He never took his eyes off her as he spoke. It was almost as if he was willing her to believe him.

"My father was *murdered* trying to deliver that information," she replied, her anger barely below the surface. "You've wasted your time and mine tonight, Mr. Taylor." There was such loathing and pain in her eyes as they met his, Robert was stunned, and looked quickly away from her as she stated firmly, "It was destroyed, along with my father when his car exploded."

Slowly, Robert took a drink to give himself the time he needed to regain his composure. He decided that, while heartless under the circumstances, the direct approach would be the most expedient, and he was running out of time. So, he responded heartlessly, "Regardless of your loss, Miss Corrigan, *you*, not your father, have what I need, and I expect you to cooperate fully and quickly. That is, unless you are ready to join your father."

"That sounds like a threat, Mr. Taylor, and I don't take kindly to threats. Nor do I intimidate easily!" Orlando replied forcefully in measured, angry outbursts. "We're done here," she said vehemently as she placed her napkin on the table and pushed her chair back. In one fluid movement, she retrieved her purse and stood to leave.

Standing up with her, Robert took a half step toward her, reached across the table and seized her arm, effectively stopping her escape. "Orlando," he said softly. "I'm sorry. I didn't mean to alarm you. Please sit down." Those seated near the pair had hushed their conversation in order to focus on their heated exchange, and were now openly staring at them. Orlando shook her arm free of him as she looked around the room self-consciously and sat down without a word.

Robert sat down too, never taking his eyes off of her. Orlando stared into his eyes, and it was almost as if she could see his soul. She knew that he was speaking the truth. Although she was still angry, she looked slowly around the room, noticing for the first time the stares and whispers they had attracted from the surrounding tables. Once the other patrons appeared to return to their own meals and conversations, she leaned across the table and stated firmly in a hushed tone, "Don't ever threaten me again." Sitting back in her seat she deliberately placed her napkin in her lap. Leaning forward once more, she continued quietly, "You've given me no good reason to believe anything you've told me. If you're not my father's killer, you could very well be working with him."

As he was about to reply, the waiter arrived with their salads. Just then, it occurred to Orlando for the first time that they hadn't been given any menus. She looked expectantly at Robert and he replied, smiling, "I took the liberty of ordering for us. I wanted to avoid as many interruptions as possible." Orlando raised an irritated eyebrow in response, but said nothing. Each course was placed before them efficiently, and they ate in relative silence until they were sure they wouldn't be overheard. Finally, Robert placed his fork on his plate and stated simply, "Orlando, I'm working for the Agency." He waited a moment for her to digest this information before he continued. "I don't know if you're aware of the work your father did for us, but I'd like to tell you about it. He acted as a courier for our government carrying sensitive information from NATO to the U.S. each time he went to Europe on business."

Taking a breath, he continued, "The reason I'm meeting with you now is rather difficult to explain, but basically what it boils down to is that the Russian Mafia is aware of your existence and the existence of the microdot. They have already made plans to recover *FILE 13,* and you haven't got much time to decide if you want to help me--or them. I guarantee that you won't find them nearly as agreeable as I am," he added with a weak smile. In a tender gesture, he lifted her hand from the table and cradled it in his, attempting to reassure her. "I'm not trying to frighten you, Orlando, but I want you to realize what kind of danger you're in."

"First of all, I told you that it was destroyed," she said slowly, removing her hand from his. "Secondly, if there were another copy and I knew where it was, I wouldn't tell you. I have no way of knowing if what you say is true or if you're a Russian Mafia operative."

Calmly, he responded, "I can give you all kinds of identification, but that won't prove anything. Trust your instincts, Orlando. If I were an operative, why would I bother to go through all of this? Why wouldn't I just abduct you and hold you--or worse-- until you gave me what I wanted?"

Orlando considered what he said for a moment as she tapped her fingers on the table. Her intuition was usually right, and this time it was telling her she could trust him. Taking another sip of her drink and feeling the alcohol warm her, Orlando asked him suddenly, "Do you know a man named Daniel Hartt?"

Robert looked surprised and more than a little angry at the mention of his name, but he responded quickly. "Why? Has he contacted you?"

"As a matter of fact, he has. Does he work with

you?" she asked innocently.

"No!" he answered with more annoyance than he intended. "What does he want?" Robert asked, unsuccessfully trying to read her expression as they spoke.

"He knew that I was meeting you tonight and told me to give you something. So, Mr. Taylor, if you're really who you say you are, why don't you tell me what it is?" She enjoyed having the upper hand for the first time this evening.

"I have no idea," he answered innocently. "He's been working as a double agent and he could've given you just about anything. What was it? A letter? Some kind of message?"

"He gave me this," Orlando replied as she slipped the velvet pouch out of her purse and placed it slowly on the table between them. "Now do you know what it is?" she asked, raising her eyebrow again in annoyance.

"I think I have a good idea," he answered, frowning. He reached for the pouch and then stopped and asked, "May I?"

"Be my guest," she replied with a wave of her hand as she sat back in her chair. She watched him open the pouch and empty the contents into his hand before continuing. "Hartt said--and I quote here: 'This one didn't contain the right information, and you'd better get the right one to him soon if you value your life.' He also said something about you double-crossing him on a deal." Orlando watched the emotions playing across his face. First he was puzzled, then worried, and finally, he became very angry. He dropped the emerald back into the pouch without another glance at the stone or Orlando, until she spoke. "Now, Mr. Taylor, don't you think it's time we stopped playing games and that you explained what all this is about?"

He looked intently at Orlando, as if he had been reading her thoughts, and finally reached a decision. "Call me Robert, please," he said, smiling indecisively at Orlando.

"Okay, Robert," she said sarcastically. "Why don't you tell me why Hartt would want another stone like that and what information he's talking about?"

"It's rather complicated," he stated bluntly. But then, in response to the angry expression on her face, he continued without taking a breath. "Okay, here goes. You know what *FILE 13* is, correct?" Orlando nodded and he continued. "Good. That'll save some time. First, this emerald is paste."

"I know that. I've already had my jeweler check it out," Orlando interrupted.

"Somehow, that doesn't surprise me," he replied, grinning. "Anyway, we've been using paste stones to carry certain delicate information from our contacts in Europe back through customs into the U.S. There's usually no way to detect the difference between these and the real stones because we have them set in necklaces, earrings, and rings, along with real stones. The courier just wears them home and no one is the wiser."

"So what has this got to do with Hartt?"

"We've known Hartt was a double agent for a long time. We've been using him to feed wrong information to the other side. Of course, we've had to occasionally leak truthful but insignificant information, or his credibility would be lost. Recently, Hartt decided it would be more profitable to go into business for himself. He'd started collecting information and then selling it to the highest bidder. The Agency wanted to trap him and put an end to it. Unfortunately, we had to use something really big, and *FILE 13* was selected as bait. We'd been trying to retrieve it from our agents in Europe, but every time we were just about to get our hands on it, it would disappear again."

"Wait a minute," Orlando said, interrupting. "There is no microdot. I told you, the only copy was destroyed when my father was killed. Are you saying there's another copy?"

"Yes, sort of. We made a mock duplicate—a fake list, which we only intended to use to flush out Hartt."

Taking a deep breath, he continued, "Anyway, we had arranged to have it brought into the country in a necklace worn by one of our couriers. We let it slip that the information would be in a rather large emerald worn by a wealthy New Yorker. We planted a counterfeit microdot in the emerald and arranged for the necklace to be stolen at the airport. We had hoped that we could trap him and close up one of the leaks we have in our intelligence network in Europe. By giving you that stone, he's telling me that he's onto our plans, and now we've lost our chance to catch him." Just as Orlando was about to ask him to tell her if there was another authentic copy of *File 13* and to explain her involvement in all of this, Paulo returned to the table and cleared the plates. Turning smoothly, he served their coffee and offered desserts, describing each expertly prepared morsel as it was presented. Robert and Orlando sat in stony silence until Paulo had completed his ministrations, each with a fixed smile on their face, looking studiously at the desert tray and purposely avoiding the other's eyes.

Thanking Paulo politely, Orlando and Robert waited until they felt he could no longer hear them before Orlando continued. "Okay. If the one in the emerald is a fake and Hartt knows about it, what are you going to do now?"

"I don't know. Hartt wasn't smart enough to engineer this whole thing by himself. We were hoping that he would lead us to whomever he was working for. Now, we may have blown it. There is only one possible way that we can come out of this ahead."

"What's that?"

"If we can convince Hartt that there really is another copy of *FILE 13,* then we may be able to continue with our original plan. If he buys it, he may just lead us to Grouchev."

"Who's Grouchev?" Orlando asked, completely engaged in the plan unfolding before her. She felt like she'd left the mundane world of big business for the fascinating life of a secret agent, and she was loving every minute of it.

"General Grouchev is a retired KGB director. He was forced to retire when the Berlin wall fell and the Cold War officially ended. His agenda for world domination became politically incorrect and he was ousted along with most of the old guard. We're pretty sure that Grouchev is the current leader of the Russian Mafia's black market operation--you know, their version of the last Don." Robert paused, glancing around him to confirm that they weren't being overheard and then continued in hushed tones. "Anyway, a while ago, Grouchev somehow obtained a copy of the list and was just about to deliver it to his superiors when the Agency 'procured' it from his office safe. We thought that we had the only copy of the list. But our best guess is that Grouchev didn't trust his own people to deliver *FILE 13* into the hands of his superiors, so he made a duplicate copy. As far as we know, that duplicate is the only remaining legitimate copy."

"So, let me make sure I have this straight," Orlando said, looking confused. "Our spies steal the real list, my father brings it home and is murdered in the process, only to find out that the guy we stole it from made a backup copy? Then, you create a fake duplicate list, put it on a microdot and place it in a paste emerald to flush out Hart…, and that's the one you're holding?"

Robert nodded silently, and she continued.

"Yes," he confirmed softly. Orlando was considering whether or not she should tell Robert about her hard copy of *FILE 13,* the one her father had made for safekeeping, when he continued. "As it turns out, Grouchev had reason to worry. Grouchev has been looking for this duplicate copy of *FILE 13* ever since it was stolen from the KGB archives. Remember when your cousin Tia went on her last mission for the Agency, the one to Moscow?" Orlando nodded. "That's when she first found out about the list. We weren't able to retrieve the microfilm just then, but we'd already put plans in motion to retrieve it from the Protectorate, the ruling party at that time. Anyway, you know what happened next, with the wall coming down and the government falling apart. The party's internal turmoil had been accelerated, shall we say, by a few well-placed agents inside their political machine. There was some uncertainty about who was the new head of the Protectorate, and in the confusion, it was relatively easy to steal *FILE 13*. We figured that whichever side won, the new head of the Protectorate would use *FILE 13* to force the U.S. into any variety of compromising situations across the globe. However, because it's still missing, neither of us has the advantage. It's a race to see who can retrieve the information first. So you see, neither side knows who to trust."

"I understand your problem Robert," she said, smiling sympathetically. "But I don't understand how I can help you. I'm not an agent." His story didn't make Orlando trust him enough to reveal the existence of her hard copy of *FILE 13,* which Sally currently had in safekeeping, and his next statement further confirmed that her woman's intuition was on target.

Swallowing hard, and looking more than a little ashamed, Robert continued, "Well, what I haven't told you yet is that the emerald that held the microdot was stolen from the Covington mansion Wednesday night. The story didn't hit the papers until this morning. We'd convinced the papers to help us by delaying publication and not disclosing all of the facts of the case. They even wrote the story in such a way that anyone reading today's paper will believe that the robbery took place last night. That gives us an extra 24 hours to try to find our thief before the Russian Mafia knows it's missing too."

"You mean some common thief has one of the most deadly piece of information to enter this country in a long time? How could you be so careless? How could you jeopardize so many people?" she asked, enraged.

"First of all, Orlando, we know who took the stone, and this guy wasn't a common thief. He had worked with your cousin in Moscow when she first found out about *FILE 13*. Second, I don't believe he even knows what he's got. No one but my boss and I knew which stone was hiding the microdot. We felt it was safer that way. Joe, the guy who robbed the Covington mansion, has been under deep cover. He's been posing as an independent operator in order to gain the confidence of the people we're trying to catch. We haven't been able to contact him because of his cover, but that's being taken care of even as we speak."

"I'm relieved to hear that. But I still don't understand what all this has to do with me. I didn't even know anything about the Russian Mafia or *FILE 13* until today," she lied. Then, without missing a beat, she added, "And my father is dead. Why should the fact that my father and cousin were associated with it put me be in any danger?"

"You see, I was the one who your father was supposed to meet when he was killed. I wish I could tell you who killed your father, but we're not sure. Only a handful of people knew that your father was involved in smuggling the information into the U.S., so we thought you were safe. We thought the Russian Mafia wouldn't come after you, but just to be safe, we've had you under surveillance since your father's funeral. Until recently, when you started making regular trips to Europe just like your father did, they started taking notice. Now you're in a position to be under suspicion too."

"But it was just business. I'm not involved in anything," she protested.

"I know that, but the Russian Mafia doesn't. Since your last trip to Europe, there's been another change in their leadership. The new man in charge knows about your father--whether from his own intelligence network, or from one of our agents who's gone bad, we're not sure. What's important is that Grouchev and the Russian Mafia have become frustrated. By traveling to Europe as much as you have recently, it appears to them that you've resumed your father's activities and thus, have valuable information that they can use. They've decided that since they can't locate *FILE 13* by any other means, they'll get the information from you."

Orlando sat back in her chair. She had been twisting the napkin in her lap back and forth, making permanent creases in the expensive linen. Finally, she asked softly, "How did my father get involved in all of this?" She paused, swirling the liquid in her coffee cup. Robert looked at her for a moment, as if debating whether he should answer her question, and then responded, "I know you knew your cousin Tia worked for the Agency, but so did several other members of your family." Orlando looked up from her cup, surprised, but said nothing. Robert didn't seem to notice, and continued speaking as if he were reciting a well-rehearsed speech. "And, as I said before, we'd been using paste stones to carry information back and forth across the Atlantic for a long time. Then, over a relatively short period, our shipments were hit by a plague of robberies, and the thieves were only interested in the paste stones. That's when we realized that we had a leak in security. Your father heard about our problem from one of your family members, and decided to get involved himself. He used his influence as Chief Executive Officer and Chairman of the Board at Investments Internationale to put special guards on all shipments to and from the U.S. He even went to Telaviv himself once. When he arrived there, he met with the NATO advisor, who explained to your father why *FILE 13* was so important. Your father generously volunteered to carry a hard copy of *FILE 13* to the U.S. just in case something were to happen to the microfilm. Unfortunately, that copy was destroyed in the accident that killed your father."

Orlando examined his face, trying to tell whether or not he was lying. She couldn't be sure, so she didn't tell him she had the hard copy of *FILE 13*.

Without hesitation, she looked him directly in the eyes and said, "Okay, Robert, I'll help you in any way that I can--on one condition. I want you to help me find my father's killer. If what you're saying is true, then I will be in danger for a long time, and I don't intend to spend the rest of my life looking over my shoulder."

He looked at the intensity in her eyes, the stubborn set of her jaw, and realized it was useless to argue with her. If he refused, she'd more than likely try go it alone. "Okay, Orlando. I'll help you find your father's killer, but we must make sure that *FILE 13* is safe first."

That's what she wanted to hear. "Good. Then Mr. Taylor, you have a deal," she said, smiling, gratified. Changing the subject, Orlando asked, "How did Hartt know about our meeting here tonight?"

"Paulo is working for him. We found out this afternoon, but it was too late to change the meeting place. Besides, it would have tipped off Hartt to the fact that we were on to him. At least this way, we were ready for them," he said, indicating the diners closest to the door. "They're with us. So is our waiter. The wine steward and two of the bus boys work for us too. Even the cab driver who dropped you off and the one who will be picking us up are with us."

Orlando tasted her dessert and then put down the fork. She'd lost her appetite and wanted to leave. Robert, on the other hand, didn't seem to have any problems cleaning his plate. "How did you know what was hanging in my closet and how did you know about the shower?" she asked suspiciously. "Do you have a camera in my apartment?"

"No," he answered with a chuckle. "Your cleaning lady is one of ours, so that part was easy. As for the shower, our microphone picked up running water. It was a lucky guess," he explained, smiling. But his look quickly changed from humor to heat as his eyes once again followed the curves her voluptuous figure from her graceful neck to her small waist, which the dress did little to hide. Orlando blushed under his intense scrutiny and wished she'd worn anything but what she'd chosen. Luckily, she was spared the embarrassment of responding to his visual attack when the waiter arrived to clear their dishes and offer the check. Robert gave the waiter his credit card; they both ordered more coffee, and the waiter left.

Orlando played with her spoon, avoiding Robert's eyes. She was unaware that she had stimulated such strong protective instincts in Robert. When he had first read her file, Robert had decided that he wanted to meet this intriguing woman. Now that he was getting to know her, he wanted to keep her safe. When he thought about this beautiful creature sitting across from him, he couldn't justify jeopardizing her life just because she was stubborn. He'd made her a promise and he planned to keep it.

However, he had no intentions of allowing Orlando to get hurt--or worse--in the process. Reluctantly, he decided to continue with the original plan to place Orlando into protective custody, even though he knew that she'd be furious with him.

Just before their coffee appeared, Robert looked at his watch and excused himself. He said that he had to make a phone call and that he would return shortly. He left the pouch Orlando had given him on the table beside his napkin and walked quickly to the back of the restaurant. Orlando was relieved to have a few minutes to herself to absorb everything that she had been told tonight. She finished her coffee and checked her watch. Almost fifteen minutes had passed, and she was becoming concerned. She decided to look for Robert. But before she left the table, she put the pouch back into her purse for safekeeping.

As she neared the exit, she saw Robert in deep conversation with Michael and Paulo. He gave each of them several large bills and shook their hands. She stepped into an alcove quickly where she couldn't be seen by the trio and watched them intently. A cold chill washed over her. Had she trusted the wrong man? He'd told her that Paulo was working with Hartt, and here he was giving him money. Orlando decided to act as if she didn't suspect a thing and walked quickly toward the three men. "Thank you very much," she heard Robert say to the others. "I trust you to make my apologies for me."

"You can make them for yourself, Mr. Taylor," Orlando said, standing directly behind him. She'd moved so quickly and quietly that none of the three had noticed her until it was too late. Before Robert could respond, Orlando turned to Michael and then to Paulo. "I trust that adequately covers the tip?" she asked, looking pointedly at the cash still in their hands.

"Y-yes, ma'am. It does," Paulo stammered. Michael's face was flushed and he wore the guilty expression of a boy who'd been caught with his hand in the cookie jar.

Ignoring his discomfort, Orlando continued, "Good. Then I will also be saying goodnight." Orlando walked toward the door without looking back at the stunned men. She didn't notice the distressed looks on the undercover agents' faces as they attempted to follow her without revealing themselves.

"Where do you think you're going?" Robert asked, grabbing her arm. His eyes were molten and his swift temper was barely in check.

"With you, of course," she answered sweetly, but her eyes dared him to try to stop her. They stood facing each other just inside the foyer.

"I'm afraid you misunderstood our agreement, Miss Corogan. If I am to keep my half of the bargain, I must have your cooperation, and that means I must complete my objective alone."

"Not on your life, Mr. Taylor. I'm going with you!" Her voice had dropped an octave and taken on a threatening tone. Her black eyes burned into his as if she could see right through him.

"How do you expect me to do my job with you tagging along, slowing me down?" His voice had now dropped to meet hers.

"I won't slow you down, and I might even be of some help! Furthermore, and I promise you this, if you don't let me go with you, I'll go directly to the press with your story!" Orlando didn't wait for a reply. She pushed past him and stormed out of the restaurant in a huff. Curious stares and hushed whispers from the customers followed her out the door, and Robert Taylor wasn't far behind.

Once outside, Robert grabbed Orlando's arms and pulled her fiercely to him. She winced as his grip tightened to keep her from squirming. When he finally spoke to her, his voice was hushed and angry. "Hold on just a minute, Orlando. I don't need you to make a scene like that. Your behavior has probably alerted everyone within a 20 block radius who has anything to do with this."

Orlando had stopped fidgeting and matched his fierce stare. "I'm aware of what I did. I'm not stupid, Mr. Taylor. I'm angry! And besides, did you ever consider that this may be just what it takes to flush out the killer?" she asked defiantly.

"Oh, if that were only true," he said with a rueful smile. "You still don't get it, do you?"

"Get what?" she asked, watching him carefully.

"I'm the agent your father was going to meet when he was killed by a double agent. It took a long time and a lot of hard work to convince the Russian Mafia that I can be bought. They think I'm getting the location of *FILE 13* from you as we speak, which is the only reason you're still breathing! If they find out that I'm not a double agent, and they see you with me, then you're in as much danger as I am--not to mention the fact that you'll blow the entire case!" Their eyes met for an instant and something almost tangible passed between them. The passion and fury were gone. All that was left was cold resolve.

Stepping back, Orlando replied calmly and coldly, "I understand your position, Mr. Taylor, but you must understand mine." She was back in control, as if she were running just another board meeting. "You've succeeded in fooling the Russian Mafia for over a year now, and I have full confidence that you could continue to do so. However, if I help you recover *FILE 13* before you find my father's murderer, there's no guarantee that you won't be killed anyway. If that happens, not only will I not find my father's killer, but the list could fall into the wrong hands again. Now, if you'll allow me to help you, I promise to stay out of your way and try to do everything possible to protect your cover. However, I guarantee you'll never see *FILE 13* if you don't let me go along!"

"Okay, fine," he said, looking straight ahead. He knew he'd lost, and he didn't like it. "You win. I guess I have no choice but to work with you. But let's get off the street. Hartt may have already figured out that I'm not a double agent and gave you that pouch as a test for me. I'm afraid it's not only marked me as an agent, but it's marked you too. Hartt and the Russian Mafia will assume that the only reason you left with me was because you knew I was your father's Agency contact here in the U.S. How does it feel to be a fugitive, Miss Corogan?"

For the second time tonight a cold chill ran down her spine and she shuddered. Ignoring his verbal jab, she said softly, "Let's get out of here. I know someplace where we'll be safe, at least for the time being. I also need to call Sally, my assistant, and let her know that I'm okay."

Robert looked at Orlando for a long moment, as if trying to make up his mind about her. Taking her arm in a more relaxed way, they walked to the curb and Robert called, "Taxi!" The taxi waiting up the street pulled up to the curb as planned. The driver waited for them to get in without turning around or making conversation. Orlando and Robert looked curiously at one another, each thinking it was strange that the agent didn't at least try to appear like a normal cab driver, but neither said anything.

Robert had no sooner shut the door when the taxi sped off around the corner without a word about their destination. "Hey, could you take it easy? You're not on the meter, you know!" he said, trying to right himself, using the arm of the door for support. While Orlando pulled on Robert's other arm trying to help him back into a sitting position, a glass wall slid quietly closed between the driver and the passengers and the door locks clicked shut.

"What's going on?" Orlando demanded, more angry than scared. She tried pulling on the door latches, but they wouldn't open. The windows wouldn't budge either. Robert looked at her panic-stricken face and swallowed his own fear. Before either of them could say anything more, a white fog started rising out of the vents near the floor. Within minutes, the entire back seat of the taxi was filled with the suffocating pale vapor.

Orlando and Robert slowly slipped into unconsciousness, still holding onto each other for support. What seemed like an eternity passed before the inky blackness began to fade. Occasionally a sound would disrupt their sleep, and as soon as they would begin to stir, the white fog would appear again, dissolving everything into a comfortable black oblivion. Robert slowly regained consciousness again, but this time he didn't move. He waited until he felt Orlando start to awaken and then slumped further down in the seat so that his mouth was next to her ear. "Don't move and don't make a sound," he whispered, "or they'll gas us again. Keep perfectly still until we stop. Then maybe we can figure out what's going on."

Orlando nodded slightly and whispered back, "Do you have any idea where we are?"

"No. Can you see my watch? How long have we been out?"

Orlando shifted so that she could see Robert's wrist, but she kept her eyes tightly closed in case their abductor was watching. After a few minutes, she opened her eyes enough to see the iridescent dial. "It's a little after four," she whispered.

"Then we've been traveling about seven hours," Robert whispered. "And, judging by the bumps, we're on an unpaved road. It's gotten considerably colder too. My guess is that we're somewhere in the country, maybe upstate New York. Of course! Why didn't I think of that before?"

"What?"

"Hartt has some relative--a cousin or an uncle, I think--scheduled to be released from Attica any day now. I'll bet that's where we're going. Hartt has a safe house someplace near there."

"If you're right, we should be there any time."

As if on cue, the cab slowed on the gravel road and turned onto a dirt driveway. Orlando and Robert could smell freshly cut grass and wild flowers, and the sun was peaking over the horizon. "It shouldn't be long now," he whispered softly. "When we get there, pretend to be asleep. Don't fight them and they probably won't hurt you."

"What about you?"

"I don't know. I guess I'll have to play it by ear. It depends on how much they suspect and how much they actually know."

The car slowed to a stop and the driver lowered his window. He pushed a button and an iron gate swung open, creaking on its hinges. The car crept up a stone driveway and then stopped in front of a very old gatehouse. The driver opened his door, stepped out, and was met by several bulky armed men. They had a brief, muffled conversation, but Robert and Orlando couldn't quite hear what was being said. Finally, the group approached the car and a key was inserted into the back door on the driver's side. The driver opened the door and growled, "Okay, you two. Get out! The boss wants to see you. Come on, move it," he said, making a waving sign with his hand. "I haven't got all night!" Orlando and Robert looked up at the driver with foggy eyes for just a moment before they were dragged out of the back seat and dumped unceremoniously onto the stone driveway. They couldn't see his features due to the poor lighting and the effects of the knockout gas.

Two of the men reached down and handcuffed Robert and Orlando together, and then grabbed each of them by their arms and dragged them to their feet.

Orlando and Robert struggled to stand, but after such a long confinement, their legs were unsteady. Orlando felt like her limbs were made of lead. "Where are we?" Orlando asked softly, still groggy as Robert helped to steady her. She rubbed her eyes and looked around for some familiar landmark. There were none.

As far as she could see in the semi-darkness, they were surrounded by trees. The dark shapes seemed to blend into each other and the shadows stared back at them as if a thousand eyes were watching. Orlando's gaze shifted from the forest to the man standing in front of her. It was the first time she'd seen the taxi driver's face clearly and he looked remarkably like a male version of the wicked witch from *Hansel and Gretel*. Maybe it was nerves or a side effect of the gas, but despite their situation, she started shaking with nervous laughter.

"What's so funny?" the taxi driver boomed angrily. His deepening frown only exaggerated the resemblance.

"Nothing. Nothing at all," Orlando said quickly, covering her mouth with her free hand.

Robert looked at her as if she'd gone mad. "Orlando, this is no time to get a case of the giggles!"

His harsh tone snapped her back to reality. "Sorry," Orlando said softly. "It won't happen again."

"Quiet!" the taxi driver yelled at them. "No talking!" He aimed his gun pointedly at Orlando and asked, "Understood?"

"Sorry," Orlando said again. The man gave her a murderous look and pushed them toward a brick farmhouse in the distance. "What time is it?" she asked Robert when she got the chance.

"It must be close to dawn, judging by the chill in the air."

"I know. I'm freezing!" Orlando said, shivering.

"Quiet, I said!" the man behind them insisted, emphasizing his point by shoving the barrel of his revolver into Orlando's back.

Robert gave him a warning look but remained silent. There was nothing he could do now. He'd have to wait for the right opportunity. "Why did I ever let her talk me into letting her come along?" he asked himself over and over again as they walked. Robert glanced at the somber morning sky. The sun would be fully up soon.

The two groggy prisoners noticed details about the farmhouse as they approached it. They felt like they must have walked two miles by now, even though it was only about a quarter mile from the car to the house, and Orlando was showing signs of fatigue. She stopped momentarily to remove heels and then continued on. The stones hurt her bare feet, but it was better than twisting her ankle on the uneven footing. They passed several pastures where the cows were still in slumber and Orlando was envious of them. The time she and Robert spent drugged in the taxi had only compounded her jet lag.

As the sun peeked over the horizon, the small group neared a large brick farmhouse. When they reached the broad wooden porch, the driver tried to get Orlando to move faster and pushed her up the steps causing her to trip and fall to her knees.

"Hey, go a little easier on the lady, will ya'?" Robert said, reaching for Orlando's arm to help her up. She gratefully accepted Robert's help, and he supported her up the steps and into the house. The sun hadn't reached the interior of the building yet and the foyer was in complete darkness. Their guides, knowledgeable in the arrangement of the rooms, directed Robert and Orlando quickly down a short hallway and into a large room. Once in the room, Orlando and Robert were blinded by massive incandescent lights. Their handcuffs were opened and the two were pulled apart so that they were separated by several feet. As their eyes adjusted, they could see that several large men stood just outside the scope of the blinding lights. One of the men walking around the perimeter of the group stubbed his toe and cursed the offending object in Russian. Robert now knew who was waiting to see them. But, before he could warn Orlando, she was taken from him and led into another room. "Robert! Robert!" she screamed in terror as she was led away.

"It's okay, Orlando," he answered her. "Just..." Robert started to say when he was hit on the back of

FILE 13   151

his head from behind with a rifle butt, and slipped into unconsciousness.

Orlando was led out of the room and across the hallway into another large, dark room. An eerie silence dominated the blackness and she could smell stale, heavy air in the room. It had the smell and feel of a musty attic. As her eyes became accustomed to the gloom, she noticed book-lined walls and someone sitting behind a huge oak desk. She was pushed forward, toward him. She progressed slowly, trying unsuccessfully to dodge the furniture. As she came closer, Orlando noticed that the man behind the desk was wearing some sort of military uniform. She was about to speak when the pungent smell of garlic distracted her. She heard the heavy footsteps and turned. Hartt entered the room, turned on the overhead light, and went to stand next to the desk. Two more heavily armed men followed Hartt into the room. One man lit a fire in the fireplace and one remained at the door. "Hartt! What are you doing here?" she asked in a hushed, angry tone.

"Relax, Miss Corogan. You're my guest. Please, have a seat," Hartt said, smiling. He looked more like a grinning Kimono dragon than a human, and his constant licking his lips made Orlando's skin crawl. He snapped his fingers and the two men by the door walked quickly to Orlando's side. Without a word, they forced her down onto the couch. "That's better. Now, Miss Corogan, or Orlando, if I may… the sooner you give me what I want, the sooner you can leave."

"I don't know what you want. What are you talking about?" Orlando asked, genuinely angry.

One of the men who had forced her down on the couch grabbed her purse from her shaky hands and handed it to Hartt, who dumped it onto the desk. The soldier behind the desk helped Hartt go through the contents, pushing several personal items aside and finally finding the pouch that contained the emerald.

"I don't understand," Orlando said, watching carefully. "That's the pouch you gave me in the board room. Why would you drag me all the way out here just to get back what you had in the first place?"

"Because, my dear, and this is key... Mr. Taylor switched the stones at the restaurant. My men had you under surveillance. This stone must be the one containing the microdot."

"I don't know what you're talking about. I gave it to him, just as you told me to do, but he didn't want it. You've made some kind of mistake. It's the same stone and the same pouch you gave me."

"Perhaps, but we'll soon know for sure." He handed the pouch to the man behind the desk who pushed a buzzer under the center drawer of the desk. The door opened and another man entered, walking silently to the desk. This man was in a grey flannel suit instead of a uniform. Without saying a word, he took the pouch and left.

"Orlando," Hartt continued in a conciliatory tone, "we've known each other for a long time. Wouldn't you rather do business with someone who understands you than with someone whose techniques are less, shall we say, friendly?" he asked, looking pointedly at the man behind the desk. Orlando looked at the uniformed man and back at Hartt, but said nothing. Her mind was laboring, trying to come up with a way to stall until she could figure a way to escape.

"Why is this stone and the microdot so important to you, Hartt? What are you getting out of this?"

"That's not important now. All you need to know is that I will get *FILE 13!*" Hartt quickly lost his slimy grin and looked at her menacingly. He leaned in closer to Orlando, adding pointedly, "You have about five minutes until the jeweler returns,. Tell me if this is the right stone before I have you shot."

Orlando lowered her gaze. She knew that she'd never tell them where *FILE 13* really was. There were too many lives at stake. She prayed for a miracle that would save her life and Robert's, but she had little hope of it happening in the next five minutes. Orlando counted the seconds quietly until she reached 100 and then started sobbing softly. She knew that Hartt expected her to be weak, so she planned to use it to her advantage. She covered her face with her hands and wept louder. Within seconds, she was giving the performance of her life, crying with the force of one condemned, all the while watching the men through her fingers. She pushed on her eyes, making them water, and the tears were now flowing liberally down her cheeks and spilling onto her chest.

"Oh, stop that blubbering!" Hartt shouted at her. As if by silent command, Hartt nodded and one of the men standing beside Orlando pulled her head up sharply by her hair.

"I... I can't help it," she stuttered. "I can't tell you what I don't know, and... and I don't want to die!" Orlando sobbed loudly and started crying all over again, hoping she sounded sincere. "Please, please don't kill me," she pleaded softly. Her red, watery gaze meekly met Hartt's and that of the man behind the desk.

The man in uniform nodded to Hartt, and Orlando was certain she would be shot on the spot. Instead, Hartt slammed his fist hard against the desk and growled, "All right!"

Orlando paused in her performance and looked up, stunned. The two men beside her dragged her to her feet and waited for instructions from Hartt. "Maybe if you spend some time with your friend, your memory will improve," he snarled. Hartt waved his right hand, saying, "Take her below." Orlando looked at the silent man behind the desk one last time, and then allowed herself to be led from the room. She was curious about that silent, stern man.

He was obviously Hartt's superior, and he had the power to kill her, yet he'd let her go. Why? she wondered. The two men led Orlando down the back stairs to the wine cellar. The guard standing outside the door unlocked it. He let them pass, and then locked it behind them. The cellar contained racks of wine from floor to ceiling, and casks lined the walls. It was damp and the air was heavy with the stench of standing, moldy water. Orlando noticed as she was led through the cavernous room that there was a cold breeze coming from the left wall. The two men led her to the far corner of the cellar, pushed her down on the floor where Robert lay unconscious, and walked out. Orlando watched them leave and then crawled to his side. "Robert? Robert! Can you hear me?" she cried as she tried to revive him.

"Ooh, my head," Robert moaned. He rolled to one side, cradling his head in his hands.

"Are you okay?" Orlando asked while gently stroking his hair.

"I guess so. I feel like a tank hit me and then left me for the bulldozer to plow under! Can you help me up?" Robert asked as he tried to stand up and slipped on the wet floor.

"Sure. Easy now," Orlando said as she tried to steady him on his feet. "There's a chair over there and a table. Do you think you can make it?"

"Yeah, I think so." Robert leaned heavily on Orlando as she helped him to stand up. The air was cool and damp and the wooden furniture showed little sign of use. The journey from the corner of the room to the table was tedious because the floor was slippery with mold. Finally seated, Robert gave a sigh of relief.

Orlando selected a bottle of wine off the nearest shelf and struggled to take the cork out of it. It gave a little pop and Orlando smelled the liquid inside. "Here, try this. It'll help clear your head."

He took the bottle from her with a smile of thanks and took a long drink. "Thanks," he said, leaning his head on his hands. Finally, he looked up at her. "What happened? Did they do anything to you? What did they ask you?"

"They wanted to know about *FILE 13*. But I didn't tell them anything. Hartt was threatening to shoot me if I didn't tell him where it was, but I started crying and they let me go. His boss said that some time with you would improve my memory," she said, smiling.

He looked at her, surprised. "You started crying?"

"Yeah, you should have seen it. It was the performance of my life," she said, smiling wryly back at him. "I knew that's what Hartt was expecting, so...." She shrugged. "What surprised me was that they fell for it."

"There may have been a reason. Let's be careful about what we say," he said, rubbing the back of his head as he looked around him.

Orlando nodded, and then asked, "What happened to you?" She adjusted a lock of hair that had fallen across his forehead while she waited for an answer.

"After they took you away," he began as he took her hand in his, "they hit me from behind. I guess they thought I would cause trouble. When I woke up, I was down here. I tried to get out, and that's when I got this," he said, gingerly touching a swollen, purple cut lip. Orlando noticed that he also had a swollen black eye. "I found out the hard way about the guard outside the door."

"Why did you do it?" Orlando asked, kneeling next to him. "You must have known that they'd put a guard on you."

"I know. I just wasn't thinking," he said, smiling weakly. "I was worried about you, and I really didn't consider the possibility of a guard or anything else. I was afraid that by the time I got to you, it would be too late."

"Well, I appreciate your concern," she said, smiling. "But I don't want anything happening to you either."

Robert smiled up at her and she continued. "Besides, all they really did was threaten me, and that's nothing new coming from Hartt."

"Have you ever seen the guy with Hartt before?"

"No. He wore some kind of military uniform, but

I didn't recognize the insignia. He never said anything the entire time Hartt was questioning me."

"If he thinks you're working with me, then my cover's blown."

"What are we going to do?"

"Well, we've got two choices. We can wait until they come back and let them do whatever it is they plan to do with us, or we can try to get out of here. I don't know about you, but I vote that we get out of here." He smiled up at her and gave her hand a squeeze.

"I'm with you," she agreed, smiling. "But how? You've already met the guard at the door, and I don't see any windows or doors."

"How old would you say this house is?" he asked, looking around him.

"I don't know. 50, maybe 100 years old? Maybe even older. Why?"

"Well," he said, smiling as he slowly stood up, "if murder mysteries and adventure novels are based on any fact at all, there should be a secret passageway around here somewhere."

"Oh, come on, Robert. Let's be serious here for a minute!" Orlando replied soberly.

"I am serious. When they brought me in here, I felt a cold breeze across my ankles. The cold air has to be coming from somewhere. Since this is a wine cellar, it's obviously below ground for temperature control. Thus, Miss Watson," he added in his best

Sherlock Holmes, "there must be a door. Let's see if we can find it."

"Okay. I guess it beats sitting here waiting for them to come back. Where did you first feel it?"

"Back here," Robert said, walking slowly back toward the middle of the room. Orlando followed him, hoping to feel the same gust of cold air. She stopped suddenly, only a foot or two away from Robert.

"Here! I think this is it," Orlando said, squatting near the ground. But where's it coming from?"

"I'll bet it's one of those wooden casks on the wall. Somewhere in this area there has to be an opening and they're the only things in here big enough for a man to walk through." Orlando and Robert moved slowly over to the three large wooden casks lining the side wall. Each of them appeared ancient. They banged on each barrel with their fists to see if there was a difference in tone. Through process of elimination, going back and forth between the barrels, they determined that the draft must have been coming from the middle barrel. Robert ran his hand along the edge of the cask, trying to locate the source of the cool air.

"If there's an opening there, then the latch must be here somewhere," Orlando said as she examined the tap and rim. "Maybe this is it," Orlando said excitedly as she reached for the tap.

"Don't!" Robert shouted as he reached in front

of her. But before the word passed his lips she had turned the tap clockwise and a loud rushing sound preceded a large volume of red wine. Within seconds, they were both slipping on the wet floor, and then suddenly, they were swept off their feet. Robert had fallen face-first onto the hard floor and Orlando landed on her backside. She rose first, but when she tried to help him up, they both landed on the floor again in a heap, Orlando looking up at Robert from his lap. They looked at each other in stunned silence and then began to snicker. "Shhh! They'll hear us!" he whispered between giggles.

They both stood up, leaning on each other to keep their equilibrium. Somehow, by the time they'd both regained their balance, Orlando was in Robert's arms, only inches from his face. Robert gently wiped droplets off Orlando's cheek where it had splashed when they fell. He continued caressing her cheek and neck, all the while never taking his eyes from hers. Orlando's hand reached out to Robert's face and she traced the strong line of his jaw around to his resolute chin, and then she slowly moved up to trace the outline of his lips. *They're so soft, so inviting*, she thought to herself. Had he heard her? Had he read her mind? she wondered.

As if answering her question, Robert tilted Orlando's head back, ever so gently, as he reveled in the silkiness of her hair and the warm smoothness of her skin. Without uttering a word, he touched her forehead with his lips, and then followed the curves of her face with feather kisses down to her cheek. He paused at each closed eyelid, cherishing the long lashes and pale shadows hiding her deep, dark eyes. As he kissed each eyelid tenderly in turn, Orlando began breathing more rapidly. Robert withdrew his head from Orlando's face, but only a few inches, and Orlando opened her eyes and stared wonderingly into his sparkling, deep blue eyes. Her own eyes were shouting her desire for him.

Holding his breath at the response he'd inspired, Robert gently touched his lips to hers. They were warm and alive, and this intimacy felt so right, as if they were meant for each other. Robert's kisses became more insistent, more demanding, and Orlando responded in kind, kiss for kiss. Neither of them was willing to be the first to draw back. Their kisses grew deeper, more passionate, and they were swept away with emotion. Robert wanted to possess her completely, and Orlando was just as anxious to prove her growing feelings for him. But they would have to wait.

Robert reluctantly released her mouth and pulled his head away from her. They had to get out of this mess first. Orlando looked at him in silence and smiled. They both knew that it was just a matter of time before they would be together. Hand in hand, they approached the cask again. Robert's bruises caused him to wince as he walked, but he assured

Orlando that he was fine. Orlando approached the tap again, but this time instead of turning the tap, she pushed down on the mechanism. She heard a cracking sound, and the draft grew stronger. Robert pulled on the side of cask and the door gave way slowly. Robert pulled out a lighter and offered Orlando his hand. "After you," she said with a smile. Robert stepped through the doorway and Orlando followed close behind him.

"See if you can close the door," he whispered. "That way, it'll take them a few minutes to figure out where we went." Orlando pulled and tugged on the door until she heard it snap shut.

The darkness was complete, and Orlando started to become claustrophobic. "I can't see a thing! Where are you?"

"Here, take my hand," Robert said, igniting the cigarette lighter. When Orlando's eyes adjusted to the suddenly bright flame in the pitch blackness, she could see his hand extended out in back of him, only inches from her face. Orlando grabbed his hand and they started walking slowly through the darkness, following the single flickering flame. The tunnel suddenly became wider, and a lighter area started to break through the darkness ahead of them.

"Obviously no one has come this way in a while," Robert said. "Look." Robert held his lighter up and they could see a silvery web that extended across the opening, with rather large black arachnids patiently waiting for dinner. Robert passed the lighter to Orlando and said, "Here, hold this."

Orlando took the lighter and asked, "What are you going to do?"

"I'm going to clear a path through here." He took his jacket off, rolled it over his right arm and fist, and started punching a hole in the web. Whispered, scurrying noises could be hard as the spiders ran for cover. Once clear of the web, Robert and Orlando tried to increase their speed toward the dim light, but the tunnel started to narrow again, impeding their passage. They had to feel their way along the tunnel walls. "I wish we had more light," Orlando said to Robert in hushed tones as she followed him down the damp passageway. "Then we could at least see where we were going."

"That's precisely why I'm glad we don't have a better light," Robert countered. "I don't know about you, but I don't think I want to know that those hairy things are crawling up my arms and legs."

Orlando was a step or two behind Robert, and just about the time he mentioned the insects, they came in contact with Orlando's bare skin. She shuddered as she brushed the furry, scratchy creatures off her stockings, arms, and shoulders. She brushed frantically at her hair and groaned miserably as they fell from the overhang into the bodice of her dress. Robert heard her squeal and noticed Orlando trying to get at the bug. "What is it?"

"I don't know, but it's biting me!" Orlando said in an anxious tone. Robert took a step forward and ignoring propriety, pulled the squirming insect out of her cleavage by the feelers. "Oooooh God!" she moaned. "If I ever get out of this place, I hope I never see another bug again as long as I live!"

Trying to distract her, Robert looked over his shoulder and said, "Come on. I think we're almost at the entrance. The light's getting brighter." Orlando nodded, but concentrated on brushing multi-legged, hairy, and slick insects from her quivering body. Orlando hurried to follow Robert and repeatedly ran into his back as he stopped to do the same. The razor-sharp clawed creatures were crawling up his pant legs and down his neck. They kept making their way toward the light, but the light turned out to be a torch, not the daylight that Orlando had hoped for. Robert extinguished his lighter and picked up the torch. They turned slowly, examining what appeared to be a junction between three passageways. The other two, unlike the one they'd traveled, were clean and appeared to be used regularly. The furry creatures abhorred the torchlight, which appeared as bright as the sun in the surrounding pitch blackness, and scampered off their victims into the security of the shadows. Shivering with relief, Orlando asked, "Which way do we go?"

"I don't know. Pick one," Robert said as he held the torch light up to each passageway.

Each of them looked equally promising. "Okay. This way," Orlando said, pointing to the right. The tunnel they had just left had been sloping downward. The passageway they now entered was sloping back up. About two hundred yards down the dry, clean passageway, they came to a dead end. Another torch lit a solid stone wall in front of them.

"Any ideas?" Robert asked Orlando.

"Well, there has to be a doorway here somewhere. The tunnel is too clean not to be traveled regularly. Besides, they wouldn't build a passageway this sturdy for no reason. Hand me the other torch and we'll see if we can find the trigger." Robert lifted the torch to hand to Orlando and the seemingly solid wall in front of them slid to one side. "I think you found it," Orlando whispered, grinning.

Robert grinned sarcastically back at her, as if to say, "No kidding," and then put his finger to his lips to indicate absolute silence was required. "I think someone is coming," Robert whispered to Orlando. She quickly replaced the torch and the door slid closed. They looked both ways and couldn't determine the direction of the voices. They were afraid to go back and they couldn't go forward. "Come here quick," Robert said as he yanked Orlando's arm, and they ducked into the shadows in a crevice in the wall.

Hartt and two other men Orlando couldn't

recognize were approaching quickly, obviously arguing about something. The echoes in the tunnel distorted their voices, but their conversation had something to do with weapons. As they lifted the torch to open the door, Robert and Orlando could hear a hammer hitting hard wood. Crates were being moved and men's voices could be heard above the hammering, as if a production line were in place. Then the door closed behind Hartt, ending his argument abruptly.

Robert and Orlando waited a few more minutes and then edged toward the door. They listened intently, waiting for more voices. When they didn't come, Robert lifted the torch and the door slid open. "Do you think it's safe?" Orlando asked, holding Robert's arm.

"Do we have a choice?" he asked, looking down into her dark eyes.

"No. I guess you've got a point," Orlando replied, mustering a smile. "After you," she said, ushering him into the room before her. Robert smiled, nodded, and then led the way. Once through the doorway, Robert replaced the torch and then quickly pulled his arm through the opening before it closed. They turned slowly and gave their eyes a chance to adjust to the light. Although dim compared to daylight, the room they'd entered was a hundred times brighter than the tunnel they'd just left. Overhead were rows of florescent fixtures illuminating the crates surrounding on either side of them. Each of the crates bore shipping labels in several languages. As they progressed through the room, Orlando and Robert marveled at the amount of ammunition piled against the walls. "There must be enough ammunition in here to outfit a small army!" Orlando exclaimed.

"Sure looks that way," Robert said quietly, looking around him.

"Well, we can't stop Hartt from using this stuff while we're trapped in here," Orlando commented as she turned her back to him and look more intently at her surroundings.

"Oh, I don't know," Robert replied, smiling. "Maybe there's a way we can change all that," he said, lifting the top off an open crate.

"How?" Orlando asked, turning to face him. They were standing very close, and they were almost consumed with the chemistry between them. It was too much to ignore, despite their desperate situation. Then, suddenly Robert's eyes left Orlando's, and he looked quickly over her shoulder, alarmed. "What's wrong?"

"Someone's coming!" Robert whispered huskily. "Come on!" He grabbed her wrist and tugged her toward the closest column of crates. They crouched down and prayed that no one would see them. Peering from behind the columns of crates, Orlando and Robert could see two men enter the room as they talked loudly in Russian. Orlando was certain that Hartt's men had discovered they were missing by now, and she figured this room was a logical place for them to start looking.

However, the two men were obviously discussing the room's contents, and not Orlando and Robert, judging by the one man's sweeping arm movements. Finally, the men turned to leave. Orlando and Robert could hear their voices recede into the hallway and then the door closed with a bang. "Now what?" Orlando asked Robert as they stood and edged their way toward the center of the room.

"Well, I doubt we'll get out of here through the remaining tunnel. It probably leads to another room just like this one. "So," he continued, a sly grin playing on his lips, "I guess we're leaving though the front door."

"Are you crazy?" Orlando asked, looking at Robert as if he'd just gone mad. "How do you expect to get past all of those guards out there?"

"Don't worry. I've got a plan," Robert replied, smiling. "Come on. Help me get some of those grenades out of their boxes. I think we might have the makings for a good diversion here. And if we can do it right, we might just be able to get out of here and stop Hartt at the same time!" Robert began filling his pockets with grenades and then handed several to Orlando.

"Hey, where do you expect me to carry these?" Orlando asked pointedly. "I don't exactly have pockets in this thing," she stated, looking down at her skimpy dress.

"You'll figure out something," Robert replied tauntingly as he grinned at her. "I have full confidence in you." Just as Orlando was about to make a sarcastic reply, Robert tossed a canvas sack at her without a backward glance and said, "Here, try this."

"Ooooooh!" Orlando groaned in frustration. "You're the most infuriating man I've ever met! I don't know why I ever agreed to work with you!"

"First of all, I agreed to work with you, not the other way around," he replied without looking back. "Second, I'm the only chance you have to find your father's killer, remember? Now, if you don't mind," he said sarcastically as he turned back to the half-opened crate, "we don't have a lot of time before they come back."

Orlando glared at his back for a moment, knowing he was right but resenting his tone. She loaded the canvas bag with the grenades and then added several rounds of ammunition and handguns. Robert draped a belt of ammunition over his shoulder, and Orlando did the same. She watched as Robert laid a fuse from the doorway to a keg of gun powder and set it. He grabbed two automatic weapons and two semi-automatic pistols, one set for each of them.

"Robert, I've never seen a handgun like this one before," Orlando stated as they hurried toward the door.

"They're imported. They're smaller than their American counterparts, and they don't jam as easily. Nice, aren't they?" he asked, holding the semi-automatic pistol up so the light could reflect off its sleek lines as he walked briskly behind her to the door. Orlando was watching Robert, pondering the attraction guns held for men, when suddenly she swung her head toward the door. "What's the matter?"

"I thought I heard something," Orlando said softly. "It must have been my imagination."

"We've got to get out of here now," Robert said, taking Orlando by the hand, standing closer to her, next to the door. "Okay, here's the plan. Once we take care of the guard outside the door, I'll light the fuse and we'll make a run for the front door. I've given us about five minutes of fuse, so we should be safely outside when it blows. The confusion should give us enough time to hot wire a car and get out of here."

Orlando just nodded. She didn't feel this was the time to point out how weak Robert's plan was, or the thousand and one things that could go wrong, so she kept silent. Robert tried the door, but the lock didn't give. Orlando said softly, "Here, let me try." She pulled a bobby pin out of her tousled mane and straightened it. Using her teeth, she pulled the rubber tip off of the two ends of the bobby pin and inserted them into the ancient lock. She only had to work the lock for a few seconds before it opened easily. "Where'd you learn to do that?" Robert asked in amazement.

"Boarding school," she replied, grinning. "They had to collect all of the bobby pins at night to keep us in our rooms," she added, smiling. "We'd all seen the movies, and we just kept practicing until we got it right. I never thought it would pay off!"

"Remind me to thank your house mother someday if I ever meet her," Robert replied, smiling. "Here goes," he said as he lit the fuse and then led Orlando out into the hall. "It's too quiet. I don't like it," he whispered.

"Maybe they weren't expecting anyone to come out of this room," Orlando replied in hushed tones.

"Maybe. Come on, we don't have time to worry about it now. We've got less than five minutes before that room blows! Stay close behind me, and don't make a sound." Orlando nodded and followed Robert along the corridor in the direction of what they hoped was the front door. They came to a wide stone staircase at the end of the corridor. They could hear voices coming from the top. There appeared to be several men speaking rapid Russian. As they got closer, Orlando heard them discussing what they would eat before they moved the guns to the ship. As the voices faded away, Robert and Orlando approached the heavy oak door at the top of the stairs. It was cracked open, which explained how they were able to hear the conversation.

Robert loaded and handed Orlando one of the semi-automatic pistols. "Do you know how to use this thing?" Orlando nodded. "Okay. Keep the grenades handy and hope we don't have to use them. Have you ever used a grenade before?"

"No," Orlando replied, momentarily allowing her fear to show in her eyes.

"It's easy," Robert said, trying to calm her and instruct her at the same time. "You pull the pin, and throw the grenade. You have about ten seconds before it goes off, so make sure you're clear. Understand?"

Orlando nodded.

"Good," Robert said, squeezing her shoulder reassuringly.

"Now can we make a run for it?" Orlando asked anxiously.

"Could we make it a brisk walk?" Robert asked, smiling grimly and holding his head where he'd been hit earlier.

"Sure. Sorry," Orlando whispered back, smiling weakly. They made their way up the stairs and to the front entranceway without encountering anyone. Just as they were about to approach the front door, Orlando stopped, dropped the sack with the grenades, and restrained Robert by his arm. "I'll go first," she said, removing the ammunition belts.

"Why you?" Robert asked surprised.

"Well, no offense," Orlando said softly, "but you're hardly in any condition to take on a couple of guys with guns, and besides," she added slyly, "I think I could get further with them than you could. After all," she added, winking, "the guards are men."

"That's sexist!" Robert stated indignantly.

"Just watch," Orlando replied with a devilish smile, and walked away without waiting for a reply. She sauntered up to the first guard outside the front door, leaving it wide open so Robert had them in full view. The guard didn't hear Orlando approach him, and when she cleared her throat, the guard turned quickly and leveled his gun at her abdomen. Without speaking, Orlando smiled charmingly at the guard. He didn't lower his gun, but he was definitely smiling back. Orlando made sure that his attention was riveted in her direction by blowing him kisses and making suggestive movements with her hands and upper body. He was so mesmerized by Orlando's seduction that his smile never faded when Robert's upper cut brought him to his knees, unconscious. His hand still held the gun, but his entire body had gone limp.

Robert picked up the sack with the grenades,

checked his watch and smiled at Orlando.

"We just might make it," he said, urging her toward the Mercedes parked in the curved driveway. She distracted two more guards patrolling the front lawn by fainting. When they ran over to see who she was, Robert gave one of the guards a Karate chop across the neck and sent him sprawling across the grass. The second turned and fired his gun at Robert and missed. Robert kicked the gun out of his hand and struck him hard across the jaw with his fist. The guard didn't fall down immediately, but rocked on his heels a moment before falling like a felled tree. A third guard noticed the commotion and ran up behind Robert.

Orlando yelled, "Look out!" But it was too late. Just as Robert turned, the guard kicked him in the ribs and Robert could feel bone crumbling under the impact. He immediately fell to the ground; he had difficulty breathing, and would've passed out from the pain if it hadn't been for Orlando. She didn't hesitate. She leveled her pistol at the man attacking Robert and fired. She hit him in the knee, and she could see blood pour out just before he fell over screaming out in pain.

Orlando helped Robert to his feet, being very careful not to put too much strain on his ribs. They walked quickly to the car, Orlando practically carrying Robert, and in the background they could hear shouting in Russian. "Keep down," Robert told

Orlando as he hot-wired the car. "They'll be here any minute. What time is it?"

Orlando looked down at her watch for the first time since they were abducted. "It's about seven-thirty. Why?"

"How long ago did we set the fuse? It should have gone off by now." Robert had no sooner uttered the words when the entire earth shook around them. Orlando chanced a look over the door panel. The house shook on its foundations, and then one explosion after another split the walls of the house open. The roof took off in the direction of the trees like a rocket. Men came pouring out of the doors of the house like rats deserting a sinking ship.

"Robert, the guards are coming out of the house, and they're armed to the teeth! And there are more of them coming from the barracks behind us. If you don't get this car started soon, we'll never get out of here!"

"Just... one... more... minute..." he said slowly. The engine sputtered and then turned over with a couple of coughs, settling down to a contented purr. Jeeps were heading toward the driveway, carrying at least two gunmen in each vehicle. The hired soldiers were firing at will. Robert and Orlando were just clearing the gate when the first rifle reports whizzed through the rear window past their ears. "Orlando, start throwing those grenades! Use all of them if you have to, but buy us some time!" Orlando pulled pins and tossed grenades at the approaching Jeeps as fast as she could. Several of the grenades made contact, exploding and flipping four of the Jeeps. Orlando quickly went through the sack of grenades, emptying it. But it had been worth it. They were now out of the range of fire from the pursuing gunmen and increasing speed. They kept checking the rearview mirror for surprises, but they seemed to be maintaining their distance from the gunmen.

"Tell me, Mr. Taylor," Orlando asked with a smile. "Where did you learn to hot wire a care like that?"

"As soon as we're out of this mess, I'll be happy to tell you all about it," he said, smiling grimly. He was in a lot of pain. It took all of Robert's concentration to stay on the road. He felt he had to find some way to lose Hartt and his men. The explosions had depleted Hartt's troops by about half, and the other half were now following them in loaded Jeeps. Robert increased his speed, maneuvering around tight curves in the country road at twice the legal speed limit. He looked down at the gas gage and uttered violently, "Damn!"

"What's wrong?" Orlando asked, concerned for Robert's health. She thought his outburst was because of his ribs.

"The gas gage," he said quietly, almost to himself. "The damn thing's on empty!"

Chapter 5

WHEN THE SMOKE cleared, Tia, Peter, and Joe were laying lifeless and still on the floor, beside and half-buried beneath the overturned couch. The helicopter quickly disappeared toward the horizon after confirming the stillness inside the apartment, which now resembled a battle zone. Sirens in the street below filled the stillness, as first responders rushed to the sound of gunfire. The shattered glass and broken bric-a-brac carpeted the floor and the remaining furniture. A full five minutes passed before any sound or movement could be detected. Finally, as if on cue, they all began moving together, easing themselves out from under the overturned couch and stood up. Joe let a slow, low whistle out from between his lips as he surveyed the damage the automatic weapons and the grenade had done. Peter just stared at the room in silence. He turned quickly to stare at Tia as she moaned softly in pain. She picked up the shattered pieces of her life. "Are you hit?" he asked anxiously.

"No!" she snapped back at him. "Would it really matter to you if I was?" she asked indignantly. Tia started trembling as memories of similar scenes from her days as part of the Agency began to surface. Turning to face both of them, she added passionately, "Joe's here now and your cover is safe. Go find your precious *FILE 13* and leave me alone. I've got to find my cousin before I lose her too!"

"Tia," Joe said softly as he slowly put his arm around her shoulder in a brotherly fashion to comfort her. "Listen, we'll take care of this mess," he said pointedly, not necessarily referring to what was her living room. Joe stared intently into her eyes, reading the pain there, and then continued. "We're alive, and for now, that's all that matters."

"And is Orlando alive, Joe? Can you tell me that?" she asked sharply as she stepped away from him. The anger and fear in her eyes touched both men as they looked helplessly at each other. Neither man had an answer for her. Peter broke visual contact with Joe and, sighing softly to himself, he turned to survey the part of the room that was closest to him. He bent over, and carefully removing his pocket knife from his jacket pocket, dug a slug out of the molding and another out of the door jam. Without taking his eyes off the spent ammunition in his hand, Peter asked Tia, "How soon can you be out of here?"

"What do you mean?" Tia asked angrily, staring at his back. The sound of approaching sirens below were quickly overcoming the normal sounds of the city alive with workday activity. "I mean, how long will it take you to collect your things an come with us?" he asked her slowly and deliberately, as if he were talking to a child, as he turned to stare at her.

"I'm not going anywhere with you. "You've got

what you want, and you don't need me anymore. I'm going to wait for the police and ask them to help me find Orlando. When I explain the situation, I feel certain they'll cooperate. And," she added pointedly, "since finding her is my priority and not yours, I think it would be best if we went our separate ways."

"Don't be ridiculous! We're both after the same thing, or didn't it occur to you that whoever has the microdot has your cousin? Telling the police anything at this point will only result in getting Orlando killed."

Looking at his watch and listening to the approaching emergency vehicles, he added, "Tia, you need to gather whatever you want to take with you, and you need to hurry. You're coming with us, and I don't want an argument. You have exactly two minutes to get whatever you're taking with you and dress, or you go as you are!" Peter's rigid tone and threatening glance left no room for discussion.

Tia, realizing that she'd lost the argument, walked quickly and silently to her room and packed a backpack with a change of clothes, some personal necessities, and some spare ammunition. She thought about Peter as she changed her clothes and her anger began to subside. She'd loved him for a long time, and even though it had just about destroyed her resolve, she had to admit he was right. Tia knew that the police would only complicate matters, and if the issue was made public, Orlando would only be the first to die. Tia remembered their arguments when they'd worked together at the Agency. They never lasted long, and always resulted in compromise and a passionate reconciliation. This time, however, Tia didn't expect any type of reconciliation. Too much time had passed, and they were both different people. While the physical attraction was still there, and she had to admit he had her best interests at heart, Tia and Peter seemed to be at crossed purposes., each with a different goal and a different path to get there. Tia quickly vanquished these unnecessary thoughts from her mind, her Agency training taking over, and slipped her revolver into the back waistband of her pants, under her jacket. Grabbing her backpack and taking one last look at her sanctuary, Tia walked quickly across the room and toward the bedroom door.

Just as Tia was stepping out of her room into the hallway, she overheard Peter and Joe discussing her in hushed tones. She pressed her body tightly against the wall so they wouldn't see her, and listened. "I think we made a mistake. Tia's gone soft. I guess it's just that she's been out of the business too long," Joe said softly. "I was hoping we could depend on her to help us, but if she's going to get so worked up about everything," he said, referring to the living room, "then we can't depend on her. She might fall apart just when we need her most, and we can't risk the success of this mission on the emotions of one woman."

Tia resisted the impulse to storm around the corner and tell Joe exactly what she thought of his opinion, and dug her fingernails into her palms instead. She waited quietly to hear if Peter shared Joe's viewpoint, or if her instinct to trust him was correct. If he agreed with Joe, she would tell them both what they could do with their opinions of women in general, and her in particular.

"Well, that leaves us with a problem, then, doesn't it?" Peter asked Joe. Joe must have nodded, because Peter continued without skipping a beat. "Since you think it's a mistake to take her on the mission, and she seems to agree with you, then I'm really left with only one alternative. For her own safety, we'll have to subdue her and hold her at the Agency until all of this is resolved." Joe groaned loudly at the idea and Peter hushed him quickly. He continued softly, trying to convince himself as much as he was trying to convince Joe. "I have to tell her the truth. When Tia finds out that the people who've kidnaped Orlando don't have *FILE 13* either and that she's their next target, she'll go through the roof! But," he added hopefully, with a sigh, "there's always the chance that she'll believe me and come quietly." Then his tone changed to one of apprehension. "You wouldn't like to take a shot at telling her, would you? I think you might avoid the thrashing I know I'll get."

"No way! Don't look at me," Joe answered with a smile, raising his hands defensively. "You know what a temper she has, and she's not going to like the idea of being confined at the Agency. Besides, the only way you're gonna get her anywhere near the Agency's headquarters is to gag her and knock her unconscious. She'll never go voluntarily. Not after what they did to her family in Moscow."

"I know," Pete said, frowning. His forehead was creased from deep concentration. "I can't think of any other way. She knows too much to stay here. The cops will be here any minute and the Russian mafia won't be far behind. If she's snatched up by Grouchev and his men, they'll know we don't have the *FILE 13* information and then we'll have another hostage to free."

"I agree," Joe said reluctantly. "The best course of action now is to drop her off at the Agency for safekeeping and then try to find Robert Taylor. Hopefully, he's found Orlando by now. Tia will just have to accept the fact that she'll have to depend on us to find her cousin and not try to take things into her own hands. But Peter, maybe you could just talk to her instead of tying her up and gagging her. I mean, you two had a thing going once, and I've seen the way you two still look at each other. Maybe she'll listen to you. Maybe if you told her..."

"Yeah, after getting her cousin involved in all

this, I'm sure she'd sit still and listen to my explanations."

Peter sneered.

"I just meant that--" Joe started.

Tia didn't wait for them to decide who was going to tell her the truth. All she knew was that Orlando was in trouble, and it was up to her to find her cousin before Grouchev's men had the chance to hurt her--or worse--and she had no intentions of waiting on the sidelines at the Agency while these two tried to manage things. She didn't even want to think about his infamous "persuasive measures" often used to get the information they wanted from uncooperative prisoners. Tia reasoned that Orlando wouldn't be able to tell Grouchev what he wanted to know because she wouldn't have a clue about *FILE 13*.

Tia crept softly back to her bedroom door and shut it softly. She heard the lock make a comforting "click" as it slid into place, and then walked quickly to the bathroom. Luckily, she'd decided to wear an old pair of form-fitting jeans that wouldn't hamper her escape. She closed and locked the bathroom door, turned on her shower, and drew the curtain to cover any noise she made, hopefully hiding her from whoever would follow.

Then, as quietly as she could, Tia opened the bathroom window and removed the screening. She lived on the third floor, but it looked like a long way down to the street below. She thought momentarily about grabbing the sheets off her bed and tying them together, and then a smile formed on her face when she saw the drain pipe less than three feet from her window. It looked old, though, and it might not hold her weight. Tia silently chastised herself for being a coward. Orlando was in trouble, and she wasn't going to allow her acrophobia to interfere with her mission.

Tia slung the bag over one shoulder so it wouldn't add any extra width when she climbed through the window. She'd considered dropping it to the ground before climbing down the drain pipe, but she was afraid the noise might attract attention. She could hear the crowd and sirens on the other side of the building, and she hoped that any nosy neighbors would be distracted long enough to miss her escape. Tia stood up on the toilet seat again and faced the window. Her sneakers didn't make any noise on the wooden seat, and if she could just get to the drain pipe without falling, she would be home free. Tia reached through the window to the outside of the building and pulled herself up until her abdomen was resting on the windowsill. She balanced her body there until she could move the backpack through the opening without dropping it. Thankfully, she hadn't put on any weight, or she and the backpack wouldn't have fit through the tiny opening. Tia squirmed and struggled until she was turned around in the window and was in a sitting position with her upper body on the outside of the building and her legs dangling inside the bathroom window. Tia paused for just a minute to catch her breath and made the mistake of looking down. The 30-foot drop looked more like 50, and Tia's breath started coming in shallow gasps. "Calm down," she said over and over to herself. "Just remember to breath and you'll be okay." Tia could feel her pulse return to normal, took one last deep breath, and continued working her way out of the window.

Very carefully, she turned until only the small of her back and buttocks were inside the window. Then, she brought up first her right leg and then her left leg, carefully bringing her body through the opening, into a crouching position on the windowsill. Holding onto the window with her left arm and anchoring her body with her left foot against the inside wall, Tia reached for the drain pipe with her right hand and foot. The backpack swung with her and caused her to lose her balance. She fell down and to the right, sliding out of the window and grabbing at the rusted metal pipe. Her right hand reached the pipe first, but she couldn't hold on. The momentum of the fall was too great, and her body swung past the pipe as her grip started to slip. Desperately she grabbed for the pipe with her left hand and held on. For a split second, her body was suspended horizontally in mid-air before gravity again took control and she started to swing swiftly the other way. Tia felt her body moving in slow motion, but her mind worked quickly. She knew that if she didn't control her fall, she could be crippled--or worse.

Tia stuck out her right foot, and whimpered as the tender flesh around her ankle made contact with the cold, sharp metal clamps holding the pipe to the wall. The bolt cut her as it slid across her skin and hooked the inside of her sneaker, jolting her to a stop.

Tia could feel the burning beginning at the point of contact and spreading all the way up her leg. *I can't think about the pain right now,* her mind kept telling her as she bit down hard on her lip to keep from crying out. She tasted blood but ignored it. She had to hold on!

Tia finally caught her breath, holding onto the pipe with both hands and her right leg, her left leg dangling helplessly in mid-air. She moved carefully until her body was placed perpendicular to the wall, forming a triangle with her hands holding onto the pipe and her feet straddled the brackets. She quickly freed her pant leg from the bracket with one hand while holding on tightly with the other. As Tia tried to slowly shimmy hand over hand down the pipe, it creaked and groaned. Her right ankle was burning and the entire length of her leg was throbbing. *I have to keep going,* she thought to herself as she saw the blood stain her white canvas sneaker. The creaking and groaning from the hollow pipe got increasingly louder with each movement. Tia forced her body to move even faster, ignoring the pain it caused because she knew that the bolts attaching the pipe to the wall wouldn't support her weight much longer.

About six feet above the pavement, the pipe finally gave way with a sickening grinding sound. Tia had just enough time to look down and see the spot where she would land before the pipe freed itself from the wall. She looked up at her bathroom window, seemingly miles above her head, and realized that she was falling backward. She landed on her back, the backpack breaking her fall and cushioning her body, but not her head, as she bounced before becoming very still. Tia lay on the ground barely breathing as the warm, comfortable blackness of unconsciousness enveloped her.

Peter and Joe hadn't heard the noise of Tia's body hitting the pavement, but they did hear the groaning and cracking of the mortar as the pipe gave way. They immediately stopped their discussion and ran to the bedroom door. It was locked. Kicking in the bedroom door, they rushed into the room. When they saw the bathroom door was also closed and heard the shower, they simultaneously came the same conclusion. Tia wouldn't take a shower at a time like this. Something was terribly wrong. Peter tried the bathroom door, but it was also locked.

He kicked in the door and pulled his gun before entering. Joe already had his gun drawn and was crouching in the doorway ready to provide backup. Peter reached for the shower curtain with his left hand and pulled hard, it immediately tore away from the plastic rings holding it to the shower rod. Peter turned with both hands on his gun, ready to shoot anyone or anything that moved. The only thing moving in the shower, however, was water.

"Look!" Joe called to Peter, motioning toward the open window with his head. Holstering his gun, Peter stood up on the toilet seat and looked down "She's down there. She's alive, but it looks like she's hurt pretty bad. We'd better get down there and quick!"

"I'm way ahead of you," Joe called over his shoulder as he ran out of the apartment. He headed down the back stairs toward the service entrance of the building, and Peter was right behind him. They came out into the alleyway where Tia was sitting up, trying to clear her vision, as two men in dark suits were approaching her with drawn guns. Tia evidently hadn't seen or heard them approach. She sat with her back to them, holding her head and trying to shake off the effects of the fall.

"Look out!" Peter shouted to Tia as he and Joe ran for cover. The two armed men looked up at the noise, distracted, and tried to locate its source. This gave Tia just enough time to pull her revolver out from under the backpack where it had landed when she fell, release the safety, and aim it at the approaching strangers. The two men looked more like four; their images kept moving in and out, swaying from side to side. First there were two men in suits, then four, and then two again. She couldn't trust her aim, not knowing which two were real, so she tried to bluff her way out of the situation.

"Get back!" she shouted, her voice shrill. "Get back or I'll shoot!" she repeated as she tucked her bruised legs beneath her. Tia was now sitting on her sore legs, using her left hand to keep herself upright. A gust of wind caught her hair and billowed it around her shoulders, making her look very young and vulnerable to the two men staring down the barrel of her gun. The men looked at each other meaningfully and continued to approach her. Either they didn't understand her, or they didn't believe she would really shoot them. One man made a lewd comment on her attire and the other smiled coldly in agreement without taking his eyes off Tia. She recognized the Ukraine dialect and responded with perfect diction.

"Stop where you are!" she shouted with all her remaining strength in the native dialect. The two men halted, exchanged glances, and appeared to be stunned at her easy use of their native language.

They moved slower now, but continued to inch closer. Tia's vision cleared, and without hesitation she shot two shots on target, hitting the first man in the shoulder and the other in the thigh. They dove for the pavement and rolled in opposite directions, positioning themselves to catch Tia in a crossfire. Tia forced her legs to move. They felt like heavy, wet logs, and they were slow to respond, but she made it behind the big metal dumpster before shots went singing past her head. One grazed her right cheek and touching it tentatively with her left hand, Tia could feel the warm, sticky wetness of her own blood. *That'll probably stop by itself,* Tia thought absently as she could feel her knees giving way, and then wondered if it would leave a scar. She was losing it; she knew it. Just as she thought it couldn't get any worse, Peter shouted for Tia to duck and took aim at the two attackers. The Russian mafia turned and fired at Peter and Joe as they moved closer to their position. Joe dove behind a parked car and Peter rolled over after diving to miss being shot. Tia was able to fire two more shots in the direction of the Russian mafia before three more gunmen came running around the corner behind Peter and Joe. Tia was temporarily forgotten by the men exchanging shots as she was now well hidden behind the dumpster. The three new Russian mafia gunmen rushed at Peter and Joe, intent on getting to them before either could fire another shot. Realizing they were sadly outnumbered and at a distinct disadvantage with three enemy gunmen pointing guns at their heads, Peter and Joe reluctantly surrendered. Silently, Tia observed the standoff.

When she fell off the pipe, she'd injured her knee and bruised her ribs. Her ankle was swollen and throbbing, even though the bleeding had stopped. She couldn't make a run for it, and she wouldn't be too much help to Peter and Joe if she was caught too, so she decided to remain hidden until the men left the alley way and then try to make it to her car and follow them. Once she'd located where they were taking Peter and Joe, she would find a way of stopping the gunmen from killing them.

Loud shouts and thundering footsteps could now be heard from the front of the building as the police and a large crowd of curious onlookers ran toward the gunshots. The five gunmen took Peter and Joe quickly to the end of the alley. Tia had followed them, limping in a semi-crouched position, toward her car. She watched closely to ensure that the gunmen hadn't heard her progress. Just then, a long, black car pulled up to the end of the alley and Tia had to dive behind a parked car to prevent them from seeing her. As soon as the car pulled away, she dragged herself to the parking garage behind the building where her car was parked. She couldn't take time to locate her keys in her bag, so she retrieved them from her secret hiding place inside the front bumper of the car. She opened the door and slid behind the wheel. Starting the engine, she pulled cautiously out of the alleyway, looking for the SUV. She saw it about two blocks away, caught in traffic.

The SUV was about to turn the corner. Tia stepped on the accelerator, ignoring the honking horns of the oncoming cars as she drove down the wrong side of the road to dodge the traffic jam. She turned right sharply, cutting off the truck attempting to make the same turn. Tia took the corner on two wheels, praying that the bald front right tire that she'd been meaning to replace didn't blow.

The tire squealed but held as Tia negotiated the corner. The SUV driver had heard her rounding the corner, but since he hadn't seen her in the alleyway, he didn't make the connection and didn't realize that she was following them. Instead, he muttered something under his breath about crazy American drivers. Grouchev heard him muttering and asked the driver to repeat himself. When the driver repeated his comment, Grouchev smiled and adjusted his girth in the back seat and turned to see who this "crazy American driver" was. By this time, Tia had gotten her car under control and was well hidden between a station wagon and a delivery truck. Grouchev couldn't identify which car his driver was talking about, but he agreed with the driver in general. The two cars continued toward the waterfront, dodging shoppers and other pedestrians as well as the heavy afternoon traffic. Following them as closely as she dared, Tia had trouble believing that this nightmare had begun just this morning. She didn't even want to consider how it would end.

As the SUV slowed down in front of Pier 35, Tia pulled quickly behind a semi across the road, parked her car, got out quickly and hid where she could watch without being seen. The driver stopped suddenly to confirm that no one was following them. He couldn't see Tia's car behind the semi so he continued driving slowly toward the end of the pier, to one of the largest yachts Tia had ever seen. She'd traveled with the nobility of Europe, but this vessel outclassed any she'd been on before. She edged back to her car, reached under her seat, and found the camera she'd left there last week when she was on a nature shoot. She popped the trunk, retrieved her telephoto lens, and crept back to her hiding place. Locking the lens in place, Tia focused the camera on the side of the yacht where the registration numbers would be. She couldn't read all of the letters and numbers, but the state designation was Florida. She swept the deck of the yacht with her camera, and was shocked by what she saw. It was more like an armed camp than a pleasure vessel. Soldiers dressed in suits patrolled the upper decks and an armed guard stood ready to welcome the occupants of the SUV at the gang plank. The men on deck looked very much like the men who had abducted Peter and Joe. Tia quickly took as many pictures of the yacht and its inhabitants as the available media in the camera would allow. She moved in closer for a better look. Limping noticeably now, clearly having lost her cat-like reflexes, Tia shadowed the various crates and vehicles on the pier. From here, she could read the name of the vessel. It was the *Golden Sun.* Just as Tia was about to head back to her car, she saw Grouchev climb out of the SUV. *So,* she thought. *He decided to go along for the ride. That means they haven't got what they were looking for.* Tia knew that if she could find Robert and Orlando, and maybe locate *FILE 13* before Grouchev's men, she would have a bargaining chip to trade for the lives of Peter and Joe. *Until then,* she thought, *I can't go to the authorities. Not even anyone at the Agency. Peter warned me that even the Director himself could be involved.* As she watched the yacht pull away from the pier, Tia knew that she was on her own. Tia needed the *Golden Sun's* destination and next port of call. She located the port authority office and then planned her attack. Limping back to the secluded spot where she'd hidden her car, Tia opened her trunk and pulled out her theatrical kit. She'd recently joined the community theater, attempting to put some normalcy back into her life, and being the pack rat that she was, Tia hadn't unloaded the costume pieces and makeup she'd used in her last performance. Opening the case, Tia pulled out a blonde wig and a sheer white blouse. It would be a bit risqué for daylight hours, but it would do the job. *In this outfit,* she thought, smiling to herself, *I should be able to get any information I need.*

She quickly climbed back into the car and, leaning down below the dashboard so she wouldn't be seen, removed first her denim shirt and then her bra. She quickly pulled on the white blouse and then looked down at herself and blushed. Her breasts were clearly defined through the thin material, and because of the cool breeze blowing through the open window, her nipples instantly became prominent. *Well,* she thought, trying to console herself, *I did worse than this when I was with the Agency.* She slipped her denim shirt over the blouse but didn't button it. She then pulled on the platinum blonde wig over her own thick honey blonde hair, carefully tucking any stray pieces under the cap where they couldn't be seen. Next she began applying extra eye makeup and lipstick. She didn't want to overdo it, but she didn't want anyone to misinterpret her intentions. Finally, to complete her disguise, she pulled a pair of blue contact lenses out of her purse and carefully applied one to each eye. She checked her appearance in the rearview mirror and was pleased with the result. She started the engine and drove the short distance to the port authority office, which was at the entrance to the waterfront piers. She could see through the large bay window at the front of the office that there was only one man on duty. She opened the door and stepped out, and her swollen ankle reminded her of her fall. She tried to walk and found that she was limping slightly. *That's okay,* Tia thought. *It will only increase my chances of pulling this off without being recognized.*

Tia reached back into the car to retrieve her backpack, and the sudden movement felt like a thousand needles cutting into her lungs. She retrieved the bag, painfully aware of her bruised ribs, and closed the car door.

She walked deliberately, and as seductively as she could--considering the limp--into the Port Authority office. Opening the door, Tia gave the officer behind the desk a dazzling smile. He was in his mid-thirties and very good-looking. *This is going to be easier than I expected,* Tia thought, smiling to herself. He took one look at the lush blonde hair and dazzling blue eyes and smiled warmly. Tia slowly removed her denim shirt and folded it over her arm. As his gaze followed her movements, his eyes were drawn to her full breasts and tiny waist. His expression reflected the hunger and lust filling his thoughts. "She'd be a handful," his expression shouted. "Hmmm," he said loudly, clearing his throat. "May I help you... uh, Miss...?"

"Collins. Teresa Collins," she drawled in a sweet southern accent. "Yes, Admiral, I do hope you can help me."

"Well, Miss Collins, I'm not an admiral, but I'd be happy to do anything I can to help," he said suggestively, appraising her figure once again.

Tia leaned closer to the man in the officer's

uniform and touched his hand with one soft finger. "Well, you see," she said softly, as if fighting back tears, "my uncle left on that yacht pulling out of the harbor, and I missed the boat. I'm sure you saw him. He's a heavy-set man in his sixties, and not very well. He had a lot of people around him. People he'd hired to take care of him." Tia smiled sweetly up at the officer, forcing a single tear out from under her right eyelid and allowing it to roll slowly down her cheek. "You see, if I don't meet his boat, he'll be real mad at me and he probably won't give me my allowance this month."

"I see, Miss Collins. But you have to understand that we can't provide you with transport to his yacht. It's a private vessel." He patted her hand comfortingly between his two strong paws, but didn't release her hand. "Why don't you step into the back room with me? Let's see if we can't work something out. My office is right there on the right," he said, smiling at her. He took Tia by the arm and led her into a small closet-like room with a desk, one extra chair, and a sofa.

Evidently he did most of his business in here, Tia thought as she paused in the doorway. She looked around and noticed that there was no window and a dead bolt on the door. *Once he gets me in here,* she almost said aloud, *it won't be easy to get back out again.*

"Please have a seat, Miss Collins," he said,

leading her to the couch. Tia did as she was asked, smiling gratefully up at the officer. After closing and locking the door, he joined her on the couch.

"I can't tell you how much this means to me. I really appreciate your helping me. I only wish there was some way I could thank you," Tia said softly, placing one open palm on his broad shoulder to emphasize her sincerity.

"Well, first of all, Miss Collins, you can call me Michael. And if I may, I'll call you Teresa," he said as he put his arm casually around her shoulders.

"Yes. Thank you, Michael." Tia smiled warmly, inhaling deeply as she did. His attention was immediately riveted downward. "I'd like that very much. Now, if I could ask you to do me a favor…"

"Certainly, Teresa. I'd be happy to do whatever I can to help. What do you need?" He was looking at her like a kid looking at a birthday present that he couldn't wait to unwrap.

This is too easy, Tia thought. To Michael she said sweetly, "If you could tell me if my uncle is still planning to sail to Miami, then I could fly down and meet him."

"Oh, Teresa, I am sorry," he said, standing up, suddenly acting very correctly. He walked around the back of his desk and sat down in his formal black vinyl chair. "You see, the destination, as well as other pertinent information on private vessels, is confidential, unless you have some official authority, like a search warrant. We can only release that information in case of an emergency or to the local police." He folded his hands to make a steeple and smiled weakly at her over the top of his fingers.

I guess I'm going to have to work at this one after all, she thought with disgust as she looked down at her lap. Tia made eye contact with Michael for just one moment before she began weeping uncontrollably. Finally, when that didn't soften his resolve, she uttered between barely concealed sobs, "But Michael, you don't understand. I've already made my uncle angry. If I don't meet him, he'll cut off my money and I'll lose everything! This *is* an emergency! These very nasty men downtown are holding my car as collateral against some debts I owe them. I had to borrow a friend's car just to come down here." Tia stood up and walked around in a circle, ending up where he was sitting. "If I don't find my uncle in time, then they said that they'll hurt me." Tia lifted her foot to the arm of his chair, lifted her tight pant leg, and showed him her ankle. "See what they did to me already?" she said tearfully.

Tia lost her balance and landed in his lap, her face very close to his. She looked up into his shocked eyes and said with a tender note of sincerity, "I'll do anything to find my uncle Michael! Anything!" He couldn't control himself any longer. He pressed her supple curves to his hard form. Tia melted automatically into his arms. She whispered into his shoulder, "Michael, will you help me?"

"Only if you'll have dinner with me tonight. My place? Eightish?" His hands were fondling the front of her blouse, his eyes hungry.

I'll probably be dessert, Tia thought to herself. But to Michael, she said breathlessly, "Of course I'll come, Michael. I can't wait!" she said with enthusiasm. Before she could move, he kissed her deeply, and when he finally released her, he was breathing hard. Tia could feel the passion rising in him and see physical evidence of his arousal. She knew she had him hooked. She confirmed her position by running her palm inside his shirt and across his chest. His quick intake of breath told Tia that she had accurately hit her mark. Michael didn't hesitate, but pulled out the file containing the *Golden Sun's* destination and chart. He opened the folder in front of Tia as if there was no longer anything to hide from her. The destination was not Miami, but Coco Beach, Florida. The *Golden Sun* was to be docked there for an indefinite period of time. The yacht was scheduled to take several stops in the Carolinas and Georgia for gas and supplies before it would reach Florida, but none of the stops would be for more than a couple of hours. If they had indeed filed a valid trip plan, then Tia could fly to Florida and be waiting to meet them when the *Rising Sun* arrives.

Tia disengaged herself from Michael's reluctant

grip and stood up from his lap. "I can't thank you enough for the information you gave me," she said, leaning over seductively in front of him to adjust the cuffs of her tight pants. "But I promise, tonight I'll try. Then, I can take an early plane to Florida tomorrow morning and catch up with my uncle in plenty of time."

"I'm really looking forward to it, Theresa. Where shall I pick you up?" he asked again, surveying Tia's form closely.

"I'll meet you at your place. I'll be dressed to the nines, as they say, so I can surprise you."

"That sounds great. Here's my address," he said, as he hastily wrote his address on a spare piece of paper and handed it to her. "I'll see you tonight at eight, at my place. I'm *really* looking forward to it."

I'll bet you are, Tia thought to herself as she smiled warmly at Michael. He followed her out into the outer office where he waved goodbye. *I wonder how long it will take him to realize I'm not going to show up tonight,* Tia thought to herself as she climbed into the car. *I wish I could see the look on his face when he realizes that his prize catch has slipped through his fingers. But alas, I'll be in Florida by then,* Tia said to herself, giggling.

Tia smiled all the way back into town. She removed the blue contact lenses at a traffic light and pulled off the platinum wig, allowing her honey blonde tresses to fall around her shoulders. Finally, she buttoned her denim shirt over the thin white blouse. "There. That's better," she said, checking her reflection in the vanity mirror. "Now, if I could only find Orlando and Robert Taylor…"

Tia pulled over to the side of the road out of traffic and pulled out her cell phone. First, she called Orlando's home. There was no answer--only her voice mail. She was about to leave a message, and then stopped, realizing that Orlando would probably not be around to hear it. Tia hung up and called Orlando's office. She was hoping to find Orlando there, since she frequently worked on Saturdays, and was surprised when Sally answered the phone. "Sally, it's Tia. Do you have any idea where Orlando could be?"

"Hi Tia! I'm so happy to hear from you," Sally said, a little breathless. "No, I don't know where she is, and quite frankly, I'm getting worried." Then, as if she was reading a script, she added, "I... I'm in the outer office now, not on Orlando's private line. I'm working today because I was hoping to get some work done while I waited for Orlando to return from her date." Sally realized that there was a high probability that the main line was tapped. She hoped that Tia realized it as well, and much to Sally's relief, Tia's understanding was evident by her response.

"Sally, your mother wouldn't like to hear you gossiping about Orlando like that. We'll talk more about Orlando's date when I see you. Now, why don't you go home and take care of those things your mother asked you to take care of, and I'll see you in a couple of days?"

"Okay, Tia. That sounds like a good idea. I'll be home if you need me," Sally responded, relieved.

Tia hung up the phone and steered back into traffic. "Mother" was code for Orlando, and "home" was the apartment at Orlando's office. Tia knew that Sally would be waiting for her in the apartment, as Orlando had directed, misdirecting anyone who might be listening on an open line who would be expecting to find Sally at her house. "A couple of days" was code for a couple of minutes, and Sally's acknowledgement told Tia that she knew she was on her way.

As Tia drove, she thought about Orlando and where she might be. She was mentally listing all of the Russian Mafia safe houses when she noticed the car following her. It was a long, late model dark sedan. The driver was obviously new because Tia lost him easily in the late afternoon traffic. She could feel all of the old training and the instincts she'd developed working with the Agency coming back to her. Peter had accused her of going soft, but she knew better; she could feel it. When she needed them, she knew that her reflexes and instincts would be as sharp as ever.

Tia pulled up in front of the Panama building

where Orlando's office occupied the top floor. Looking in her rearview mirror, Tia saw the car that had been following her. "So," she said aloud, "That's why I lost him so easily. He knew where I was going all along. I guess that means the line was definitely tapped--and they've figured out our code." Before climbing out of the car, Tia checked her revolver to confirm that it was loaded. She released the safety, carefully replaced the gun in its holster in her purse, and approached the building as if she hadn't noticed the car pulling into the parking lot across the street. Tia quickly climbed the concrete steps and, entering the lobby, stepped quietly behind the closest marble column across from the empty security desk. She pulled her revolver out of her bag and allowed the bag to slide quietly to the floor next to her. Almost holding her breath, Tia anxiously awaited her assailant's arrival.

The hunter became the hunted as Tia let him pass her. Once he'd presented an unsuspecting back to her, Tia sprung into action. She quietly slipped up behind him and hit him firmly across the back of the neck with the butt of her gun, both hands clenched tightly into a fist around the grip. He grabbed his neck instinctively with his right hand as he moaned and turned around to face her. Tia saw her opportunity and kicked him as hard as she could in the groin. When he doubled over in pain, she brought her knee up, pounding his chin like a sledgehammer. Tia's would-be attacker fell at her feet in a crumpled heap, groaning loudly, holding his groin. His legs were curled up tightly to his chest in the fetal position to protect his lower body from any further assault.

He won't be following me again anytime soon, Tia thought to herself, smiling as she retrieved her purse and stored the gun. As she walked to the bank of elevators, she swiped a security card that activated the cars. Once in the elevator, she chose one floor down from the top so that she could enter the penthouse from the stairwell and avoid anyone who would be watching the elevators. Pulling her revolver out of her bag again, Tia slowly cracked open the stairwell door. Just as she'd suspected, there was an armed man standing guard outside the Investments Internationale door and one positioned near the elevator. They probably weren't expecting Tia to arrive at the office via the back stairwell, especially 14 floors above street level. Tia peered through the cracked door again. The two men guarding the hallway were dressed alike, in black trousers and turtlenecks, as if they'd just stepped out of a grade-B spy movie. They were definitely muscle-bound, and didn't appear to be too mentally alert. Tia decided that the direct approach would be the least expected, and therefore probably the best. Tia closed the door softly and went to work.

She reached down and unbuttoned her blouse to

reveal ample cleavage. *Here we go again,* she thought with disgust. *Just once, I'd like to use the direct approach without using these,* she thought as she looked down at her blouse. Just to be sure, she undid one more button on the white blouse and pulled it out of her painted-on jeans. Tying her denim jacket around her waist by the sleeves so that it hung down the back of her thighs, Tia took a deep breath and opened the door. When the guard at the door heard her open the stairwell door, they turned in unison. The guard at the elevator turned to face the two at the office door with his gun drawn, ready to shoot at the first sign of trouble. Tia leaned close to the man at the office door so that his view down the front of her shirt was unobstructed and whispered, "Why don't you tell your friend to disappear for a while, and we could go inside and get better acquainted?"

Without speaking, a slow grin appeared on the man's face. He waved his comrade off, saying that he was going to have a "snack" in Russian. They stepped into the outer office and he shut the large wooden door behind them. He quickly pressed his hard body against Tia's soft, pliable figure. Tia could feel the roughness of the wooden door against her back as he pinned her there and lowered his mouth to roughly possess hers. She moaned with feigned desire and put her hands up around his neck. He lifted his head slightly and glowed at her with self-satisfaction. She returned his smile just before pinching the nerve in his neck that controlled the blood flow to his brain. She watched him slowly fall into unconsciousness, looking shocked and confused as he slumped to the floor at her feet. The surprised look never left his face. Quietly, Tia edged her way into the main office, watching for any more gunmen. There didn't seem to be anyone in sight, and as Tia breathed a sigh of relief and began to relax, she let her guard down. Just at that moment, she heard a noise in the room off the main office where Orlando kept the refreshments. Pulling her revolver out of her purse, she crept along the wall to the entrance. The man in front of the refrigerator was obviously so occupied with the selection he was making from the food inside that he didn't hear Tia approach. Tia stepped back around the corner of the alcove and pressed herself flat against the wall. The man evidently didn't see her when he stepped out of the kitchen area because he sauntered out of the alcove, softly humming to himself as he bit loudly into a green apple. Tia would never forget his surprised gasp as she jammed the gun into his back. The expression on his face as he turned around slowly and raised his hands above his head was one of complete surprise. His pupils were the size of quarters, and he still had the apple gripped firmly between his teeth.

"Move!" Tia said in Russian, trying to cover her nerves with anger. Tia maneuvered the man to the center of the office where there were no readily available retaliatory weapons. "Now, turn around and put your hands on you head," she added. With one hand pressing the nose of the gun firmly into the small of his back, Tia used her other hand to search him for weapons. She found a snub-nosed pistol in his shoulder holster hidden beneath his left arm and slipped it into the waistband in the back of her jeans, under her jacket. Finding no other weapons, she motioned him over to the couch. She kept her voice low, conscious of the guard still outside near the elevator.

Speaking fluent Russian, Tia stated in hushed tones, "If you make a noise or in any way attract your friend's attention, I'll put a bullet between your eyes. Now, where's Orlando Corrigan?" Tia demanded. She remained standing with her revolver aimed directly at his forehead.

"I don't know what you're talking about," he said slowly with a heavy Russian accent.

"Yes, you do," Tia responded, getting angry. "Now, tell me what you know, and fast, before I lose my temper!" She emphasized her point by jabbing her gun at his face. "I don't know what you're talking about," he repeated, getting louder. "That's true, Miss Johnson," a heavy, masculine voice stated

behind her said. Tia turned quickly and looked up at
the second man who had walked into the room. It was
the man by the elevator, and she hadn't heard him
come in. The man on the couch in front of her stood
up confidently, and Tia, looking slowly from one to
the other, reluctantly lowered her gun. The two men
were quickly joined by a third man--not the one who
she had assaulted. They had her trapped, and there
wasn't anything she could do about it. Peter was
right; she'd allowed herself to get sloppy. But, she
vowed to herself as she stood silently looking from
one man to the other, it wouldn't happen again.

"Now, Miss Johnson," the second man said in
Russian, "if you will please hand me your gun, butt
first, and sit down…" He motioned to the seat on the
couch that the other man had just vacated. Tia sat
down and slowly handed over her gun, which the
man accepted with a satisfied grin. He hadn't
mentioned the gun in her waistband and Tia was
hoping that he hadn't noticed it. "Sir," the first man
said in Russian.

"Not now," he answered him quickly. "Leave us!
Both of you," he ordered. The first man started to
speak again, but he was interrupted. "Not another
word. Get out!" The first man shrugged his shoulders
and walked out of the office. The third man followed
him slowly, closing the door behind them. "What are
you going to do with me?" Tia asked angrily in
Russian.

"Nothing, Miss Johnson, as long as you tell me what I want to know," he responded in perfect English, with no sign of an accent.

"And just what is that?" Tia asked, surprised, also in English, as she watched his face warily. "Oh, don't worry. I'll let you know when I'm ready." He smiled smugly down at her. Tia studied him carefully. He was a tall man, but he appeared squat because of the breadth of his shoulders, and the equal width of his waist. His head was balding and the few strands of hair crossing the expanse of shiny skin on the top of his head were equally as shiny, as if he hadn't bothered to wash them in several weeks. His pale skin matched his hair in oil content, maintaining an overall greasy glow. The large pores around his nose and across his cheeks added to the repulsive image he projected. The shifty way he moved his beady eyes from side to side gave him a sinister look. "Who are you?" Tia asked suspiciously.

"My name is Hartt. I doubt you know me, but I know all about you and your cousin Orlando. But that's not important now. What is important is that you're going to go for a ride with me, and Miss Johnson, I would suggest you come peaceably." "And if I don't?" Tia asked, raising one eyebrow in defiance.

"I wouldn't even like to suggest the alternative," he said, smiling through the space between his green teeth.

"Alright, Hartt. I'll go with you, but I need to use the bathroom first. It's been a long time since I last... well, you know. Besides, your men already searched me," she lied, "so you shouldn't have a problem with me taking care of certain necessities."

"Fine. Use the one here in the office, but don't be long. And don't try anything. I'll be watching you."

"Thank you," Tia responded with a stiff smile. "I'll only be a minute." Tia stood up slowly and adjusted the jacket around her waist to better conceal the gun. Once he was satisfied that she was securely in the bathroom with no means of escape, Hartt summoned the two guards he'd dismissed earlier.

Inside the bathroom, Tia quickly took the gun out of her waistband and, raising her right leg, slid it into her boot. She fervently hoped that they wouldn't think to look there should they decide to search her again. She flushed the toilet, washed her hands, and took her lipstick out of her pants pocket. Tia dabbed a little on her lips and then, using a firm, steady hand, wrote the following note on the mirror: *"Hartt has kidnaped me. Call the Agency and tell them to send help. Tia."* Turning out the light, Tia left the bathroom and shut the door behind her. She calmly walked across the office, never losing eye contact with Hartt, and sat softly on the couch.

The two gunmen Hartt had ordered out of the office returned when he called to them. Following

Hartt's directions, they walked over to Tia and lifted her off the couch by her arms. Before they led her out of the office, Tia was allowed to see, firsthand, how Hartt dealt with people who didn't follow orders. Hartt had instructed the other gunman to pick up the man who Tia had knocked out. Hartt, speaking in fluent Russian, ordered the man who held the still unconscious, muscle-bound gunman to step forward and roughly slap the man to consciousness.

When the man was aware of his surroundings, Hartt spoke loudly to him, violent curses interjected between each phrase. Within minutes, he had the gunman groveling at his feet for mercy, but Hartt just laughed at him, as if he were some pitiful insect hardly worth noticing. Without warning, Hartt removed his revolver from his shoulder holster, screwed on a silencer, and aimed it at the poor man's head. One of the men holding Tia walked around behind the cowering man and yanked his head up by the hair so he could see what was coming. The man screamed one last time as Hartt laughed coldly at him, aimed the gun, and without a moment's hesitation, shot the gunman twice between the eyes. His cries for mercy ceased immediately, and the silence that followed was deafening. Tia could feel each of the shots, even though the silencer on the gun kept the noise from traveling too far.

Before the man's face hit the floor, Hartt had unscrewed the silencer and returned his gun to its holster, and was walking toward the door. The two men who had been holding the now dead gunman dragged him out the door behind Hartt. *His blood must be like ice*, Tia thought as she was led by the third gunman out the door behind the dead body. Would this be the way she would end her life too? Evidently her thoughtful mood didn't go unnoticed by Hartt. He turned at the elevator and took her two soft cheeks between his rough, blistered fingers, using the same hand that had just pulled the trigger. She could smell the gunpowder on his hand.

He smiled the same slimy, green-toothed smile he'd used on her in the office. "Don't worry, my dear," he said, the false smile permanently cemented on his face. "After you tell us what we want to know, I'll take care of you, personally. Not like that messy business in there," he said, casually waving in the direction of the office they'd just left. "I'll spend some time with you first. Give you something to remember," he said, smiling as he ran one rough finger down inside her blouse, following the swell of her heaving breasts. His breath was warm and moist on her cheek now as he continued smugly, "I'll give you a night you'll never forget! Now you'd like that, wouldn't ya?"

"Get your greasy hands off me!" Tia spat at him. She was beyond fear of being killed now. The mere thought of having to spend any time alone with this slimy toad standing in front of her nauseated her beyond description. "One more finger on me, Hartt, and it will be your last!" The fire in Tia's eyes, along with the angry flush quickly spreading across her cheeks, simulated the passion that Hartt wanted to inspire in her. She was livid, however--not aroused. But Hartt didn't see it that way. He traced his finger down the open "V" of her clear blouse while the man behind her held her arms. She automatically pulled away from his touch, her entire body repulsed by the contact. He started to unbutton the top button of her blouse and then stopped, as if he remembered the real reason he had come there.

"Later, Miss Johnson," he said, licking his lips. "Yes. I think I'm going to enjoy getting to know you better." They walked out of the building as a group and silently entered his waiting SUV. Anger and the need to escape filled Tia's thoughts as she rode silently beside Hartt. She didn't want to spend a minute more with him than absolutely necessary, but maybe she could find out some information from him to help Peter, Joe, and Orlando.

They drove for what seemed like hours as he stole her away to a house outside the city, but Tia didn't doze off. She paid close attention to the residence as they made their way down the long driveway. With the accuracy of a photographic memory, she took in the details of the house and the surrounding area, including the number and placement of the armed guards encircling the grounds. The brick house was set in the middle of three acres of manicured lawns and tediously maintained ornamental shrubbery and flower beds. Everything about the white-washed retaining wall surrounding the property, to the freshly painted wrought iron gate, lent an air of security and privacy to the estate. The spell was broken, however, by the sound of a troop of armed guards marching loudly as they patrolled the grounds with unceasing rhythm. The wall too, upon closer examination, was patrolled by vicious guard dogs and armed men. Tia didn't know who this man was who was waiting to see her, but she was quickly becoming consumed by an overwhelming sense of dread. She could smell the almost palpable odor of death all around her.

The car glided to a stop outside the front door, and the driver opened the door for her to get out. She hesitated only a moment, when Hartt wedged the nozzle of his gun between her ribs to brutally remind her that she didn't have a choice. As she moved out of the car, she could feel the muzzle of his gun pressing into the fleshy area of her back, just below her rib cage near her waist. Once outside the car, one of the guards trained his gun on her and Hartt holstered his and led the way. Reluctantly, Tia followed her beaming host into the house. He instructed some of the household staff to bring refreshments for three into the library, and led the way, signaling for Tia to follow. Hartt was again wearing his trademark reptilian smile.

Hartt opened the door of the library and Tia noticed the third person he had mentioned to the staff. His coloring and figure were lighter than Hartt's, and his slender frame supported an angular head with sharp, high cheekbones. The sardonic smile that he gave Hartt and Tia implied that he enjoyed his work immensely, and Tia had a pretty good idea of what type of work that was.

He appeared to be someone who received great satisfaction from causing others discomfort. "Miss Johnson," Hartt said formally, "I would like to introduce Mr. Krosky. Mr. Krosky, Miss Johnson." Krosky nodded at Tia, scrutinizing her from head to toe as she surveyed him discretely from behind lowered lashes. He appeared to be trying to read her mind, and it was obvious that the man sensed her discomfort. Hartt continued chattering non-stop, oblivious to their non-verbal exchange. "Tia, my dear, Mr. Krosky is my house guest." He assumed an annoying familiarity with her. "Honey, why don't you to tell Mr. Krosky everything you know about your friend Joe Cramer, and the items he stole from the Covington mansion?"

"I don't know what you mean," Tia replied softly. She watched his face closely, hoping that her nerves wouldn't give her away.

"Oh, I think you do, Miss Johnson," Krosky said,

walking over to her. "Mr. Hartt foolishly gave an emerald from that robbery to your cousin to deliver to the Agency's contact, Joe Cramer. This emerald contained a microdot, disguised as a natural inclusion, which was supposed to have contained *FILE 13,* a current list of all of NATO's double agents throughout Europe. As it turned out, when we asked Mr. Taylor and Miss Corogan where the correct stone was, the one with the real *FILE 13,* they were less than cooperative. The emerald we gave to your cousin was exactly like the one that had the correct information stored in a microdot sealed in it. The only difference, of course, was that the emerald we gave Miss Corogan had a false list on the microdot. We must conclude, therefore, that since Mr. Cramer was the principle involved, he must know where the right stone is." Krosky leaned in closer to Tia's face and continued in a soft, almost menacing whisper: "You see, Miss Johnson, it's embarrassing to admit, but we're not even sure if the correct stone is an emerald. It could have been one of the diamonds or sapphires stolen from the Corogans. I'm depending on you to obtain the correct stone from Mr. Cramer."

"But why me?" Tia asked innocently.

"We know he's worked with you in the past, and we know that he was at your apartment when my men arrived," responded Krosky. "We followed him to you. Now, we don't want to cause you or your friends any unnecessary pain, so Miss Johnson, if you will just tell us what we want to know, you can be on your way."

Tia just stared at him incredulously. Why would he ask her for the information on the stone that Joe stole from the Covingtons unless he didn't know Grouchev had Joe and Peter on the *Golden Sun*? Tia knew Grouchev's tactics, and she didn't doubt that he'd have the information he wanted by now. It didn't take Tia long to conclude that either Krosky wasn't working with Grouchev, or he didn't know Grouchev had Joe and Peter. She decided to tell him about Grouchev and see where it led her. "If I'm not mistaken," Tia began demurely, "your own people have him. How is it possible that you don't know that, Mr. Krosky--unless you aren't as important to Grouchev as you'd like us to believe?"

"What are you talking about?" demanded Krosky. His steel blue eyes flashed and his hard face flushed with anger. "Explain what you are talking about, and I warn you, Miss Johnson, be brief!"

"I had assumed that you were working with the Grouchev's men. And I had assumed that you'd know that they have Joe. Now, since I've told you where Joe and the stone are, I'll be going," Tia said with false aplomb as she turned to leave.

"Wait!" Krosky shouted hoarsely. He was beginning to perspire. He even looked a little nervous. "Who did you say has Mr. Cramer?"

Tia turned slowly, appearing puzzled. "Grouchev." Her one word answer floored him. His face became a blank mask.

"That will be all. Thank you," Krosky almost choked, whispering the words. His composure was slipping. Hartt was unusually quiet under Krosky's icy gaze. Neither man seemed to notice Tia until she spoke.

"Mr. Krosky," Tia asked boldly, "I have one question I'd like to ask you before I leave." Tia stood very still, expecting a cold rejection. She was surprised at the calm in Krosky's voice when he spoke.

"What is your question, Miss Johnson?"

"If you and Grouchev are working for the same people, why didn't you know they had Joe?"

"A legitimate question, Miss Johnson." He offered a false, warm smile to her as he continued. "Of course, I never said I was working with Grouchev. You did. But I guarantee, Miss Johnson, that I will know the answer to that question before the day is out. You know, you are quite inquisitive and quite bright for an American woman, qualities I would normally admire in someone so beautiful. But for now, my dear," he added with condescension, "I would suggest you curb your curiosity and suppress those qualities if you want to retain your excellent state of health."

"I don't understand," Tia pushed, ignoring his

warning. "Why is the Russian Mafia interested in covert Cold War operations since they aren't even supposed to exist anymore? I mean, since the Cold War is over and we're all friends now, there's no need for the Russian Mafia to search for NATO secrets or even for *FILE 13,* right? So why do you want it so badly?" she asked, hoping that her feigned ignorance could pull some information out of him.

"Let's suffice to say that certain members of the Russian Mafia have different views on what is the best direction for the organization to be moving in. What happens to *FILE 13* may just determine that direction, and the person who solves the puzzle the fastest may be instrumental in determining that direction. I hope that answers your questions," he said, purposely looking down at his paperwork as if she'd already left the room. "Good day, Miss Johnson," he concluded abruptly, turning his back on her, signaling the end of the conversation. Krosky didn't even address Hartt; it was as if he didn't even exist.

Tia was ushered out of the house, without any of the much-discussed refreshments—and without Hartt. After she left the office, Krosky ordered Hartt to find Orlando Corogan and Robert Taylor and eliminate them. Then, Krosky ordered Hartt to have his men follow Tia in case she knew where Grouchev had taken Cramer and the stone. He prided himself on being able to read in a person's eyes whether they were telling the truth or not, and he believed Tia's explanation.

Krosky turned to Hartt and added, "If she finds Grouchev, eliminate her. If she fails to find Grouchev, eliminate her anyway. She knows too much. I don't want her around to ask any more embarrassing questions. Make it look like suicide or an accident. Just take care of it. And Hartt, if there are any more complications, I'll take care of *you* myself," he promised with a cold smile. "I'm starting to think I'd rather enjoy that." Hartt's face turned ashen as Krosky turned his back on him again, terminating the exchange and dismissing any unspoken protests Hartt might have considered.

Hartt slowly walked out the door, shoulders slumped over and head bowed. He had the look of a man defeated. As Hartt followed her out of the house, Tia's face was solemn, but her eyes peered triumphantly at him. She was on her way to freedom––or so she thought. Hartt had overplayed his hand and he'd lost. Whatever game Krosky and Hartt were playing with Grouchev, Tia was certain that it no longer involved her and that she was free to resume her search for her cousin and her friends. Several of Krosky's men loaded automatic weapons into the trunk of a second car and climbed in. They followed Tia as they had been ordered, keeping their distance and remaining undetected.

Chapter 6

ROBERT TURNED OFF at the first side road he came to. The troops following them continued on the main road, not seeing Robert and Orlando. "We don't have much time," Robert told Orlando. "They'll discover we turned off before too long, and then they'll be back here looking for us. We've got to ditch the car and make a run for it. The only thing is, there's no place around here to hide it in a hurry," he added, looking around him.

"How about up ahead?" Orlando said, pointing to the next bend in the road. "There's a bunch of pine trees and maybe we could hide it in the undergrowth. You know, you could drive it off the road and maybe hide the car behind some of those trees."

"Sounds good, but I don't think the car will make it that far," Robert said as the car slowed of its own accord. The engine died as they approached the turn in the road. "Say a prayer, Orlando. We might just make it." The car did make it to the turn, but within thirty seconds after leaving the paved surface, the car ground to a halt. Robert tried valiantly to re-start the engine, but there was no response. "Looks like we'll have to get out and push," he said, opening his door.

"All right," Orlando replied unenthusiastically, opening her door and removing her shoes, and getting out to help Robert. Pushing the car through the brush was more than difficult. The vehicle seemed immovable. Between grunts, Orlando tried to lighten his mood. "You know, Robert, I'm sure you've been in worse jams than this, right?" She looked at him, but there was no response, so she continued. "I mean, I'm sure things were much worse than this overseas...." But when there was no acknowledgement, only silence, she stopped talking.

"Oh, sorry," he replied, looking up at her, bewildered, with a weak smile. "Were you saying something?" he asked, breathing in short gulps of air and breathing hard. "Nothing," Orlando replied softly, and went back to pushing.

"Listen," Robert continued without really waiting for a reply, "I'm going to have to rest for a minute, okay?" They both stopped pushing and Orlando looked quickly at his face. It was almost grey, and he had broken out into a cold sweat. His breathing was also becoming quite shallow. His ribs must be cracked, or even broken.

"Robert, are you wearing heavy socks or light socks?" Orlando asked as she walked quickly around the car to his side.

Robert had opened the door as wide as it would go and was sitting on the driver's seat holding his side. At the question, he looked up at her as if she'd finally lost her mind. "What?"

"Never mind. Just answer the question," Orlando said, looking at his chest rise and fall slowly and the pain on his face as he fought to breath.

"Heavy. Why?" he asked, looking up at her puzzled.

"Let's take them off, and give me your pocket knife." Kneeling down, she helped Robert remove his shoes and socks as he lifted first one foot and then the other. Then Orlando put his shoes back on and handed him one of the socks. Without speaking, Orlando quickly took the pocket knife from his hand and slipped it into the other sock. She split the first sock in half and, taking the second sock from Robert's, repeated her movements. Orlando now had four long, spandex reinforced cotton strips to work with.

"Did you learn this in boarding school too?" Robert asked, a sardonic smile playing around his lips.

"No, at the movies," she replied, smiling up at him. "I love old movies. Don't you?" she asked nonchalantly as she sneaked a look at his face. It was beginning to turn ashen. Orlando figured that his ribs must be pressing on his lungs, or maybe they had even punctured one of his lungs; he was definitely having problems getting enough air.

"Now, stay still," she said gently. "We don't have much time." Orlando tied all four strips together to create a makeshift ace bandage and, with the aid of his good arm, wrapped it around his ribcage, securing the injury. She then took a bobby pin out of her tousled hair and made a hole in the free end of the strip, hooked it through the last layer of the socks, and then, making another hole, hooked it on the outside of the socks. Then, she twisted the bobby pin back on itself so that it wouldn't come loose. "There. How's that?" Orlando looked up at him, smiling.

"Better," he said softly. Robert tried to manage a smile, but only succeeded in grimacing. Orlando could tell he was in a lot of pain, but at least the grey color was fading from his face. "I can actually breathe again, as long as I don't take a deep breath."

"Good. Now, I suggest that we give up the idea of moving the car and try to get as far away from here as possible." Orlando gave Robert her left arm to lean on and, with her right arm around his waist, helped him stand up.

"I agree, but we can't get away from them on foot. They'll catch us before we've gone half a mile. Our best bet is to find some place to hide and hopefully they'll think we made a run for it. Then, after they're gone, we'll try to make it to a house or farm, but we'll have to stay close to the trees in case they come back." Robert and Orlando were walking slowly toward the trees as they spoke. She was carrying her shoes so there wouldn't be any marks in the soft shoulder of the road.

"That's a good idea. Are you feeling any better?" Orlando asked, surprising herself by her controlled tone.

Her voice had taken on its own personality. Her stomach was tying itself in knots with worry, but her voice sounded like the cool professional. "I'm okay," he replied without enthusiasm. "Let's get to those trees before they get here. I think I hear a car coming."

Orlando nodded, and with him leaning heavily on her, they found a good hiding place near the edge of the woods. Orlando helped Robert lay down in the grass, hiding his body under a bush, behind a pine tree. Once Orlando had helped Robert get settled, she lay down beside him. They could see the road from where they were hiding. Robert had been right about an approaching car, but he had underestimated the number of vehicles. They'd just gotten situated when three Jeeps carrying armed men came racing around the curve in the road, and then screeched to a stop next to the abandoned car. The dirt the Jeeps kicked up as they pulled onto the dry shoulder momentarily hid the number of occupants exiting the vehicles. When it cleared, Orlando was surprised at how many men there were. She was hoping that her imagination had gotten the best of her and exaggerated the number of soldiers who were after them. Unfortunately, her guess was terribly accurate. The men didn't immediately head for the trees, but seemed to be having a debate as to which would be the best strategy to take.

Finally, most of the troops climbed back into

their vehicles, and all but one Jeep full of men drove off down the road. From the snatches of conversation Orlando and Robert could hear, the soldiers following them evidently felt that they'd had help in escaping and that there had been another car waiting for them. The remaining gunmen approached the abandoned car carefully, guns drawn and ready to shoot at the first sign of movement. While they searched the car, Robert reached into the waist of his trousers and withdrew two pistols. He handed one to Orlando, and she looked at it as if it were some foreign object. "Where did you get these?" Orlando whispered.

"Shhh! I borrowed them while you were distracting the guards back at the house. You do know how to use one of those things, don't you?" he whispered, smiling warmly at her.

"I'm not an expert," she replied, smiling, mocking him, "but if those guys get close enough, I think I can hit them."

Robert grimaced in reply, and they turned their attention back to the men by the road. They watched the soldiers thoroughly search the car and the trunk. Once they were satisfied that there was nothing else to find in the car, the men began arguing among themselves about where they should begin their search. Finally, they split up into two pair and spread out, heading toward the trees. Orlando held her breath as two men walked right past the spot where she and Robert were lying. His pants nearly brushed her cheek, but he didn't notice her because of the dense undergrowth. The two men passed Robert and Orlando and continued on. Orlando had lifted her chest off the ground, preparing to get up and make a run for the Jeep when Robert grabbed her upper arm and restrained her. Without speaking, he pointed to his legs. Orlando turned to see what the problem was and inhaled so quickly that she made a small gasp. A diamond-back rattler was slithering over Robert's outstretched legs, heading for Orlando's. By the time she'd turned around, the snake had crossed the short distance between her and Robert, and was climbing the side of Orlando's left calf. Orlando was deathly afraid of any kind of snake, and she was about to let out a scream when Robert clasped his hand over her mouth. He shook his head and pointed to a spot behind Orlando. The two men who had just past them were heading back toward the Jeep. If she'd uttered even a whisper, they'd have heard it and would have been on Robert and Orlando before they could take aim.

The snake slowly slithered over first one shapely, stocking-clad calf and then the other. Less than a minute had passed, but to Orlando it seemed an eternity. She was petrified of the snake, and all that kept her from screaming in horror was Robert's arm around her shoulders and his hand over her mouth. She didn't dare move a muscle in case the snake became frightened and decided to attack. Her legs, hips, and torso were becoming cramped from maintaining her twisted position. Trying to take her mind off the pain and the snake, Orlando looked toward the road. All of the men had returned to the Jeep by now, but instead of leaving, they obviously had decided to take a break, and were passing around cigarettes and a flask.

The midday sun was warming the woods and the insects were beginning to stir. The snake continued on its way, and Orlando could finally shift positions, stretching her legs. "Robert, we've got to get out of here," she whispered softly.

"Yeah, but where? The car won't go another half-mile. It's out of gas. You could try to make it on foot. You'd stand a chance without me slowing you down. I could stay here and create a diversion and give you enough time to sneak away. You could go for help." He was breathing hard from the exertion of talking.

His ribs are surely broken, Orlando thought. "No way, partner," she said, smiling reassuringly at him. "We're in this together."

"I hate to admit it, but I was hoping you'd say that," Robert said, grinning.

"Besides," Orlando quipped, teasing him, "if you were telling me the truth last night and you are working with the Agency, I don't want to lose you. You're the only link I have to my father's murderer."

"Well, I'm glad I'm so valuable to you," Robert responded with a smirk. Then seriously, he added, "So, have you got any ideas?"

"Yeah. Why don't we 'borrow' their Jeep?"

"And how do you propose we do that?" he asked, shifting position to ease the pressure on his ribs. Then, looking up at her, he said slowly, "Orlando, I don't like that look on your face."

"I think I could distract them long enough to get the Jeep away from them, but I'll need your help. I'd like to lure them one at a time into the woods, where you'll be waiting for them from behind a tree with your gun. I'll walk past you and you clobber each man over the head with the butt of the gun."

"How do you plan to lure them here one at a time? Or are you planning to invite a gang rape?" Robert asked angrily. "Do you have any idea how long these guys have probably gone without a woman? And dressed like that... well, you'll be asking for a lot more than you can handle!" His annoyance was out of genuine concern for Orlando's safety, but she didn't see it that way. "Besides," he continued without waiting for a reply, "after the first guy, they're not going to keep falling for a line."

"You know, *Mr. Taylor,* I don't appreciate your attitude," she replied, speaking a little louder and with a sharper tone than she had intended. She continued more softly, but with no less passion, "I know I'll have to be careful. I can convince them to follow me. After all, I did get us past the guards at the house, didn't I?" She paused briefly and, moving closer until her face was inches from his, looked directly into his eyes. "Now, are you going to help me or not?"

"It seems I don't have a choice." Robert sounded sarcastic but looked defeated. "I'm not really in a position to argue, am I? And," he added in a conciliatory tone, "you're right. I haven't come up with a better idea. And if we don't get out of here fast, the others will be back to search the woods again, and I don't think we'll be as lucky next time."

"Okay, here we go," Orlando whispered, quietly moving to a kneeling position.

"Orlando," Robert said huskily as he reached for her arm. He stopped her movements with his tone. His eyes held her prisoner. In that instant, they were the only people in the world. He pulled her down to him and kissed her hungrily. His warm, soft kisses became more demanding, and Orlando gladly surrendered to them. He allowed himself the luxury of savoring her sweetness for only a moment more, and then withdrew reluctantly. "Sorry. I had to do that... just in case. Be careful," he added softly.

Orlando replied with a smile, "It's okay, Robert. I'm glad you kissed me. I was beginning to wonder if you ever would." She smiled even more broadly at his surprised expression. "Don't worry," she added. "I'll be careful. Are you sure you're up to this?" she asked with genuine concern. His face was starting to show the pain he was in.

He didn't answer her, but he nodded, grimacing. Orlando grinned reassuringly back at him. Then she again moved to a kneeling position and began ripping the side seam in her dress. Standing up quietly, she adjusted the dress so that a good portion of slender, smooth thigh was visible. "Wish me luck," she said softly to Robert as she helped him up. She straightened her shoulders and, without looking back, started walking toward the Russian soldiers. As she walked, she swayed from side to side as if she was exhausted from running, creating a lot of noise so they would hear her coming and not shoot her accidentally. The four men, dressed in fatigues, turned as a group to face her when she emerged from the trees. Her hands were raised above her head, stretching the thin material of her dress to skin-tight proportions. As she approached their position, the attention of the four men was riveted on her swaying figure, no movement going unnoticed. She walked directly up to the men and pretended to feel faint. Just as she was about to collapse, one of the men rushed to her aid and grabbed her around the waist.

He lifted her into his arms, supporting her full weight as gently as if she were a mere child. Orlando looked up into his face sweetly. She could smell strong liquor on his breath. He'd evidently been drinking, trying to stay warm. The gunman, realizing where he was, righted her on her feet while Orlando removed the flask from his pocket in one smooth movement. She opened the flask and, saluting the small group, took a long, healthy swig. She then closed the flask, placed it back in his pocket and, smiling, gave it a small pat. The soldiers stared at her open-mouthed, as if they were in a trance. Finally, the soldier in charge decided that this was no way to treat a prisoner and ordered his other men to stand away from Orlando. He then pushed her to the back of the Jeep and with his gun pointing in her direction, ordered her to sit on the fender. "Where is the man who was with you?" he demanded in broken English.

This isn't going at all like I planned, Orlando thought. She looked up at him sadly and said softly, "Gone." Then she began moaning, and doubled over with her head resting on the spare tire.

"Where?" he demanded, grabbing her by the shoulder and pulling her up.

"Back there somewhere," she replied, waving her arm in the direction of the highway. "He left me here. He said I was on my own when the car died, and he just took off, leaving me here!" Orlando began sobbing softly, praying that she was convincing them she'd been abandoned.

"But you were coming from the trees," he stated suspiciously.

"I tried to find my way to a house or a farm, but there were snakes and crawly things in there," she answered, shuddering. "I decided to take my chances with you."

Grunting in disgust, the head gunman ordered a guard to be put on her and called the other men into a small group some feet away, talking softly in Russian. Orlando waited patiently for the right moment. Her thoughts were constantly with Robert. She couldn't see him from where she was sitting, but he was never out of her thoughts. For some strange reason, he reminded her a lot of her father. He was strong-willed, arrogant, and more than a little bit of a rogue. But his heart was good, and even though she'd only known him for less than 24 hours, she knew that she could trust him. Now, his life was in her hands. She knew it was love at first sight, even though she'd never tell him so. Taking a deep breath, Orlando snuck a glance at the man guarding her. He seemed distracted, trying to light a cigarette. Slowly, she stood up, stretched, and snuck a look at her slim watch. It was after 2 p.m. They must have been hiding in the woods longer than she'd realized. Time had slipped by, and her limbs were stiff. As soon as Orlando stirred from her resting position, her guard stepped closer and raised his gun. Orlando motioned to him to come closer to her. He did so cautiously, keeping his gun raised. "Vat do you vant?" he asked in an annoyed tone.

"Oh, you speak English?" Orlando asked sweetly.

"Ov course I speak Eenglish," he answered emphatically, as if he were insulted that she would even ask.

"Then, may I tell you something?" Orlando asked, moving closer. He didn't answer, but eyed her suspiciously. "I think you are possibly the most attractive man I've ever met. I love your accent, and you have the cutest little dimple, right there." She touched his right cheek softly as she spoke. "In fact," she added, moving closer to him, "I would really like to get to know *you* better."

He watched her closely, as if trying to read some form of deception in her face. But her face was the picture of innocence and sincerity. Holding his eyes with hers, Orlando took one final step and pressed her upper body sensually against the soldier, his rifle pinned between them. Her soft, supple body molded itself to the hard lines of his lean, muscular frame while she looked up into his face invitingly. She could feel his desire for her growing by the minute, and the raw hunger that he was feeling for her was reflected in his eyes. Orlando felt victorious. She'd succeeded in arousing him to the point where he'd follow her anywhere, just so long as they could be alone. Straining against him, Orlando stood up on tiptoe, and whispered in his ear huskily, "Not here. Let's go into the woods, behind the trees where we can be alone."

He didn't answer her, but grinned broadly down

at her. He took her by the forearm and led her toward the trees. Speaking loudly in Russian, the soldier in charge demanded, "Where do you think you're going?" The soldier holding onto Orlando responded, also in Russian, that he was going to show the "woman" why Russians were superior to Americans. His commander smiled and warned him to be careful since they still hadn't found the man.

Orlando had learned enough Russian from her cousin Tia to understand what had been said. She decided to use their nonchalance to her benefit and lure her first victim to the proper location. Pretending to stumble, Orlando waited until the soldier reached for her waist to prevent her from falling, and then whispered, "This way." Orlando smiled softly up at him as she led him to where Robert was waiting for them. The soldier grinned back and picked up the pace across the grassy expanse in front of the forest.

The other soldiers were standing around snickering and discussing their friend's imminent success. Then they began arguing about who would have the beautiful American woman next. One of the men commented that he could think of worse ways to pass the afternoon, to the laughter and jeers of the others. The man with Orlando was so intent on his catch that he never even noticed Robert standing behind the first cluster of trees. He had a heavy rock in his good hand, and he used it to silence his opponent.

"Why didn't you use the gun?" Orlando asked as she grabbed the falling soldier. He fell on top of her and moaned loudly as he slipped into unconsciousness. Evidently, the other men by the jeep only heard their comrade's moan and then the two of them falling in the dry underbrush. Misunderstanding, they cheered wildly at their friend's success.

"I found the rock and I figured it would guarantee results," Robert replied as he helped her push the now unconscious body off hers.

"Good idea," Orlando said, smiling as they dragged him out of sight. Breathing heavily, they sat back to rest and wait a respectable amount of time. They were still only two against three, so she'd have to go back out to the remaining men and do it all over again. After about 30 minutes, Robert moved back into position and Orlando emerged from the trees looking exhausted and vulnerable. She stumbled and fell forward into the grass a few feet past the trees, as if she were worn out from her afternoon's activities.

"Vere's Schmidtt," one of the lead men called to her. He obviously was uninterested in her condition.

Orlando tried to stand up as he approached her. When he reached her, he noticed that her dress had been pushed off her shoulders and was barely covering her breasts. She clung to him in much the same way she'd clung to the first man, looking up soulfully into his eyes.

"He told me to leave him," she answered him breathlessly. "He said he was satisfied and tired, and he needed to rest." Orlando looked as sad and ashamed as she could. "Help me, please," she said, looking up into his face.

"*Ya*, I vill help you," he said sarcastically, as he yanked Orlando by the arm and dragged her with him to the trees. "As soon as I have dealt vith that lazy rat bastard." They headed toward the same place where he'd watched Orlando enter the trees with his subordinate. But they were going too fast for Orlando to position him so Robert could knock him out, so she pulled up short, pretending to trip, and caught him off balance.

"I can't go that fast. You're hurting me," she said, pulling her arm loose from his grip and standing away from him. "I'll show you where your friend is. Just don't pull me around like a sack of potatoes," she added angrily. "He's over here," she said, walking ahead of him.

The soldier walked behind her, his gun ready, a suspicious look on his face. Orlando couldn't hear the men by the Jeep any longer, and she knew that they wouldn't waste any time coming after her if a second man disappeared in the woods. They were already becoming suspicious. The gunman stopped shortly and pulled Orlando around to face him. "Dat's far enough. Vere is he?" he asked angrily.

Orlando was just about to answer him when

Robert stood up behind him. He swung the same rock, which came down with a thud on the Russian's head. The Russian collapsed to the ground slowly like a slow-motion playback in a football game. There was a look of disbelief on his face just before he lost consciousness. "We don't have a lot of time. The other two will be in here any minute to find their comrades," Orlando said softly.

"I know," he answered shortly. "Have you ever shot a rifle?" Robert asked as he handed her the soldier's AK-74. "It's not much different from the revolver, but it's got a kick. Just make sure you put the butt end into your shoulder or you'll land on your backside."

"No problem. How hard can that be?" Orlando asked back, smiling. "I just aim and pull the trigger, right?"

"Yes, that's right," Robert replied, smiling. "Once the safety is off." He reached over and disengaged the safety adding, "Just try to hit one of them, and not yourself or me. Oh, and be sure you use two hands to steady it. We're not going to Rambo it today!"

"Okay. Where are we going to hide?" Orlando asked quietly, anxiously looking toward the Jeep. The two remaining men were calling for their comrades while checking their weapons, getting ready to enter the woods.

"Over here," Robert said, taking Orlando's hand

in his. "Be careful not to trip or break any twigs. Our only advantage is surprise. They're expecting you to be alone in here. I want to catch them in a crossfire. Otherwise, they could hold us off in here until help arrives."

"Okay," Orlando agreed nervously. She didn't want to think about what might happen if Robert's plan didn't work. This whole thing had seemed almost like a game of intrigue until now. She'd never killed anyone before, and she wasn't sure she could. She knew, however, that if it came down to her life or that of the Russian soldiers, she'd fight with every ounce of strength. She looked over at him. "Oh, how I wish I'd told him how I feel. What if we don't make it?" The thought kept her strong. She resolved herself to be strong and to face the situation at hand. Somehow, she knew they'd both have to make it.

It didn't take long for the two remaining Russians to become suspicious about the prolonged absence of their friends. They moved slowly toward the trees, guns lowered and ready to shoot the first thing that moved. They took turns calling their comrades by name--in Russian, not English. Robert, trying to lure them closer, answered, "Over here!" in Russian. The two men looked at each other, confused, and moved closer. They took cover behind some undergrowth. It appeared they were going to wait for help. Orlando decided that the time had come to do something. The tension was becoming unbearable. "Help! Oh, please help me," she cried out faintly. Robert shot her an angry look. She was setting herself up as a target.

One of the two men moved around the trees in Orlando's direction. When he reached the spot between Orlando and Robert, he heard another cry. "Help, please!" This time it was more faint, but definitely to his right. The soldier closest to Orlando turned quickly, his gun aimed in the direction of the sound. He never got the chance to fire, however, because Robert placed one shot squarely between his shoulders. It spun him around like a marionette on a loose string. He was suddenly facing Robert, wobbling on unsure legs as if gravity had been temporarily suspended. Robert shot him again, this time in the heart. The soldier fell over, dead before he hit the ground. The gunshots brought the last Russian running swiftly but cautiously in their direction, moving quickly through the trees. He called frantically for his friend to answer him, but was met with a deadly silence. He slowed down and crouched low behind a rock. Orlando sensed his fear. She could feel fear's numbing cold run through her bones, too, and smell the extreme crispness in the air. Slowly, the Russian inched toward where Robert and Orlando were hiding. He was headed directly toward Orlando, and she couldn't do anything to get out of his way. One more foot, and they'd be eye-to-eye. Robert suddenly yelled at the Russian soldier in his native tongue. He hesitated. He didn't recognize the voice, but the dialect was familiar to him, and it confused him. His momentary hesitation was his downfall. Orlando clenched her teeth and held her breath, and, raising the rifle, squeezed the trigger. She hit the last soldier squarely in the forehead. He didn't move at first. He just stood perfectly still, staring dumbly ahead of him. His mouth opened, but no sound came out; then, his face contorted of its own volition, just before his knees buckled and his torso hit the ground inches from her feet. There was very little blood, for which Orlando was very grateful. She started to tremble, and let the rifle hang loosely from her fingers, dangling at her side. She would've passed out from the shock of actually shooting a man dead, if it hadn't been for Robert. He stood up and moved quickly to her side.

Are you alright?" he asked, genuine concern and affection mingled in his eyes.

"Yes, I think so," she answered softly, not yet sure of her own voice. She was still shaking, and the gun was swaying slowly back and forth in her limp hand.

"Good. Then let's get out of here. Now, let me help you," he said, lifting her right arm slowly in his two hands, making certain that the gun was aimed away from his body. "Good. Now, give me the gun," he said softly, and Orlando's arm went rigid, holding the rifle in a death grip. "Look at me, Orlando," he said more urgently. "It's me, Robert. I'm going to take the rifle now." Orlando looked up slowly and stared into Robert's eyes as if she was trying to return to the present. Without losing eye contact, Robert carefully pried her fingers from around the trigger. Reluctantly, Orlando released the gun to him.

Once the weapon had been removed from her hand, everything came flooding back. "Oh, Robert," she cried, and flung herself into his arms, sobbing hysterically. "I killed him! I killed him! Oh my God, what have I done?" Robert just held her until she calmed down. "I'm sorry. I shouldn't have fallen apart like that. It's just that I never…" she said softly, pointing at the dead man on the ground. Then, hearing Robert's ragged breathing, she turned to him and quickly added, "Robert, your ribs!"

"I'll be okay," he said, inhaling sharply. "Let's get to the Jeep." He didn't want to let her see the pain he was in.

That last effort to distract the Russian had done something to his cracked ribs. Now, he was getting a sharp pain every time he inhaled, and it was becoming increasingly difficult to get enough air. They walked as quickly as they could toward the Jeep. When they reached it, Robert said with a struggle, "You'd better drive, Orlando. I'm afraid I'm not up to it."

"No problem. I was planning on it," Orlando said as she turned and looked at his pale complexion and the glassy look in his eyes. She took the gun out of his hand and put it in the glove compartment of the Jeep, and started the engine. Her heart went out to him. Her anxiety and guilt about what had just taken place disappeared in a single breath. "Sure, Robert. No problem. Here, let me help you," she added as she gently eased him into the passenger seat. Robert didn't argue, and gladly leaned heavily on her. He couldn't speak without extreme pain, and he decided that it would be better for them both if he conserved his energy. As Orlando helped Robert into the passenger seat, she took a quick look at his face and really started to worry. His eyes were closed, and his breathing was shallow and rapid. He was becoming more pallid by the minute, and his arms lay in his lap like those of a broken doll.

Orlando spun the tires on the gravel, and dirt flew into the air as she swerved on the side of the road. Not really knowing where she was going, Orlando jammed the car into gear and headed back toward the house. She drove in the opposite direction than the one the soldiers had taken, just in case they doubled back. She had no idea where they were going; she only knew that they were heading away from Hartt's soldiers, and hopefully toward civilization. While she was driving, the scene of the killing kept playing over and over again in her head: the last soldier standing there face to face with her. If it hadn't been for Robert, standing up just in time and drawing his attention... she didn't want to think about the alternate ending. She couldn't get the smell of gun powder and burning flesh as the bullet entered his body out of her mind. The dull popping sound of the bullet cracking the bone in his forehead continued to ring in her ears, and she was sure she would be haunted by the hollow look on his face just before he fell to the ground for the rest of her life.

"Where're we goin'?" Robert murmured. His speech was slurred as he drifted in and out of consciousness.

"To get you to a doctor. You don't look good, and you sound even worse," Orlando said, smiling weakly.

She didn't add that she was afraid that his cracked ribs had punctured his lung and that he wouldn't make it much further. "You're just full of compliments, aren't you?" Robert said, closing his eyes again.

"Never mind. You just rest and leave the driving to me. Besides," Orlando added, trying to reassure him, "we'll be there soon."

"Must get to Hartt. Must stop him... no time..." Robert was mumbling to himself, his eyes closed tightly and his face contorted with pain. His color was becoming ashen. When Orlando could sneak a look at him a few minutes later, Robert was half sitting, slumped over in his seat, unconscious. Orlando pushed the Jeep to go even faster. The speedometer edged up to 70, then to 80, and then past 80. She had to slow down because of the curves in the country road, but she was driving like a woman possessed. The only goal she had was to get Robert to a doctor before he passed the point of no return.

The miles sped by and Orlando finally saw a road sign up ahead, stating *Bridgeport 37 Miles. Thank God. Now all we need is an emergency room,* she thought. When Orlando reached the city limits, she slowed the Jeep down to a safe speed. She looked frantically for some sign of a hospital or doctor's office. Finally, frustrated and more than a little angry, she pulled into a gas station. When the attendant approached her, Orlando asked excitedly, "Where's the nearest hospital?"

"About three miles ahead on the right. But there's road construction between here and there, so you'll have to detour." He continued on with detailed instructions about which way she should turn to avoid the barricades. "What's wrong with your friend?" he asked curiously, looking past Orlando to where Robert was slumped unconscious.

"He's had an accident. He fell off a horse and broke some ribs," she lied smoothly. "I think it's pretty serious. So, if you'll excuse me…" Orlando said shortly as she shifted into first gear.

"Sure. Good luck," he said, stepping back from the Jeep. Orlando stomped on the gas without even looking to be sure the attendant's feet were clear of the tires. She followed the gas station attendant's directions to the letter and arrived at the University Hospital Emergency Room a few short minutes later. She left Robert in the Jeep and ran into the emergency room. She grabbed the first nurse she came to and explained the situation. The nurse in turn called for two orderlies to bring a gurney and follow her. They carefully lifted Robert out of the Jeep, placed him on the gurney, and wheeled him into one of the exam rooms. The doctor asked Orlando to wait in the waiting room and told her that someone would be out to take all of his information.

The next couple of hours went by in a blur. She was asked for insurance information and about her relationship to Robert. That question stumped her. She told them she was his wife because it was the first thought that entered her mind. Then she was asked about his allergies, any medical history she might be familiar with, who was his next of kin, etc. She was sorry that she hadn't taken the time to find out more about him before they'd met for dinner. The only information she could provide them with was what she'd found out about Robert's professional background, and that wouldn't be much help at this point, so she lied and said that he had no family and that she was his next of kin.

Finally, the doctor called Orlando back to the exam room and told her that she could see Robert if she wanted. She walked quickly into the exam room, knocking on the door as she entered. Robert was lying on the table. His ribs were taped, there were wires and tubes attached to every part of his naked upper torso, and his bed was raised to support his frame. Thankfully, his color was returning to normal. He'd obviously been given some strong painkillers, because he was smiling. The doctor walked in behind her and, without ceremony, began speaking. "His rib was pressing on his lung, but after looking at the CT scan, we're confident his lung wasn't punctured, and he should be alright in a couple of days. We're going to run some more tests, but he should be able to go home today. Once you take him home, you'll have to give him some TLC for about a week—no lifting, no bending, and no exercise of any kind. And Mr. Taylor, I don't want you doing *anything* strenuous for the next few days, if you get my drift." He gave Orlando a pointed look. "Nothing that will raise your blood pressure or cause you to breathe heavily. After that, start with light exercise, and then in about two weeks, you can return to your normal activities. In the meantime, I want you to follow up with your regular doctor, and if you feel any discomfort, I suggest you come back here or see your doctor as soon as possible. I'll forward your CT scan and other test results to his office so he'll be familiar with your status. Do you have any questions?"

Robert shook his head no.

"I would be happy to play nurse to Mr. Taylor, doctor, and I promise he will do *nothing* strenuous,"

Orlando said, stressing the word "nothing," and they all smiled. It only took about an hour for them to release Robert, and after they'd signed the necessary papers, they were on their way. "Okay. Now what?" Orlando asked, helping Robert into the Jeep before climbing into the driver seat.

"Well, I thought we might go shopping in New York, get a change of clothes, and then get started on that R&R that the doctor mentioned," he replied, grinning.

"New York?" Orlando asked, surprised. "With everything going on right now, I don't think that's a good idea. Won't Hartt be looking for us there? I think we need to get away for a while."

"Yes, I guess that's true," he said, smiling. "I was just kidding. We need to get away from the city and go somewhere no one can find you. My family's got a house in Florida. We could go there. It's not anything fancy, but it'll do for a short vacation. It just happens to be near Walt Disney World. There's a small town nearby. You might have heard of it? Orlando?"

His sense of humor was returning. "Yes, I've heard of it," she replied sarcastically, smiling.

"Well, then, it's settled," he said with a nod. "We'll need enough clothes for about a week, but I wouldn't suggest we go back to either of our apartments. We'll need to go shopping once we get to Florida. I don't think we should fly commercial since

Hartt will probably have the airport under surveillance. We can't use an Agency plane either, since we don't know who's working with Hartt. Can you call the airport and have your pilot and the company jet ready? That way, we can drive straight to the private area of the airport and take off."

"We can use my jet, but what makes you think Hartt won't be waiting for us at the hangar? Besides, I can't leave town for an entire week without any notice. I have to get in touch with Sally and let her know where I can be reached, and I have to reschedule some of my appointments, and I have to..."

"Don't worry about all that," he said, interrupting her. "First of all, we'll watch for Hartt's men. They all dress alike, so I can probably spot them from a block away. Second, the phone line to your office is probably bugged, if they're not already in your office babysitting your assistant. You can call Sally from the plane and let her know you're okay. It's safer that way. And you'll have to let her handle the business meetings. No one else can know about us leaving town--just Sally. That's all. The fewer people who know where we are going, the safer we will be."

"Yeah, I guess you're right. I almost forgot about *FILE 13* with everything else that's been going on. God, I wish this whole mess was over and we could get back to a normal life."

"Don't worry. It'll all be over soon enough. As soon as we secure *FILE 13,* you can get back to your normal routine, and you won't have to worry about men like Hartt bothering you again."

Orlando didn't answer him. She knew that as soon as they'd securely placed *FILE 13* in the proper hands, she wouldn't have any reason to see Robert again. They drove the rest of the way into New York in silence, each occupied with their own thoughts.

Most of the day had passed by the time they'd gotten through the city traffic. Orlando drove on the Long Island Expressway (LIE) toward Kennedy International Airport where her corporate jet was waiting. Robert would occasionally open his eyes and look around to see where they were, but he was too groggy from the pain medicine the doctor had given him to talk. He sat back in silence, brooding. Just before they reached the JFK Airport exit off of the LIE, Orlando spotted a store where she could pick up a burner phone. She pulled off of the LIE and into the parking lot quickly, trying not to wake Robert. When she left the Jeep, he was still sleeping, so she locked it and slipped inside quickly. After about five minutes, she re-entered the Jeep just as quietly, and headed back out to the highway.

Orlando looked at the time. It was already 10:00 p.m. It was much to late to try to call anyone, but she had to get in touch with Sally. She was sure that Sally would be frantic, because Orlando never called her. How could it be possible that only a little more than 24 hours had passed since she'd left for her dinner date? They hadn't eaten since dinner the night before, and now her stomach was starting to complain. *Well,* she thought, *as soon as I get a hold of Sally, I'll get us something to eat.* Orlando first called Sally's apartment, and then her sister's house. Orlando apologized to Sally's sister for calling so late, asking if she'd seen her friend. Her sister hadn't heard from her, but said that they were planning to have lunch together the next day. Orlando wished her a good evening and hung up. Sally didn't date much, and if she'd had a date planned, Orlando was sure she would've told someone. Sally wasn't a spontaneous person, and Orlando was starting to get worried. Now, her imagination was starting to work overtime. What if Hartt had done something to Sally? What if he had tried to force her to tell him something about *FILE 13*? Orlando called her office. She got the after-hours operator on the main line, and there was no one on the back line. Finally, Orlando tried her private line to her office apartment, and the phone rang twice before Sally picked it up.

"Hello," she said groggily, as if just awakened from a deep sleep.

"Sally?" Orlando asked anxiously.

"Orlando?" she answered.

"Yes, it's me. Are you okay?"

"No. No, I'm sorry, Orlando isn't here. I don't know where she is or when she'll be back," Sally responded quickly, sounding scared.

"Sally, are you okay?" Orlando asked. She was becoming frightened. Sally's response didn't make any sense. Then it occurred to her. "You're not alone, are you?"

"That's right. If I could have your name and number, I'll be happy to give her a message when I hear from her."

"Sally, don't worry. We'll be right over. Just hold on, okay?" Orlando was really scared now. Hartt and his men must be holding her.

"No!" Sally said emphatically. Then, returning to her normal friendly, calm demeanor, she added, "You don't need to do that, sir. I... I don't know when she'll be back. If delivering the contract is that time-sensitive, I can give you her email address and you could send it to her. Yes, she'll be out all week, but I will be checking her email address. No, I'm not sure where she is at this moment, but I believe she will be at a ski resort in Sun Valley."

Orlando hesitated before she spoke again. That was the cover story she'd left with Sally in case there was trouble. "Okay, Sally, I understand. I won't come over there, but I'll send help. Once the police get there, follow the plan we'd discussed before I left last night. Okay?"

"Yes. Thank you," she replied, sounding

relieved. "I'll give her the message, and you can depend on me to be sure she gets it. Thank you for calling," Sally said quickly as she hung up the phone.

Orlando didn't waste any time. She called the police as soon as she hung up with Sally and reported an attempted robbery in her office. She explained that her assistant was working late and had heard someone enter the office when she was supposed to be the only one there. Orlando elaborated, saying that she was on the phone with her assistant when she heard the men come in, that she had heard multiple voices, and that she was afraid they were armed. Next, she called her pilot so that the jet would be fueled and ready to go. After another 20 minutes of fighting traffic, Orlando pulled into the airport and drove toward the private area of the airport. She didn't drive directly to her hangar, however, as she was worried there might be someone waiting for her there. Orlando drove behind a nearby fuel truck and stopped the Jeep. She waited a few minutes, watching the hangar for any unusual activity. She didn't see anyone, so she slowly circled the hangar and parked out of site on the side of the building. Gently, Orlando roused the sleeping man next to her. "Robert, we've gotta go." "Okay, I'm up. Once we're in the air, I can call my boss at the Agency and we can make arrangements to pick up Sally and..."

"No. We don't have time for that," Orlando said,

interrupting him. "I finally reached her. She's in trouble. Hartt must've decided to hold her to get to me. Us. He's there with her right now. He and a couple of his men are in my apartment with her. I was going to go over there to help her..."

"No! Absolutely not!" He grabbed her forearm roughly and looked intently into her eyes before he continued. "You're not going anywhere near that place. If Hartt gets his hands on you again, he won't be satisfied with just questioning you. He'll make an example of you--and make sure you don't tell anyone else about *FILE 13* or him! Sally will be okay as long as he thinks she'll lead him to you. He didn't realize you were the one calling, did he?" Orlando shook her head no. "Good. Then she's not in any real danger yet. As long as he thinks that you don't know about her, he can't use her as a hostage."

"I told Sally I'd send some help. I called the police and reported a break-in. They should be there by now." Orlando looked at him, worried.

"I'll send my men too. Exactly where in the building are they, and where can my men gain access into the building without being seen?"

Orlando told him about the private apartment, as well as the secret entrance. She was surprised to find out that he didn't know about it. "If you didn't know about the apartment and how to get into it, how did you know what was in my closet?" she asked, confused. "I bribed one of the cleaning ladies," he admitted with a weak smile. "I got her to look for me the last time she cleaned in there. She told me the only way she'd let me know what was in your apartment was if I promised not to ask where it was. She's obviously very loyal to you, but she thought that it was very romantic that I'd want to buy you a dress and not duplicate one of the dresses you already had in your closet."

Orlando just smiled at him. She knew the woman he was referring to. The woman was one of Orlando's oldest employees, and she knew that the woman would've never gone along with Robert's scheme unless he'd convinced her that he was a romantic suitor trying to win her heart. Mrs. Philippe was a very shrewd woman, but she was a pure romantic at heart. *Robert must be a very accomplished liar,* Orlando thought. *I'd better watch him closely.* After Orlando had told Robert everything she knew about the alarm system in her office, the various entrances and security guards, he called the Agency. He explained what was going on and where they were going. He said that in an emergency he could be reached at his Florida residence. He then asked this team to leave an agent with Sally to protect her, gave them the number at Orlando's office apartment, and told them he'd call them within the next couple of hours to make sure that Sally was alright.

Thinking about what could happen to Sally, Orlando began to imagine the worst. She pictured a scene like the one they'd recently left behind in the interrogation room, with Sally as the victim and Hartt's men torturing her for information. She knew her imagination was getting the better of her. Sally had sounded fine--a little scared, but no worse for wear... so why couldn't Orlando shake the feeling that something really awful was about to happen? She had a flashback to the woods and the gun battle there. She waited for the chill to pass as she remembered shooting the soldier at point blank range. "You know, Robert, I wish I could tell you that I'm not scared of the danger involved in all of this, but I won't lie to you. I'm terrified!" Orlando looked directly at Robert. She felt that this was the turning point for them. She wanted to be able to trust him, but she'd only known him for such a short time, and she really didn't know that much about him. "I would like to think that we're in this together, but the fact of the matter is, Robert, I'm not sure I can trust you."

"What?" It was a one-word question, but the single expression was filled with puzzlement mixed with indignation, and it spoke volumes.

"There are several reasons," she responded slowly, "but primarily, because I know nothing about you except what you told me at dinner. Besides, I've seen your ability to deceive, and I don't want you to practice your deceptions on me." Orlando stopped and looked him directly in the face.

Robert stopped too, and, smiling at Orlando, responded, "Okay. I'll make a deal with you. If you'll postpone this discussion until we're on the plane, I'll tell you anything you want to know."

Looking around the hangar and surrounding air strip, Orlando remembered how vulnerable they were in their current location. "Okay, you've got a deal. But I'm going to hold you to it."

"Deal," Robert said, smiling. He turned and took her two hands in his, and looked at her squarely in the face. "I'll tell you anything you want to know. Look, I don't know what there is between us yet, Orlando, but I know you've felt something too. I want to give us the chance to find out just what it is. It's very important to me that you trust me."

Orlando looked at him, trying to discern some form of deception in his eyes, but there was none. He looked completely sincere. *But,* she thought, *wasn't that part of his charm?* Then, to Robert she said softly, "I want to trust you, but you do have a way of turning events and people around to your advantage."

"It's part of my job. Just like finding *FILE 13* is part of my job. But Orlando, if you'll just give me the chance, once all of this is over, I'd like to take the time for us to get to know each other *a lot better."* His tone more than his words conveyed his meaning, as he ran his finger along her cheek, tracing its silky curves down to her trembling lips. "I'd like that," she replied breathlessly. "I'd like the chance to get to know you well enough to trust you." She stopped herself before she added that she'd like the freedom to fall in love with him.

"Then just give us a chance," he replied. "Let's get through this and then we can take it from there."

"Okay," Orlando said, smiling at him. Gently, he leaned forward and kissed her. His lips touched hers softly at first, exploring her full, sweet lips. Then, his kiss became more demanding, filled with burning passion. His lips demanded a response from Orlando, and he got it. Their kisses and caresses were brief and unsatisfying, but they promised something wonderful to come later.

Time was passing quickly, and they had to get on the plane. Orlando opened the glove compartment and retrieved the pistol she had used earlier in the day. It seemed like a year ago now. Pushing the images of the fire fight in the woods from her mind, she quickly shoved the gun into her purse and closed the glove compartment. She helped Robert out of the Jeep, and they walked arm-in-arm toward the plane. Since it was a private plane, there was no security or body scans to go through, so there was no search to worry about. Orlando and Robert were the only ones who knew about the pistol and the real reason for their flight to Florida.

True to his word, Robert told Orlando all about himself while they were in the air, from his early childhood right up until the time he joined the

Agency. He told her about his parents' death in a car accident when he was six, and he detailed his journey into adulthood at the hands of a cruel uncle who enjoyed beating him whenever he disobeyed. He told her how he had run away at 14 and lived on the streets until he was 18, when he joined the Army. He explained how he couldn't even read and write well when he joined the Army and that he received not only a high school diploma, but his college degree as well, thanks to Uncle Sam and a very supportive recruiter. It was while he was in the Army that his talent for subterfuge was discovered. Frustrated by Robert's constant meddling, his commanding officer offered him the choice of going to the stockade or doing some work for the Agency. "Naturally," Robert said, smiling, "I chose the Agency. Now, the rest of the story is classified. That is," he said, running his finger along her jaw bone up to her ear, "until we get to know each other better."

Orlando smiled at him and said sarcastically, "Oh, Mr. Taylor, I can't wait." To her surprise, he just sat back in his seat and roared with laughter. Orlando joined him, and she felt the stress melt away from her body. Their conversation for the rest of the flight was light and filled with good humor. The jet landed at the Orlando Executive Airport just before midnight. They'd made good time. Before taking Orlando to his house, he insisted on touring the city bearing her name.

"I want to see the city as much as you want to show it to me, but if I don't eat something soon, I'm going to pass out. Aren't you hungry?"

"Yes, as a matter of fact, I am. That's why our first stop is the Citrus Club."

"The what?"

"Come on. You'll see."

The quick 10-minute drive from the airport to downtown Orlando was comfortable in Robert's red Jaguar. They talked companionably, and laughed when first Orlando's stomach rumbled and then Robert's gut spoke up. "Won't the Citrus Club be closed by the time we get there?" Orlando asked, looking at the clock on the dashboard.

"Probably, but don't worry about it. The manager is a friend of mine. I had the pilot call ahead and tell him we were coming. He'll have a sumptuous meal ready and waiting for us. Wait 'til you see the view from the eighteenth floor of the CNA building." Robert was enthusiastic about the city he liked to call home.

"I'll appreciate the view a lot more after I've eaten," Orlando said, smiling. "How much farther?

"Not far now," Robert said, pointing to the Merita Bread Company. "Open your window."

"Why?" Orlando asked, puzzled.

"Just do it," Robert urged gently. Orlando did as she was told and much to her delight she could smell fresh bread baking.

"It smells just like our house did when I was growing up," Orlando said, smiling as she sat back and closed her eyes. She inhaled deeply, enjoying every tantalizing breath. Opening her eyes, Orlando turned to Robert and smiled. "You know," she said, turning to Robert, "this wasn't such a good idea."

"Why?" he asked, puzzled.

"Because now I'm even hungrier than ever."

"Okay, okay. We'll be there in just a minute." Robert pulled off the interstate and into the downtown late-night traffic. The CNA building faced Orange Avenue, but was is one way, and Robert would be going the wrong way.

He circled the block and then pulled into the covered parking garage. They were the only people in the garage, and they could hear their voices echoing in the cavernous room on their way to the elevators. They rode silently to the eighteenth floor where the Citrus Club was now quiet. "Hello? Anyone here?" Robert called out.

"Over here," a male voice called from around the corner.

"Robert, this is beautiful," Orlando said, examining the rich carpeting, oil paintings, and antique furniture. Through the tall windows she could see the outline of the city and the twinkling lights of the cars driving by on Interstate 4 below them. "I had no idea it was such a beautiful city," Orlando remarked as Robert led her to their table. It was a small window table, lit by candlelight and surrounded by greenery. Fresh flowers decorated the center of the table.

"Tony, I'd like you to meet a very special friend of mine, Miss Orlando Corogan. She's from New York City. Orlando, this is my friend Tony. Tony is the one who's responsible for the delicious food we're about to eat. And Tony, since we haven't had anything in over 24 hours, we're ready to eat now. What do you have ready?"

"All your favorites," he answered, smiling.

They feasted on hot spinach salad and cold potato soup, followed by fillet mignon and poached asparagus. Cherries Jubilee for Robert and Baked Alaska for Orlando topped off the meal. They toasted each dish with a glass of champagne, and sipped cordials after dinner. Feeling full and satisfied, they strolled arm in arm around the empty restaurant, looking out at the city. "Fair lady," Robert said with great flourish as he turned Orlando to face him. "I think we'd better be heading back. It's after one in the morning and we've got a long drive ahead of us."

"Okay," she agreed softly. "I am getting sleepy," Orlando said, stifling a yawn. She smiled up at him in embarrassment.

"You need to stay awake until I can get you there. So, let me tell you a little story," he said, laughing, as they exited the restaurant. "Goodnight, Tony, and thanks!" Tony said to the man watching them as he waved goodbye. Tony waved back with a nod as he cleared the table.

"So what's this story?" Orlando asked while snuggling closer to him in the elevator.

"Well," he began slowly, looking down at her upturned face. "There was this young lady I met, not too long ago, who had a very unusual name. Like you, her name was *Orlando* and like you, she was very beautiful."

"Thank you," she said, smiling.

"You're welcome," he replied, smiling. "Anyway," he continued, "she was born in the northern part of the beautiful state of Florida. Shortly thereafter, her family moved with this beautiful young lady, to Orlando, the very city in which we are standing. Now, why would they come here, you might ask?" he said, waiting for her to ask. When she didn't, he tweaked her nose and made a face of exasperation. He continued, "Well, someone might ask." He paused again, waiting for a reply. When he received none, he continued, "Anyway, they came back here because that's where this young lady was conceived, thus her name: Orlando. When her father's business expanded, they moved to New York and he eventually became a very wealthy and influential man."

By now Orlando was becoming uncomfortable. Her family's story about her father's success in the business world was well-known, but the other information about how she'd gotten her unusual name was not. Robert continued to tell her about his rise in financial circles, and his international fame as the new Madison Avenue wiz kid. He also told Orlando about her desire to come back to her namesake, nicknamed the "City Beautiful," and settle down with her own family.

"Very funny," Orlando said, climbing into the car beside Robert. "How did you find out all that information?"

"I have my sources," he said, reaching for her hand. He caressed her long supple fingers with his own lean, strong ones. Just this simple touch sent shivers up and down her spine. She knew that what was building between them was inevitable, and that she was powerless to stop it. Her body cried out for Robert, and it was obvious that he desired her too. She only wished she knew if it was just chemistry, or if there was something more between them. But, regardless of the reasons, Orlando resigned herself to the fact that it was just a matter of time before they became lovers. Her body had been telling her so for some time now. Only after this long period of intimacy with him was she was prepared to admit it.

"Seriously, Robert, how did you find out about my mother and father? No one knew about how I got my name but my mom and dad, Sally, and a few close friends."

"Seriously, Orlando," he answered her, smiling

as he mimicked her tone and phrasing, "I told you-- your father and I were very good friends. He wouldn't have told me about you if he didn't trust me. And if he felt that he could trust me, don't you think you could risk it?"

"Let's get going," Orlando said quietly, as she turned in her seat and reached for her seat belt. Without another word, Robert started the car and pulled out of the garage. He pulled onto the city's most scenic road, Orange Avenue. "It's beautiful," Orlando said softly to herself, as she looked out the window at the shops, the gas-style street lamps, the brick intersections, and cobblestone decorated sidewalks.

"You know, there's a magic here I haven't found anywhere else, not even in the cities of Europe," Robert commented. "Oh, they have their old-world charm, but this city, Orlando, has something I can't describe. It's... well, it's magical," he added, looking at her. "I've been here before. It was a long time ago, right after high school, and the people were so friendly. I know I sound foolish, like a typical tourist, but it's true. I really would like to live here someday," Robert concluded as he smiled at her.

They had stopped by Lake Eola, the heart of Orlando, with its colorful fountain and band shell. Robert took her in his arms and kissed her. His hand touched the hollow of her neck where her pulse was beating wildly. He traced her silky skin slowly down

to her breasts. He toyed with the top of her low-cut
blouse, but was careful not to push too far too fast.
Orlando was experiencing sensations she'd never felt
before. Her pulse was racing so loudly she could hear
it, and her head was spinning so wildly that she felt
she would leave the ground at any moment. A slow
burning had started at the core of her being and was
spreading outward to fill her with an incredible
warmth. Her toes and fingertips were tingling, and
every cell in her body seemed to come alive. Then, as
suddenly as it had begun, it was over. Robert sat
back, breathing hard, and put the car in gear.

"Where are we going?" Orlando asked, confused
and more than a little shaken.

"I want to show you something," he said without
looking at her. What he didn't tell her was that while
he was kissing her, he'd noticed a long, black sedan
pulling up to the curb several cars behind them. It
was just then that four men, also in black, got out of
their car and started walking toward them. That's
when Robert had noticed them in the passenger side-
view mirror, and that's why he had pulled away from
Orlando. He didn't mention it to her, not wanting to
scare her. To cover, he started a conversation as he
quickly moved the car.

"Have you ever seen Church Street Station?" he
asked her as he stepped on the accelerator.

"No. What is it?" Orlando asked, regaining her
equilibrium.

"It's a historic U.S. depot, built around 1890, and it actually functioned as a major train station for the city. I think it still does today, but it's also a collection of clubs that are situated alongside the railroad tracks, and each has a different theme. They have a cool saloon called the Cheyenne Saloon, a dance club, a country bar, and a really nice restaurant. They've had all kinds of top performers put on shows there, and even a few political rallies back in the 1980's. We'll come back to the restaurant when they're open, and I'll take you to dinner and a couple of the shows. They even have an attached mini-mall that has two stories full of boutiques."

"That sounds great! I know it's probably near closing time, but I would love to see it," she said, grinning. Oblivious to the impending threat, Orlando was looking forward to the adventure. Robert drove the few short blocks and parked the car under Interstate 4 in the public parking lot, and then they walked across the street to Church Street Station. The typically large crowd trying to get into the shows in the main room was gone and the street was eerily quiet. Only a few couples like themselves were strolling along the street. As they walked slowly down the side of the quaint brick buildings, Robert told Orlando some of the history behind the restaurants and clubs which encompassed the 'Good Time Emporium' and the man who'd built it.

"It looks like they'll be closing soon. Would you

like to stop in for a couple of minutes, or are you too tired?" Robert asked Orlando, looking lovingly down into her eyes.

"No, I'm not tired anymore," she replied, smiling up at him. "I'd love to see it."

Robert and Orlando made their way inside, paying their admission at the door, and finally found a seat near the bar. While Orlando watched the singing group perform, Robert watched for the men who'd been following them. Just about then, the four men dressed in black entered the club. They'd taken off their jackets so that they would look less conspicuous among the tourists and revelers, but it was definitely them. No matter how hard they tried to blend in, they still looked very much out of place. Robert could pick them out anywhere, no matter what they were wearing, just by the way they moved in unison, as if they were one individual and three mirror images. It was as if they didn't know if they were supposed to be tourists or natives, and it was obvious that at least one of the men had never been to a club like this before, as he couldn't take his eyes off the singers. One of his companions was forced to continually jab him in the ribs with his elbow to get his attention. The four men, one slightly taller than the other three, and a bit darker, looked as if they were Eastern European. As they made their way to where Robert and Orlando were sitting, they casually pushed people aside, ignoring their stares, loud objections, and dirty looks. One of the women whom the four men pushed as they walked by grabbed the last man's arm and loudly reproached them, just before hitting them with her purse. This brought the man's presence to the security guard's attention, and bought Robert and Orlando some time. "Orlando," Robert whispered in her ear, "we're getting out of here. I'm afraid we've got company." He motioned with his head to where the gunmen were trying to get away from the woman with the purse. "Who are they?" Orlando asked, alarmed, as she stood up quickly.

"They're probably friends of the guys we left up North. I don't think they were too happy about the way we left their little party, and they've come to take us back. Come on, take my hand, and stick close." Robert didn't wait for a reply. Orlando had just picked up her purse when he literally pulled her out of the bar area and jerked her toward the door.

Robert quickly circumvented the crowd, and was heading toward the back of the building. He opened the EXIT door at the back of the room, and the fire alarm started going off. People immediately started to run out the doors, not waiting to see if it was a false alarm. Robert and Orlando took advantage of the large crowd and the confusion to make their escape. They looked for the four men in black and couldn't see them, so they ran in the opposite direction, out the front door and down the alley to the street. They ran toward the public parking area where they had left their car, carefully ducking between the cars.

When they finally arrived at Robert's car under Interstate 4, they paused only a moment to see if the four men were chasing them. They were.

Obviously Robert's trick with the fire alarm hadn't fooled them for long, and they'd somehow managed to escape the woman with the purse, the crowds, and the bouncers. They spotted Robert and Orlando from across the street, and were headed toward them at a full run. They ignored the cars and busses that had almost hit them several times while crossing against traffic. "Get in! Quick!" Robert shouted. Orlando didn't have to be told twice. She got into the car and locked the doors as Robert quickly jammed it into reverse. He nearly ran down two of men as they approached his car from the rear. Robert shifted the car into first, and then second as he roared off in the opposite direction. He could see the two men still chasing them, but falling behind as their companions joined them, yelling at him with raised fists.

"It'll take them a few minutes for them to get to their car and get it started. That'll give us the advantage we need," Robert said to Orlando without turning to look at her. He jumped up on Interstate 4 and then got off at East Livingston Street, north toward Colonial Drive. He was heading east, and picking up speed with each mile. "Where are we going?" Orlando asked. She felt like she was constantly asking that question.

"Back to the Executive Airport. I was planning to drive to the ranch, but I think we'd better take a helicopter out of here so we can get back there before they catch on to what we're up to. They'll be expecting us to try to out-run them on Interstate 4, and they'll be waiting for us. If we can get to the ranch before they do, we can get some help. I've got enough men there that they won't try to take us away."

"A ranch?" Orlando asked, confused. "You said it was a little house. Just how big is this ranch?"

"Don't worry how big or small it is now, Orlando," Robert responded, annoyed. He wasn't angry with her, however. He was mad at himself. He felt he should have anticipated that they'd be followed down to Florida. "Well, we're here," he said, pulling into the airport. "Do you see a helicopter anyplace?"

"Over there," Orlando said, pointing to where a small bubble helicopter that was parked outside the hanger.

"That's it," Robert said, relieved, pulling the car into the hangar. "Come on. Let's go." Robert had stopped the car next to some boxes covered with tarp. He removed the tarp from the boxes and covered the car with it. "That should buy us a few minutes. If they send someone to the airport, they won't be certain we were here unless they discover the car. Now, let's get out of here and get to my ranch." He grabbed her hand as she ran alongside of him toward the helicopter.

"Robert, I can't believe you're stealing this thing! Besides, do you even know how to fly it?" She was quickly buckling the belt around her as she spoke.

"Of course I can fly it! Don't worry. It belongs to a pilot friend of mine. We have an agreement that whenever I need it I can just take it. In return, I help finance his flying school. It works out very nicely, especially when I need to leave town quickly."

"Is that often?" Orlando asked, shouting over the engine.

"Later!" Robert said anxiously. He prepared to lift off and called the tower. Robert identified himself and the aircraft, and then told the tower his intended destination. The tower gave him clearance and he lifted off. "Won't the flight plan tip off the men following us as to where we're going?"

"Nope. The airport I designated as our destination is in Daytona Beach. By the time they figure out where we're really going, they'll have some catching up to do. Besides, they have to figure out if I'm driving or flying. Granted, the guys driving down Interstate 4 won't be too far behind us, but I think we'll beat them to the ranch with a few minutes to spare. And, just about now, they should be second-guessing themselves, wondering if we drove or went to the airport. Those four following us didn't look intelligent enough to figure it out for themselves, so they'll have to call and ask for instructions. That should buy us a few more minutes."

"I agree with you, but Robert, this whole thing doesn't feel right. I mean, getting away from those guys was too easy. It doesn't seem right. I mean, if they could find us downtown, they might have known where we would run. It's almost as if they let us get away," Orlando said, frowning.

"Well, don't worry about it now. We're on our way to my ranch and safety. It'll be alright, I promise." He smiled, reassuring her with his calm manner.

"Oh, I know I sound foolish," she said, embarrassed. "But it just doesn't feel right. Call it woman's intuition, but something's wrong." Her frown deepened, and her expression was troubled.

"Hey, come on, don't go getting shaky on me now. Not after all we've been through." He smiled and squeezed her hand.

But before he could continue, the engine started making strange sounds. It started choking and bucking as if the fuel lines had dirt in them. They were about two miles from Robert's ranch. It was, in reality, a sprawling ranch house with several out-buildings surrounding it. The helicopter started a slow and spiral down as it descended of its own accord. Robert fought with all his strength to stop it, but to no avail.

"Hold on," Robert said, holding onto the controls with both hands. "We're going in, and there's nothing I can do about it." He stopped speaking for a moment and tried vainly to control the helicopter, but it only spun faster. "Cover your head with your hands and tuck it between your knees. You might just survive that way."

She looked at him and then suddenly felt compelled to tell him how she felt. She might not get another chance. "Robert, there's something I've got to tell you."

"Not now," he shouted at her sharply. "Get your head down, and don't look!" Orlando did as she was told.

She'd missed her chance. Neither of them spoke after that. Robert concentrated on trying to make a controlled crash landing. Orlando peaked out from her crouched position and could see the trees coming at them faster and faster. She knew that they wouldn't clear them, and she waited in horror as everything seemed to happen in slow motion. The ebony of the night sky gradually gave way to the dark, emerald green of the dense set of trees and underbrush. There was a loud roaring noise and a rushing in her ears as they neared the ground. The sound of metal splitting wood and glass shattering got louder and louder as they fell like a heavy stone. The birds who had been occupying the upper limbs in slumber screeched as they fled in fright when the helicopter made contact with the pine forest. Orlando covered her head again and held on tight, as Robert had told her to do, trying not to scream. She heard the piercing cry that came from her mouth, but it sounded like it had come from another person. Robert let out a gut-wrenching yell of terror in response to Orlando's scream. But their screams were short-lived. The creaking and groaning of the trees straining against the plummeting intruder was followed by grinding metal and the splintering crash of wood and broken glass. When the helicopter finally left the trees and made contact with the hard ground, the loud, booming thud drowned out all of the other, natural sounds. The birds and wildlife continued screeching and, in general, producing a cacophony of sounds for several moments as they ran away in terror, and then there was complete silence. It was a reverberation more terrifying than any the forest had ever known. The vibrant forest had become deadly quiet.

Chapter 7

KROSKY'S CAR PULLED up in front of Investments Internationale, next to the spot where Tia's car was parked. The driver stayed in the car and the gunman assigned to keep an eye on Tia opened the door let her out of the car. They didn't speak to her, but stood as quiet and alert as a jungle cat, waiting for her to start her engine before pulling away. As soon as Krosky's car was out of sight, Tia pulled around the corner to the underground garage and parked the car. She walked quickly out of the garage, crossed the street, and entered the building. At the security desk, she asked to use their phone, explaining that she was Orlando's cousin and that she was supposed to meet her at the office. Tia called the main number to Orlando's office and there was no answer. Then, remembering it was not unusual for Orlando to work alone in her office on Saturdays, even though the rest of the work world shunned weekend hours at the office, Tia decided to try Orlando's back line and Sally answered.

"Hello, Orlando, is that you?" Sally asked quickly.

"No, Sally, it's Tia," she replied. "Where you? Are you all right?" Sally asked, sounding a little panicked.

"Yes, I'm fine," Tia reassured her. "Are you

okay? I'm looking for Orlando."

"I'm so glad," she said with a sigh of relief. "I heard the commotion in the outer office, and I saw some men come in and take you away with them. The cleaning crew saw your note in the bathroom and told me about it, and I was going to call the police, but I didn't see who they were or where they were taking you, and I was afraid they'd think I was nuts. They didn't hurt you, did they?" Sally asked. "No. I'm fine, really," she responded. "Are you okay?"

"Yes," said Sally. "They didn't hurt me. They held me for a while and then let me go."

"Good. I'm glad you're okay," Tia answered. "Now, listen, Sally, this is important," Tia said with urgency. "Have you heard from Orlando or a man named Robert Taylor?"

"Yes, and Tia, it was so frightening!" Sally exclaimed.

"What do you mean?" Tia asked, getting anxious. She was becoming annoyed with Sally's roundabout way of putting things. "What happened? Is Orlando in danger? Is she hurt?"

"It all happened so fast. Yes, I think she's in danger," answered Tia. "But she sounded fine when I talked to her a while ago." Then Sally sounded as if she was going to cry and started talking even faster.

"Okay, Sally, I want you to calm down," Tia said, trying not to get irritated. "Sally, slow down and take it from the top. Now, when did you speak to

Orlando?"

"Well, it was right after Mr. Hartt and some god-awful men with guns showed up. They figured out how to open the door behind the bookcase and came right in here, expecting to find… I don't know what. Anyway, one of them told me to sit down, and pushed one of those long, cold guns up against my cheek. Then Mr. Hartt started asking me where Orlando and that Mr. Taylor was. Well, of course, I wasn't going to tell them. I mean, I love Orlando like she's my own kid! I'm not going to let those thugs get their hands on her if I can help it," Sally explained emphatically, as she paused for a breath. Then, inhaling deeply, she continued, "Anyway, right in the middle of all of this, as if by some omen, Orlando called me. Of course, I didn't let on that it was her," Sally explained with pride. "I told the person on the phone, even though it was really Orlando, that she'd gone skiing. I played dumb just like she told me to do. She guessed I wasn't here alone and said that she'd send help. And I guess she did, because about ten minutes later, the phone rang again. Hartt got mad and answered the second call himself. While he was listening to the other person talk, his face got very red and he started cursing under his breath. Then, he thanked the person on the other end of the phone and slammed it down. He yelled at the gunman standing by the door, in Russian. He said that they were on their way over here right now! Then Hartt, along with the gunman who was holding the gun against my face, got out of the office as fast as they could. They forgot all about me, which was fine with me, if you know what I mean."

Tia smiled to herself and said, "Sally, I'm glad you're alright." Then she took a deep breath and asked Sally patiently, "Sally, what did Orlando say when you talked to her?

"She told me to get the letter to the person we'd discussed, and that's what I'm going to do," she replied emphatically. "Once we get rid of it, then this whole mess will be cleared up. I think Orlando was foolish to hold onto it as long as she did. I didn't even know she had it until yesterday, but if I had, I would have insisted she get rid of it. I mean, as far as I can see, it's only caused her trouble."

"I think you're right, Sally," Tia said. "You should do what Orlando told you to do, and whatever you do, don't mention what's in the letter or anything about it on the phone or to anyone else," Tia said. Then, almost as an afterthought, Tia added, "And Sally, I can't emphasize this enough… I don't know who the person is who's supposed to get the letter, but whatever you do, don't give it to anyone besides the person Orlando said should get it! Do you understand?" Tia asked.

"Yes, Tia, I understand," Sally responded soberly.

Tia continued, "And if anyone tries to take it

from you or prevent you from giving it to the right person, destroy it. It could cost a lot of people their lives, including Orlando!"

"Oh my God," Sally exclaimed. "I thought she was safe! I mean, since I talked to her and she sounded okay, I thought she was okay. Tia, if anything happens to her because of me I'll… I'll… well, I could never forgive myself!" Sally replied, almost in tears.

"Sally, pull yourself together! I need your help," Tia said sharply. "Orlando will be fine. I'll find her and everything will be okay. Understand?"

Sally responded to Tia's tone like a child who'd just been pulled up short of a temper tantrum. "I'm sorry, Tia. You're right."

"It's okay, Sally. I know this sort of thing isn't in your job description," Tia said, softening her tone a bit. "Now, can you cover for Orlando at the office? I don't want anyone to become suspicious about her absence. The fewer people we have asking questions, the better."

"No problem," she responded. "I had already cleared Orlando's calendar for the rest of the week, just in case something like this happened. All I have to do is reschedule some of her meetings."

"Good," Tia answered. "I also need you to trace a yacht called the *Golden Sun.* It's scheduled to dock in Coco Beach, Florida later today. I'll get a flight into Orlando International for later today and drive over. I need you to find out who owns the yacht and tell the person you're giving the letter to about everything we've discussed. You also need to tell him that a man named Grouchev has two of his operatives aboard the *Golden Sun.* Make sure you write down the name so you won't forget it. That's G-R-O-U-C-H-E-V. Got it?"

"Yes, Sally responded. "Anything else I can do to help?"

"Yes, please," Tia answered. Can you remember if Mr. Taylor had another residence besides the one in New York?" Tia asked. "I can't think of another place, other than his home, where he might have taken Orlando. If I'm lucky, I might be able to beat our friends to them."

"As a matter of fact," Sally responded, "Orlando had ordered a background check on him, and I think I remember something in the report about a ranch in Florida. Can you hold on a moment, Tia? I've got the report right here."

"Sure," Tia answered.

After several minutes of silence, Sally was back on the line, and her mood was noticeably improved. "I was right!" she said with a triumphant tone. "The report says that he has a ranch just south of Buena Vista, Florida. That's near Disney World, I think. I visited there last summer on vacation, and I think it's just outside the theme park."

"Yes," replied Tia. "Yes, it is, Sally. Thank you

so much for your help with this," Tia added excitedly. She couldn't believe her good fortune. She was finally catching a break. "I'll call you from the ranch," Tia added. "Thanks, Sally. Thank you very much!"

"You're welcome, Tia," Sally said. Then she added, "But Tia, don't go disappearing on me like your cousin did."

"Don't worry about me, Sally," Tia responded. "I know how to take care of myself." Then, she added quickly, "Listen, I don't know if Orlando would want you to know this, but I think I ought to tell you. For your own safety, I think you should go visit your sister for a while. The Russian Mafia is involved in this, and they're not as nice as Hartt."

There was an audible intake of breath on the other end of the phone. "Then the men..." Sally started.

"That's right, Sally," Tia interrupted. "The men you saw leading me away were Russian Mafia. Hartt, the American who came there to the office, was working with them."

"That explains everything now," Sally said slowly. "Hartt gave Orlando an emerald yesterday."

"I know," Tia interrupted. "I know all about it. Listen, Sally, I don't have time to explain what's going on right now, but if Orlando gets in touch with you again, call me immediately on my cell phone. You have the number. Orlando's in a lot of danger, so

I need to get in touch with her right away."

"Oh, okay," Sally replied.

"I'm going to Robert Taylor's ranch," Tia said quickly.

"Will you be flying commercial or taking the family jet?" Sally asked, interrupting Tia.

"I'll be flying commercial," she answered. "I don't want to draw anymore attention to myself than I already have. I've already got a shadow. That's why I'm not using my cell phone to talk to you now. It's harder to tap a land line than a cell phone, and I'm pretty sure this one is relatively secure. I'm hoping to lose my shadow at the airport, and I'll call you if I can with my flight number and my ETA. If you hear from Orlando before I take off, have the airline contact me at the gate and I'll get off the plane. I'll be traveling under the name Samantha Johnson. If you have to call, ask for me by that name. Have you got any questions?" Tia asked.

"No, I've got it. Anything else?" Sally asked.

"No, I don't think so. I'll call you from the ranch first thing," Tia responded. Then she added quickly, "Don't forget. Get that information to the person we talked about as soon as possible, and NO ONE ELSE!" Tia paused a minute and then continued. "Sally, be careful, okay?"

"I will, and you too," Sally answered. "And Tia…" Sally said, pausing.

"Yes?" Tia responded.

"When you see Orlando, give her my love," Sally said softly.

"I will. Take care," Tia said before she hung up.

"You too," replied Sally.

Tia thanked the security guard and then walked back outside the front door and halfway down the steps before she bent over, as if she was tying her shoe. As she did it, she covertly looked around for her shadow. She could see the front left fender of the black SUV behind a delivery truck on the next corner. She casually stood up and walked back to the parking garage and got into her car.

As she was pulling out of the garage onto the street, she wondered if they were just careless about their surveillance or if they wanted her to know they were there. Either way, she wasn't in the mood for playing games. Tia had just under three hours to catch her plane. With the new security procedures in place, that gave her just over an hour to pick up what she needed and get to the airport. Once on the street Tia took off into traffic, trying to lose them long enough to affect a convincing disguise. She half-expected her shadow to be waiting for her at the airport. Her disguise would have to be really good to lose them before she boarded the plane.

Tia knew there was only one place she could go to lose him. She ducked into one of the alleys in the garment district with the SUV not far behind her. She dodged vendors and pedestrians and men pushing racks of men's and women's clothing. The SUV wasn't as lucky. It drove right through one of the racks of clothes. The driver tried to steer the car with his right hand while frantically trying to remove the garments with his left, but the clothes that had spread out across the windshield successfully prevented him from seeing anything. He swerved right and left, but for all his efforts, he only succeeded in scattering people and clothes in every direction before the car careened into a large dumpster. A seething man who'd been pushing the rack and about 30 other angry people ran after the SUV down the alley. They were ready to teach the driver a lesson. Curious pedestrians and a few barking dogs joined the screaming, running throng. The scene would have been hilarious to anyone not involved in the chase.

Once the SUV had come to a complete stop, the crowd jumped upon the vehicle, yelling at its occupants. The man who had been pushing the clothes was banging on the driver's door, yelling for them to come out. The rest of the people were crushing around the car, and several young men were screaming profanities about the injustices done to the poor by the wealthy. The driver had quickly raised his window and secured the car. They were not leaving the safety of the SUV under any circumstances. The roar of sirens dispersed the crowd quickly, and the man banging on the driver's door stopped to listen. Then, as he slowly backed away from the car, he added, "Now you'll see what's done with trash like you!" He continued making threats to the SUV driver, shouting at him from a safe distance.

The arrival of the police and the general confusion over the SUV and the clothes, and the irate man gave Tia the time she needed to get away. She pulled into another alleyway, and then out onto the parallel street. She drove about a block and pulled into yet another alleyway leading away from the accident. She stopped at the end of the alleyway and honked three times, paused, and then honked twice more--one long and one short. A garage door slowly raised, opening to a space large enough for a car with no room to spare. Tia pulled all the way in and the door closed silently behind her. The small opening quickly became an elevator, rising with Tia in her car, to the second floor of a large warehouse. Once the elevator stopped, Tia pulled forward into a cavernous room with wooden floors and old plastered walls.

"Hi, Harry. Where's Kathy?" Tia asked the man who'd been waiting to greet her as she climbed out of the car.

"Upstairs. Where do want the car put?" he asked Tia as he climbed in behind the wheel.

"Anywhere out of the way," she replied. "I also need you to call Orlando International Airport and have them deliver a helicopter to the Delta terminal, or as close as they can get to it. I need to get to a ranch south of Buena Vista, near Disney World, as fast as possible. And Harry, I need a trustworthy pilot. One who knows how to keep his mouth shut."

"Will do," he said, grinning, giving her a mock salute. "So, are you in trouble again, or are you back with the Agency?" he asked her through the open driver's window.

"Ha, ha!" she replied, smiling back at him. "You know better than to ask such foolish questions, especially when you know I can't answer them." His chuckles followed her all the way up the stairs. Harry's fashion house was very successful in its own right, but he was also a strong supporter of the Agency, and a close personal friend of Tia's. They'd worked closely together in the past, and Tia knew she could trust him implicitly whenever she needed help and she couldn't go to the authorities.

As Tia made her way through the building, she passed the cutting rooms of the design house and the sewing rooms. These were the heart and soul of Harry's business. There were elevators, but Tia preferred the old, narrow spiral stairway that led from the warehouse downstairs to the workrooms upstairs. Each of the rooms was like a small auditorium, noisy and busy. But this was no sweathouse. The employees were well-paid and the work rooms were cheerfully decorated and well-lit, with attention to detail when it came to the workers' comfort. As Tia walked from room to room, she could hear the radio playing somewhere in the background, accompanying the noise of the sewing machines. The people operating the machines didn't seem to notice her, as they were completely absorbed in their work.

Harry had very little turnover in staff, and most of his seamstresses and tailors had been with the company a very long time. He believed that a happy employee produced twice as much as an unhappy one, and so far, his theory had proven to be correct. His factory was producing as much as competing larger factories, many with three times as many employees. There was even a waiting list for job openings, mainly because very few of Harry's team ever left. He was a kind, generous man who treated his employees like members of his family. He had helped Tia many times in the past and she was indebted to him, as were most of his employees. She knew that she could trust him. Harry and his employees were known to be discreet.

Tia traveled quickly through the design room, pausing a moment to look at the sketches on the work boards.

The designers were at lunch, so the room was very quiet. Tia climbed another flight of stairs to the fourth floor where Kathy's office was. Where Harry was the heart of the organization, Kathy was the financial genius behind the business. She handled the books and the vendors, the shipping, the vendors, and just about everything that had to do with the company's operations. Harry said he couldn't stand that side of the business, preferring instead to manage the designers and the creative side of the business. "KNOCK, KNOCK! '" Tia said, rapping on Kathy's office door.

"Come in. The door's open," she heard from the other side. Tia opened the door and was immediately made to feel welcome with a big hug.

"Tia! What a nice surprise. Come here, let me look at you," Kathy said with joy in her voice. She was like the mother Tia had never known, and Harry thought of himself as her stepdad.

When Tia was in school, she knew that if she had a problem, she could turn to Kathy and Harry. They had even screened her dates, helped to pay her way through college, and gave Tia her first job out of school. The grey hair and even the age difference went virtually unnoticed in their time they spent together. They only argued over one subject as far back as Tia could remember, and that was her career choice. When Tia decided to join the Agency, they strongly objected. They were concerned about how dangerous the missions would be and that she wouldn't have time for a private life or a family of her own. Tia had to admit that many times while in the middle of a mission, those arguments would haunt her. She finally had to admit they were right, and that was when Tia left the Agency.

"Hi, Kathy. I've missed you," Tia said, hugging

her impulsively. She meant it, too. Every time she went to see them she felt like she was coming home.

"I've missed you too, Tia," she said softly. Stepping back and looking intently into her eyes she added, "Now, why don't you tell me what's going on. Lately, the only time you come to see me is when you're in trouble."

"That's not true!" Tia protested with a smile.

"Oh, yes, it is. Now come sit down and tell me all about it. What can I do to help?"

"Kathy, have I told you lately how wonderful you are? Tia asked sincerely. Kathy smiled and shook her head. "Well, you are!"

"Boy, Tia," Kathy said, laughing. "You must really be in trouble! Tell me what's going on."

"Okay," Tia said, smiling weakly. "Some men are following me and I need a disguise. You see,

I need to catch a plane out of town, and I don't want them to follow me. I'm sorry I can't tell you more, but you know how it is. Will you help me?"

"Of course I will," Kathy answered. "You know all you have to do is ask!"

"Thanks, Kathy," Tia reassured her. "I never doubted you. I'm just in a rush. I only have an hour to get to the airport."

"Okay then. Let's get started," Kathy said, taking Tia by the arm.

Sharing a conspiratory grin, they walked arm in arm downstairs. Kathy found Tia a platinum blonde wig, about medium length, just long enough to cover her long, dark tresses. Next, Kathy found a large dress, one about three to four sizes bigger than Tia, and designed for a woman at least 20 years her senior. Padding, a light sweater, a hat, and tinted fake bifocal glasses were added. Tia now looked like a solid but stylish middle-aged housewife off to visit relatives. Kathy finished off the outfit with sensible black flat shoes and a box-style purse.

Tia's face and hands might give her away, so Kathy suggested she wear special theatrical makeup to age her. It had to be authentic up close so that the TSA agents would not be suspicious when she went through security. As the makeup base dried, it tightened Tia's skin and formed wrinkles around her eyes, mouth, and jaw line. It had the same effect on the tops of her hands and fingers. Next, Kathy brushed a light, waterproof brown powder over Tia's face and hands. The color collected in the lines formed by the base and emphasized the wrinkles. Next, Tia inserted dark contacts into her eyes to change their color from blue to brown. Finally, Tia donned several cubic zirconia rings to simulate a wedding set on her left hand and an expensive cocktail ring on the right.

"Well," Tia said, looking into the full-length mirror, "the acid test will be Harry. If he doesn't recognize me, no one will." She turned to look at Kathy, and asked, "What do you think?"

"You're right," Kathy said, smiling. "I think you look great, but let's see if we pass the test." She pushed the button on the intercom and asked Harry to come to the office. "Harry, could you come to my office for a moment? I have a buyer in here I'd like you to meet." She then turned to Tia and said, "We'll make your ID once Harry has seen you, to make sure we're good and don't have to make any changes. What are you going to do about transportation? You can't take your car; they'll be looking for it."

"I was sort of hoping you'd let me have a ride in the van. It leaves every day about this time, and it would go virtually unnoticed," Tia said. Before Kathy could get an answer, Harry knocked on the door and walked in.

"Watcha need, girl?" he asked, beaming at his wife. Before she could reply, Harry turned and saw Tia. "Oh, hello. I'm Harry. It's nice to meet you," he said, smiling and extending his hand. "Harry, I'd like you to meet..."

"Samantha Johnson," Tia supplied. She affected an Irish accent, and spoke slower than she usually did.

"Nice to meetcha," Harry said again, grinning. "I didn't know my wife hid her most beautiful business associates from me so well."

"Ho, you were right," Tia said to Kathy snickering. "He can be a charmer when he wants to be."

"Wait a minute!" Harry said, his forehead creased in a deep frown. "I know that voice!" He walked around her, looking at her closely. Tia couldn't control herself anymore and neither could Kathy. They burst out laughing and confessed to Harry. Tia now felt confident that her pursuers wouldn't recognize her and that she could fly to Florida without being slowed down. Tia quickly tucked a change of clothes into her big purse and headed toward the door.

Tia thanked Kathy, and Harry and was about to leave when Harry insisted on driving her to the airport himself. "I'm going to see to it that you get on that plane safely. Besides, they'll be looking for a woman traveling by herself, not a woman with a handsome devil like me."

Kathy also insisted that Tia allow Harry drive her to the airport. "He'll take good care of you, child," she said, waving goodbye. "Besides, if you're the only *other* woman in his life, I won't worry so much." They all laughed at that.

Harry drove her to the airport in the company van and never asked why she had to go to Florida. He and Kathy had learned a long time ago that any inquiries were futile. He kissed her goodbye at the entrance to security and waited for her to go around the corner in the TSA line before leaving. He noticed two men in dark suits also watching the security line, and they seemed unsure about what to do. Finally, they headed for a quiet area where they could use their phones, and Harry followed them. He pretended to be calling someone near them and kept his back to them to avoid suspicion. He heard them telling the person at the other end of the line that they didn't see "the girl." They said that they weren't sure if she was still going to Florida by plane. The flight Tia had caught was the last one for several hours, so the two men were told to wait at the airport in case she showed up there. They confirmed the fact that they would have someone waiting for her in Orlando. Harry was satisfied that their plan to fool Tia's pursuers had worked. He was concerned, however, about the two men waiting for her in Orlando, but he figured they wouldn't have any better chance of recognizing Tia than these guys in New York.

Tia's flight to Florida was uneventful. Kathy and Harry had done a good job of disguising Tia's true identity. When Tia arrived at Orlando International, she called Sally while pretending to be waiting for her bags to be unloaded. She confirmed what Tia had found out about the *Golden Sun*'s destination and time of arrival. She also told Tia that the yacht was registered to a Samuel Goldman. Tia told Sally that that was the name Grouchev used in the United States. Tia asked Sally to try to contact Robert and Orlando at the ranch and tell them of her plans. She also instructed her not to divulge her plans to anyone but Robert or Orlando. Finally, Sally told her that

Harry had contacted the Agency helicopter pilot which Tia had requested. Sally gave Tia directions to the helicopter, which would be waiting for her at a discrete location outside the main part of the Orlando International Airport. Harry had also arranged for the gun and ammunition Tia had requested, and they would be waiting for her in a bag on the helicopter.

Walking back away from the baggage pick up area, Tia considered her plan. She hoped to rescue Peter and Joe from the yacht and ask them to help her get Orlando out of this mess before she got herself killed. In return, she would agree to help them recover the emerald with the information. Tia knew that even if the right person received the letter in time to warn the people whose names appeared on the list, *FILE 13* could seriously damage the United States' status with NATO.

As everyone left the baggage claim area, Tia quickly joined the throngs of tourists exiting the airport. Once outside, she paused to see if she was being followed. Satisfied that her ruse had confused her shadow, Tia headed for the waiting helicopter. Once at the hanger, Tia met the helicopter pilot and explained that her plans had changed. She told him she needed to get to Port Canaveral as quickly as possible. "No problem, ma'am," he said to Tia as he helped her into the small craft. "You're in good hands. Harry told me to take good care of you, and that's just what I'm gonna do. By the way, the bag

Harry asked me to have ready for you is waiting in the chopper. It's on the floor next to your seat. You might want to check it to make sure everything is there."

"Thank you," Tia answered him, smiling. She reached down and opened the duffle bag next to her seat. Inside, she found a .357 Smith & Wesson Magnum and three boxes of Glaser Blue Safety Slug Ammunition. Each box contained 20 of the 38 Special +P 80 Grain Safety Slug #12 compressed shot bullets. Tia preferred the Glaser Blue Safety Slugs because they were designed for maximum stopping power, producing immediate energy dispersal into the target with reduced penetration. Each round is exceptionally accurate and has minimal ricochet, which allowed Tia to focus on personal protection in populated areas where over-penetration may be a concern, but performance was still important. After checking the gun and boxes of ammunition, Tia added, "I think it's only fair to warn you, though, it could get dangerous."

"No problem," he answered, grinning. "I used to fly during the war, you know." He continued reminiscing as they lifted off. He was so captivated by his own stories that he didn't even notice Tia removing the wig and the padded form from the top of her dress. It wasn't until she slipped the dress down over her slender hips that he realized a transformation was taking place. "And I said to the major... hey! Just what do you think you're doing?" he said, turning toward her.

"Don't worry," Tia said, looking at him while she disengaged her feet from her sensible shoes. "Please keep your eyes on the instruments!" She stripped down to a pair of lacy black bikini briefs and a matching camisole. "I'm getting changed. Hey! Watch out!" Tia shouted. The pilot looked up in time to see the helicopter heading directly for a power line. He pulled up on the controls just in time, but not before nearly emptying Tia's stomach. After she recovered from the near catastrophe, Tia said, "I think you'd better keep your eyes on where we're going, and not on what I'm doing." She couldn't help but smile at his reddening face.

"'I'm so sorry. I... I never intended any offense, ma'am. It's just that I... I never had any woman get undressed in my helicopter before, and none that ended up looking like you!" His face was getting even more crimson. The more that he tried to explain, the worse it got.

"Please stop! You're not making it any better," Tia responded, smiling. She was trying not to laugh. As she slipped on her shirt, she added, "I don't usually get undressed in front of strangers, but I'm under a tight timeline." Tia paused, smiled weakly, and then continued. "Well, I guess it's only fair that I let you know what you're getting yourself into. You see," she continued, speaking as she pulled on a black polished cotton jumpsuit, "I work with the government, and the boat we're meeting at Port Canaveral belongs to some criminals. They are illegally holding two of my friends on board. I am going to get them back. I am hoping you'll help me." She finished speaking as she zipped closed the front of the jumpsuit.

"Well," he said, smiling conspiratorially at her, "it's after four o'clock, and I haven't had any excitement yet today. Maybe I could help out a bit. What do I have to do?"

Tia quickly explained what she needed him to do, smiled gratefully, and gave him a quick peck on the cheek. "Oh, and what you just saw," she said, smiling shyly, "is top secret, okay?"

"I didn't see anything," he said, smiling back at her. "By the way, my name's Mel."

"Nice to meet you, Mel," Tia said, offering her hand. "I'm Samantha Johnson." He looked over at her and then reached across and shook hands with her. "How long 'til we get there?"

"About ten more minutes," Mel said, checking his instruments. "Do they know we're coming?"

"I hope not," Tia answered him. "There were a couple of them following me in New York, but I think I lost them at the airport with this disguise. They might have had my cousin's secretary's phone tapped, and if that's the case, then they'll know where we're going and they'll be waiting for us."

"Okay," Mel replied, considering the situation. "Good to know. Is your cousin one of the people they're holding on the boat?"

"No," Tia explained. "Neither of the men being held on the boat is my cousin." Mel was looking more confused by the minute.

"Mel," Tia said reassuringly, "it's a long story, and we really don't have time to go into it now. The Russian Mafia is holding two of my friends and we need to get them off that boat fast! My cousin isn't on the boat, but she's in a lot of trouble, and I need my friends to help me rescue her. For now, that's all I can tell you. Can you just trust me on the rest?" She put her hand on his arm again.

"Okay," he replied. "But Harry's gonna owe me for this one!"

"So will I," Tia replied with a grateful smile. Tia had Mel radio ahead for a car since the helicopter couldn't land at the dock. It was a short five minute drive from the helipad to the dock. The *Golden Sun* hadn't docked yet, so Tia and Mel decided to get something to eat. They stopped at Flo's Place, a little roadside diner, and had their chopped steak special.

"Just to satisfy my own curiosity," Mel said, as he swallowed his last mouthful, "will you tell me if your cousin has anything to do with these men holding your friends on the boat?"

"I don't know, Mel," Tia answered him honestly.

"My cousin disappeared two days ago and no one has seen her since. I'm hoping my friends will be able to help me find her. You see," she continued cautiously, "the guys we're going to save used to work with me. I'm afraid that's all I can tell you for right now. If you want to back out, there's still time. I'm asking a lot, and I'll understand if you do."

"No, I'm not going to back out," he answered her slowly. "But there is one thing that's been bugging me."

"What's that?" Tia asked with her mouth full.

"I don't even know your name...your real name. I know you're not Samantha Johnson."

"What makes you say that?" Tia asked, looking surprised.

"You wouldn't have given me that name so easily if that was your real one," Mel said seriously. "Harry told me what you'd look like, but he never gave me a name. And I figure if he'd wanted me to know your name, Harry would've given it to me." Mel paused and waited, but Tia didn't respond. She just smiled down at her plate as she finished her food. Mel continued, "Now, the way I figure it, if I'm going to go into a dangerous situation with a lady, I'd like to at least know what name to shout out if she needs to duck!"

Tia couldn't help but chuckle. She looked up at him and saw sincere concern in his eyes and decided to answer his question "My real name is Tia Johnson.

I am afraid Harry was just complying with my wishes when he didn't reveal any information," Tia added apologetically.

"Well, Tia, I'm glad to know you. And don't worry, I won't ask any more questions," Mel said. "If you're a friend of Harry's, then that's all I need to know."

"Thanks!" she answered, sipping her coffee. "I think we'd better get going if we want to get to the pier before the yacht docks."

"Okay," Mel said, picking up the check.

"I'll take that," Tia said, reaching for the check. She couldn't get it away from him.

"No! It's mine," Mel's tone abided no argument. "If we get out of this mess you can buy me dinner. And you can bring along that cousin of yours. After all this, I'd like to meet her."

"You've got a deal," Tia answered, smiling. They walked together to the register. Several sets of eyes followed them, and when they left the diner and walked to their car, a man in a dark blue suit followed them.

Chapter 8

THE SUN WAS shining brightly in the eastern sky when Robert regained consciousness. The natural sounds of the forest had returned sometime during the night, and they filled the quiet trees. Robert sat up slowly and looked around him in disbelief. He saw Orlando tangled in the seat belt and some of the wiring from the rotor. He climbed gingerly out of his seat and disengaged himself from the belt and wiring holding him in the cockpit. He felt something running down the side of his face, and when he reached up to touch it, he noticed it was sticky. He examined his fingers and found his own blood staining them. He wiped his hand off on his pants and took out his handkerchief to dab at his forehead. It was bleeding steadily and it was starting to sting. When he started to walk around the wreckage to Orlando's side, he felt light-headed and slightly woozy. His head was starting to pound in rhythm with his heart. Ignoring the pain, he reached Orlando and felt for a pulse. There was one, and it was strong. He shook her until she regained consciousness.

"Are you alright?" Robert asked Orlando when he leaned over to help her out of the wreckage.

"Yes, I think so," Orlando said, groaning and holding her head. "How about you?"

"I'm okay," he said quickly, ignoring the pounding in his head and the dull throb in his ribs. He helped Orlando to get up easily, as if she were a small child, and led her out of the broken helicopter. He helped her sit down on the grass near the only standing tree in the area. "I wish I could say the same for the helicopter," he added, turning and walking a few feet back toward the wreckage.

"Robert, your head!" Orlando cried when she saw the red streak on his temple. She stood up slowly and walked over to him. "You're bleeding!"

"It's okay," he said, dismissing her concern. "It's just a scratch." Then, turning to examine the helicopter again, he added, "The problem is, where do we go from here?"

"How far is it to your house?" Orlando asked as she brushed bark and twigs off her clothes. She walked over to the helicopter to look for her purse and overnight bag. Digging through the multitude of wires, straps, and twisted metal, she found the items she was looking for. She also found a first aid kit, but it only had small band aids, an ace bandage, and some antiseptic. Not finding anything large enough to suit her purposes, Orlando opened her overnight bag and pulled out a pure white silk baby doll nightgown.

Robert turned to answer her question, and looked at her curiously. "What is that for?"

"It was for the first night at your house. Now, it's for your head," Orlando replied simply before she ripped one of the seams open, ripped the back of the gown in strips, and then tied the pieces end-to-end.

"Come here and sit down," she said firmly, guiding him by the arm. The fact that he didn't argue told Orlando a lot more than anything he could have said. Orlando carried the shredded silk and the antiseptic from the first aid kit in one hand and held onto Robert with the other as they approached a grassy area where she helped him sit down on the ground.

Robert's head was really starting to hurt now that the shock of the accident was starting to wear off. He was holding his head in his hands, rocking back and forth trying to stop the pounding. Robert moved his hands out of the way as Orlando approached. Orlando tried to sound better than she felt as she dabbed at the cut with the rag. "Hold still. This is going to hurt."

The cut wasn't as deep as she'd originally thought it was, but it wouldn't stop bleeding, and it was caked with dust and dirt. Once the wound was clean, Orlando applied some antibiotic cream and tied the remaining strips like a bandana around Robert's head, securely covering the wound. "There," Orlando said when she was done. "Does that feel better?" she asked, sitting back on her heels.

"Yes, thank you. But I'm sorry you had to sacrifice your nightie. I'd rather have seen you in it," Robert said, smiling up at her. "You know, that's the second time you've patched me up. You're going to have to give me a chance to thank you." His arms encircled her waist and pulled her closer to him.

"Oh, I'm sure I'll think of something," she said,

smiling back at him. "Speaking of patching you up,"

Orlando said, pulling away from him, just far enough to read the expression on his face, "how are your ribs?"

"They're fine," he said, automatically reaching for his side with his other hand.

"So I see," Orlando said pointedly, looking at the spot where his hand covered the bandage beneath his shirt.

"I'm fine. Don't worry about it," he said, sounding annoyed. "We've got more important things to worry about right now. We have to find a way to get out of here."

"Okay. Any ideas?" Orlando asked, changing the subject.

"Well, I could see the house lights just before we crashed last night, and we came in pretty straight. Judging from the sun, this way is east, so I figure the ranch is about two miles in that direction." Robert pointed in the direction the remainder of the helicopter nose was facing. "We're going to have to walk, and I'm afraid there are some pretty unfriendly things out here. We have a long way to go and it's going to get pretty hot. Don't bring anything except what you absolutely need so we can travel faster."

"Okay. Everything I need is in my purse," Orlando said, slinging it over her head and across one shoulder. You didn't by any chance bring anything for bug bites, did you?" she asked, rubbing her exposed arms.

"No," he replied absently as he stood staring at the ground, deep in thought.

"Okay, I'm ready. Feel like takin' a walk?" Orlando asked, faking cheerfulness.

"You don't look like you're up to it," he observed, as if he was looking closely at her for the first time.

"Your clothes aren't exactly what I'd call practical, and you'll never make even a half mile in those heels."

"Well, I don't really have a choice, do I?" Orlando asked, annoyed.

"I'm sorry. Here, take my shirt," he said, taking off his jacket and handing it to her. "You'll be more comfortable in this." When Orlando started to object, Robert interrupted her by raising his hand. "It's chilly now, but it'll warm up once we start walking. I'll be fine. Besides, it'll hide those bruises on your arms," he said as he ran a smooth finger down along her exposed skin. Her flesh instantly developed goosebumps, not entirely from the cool air.

"Thank you," she said softly, looking up into his face as she quickly slipped her arms into his jacket.

"You're welcome," he answered just as softly. He put his arms around her shoulders and pulled her close. He watched her face very closely, and he was shocked by the clear intensity of her eyes, the open affection he saw in her smile. He took her chin between his thumb and forefinger and looked even deeper into her eyes. He could see his own reflection there, and something more. He didn't dare speculate that it was love. It was far too soon, wasn't it?

The longing within him was obvious to Orlando too, and she could feel a delicious warmth spreading to her arms and legs from deep within her. His lips lightly brushed hers, tentatively at first, and then with more intensity, more possessiveness. It was an open, if silent, declaration of love, and it caused Orlando to gasp. He drew back long enough to look into her eyes again, as if asking permission. He saw what he was looking for, and this time Orlando responded with every ounce of strength, every bit of affection she felt for this man who had dominated her mind, her body, and her emotions. They were both swept away to a quiet haven, and then drained by the intensity of emotion they felt for each other. Orlando and Robert drew away slowly, reluctantly, silently agreeing not to examine these new feelings too closely. Orlando rested her head on Robert's shoulder, suspending the cloud of desire and allowing the reality of their predicament to invade again.

"Robert," she whispered into the hollow of his neck, just above his collar bone.

"I know," he whispered back. "Hush," he said just as quietly. "You don't have to say anything." He too was searching for words to express his new found feelings toward her. But there weren't any. Then,

Robert gently lifted Orlando's chin to look into her eyes again. He said mischievously, "We'll continue this conversation later."

She answered with just a smile as she breathed in the sweet muskiness that was uniquely him. Her face hovered just above his chest at the opening of his shirt, and inhaled deeply as she rested her cheek on his chest. "Sounds good to me," Orlando responded softly, lifting her head and looking up at him smiling. She was as relieved as Robert was that the moment of awkwardness had passed. "Besides, we can't forget why we've come here. What are we going to do about *File 13*?"

"I've got a plan," Robert said quickly. He kissed her once more, quickly, on the forehead, and then he turned his attention to more practical matters. "Let's get going," he said as he helped her stand up. He scanned the immediate area, quickly assessing the situation. "I'll lead the way, and you stay close behind me," he said, offering her his hand. "We're going to have to go the rest of the way to the house on foot. Are you ready?"

"About as ready as I'll ever be," Orlando said, looking around her at the thick underbrush. The palmettos looked sharp, and several of them were taller than she was. The ground was damp, and puddles of standing water could be seen in almost every direction. "How do you know which way to go? It all looks the same to me."

"I think I have a compass in the helicopter--or what's left of it. Worst case, we can navigate by the sun. When we were coming in, we were heading east, so as long as we continue in that direction, we should be okay." He and Orlando started to walk, and her heels stuck in the soft, wet grass. "Wait," Robert said, offering her his hand again. "You'd better give me your shoes," he responded to Orlando's puzzled expression. She took off her heels and handed them to him. Robert took them over to a tree stump, found a small rock and, one by one, hammered away at the heels until they came off. "I saw this in a movie once," he said, grinning up at her when he was finished. "Works pretty good, doesn't it?" he asked, holding up the rock and the now roughed-up flat shoes.

"Nice!" she said, glaring at him with annoyance. "I paid $480 for those shoes and now they're ruined!"

"Well, now they're $480 flats," he replied in a matter-of-fact tone. "Just add them to the list of things I owe you. Besides, you know you wouldn't have gotten very far in those shoes. Now they should be a little more comfortable."

"I know, but..."

"No buts. You couldn't walk barefoot through this stuff," he said, motioning to the undergrowth. "If the snakes and insects didn't get to you, the palmettos would have. As it is, your arms and legs will probably be scraped pretty badly before we get to my house."

Orlando took the shoes from him and put them back on her feet without comment. She didn't want to admit it, but she knew that he was right. "Do you want your shirt back?" she asked.

"No. I'll be fine. I grew up down here, and my skin isn't as tender as yours is. The bugs won't find me such a tasty meal."

"Thanks," she said, frowning. Orlando didn't like to think of herself as the weaker sex in any way, even if she was in a situation where circumstances were out of her control.

"Come on now, no sulking," he said, tapping her cheek. "It doesn't become you. Let's get going." Robert took her hand and started leading her away from the plane wreckage and into the woods, in the direction of his home.

"Wait!" Orlando said, pulling free from him and running back to the helicopter.

"What did you forget now?" he asked, becoming agitated.

"My pistol!" she said, as she pulled it out from under her overturned seat. "Remember?" Orlando looked up at Robert, smiling as she pulled it out of the crumpled bag. "This might come in handy."

"Come on," he said, grinning at her. Robert took her hand again and they started walking toward the trees. "What am I going to do with you?"

"Get me home safely and I promise to give you

some suggestions," Orlando replied, smiling up at him devilishly. They walked slowly, picking their way through the broken tree limbs and underbrush. Orlando followed Robert closely through the woods, without speaking. Each of them lost in their own thoughts. At first, the dampness in the forest held the coolness of the morning air, but as the day wore on, it became increasingly more uncomfortable. Orlando found herself wishing she could shed her clothes and stand under a nice, cold shower. They had been walking for about two hours when Robert told Orlando to take a rest.

"How far do you think we've gone?" Orlando asked, sinking disgustedly onto a moldy stump.

"About a mile, if we haven't been walking in circles," Robert answered as he sat down beside her.

What do you mean? I thought you knew the way," Orlando asked, confused.

"It's difficult to keep your bearings in the woods, especially when the only sunlight you can see through the trees is filtered."

"How much longer do you think it will take to get there?" Orlando said, standing up and stretching.

"I don't know," Robert said, mopping his forehead with his forearm. "When we get to higher ground, we'll know we're heading in the right direction. I built the house on a hill and the ground slopes down to a lake from the house on one side and down to the woods on the other. I've cleared about 20 acres around the house and we landed on the side of the house ringed by trees, not water, so we should be out of this stuff pretty soon."

Orlando didn't reply immediately. She was thinking about getting to the house. She'd been thinking a lot about a lot of things during the last 24 hours. Orlando guessed that whoever had sabotaged the helicopter had to have had a lot of information about Robert. It only made sense that whoever was trying to kill them had figured out where they were heading, regardless of Robert's flight plan, and it only stood to reason that whoever that person or persons turned out to be would probably be waiting for them at the house. Robert had deduced the same thing, but neither of them voiced their fears. Each of them was trying to be brave for the other.

"Just how big is your ranch, Mr. Taylor?" Orlando asked, feigning formality to lighten the mood.

"Well," he replied proudly, "the house is your typical one-storey ranch style. No pun intended. There are several out-buildings and sheds, and a barn, and the land around it is big enough for a few head of cattle and some horses."

"And how much land is that?"

"About a 100 acres."

"Impressive," Orlando said, smiling. "Do you know how much a piece of property that size around here goes for these days?"

"Yes, I do, but my grandfather bought this land long before anyone had ever heard of Disney or Orlando. He paid about $10,000 for the land, the house, and the barn. I'd say he made a pretty sweet deal."

"Sounds like it. But I'll reserve judgment until I see it," Orlando said, smiling again.

"Okay," he said, standing up. "If you're ready, let's get going." Orlando nodded and followed Robert single file through the underbrush. They walked along the slope of the land to higher ground. Before another hour had passed, they had reached the edge of the cleared land Robert had talked about. They were both relieved. There was a sense of peace about the place, as if they were the first people ever to lay their eyes on it.

"What do you think we'll find when we get up to the house?" Orlando finally asked quietly as they headed toward a small stream crossing their path.

"I'm not sure," Robert said, avoiding her gaze. He decided it was time to level with Orlando and try to prepare her for whatever, or whoever, they might encounter. "I would guess that the men who were chasing us last night are already there, and they're probably pretty heavily armed. I only hope that they figure we couldn't have walked away from the crash and they're not expecting us. I would've expected them to have started a search for us by now, just to be sure that we're dead. That should reduce the number of men waiting for us at the house."

"Once they figure out we walked away from the wreckage, won't they come looking for us here?" Orlando asked.

"I hope not," he replied. "I'm hoping that they wouldn't expect us to double back to the house since the highway is only about a mile in the other direction. They probably figure that if we're able to walk at all, one of us would be seriously injured and we'd be heading toward the highway to get help. They've probably got people searching up and down the highway already. Let's get to the house before they realize they've made a mistake."

"Won't the men inside the house see us? There's no shrubbery or anything to block their view," Orlando asked, concerned.

"They might, but we don't have a choice," he answered. "Keep low and try not to make any noise. If I'm guessing right, no one will be looking in our direction and we should be able to make it to the house without being seen. Are you game?"

Orlando nodded and smiled weakly.

"Okay, let's go," Robert said, squeezing her hand. They ran across the open ground, scurrying in a zigzag pattern and taking cover wherever tall, uncut grass allowed. They were about a 100 yards from the house when they heard a loud whooshing noise overhead. "Quick, get down!" Robert yanked on

Orlando's arm and they both landed on their stomachs, laying absolutely still with their faces buried in the dirt.

A helicopter flew low overhead, stopping behind them at the treetops, near the spot where they had emerged. It stayed there for several minutes, hovering as if searching for someone. "Do you think they saw us?" Orlando asked anxiously after it had passed.

"I don't think so," Robert replied. "They would've landed if they had. But I think we'd better hurry just in case. Keep low, and if you see anything, let me know."

"Robert..." Orlando said slowly.

"Yeah?" he asked, turning on her sharply.

"Never mind," she answered, changing her mind. "It can wait." Orlando knew that the odds of them coming out of this situation alive and unharmed were very slim, and she desperately wanted to tell Robert how she felt before something terrible happened to one or both of them, but she wasn't sure if he shared her feelings. So, she stopped herself. To cover her mistake, she said, "Here Take my revolver." Orlando spoke softly without making eye contact.

Robert gave her a puzzled look but didn't press the issue, and took the gun without comment. He was more concerned with how they were going to get to the house and call for help without getting caught. He hadn't counted on aerial surveillance. Robert nodded to Orlando as if to silently ask if she was prepared for their assault on the house, and she nodded back her assent. They ran quietly, in a crouched position, to the outer farm buildings and stopped behind some hedges to catch their breath and evaluate the situation. Orlando looked back over the distance they'd just run. *My gym teacher would have been proud,* she thought. They'd just run a good quarter mile in less than five minutes. *Well,* Orlando thought, smiling to herself, *for me it's a record.*

"I don't like this," Robert whispered softly. "It's too quiet."

"What do you mean it's too quiet?" Orlando asked, puzzled.

"It's like nature is holding its breath waiting for something to happen. Listen. Do you hear anyone working? Any birds? I don't even hear any insects."

"Now that you mention it, you're right. You know," she whispered, "ever since that helicopter flew over, I've felt like we weren't alone. Like we were being watched. I thought it was just my imagination, but now that you mention it, something seems seriously wrong."

"Let's hope Sally followed your instructions and delivered that letter to the right person," Robert said, checking the revolver. Then, holding that pistol in one hand, Robert pulled a second gun out of his leg holster under his trousers. Orlando looked surprised but didn't say anything. "I always keep a spare, just in case. Here, take yours back. I have a feeling you're going to need it."

Orlando just nodded and took back her gun. "How do we know who the right person is—to turn over *FILE 13,* I mean?" Orlando asked as she checked her gun to see that it was loaded and the safety was off.

"Well, I figure that if you go high enough, someone's gotta be honest. I'm hoping she's taking it to the White House and to the President himself." Robert's mouth was set with grim determination as he surveyed the landscape.

"I only hope he'll see her," Orlando replied. "If Sally follows her instructions, she shouldn't have any problems."

"Let's hope. But for now, we have more important things to worry about, like staying alive," Robert interrupted.

One look at his expression told Orlando not to question his statement. "Right. Okay, where do we go from here?" she asked quietly.

"See that building over there?" he asked, pointing to a small shack about two hundred yards away, directly in front of them.

"Yeah. What is it?

"It's the munitions shack. I'm sure it's well-guarded. But if we can secure it, we might stand a chance of getting the upper hand on these guys."

"But Robert," Orlando said, stopping him with a concerned hand on his arm, "if you're right, and it's too quiet, then what's happened to your employees? Where are all the ranch hands?"

"I don't know. But I hope they wouldn't have killed all those innocent people. These guys are professionals and all they're interested in is getting what they came after. They still might kill them, but not until after they secure *FILE 13.*"

"Okay, assuming you're right, how do we take the ammo shack?" Orlando asked, ready to move.

"Follow my lead. I think a frontal attack will be the most effective. They won't be expecting it from just the two of us, and that means we'll have the element of surprise on our side."

"Tell me when," Orlando said, nodding her agreement with his plan.

"Now!" Robert said in a loud stage whisper. They ran from behind the hedges, behind the storage building across from the munitions shack, and ducked behind a huge oak tree leaning over the munitions shack roof. They had just stopped moving when Robert spotted an armed, uniformed guard walking slowly toward them, his gun slung casually over one shoulder. The guard obviously hadn't seen or heard them, and continued on his way, around the corner and out of sight. Orlando stood very still and watched as Robert followed the guard around the corner. She heard a sharp whack and then a thud. Robert had obviously given the man a swift blow to the neck from behind. He then dragged the still body back to the bushes. Orlando hurried over to help Robert cover the still form with fallen branches and leaves from the nearby trees.

Within minutes, heavy footsteps followed the path recently taken by the unconscious man. Robert sprinted back to the tree and hid, prepared to repeat his attack. Orlando continued working quietly, carefully placing branches over the man's clothing and face. She had to work quickly before the next man reached her location. She stripped the body of guns and ammunition, and then she finished hiding it under the shrubs. She checked his boots before covering his feet and found a large knife, still in its sheath. Orlando removed it carefully and hid it underneath her clothes where it wouldn't be discovered if she was captured and searched later.

The second uniformed man walked down the path much more slowly than the first, as if he were looking for his friend. Just before he passed the tree where Robert was hiding, the man paused and listened. Robert waited patiently, standing as stiff as a board, and Orlando held her breath, afraid to move. Suddenly, the man stopped and drew his gun, looking around as if he'd heard something but wasn't sure where the sound had originated. Slowly, very slowly, he edged forward proceeded by the barrel of his gun. He was on edge and had just turned his back on Robert to look in the other direction when Robert hit the guard in the neck, just under his ear with the grip of his gun. When the guard turned to shoot his assailant, Robert grabbed the barrel of the gun and pulled hard. The guard, caught off balance, was propelled forward by the inertia and slammed into the side of the tree, dropping the gun. Robert grabbed him by the hair on the back of his head and slammed his head into the tree again. The guard groaned and landed on his back with his arms and legs flung wide, unconscious. Orlando ran from her hiding place behind the bushes and straddled the man's chest, placing one knee on each forearm, using her weight to secure him. She pointed the gun she was carrying directly between his eyes. If he moved so much as a muscle, she was ready to pull the trigger.

The man started to stir and found himself staring directly into the barrel of Orlando's gun. He glanced nervously from the gun to her eyes, and then to Robert's face, all without moving a muscle. It was obvious that he'd evaluated his position in an instant and decided that it would be in his best interest to stay perfectly still.

Looking closely at the man's face for the first time, Robert recognized the prone man. He held up his hand to stop Orlando from shooting him as he whispered anxiously, "Orlando, it's okay. Let him up." He continued quickly, "It's Henry. He's one of my men. It's okay. Let him up," he repeated softly as he pushed the gun away from the Henry's face. Robert pulled her off the relieved man, helped her to her feet, and took the gun carefully from her hands. He held Orlando's shoulders tightly and looked deeply into her eyes, trying to will Orlando to stop trembling. Henry scampered to his feet, grabbed his gun and all three took cover again behind the tree.

"I am so sorry," Orlando said softly to the man. "I could have killed you!"

"It's okay," Henry said. "I'm just glad you don't have a hare trigger."

Orlando started to apologize again, but Robert interrupted, "Where is everyone?"

"They're trapped in the root cellar and the trailers up at the house. So far they haven't hurt anyone, and they don't seem to be in any hurry to do anything. They appear to be waiting for someone to arrive. I was out patrolling the south perimeter when they got here, so I wasn't with everyone else when they took them hostage. I was just returning to the house when I spotted them. I did some snooping, got what I could, and headed out this way. I don't think they've noticed I'm missing. I was trying to get to the road to get help when I… uh, ran into you and the young lady."

"Don't bother," Robert replied. "They've got a helicopter out looking for us, and the last time I saw it, it was heading toward the road. If you'd kept going, you'd have probably been captured or shot."

"Well, in that case," smiled Henry, "I guess I'm glad it was you two who ambushed me."

"What's with the uniform?" asked Robert. "I noticed it on the first guy we nailed."

"Yeah, they were all wearing them. When I escaped from the house, I knocked out one of the guards and took his uniform," Henry answered, smiling. Then, noticing how quiet Orlando was Henry asked, "Are you okay?"

She just nodded without replying. All she could think about was how close she'd come to actually killing someone, and an innocent man at that. Two days ago, the thought of picking up a gun, even in self-defense, had repulsed her. Now, her whole world was upside down and she'd found she was capable of doing things she'd never dreamed of doing before.

"Well, I'm glad you didn't shoot," Henry said to Orlando as he squeezed her shoulder reassuringly.

"And is it good to see you too, Robert," he added, shaking hands with Robert. "Quite a partner you got there. I don't think I'd want to run into her if I was the opposition."

"I know what you mean," Robert said, smiling at Orlando. She looked first at Robert and then at Henry and smiled self-consciously. "I'd trust her with my life," Robert stated confidently.

"Well," Orlando said softly, embarrassed, "let's hope it doesn't come to that."

"I'll agree with that," interjected Henry. "No offense, ma'am, but I'd rather not have any of us risk our lives if we can help it."

"No offense taken, Henry," Orlando said, smiling. "By the way, my name's Orlando."

"Nice to meet you, Orlando," Henry said, offering his hand. "I'm Henry."

"Not to break this up," Robert interjected, "but Henry, do you think you could fill me in on what's been going on?"

"Sorry. Sure," Henry said, swallowing hard, "Well, last night, just after you called to let us know you were on your way, a SUV pulled up to the house and a man in a very expensive-looking dark suit got out. He talked to Maria." Turning to Orlando, he added, "She's the housekeeper. Anyway," he continued, "he asked if you were here. When Maria said that you'd gone out for the evening, he pulled a gun and forced his way into the house. He said he'd wait for you to come back. Then he told Maria to ring the chow bell, even though it wasn't chow time, and naturally all the men came to see what was wrong. When they came out of their trailers to the main house, there was a regular army waiting for them. I don't know where they all came from, but these armed men in uniform came scurrying out of the bushes like roaches. They rounded up all the men and locked them in the root cellar. Then they went around to all the trailers and took the women and children and put them into the bunk house. As far as I know, they're still there. Whoever they are, they're smart. They know the men won't try anything as long as those guys are holding their wives and children."

"How did you get out then?" Robert asked, puzzled.

"Well, you see," he replied, looking at Orlando, "it's kinda embarrassing."

"I need to know," Robert said, trying to hide his amusement at Henry's discomfort. "Well, you see," he said, leaning closer to Robert, "first I..." Orlando couldn't hear the remainder of what he said because he was whispering to Robert. She didn't press the issue because she could see Henry blushing furiously while Robert was stifling a chuckle.

"Henry," Robert said, tactfully changing the subject, "is anyone watching the ammunition shed?"

"Nope," he said proudly. "As soon as I saw what was happening, I took down the *Ammo Shed* sign and put up the *Port-o-let Storage* sign. I waited and watched one of the gunmen walk by, take one look at the sign, and keep going. He didn't even bother to look inside. I'll tell you Robert, they're a conceited lot. They didn't think, even for a minute, that anyone would get to the ammo shed before them, or that anyone could outsmart them."

"Then the guy we just took out was just on patrol," Robert said.

"Right," Henry confirmed.

"How many men do they have patrolling the perimeter?" Orlando asked.

"About half a dozen," Henry answered.

"And where are the rest?" Robert asked.

"There's about a dozen around the house and in the compound, and the guy in the dark suit sent out the rest to look for you two. They left about an hour after sun-up, so I figure they'll be gone a while."

"Okay, let's not waste any time, then," said Robert thinking out loud. "I'll take the lead. Orlando, I want you to stay behind me, and Henry, you bring up the rear. We're going to secure the ammo shed first. Once we've got some weapons, then we'll work on freeing the men and their families. If we're lucky, we should have a nice surprise waiting for them when they get back. Orlando, do you still have the knife?"

She nodded.

"Good. If we run into trouble, do you think you can use it?

Orlando pulled the knife out of its sheath and took a long look at the long, sharp, glistening blade. She doubted that she could actually stab a man to death, but she wouldn't admit that to Robert. Finally, Orlando slid the knife back into the sheath and slipped it into the back of her pants, just below the waist so it wouldn't move around. She looked directly at Robert and nodded silently.

"Okay. Let's get going," Robert said.

"Just a minute," Orlando said, putting a hand on his arm. Both men watched as she silently crept over to the man lying unconscious on the ground, mostly covered by the bushes. Orlando quickly brushed aside the branches she'd used to cover his body and dragged him a few feet to the nearest tree. She propped him up against the tree as if he'd fallen asleep. Henry, seeing what Orlando was up to, pulled a silver flask out of his shirt and took it over to where Orlando was working. Winking at her he pulled the top of the flask off, poured a little in the man's mouth, allowing it to dribble down his chin and onto his shirt. Henry then emptied the flask over the man's head and clothing, and placed it in his hand. "Good idea. That should buy us a couple of extra minutes," Orlando said smiling at Robert and Henry.

"Like I said, Robert," Henry said, putting his hand on Orlando's shoulder, "smart little lady."

"Thank you," Orlando said, smiling at him. "You're not so bad yourself. Now let's get out of here. That guy," she said, pointing to the man propped against the tree, "is starting to give me the creeps."

They ran crouched over to the front of the ammo shed, but there was no need for silence. There was no sign of a guard outside and no one inside. The door was still locked, but it didn't take Robert long to break in.

Once inside, Robert said, "I wish Peter was here." He examined the boxes of dynamite. "He's the best demolition man I know."

"What do you mean?" Orlando asked curiously.

"He's one of the best. You know, the secret agent type? He'd know how to get around these guys better than anyone."

"Well, if he's as good as you say he is, then I look forward to meeting him," Orlando responded. "But for now, all you have is Henry and me. I hope we won't disappoint you too much."

"No. You'll do fine," he said, pausing to smile at her. "Now, let's get this stuff out of the crates. Henry, take these," Robert said, handing Henry a half-dozen grenades. "We'll use these for a diversion. We'll take a few of these semi-automatic pistols, and a couple of the rifles, and some extra boxes of ammo. We'll need to stash this stuff out of sight until we're ready for them. Here, fill these gunny sacks with the dynamite and ammo."

Orlando helped Robert fill the sacks with the dynamite, grenades, pistols, and spare ammo. When they had all of the sacks ready to go, they left the ammo shack as quietly as they could, and Robert closed the door. Watching for patrols, the three of them ran quickly and quietly from shrub to shrub, and then from vehicle to vehicle, until they'd reached the eight foot stack of firewood near the main house. So far, they had avoided all of the armed men in and around the compound. Robert, Henry, and Orlando hid some of the dynamite, extra boxes of ammunition, and several rifles under the loose pieces of wood. Orlando was starting to get the feeling that she'd just been inducted into the military, quickly learning the hand signals for advance, hold, and hide, and she was handling guns and ammunition as if they were bags of groceries. Before yesterday, the closest she'd ever come to seeing anyone get killed was watching it on television. Today, she was not only prepared to kill; she was helping two men she barely knew launch an all-out invasion on the Russian Mafia in order to free some ranch hands and their families.

Orlando was starting to get a sick feeling in the pit of her stomach. As the three of them hid the ammunition, she was desperately trying to convince herself that she was going to wake up from this nightmare any minute and find herself safely back in her own bed, snuggled under her down comforter. She started sweating and feeling dizzy. "Are you alright?" Robert whispered anxiously. "You're as white as a sheet."

"I'm fine," she replied quickly, almost indignantly. "I'm just fine. I'm just anxious to get this over with," she said more contritely.

"I'll be over soon," he said, squeezing her hand. "I know you'll be fine. You're doing great! If we run into trouble and you have to defend yourself, don't stop and think about what you're doing. Just do it. I've watched you. You've got good instincts. Trust them and they'll get you through. When everything else seems to have left you and you're afraid you're going to buckle under, just take a deep breath and trust your gut."

Orlando smiled at him warmly, a silent thank you for understanding. Just then, a guard rounded the house on patrol and they had to duck back down behind the wood to avoid being seen. Orlando was holding her breath, and didn't realize it until the guard had passed and she exhaled loudly and Robert stared at her in amazement. Robert waited until he was sure the guard wasn't returning, and then he gave Orlando her instructions. He sent her to the bunk house to free the women and children and lead them out of danger. He gave her very specific directions to the safest place to hide them.

"We have to get them to safety first so they can't be used as leverage," Robert explained. "If the gunmen aren't stopped on the first attack, then they'll head for their best negotiating tool: the men's families. If they get their hands on them, they'll use them against my men, and none of us will get out of this alive. So I'm depending on you to get them to where they can't be found."

"I understand," Orlando said, smiling. "I won't let you down."

Next, Henry told Robert and Orlando that they had only stationed one guard in front of the bunkhouse, since the only way in or out was through the front door. "Just do to him what you did to me," Henry said, smiling at Orlando, "and you won't have any problems."

Orlando smiled at him and then made her way carefully across the compound. She ran, crouched down, from one parked vehicle to another until she was in line with the bunkhouse. The guard that Henry had told her about was lounging around the front door, leaning against one of the building's support beams. Orlando was hoping that her luck would hold out and there wouldn't be a second guard around back. She took one last look at the guard before sneaking around the back of the bunkhouse. He was intently cleaning his fingernails with a knife and seemed to be oblivious to everything around him. Orlando crept around to the back corner of the bunkhouse and, not seeing a second guard, quietly approached the first window. She didn't see any men in the large interior room, so she tapped softly on the window with her fingertips. One of the women toward the back of the room heard the noise and came closer to investigate. Luckily, once the woman saw Orlando, she opened the window without calling out.

"I'm here to help," Orlando told her. "Is everybody okay?" Orlando asked.

"Yes, just scared," she whispered. "The children are complaining about being hungry. They haven't let us have anything to eat since yesterday. Where are our husbands? Are they okay?"

"Yes, they're fine," she lied. She had no idea

where they were, or even if they were alive, but this wasn't the time for that discussion. "Don't worry about them," Orlando said softly, trying to reassure her.

"Mr. Taylor and some friends are working to free them right now. The best way you can help your husbands is to help me get you guys out of here safely. Now, there's one guard at the front door. Have you seen any others?"

"No. What do you want me to do?" the woman asked.

"Have you got anything to defend yourselves with?" Orlando asked. "Do you have any knives or something sharp? Did your husbands leave any type of weapons behind when they were taken out of the bunkhouse last night?"

"I don't know, but I'll try to find something," she whispered anxiously. "They searched every room and dumped everything out of the drawers before they let us in here, but they may have missed something." The woman started to turn away, and then suddenly turned back to Orlando and added, "I'll tell you one thing. If you gave me a knife, I'd be happy to kill that bastard Krosky myself. He's been after the little girls, especially my Becky. She's just turned 11, but she's big for her age, and he's been trying to get her alone, if you know what I mean. But I won't let him get near her. I'll kill him first!" Her voice was hushed, but it held a violence that was terrifying. Orlando didn't doubt the woman's sincerity for a minute. You could see the anger and fear in her eyes. Orlando didn't want to inflame the woman even more by saying the wrong thing, but before Orlando could think of an appropriate response, the woman seemed to recover her calm as abruptly as she'd lost it. "I'll see what I can find, and I'll try to recruit some of the others to help."

"Here," Orlando said as she pushed open the screen enough to hand two knives through the window. "This is all I have right now. Find what you can to defend yourselves, and get ready. Do you think you can arrange a diversion inside the building in about three minutes? I would rather we did this quietly, so he doesn't have time to call for help."

"No problem. Just leave it to me," the woman replied, smiling.

Orlando nodded and then started back toward the front of the bunkhouse. She wasn't sure what the woman had in mind, but instinct told her that she wouldn't be disappointed. Within three minutes, from where she was hiding around the corner by the front door, Orlando could easily hear grunts, shouts, and sounds of breaking furniture coming from inside the bunk house. Then all of a sudden, the noise abruptly stopped. A long moment of eerie silence was followed by a loud, wood-splintering crash and a very loud scream. The women were obviously fighting, close enough to the door for the guard to notice. The guard at the door called over a second guard who was patrolling close by, just as one of the women in the bunkhouse broke a chair against the inside of the front door. The guards readied their guns and passed a derogatory comment between them in Russian before opening the door. The only phrase Orlando could hear clearly referenced "stupid American bitches" as they approached the door carefully.

The two men were standing close together, listening for a moment at the door before they opened it. Just as they unlocked the door, Orlando ran out from her hiding place and jumped both men from behind in a flying football tackle. The momentum of her weight flying through the air and landing squarely on the backs of the armed men, combined with the open door, pushed them through the door and into the room, and sent them crashing to the floor face first. The women Orlando had addressed through the back window and two of her friends were waiting for them near the door. When the men landed on the floor, Orlando rolled quickly off them to one side and the other women jumped on them to take her place.

The woman Orlando had spoken with saw her target and used the opportunity to exact some revenge. Screaming obscenities and threats at the man who had pursued her young daughter, she plunged a butter knife deep into his back, between his ribs, and punctured his lung. He screamed out in pain, and as he tried to roll away from her, his hand squeezed the trigger of his gun out of reflex. Luckily, the other women and children in the bunkhouse had taken cover and stayed low, so no one was hurt. The man the woman had stabbed lay still at Orlando's feet, trying to breathe. Orlando bent over to retrieve his gun from his limp hand while the other guard pushed her back with the gun he had pulled out from underneath him, ready to fire.

The room fell silent and all of the women froze in place, transfixed. Orlando stared up at the man. His expression was fierce and his eyes held no mercy. His cold, calculating stare was enough to chill the most warm-blooded person to the bone. Orlando was trying to think of a way out of the situation, while simultaneously making her peace with God. Just as she was sure she'd never see tomorrow, the man holding the gun inhaled sharply, looking surprised, and then silently opened his mouth wide, as if to scream, and fell forward. The gun discharged harmlessly into the wood floor near Orlando's left foot, just before it and its owner hit the ground with a double thud. Orlando looked up, stunned. Facing her was another woman, much more frail and older than the first woman. She pulled herself up to her full height of four feet, 11 inches, standing tall and proud behind the still body, bright red blood covering both of her hands. She was smiling at Orlando. "Are you alright, dear?" the woman asked quietly, as if she was addressing her granddaughter, obviously numb by what she'd just done.

Orlando looked from the old woman to the dead body beside her and her eyes focused on the large pair of scissors protruding from his spine. She looked back at the woman and nodded. "I think so. Thank you. Are you alright?"

"Good now," she said, smiling at Orlando in a reassuring, motherly fashion. It wasn't until Orlando looked more closely at the woman that she saw the bruises on her right cheek and her swollen eye. "My name's Sarah. What's yours?"

"Orlando. Orlando Corogan," Orlando replied slowly. Everyone, including herself, was shaken, but they began to calm down when the women started to speak. The women and children who had been hiding started to stand and approach them. In light of what had just happened, standing there over a dead body holding a civil conversation seemed a bit odd. Orlando felt like she'd entered an episode of *The Twilight Zone*, but then she quickly remembered why she'd come to the bunk house. Orlando and Sarah looked around the room to reassure themselves that there were no other victims. The other women and children stood in stunned silence, looking first at Sarah and then at Orlando. They were waiting for someone to tell them what to do next.

Orlando first bent down and examined the guard's dead body and retrieved his pistol. The other man with the punctured lung lay still on the floor, and he wasn't breathing. She felt a wave of nausea flow over her, and pushed it back down. She averted her eyes and turned to face the women and children. "Is everyone okay?" she asked, looking around her. The women and children moved a few steps closer and nodded. Their faces reflected the fear she was feeling, but they were hopeful too, expecting Orlando to rescue them. "Good," Orlando said with more confidence than she actually felt. "Mr. Taylor and some of his men are going to be freeing the others any time now, and I've got to get you guys out of here. Otherwise, they could use you guys as leverage against them."

But before she could say anything else, an explosion in the direction of the house shook the entire bunkhouse and all its occupants, knocking them all off their feet. "Okay, everyone needs to stay calm," Orlando said, quickly standing up. "It's started. We need to move quickly and quietly, so don't take anything with you. Everyone, follow me. Please help carry the smaller children so that we can move quickly. We have to hurry!"

"Where are we going?" Sarah asked as they ran out the door.

"To the old maintenance shack. We have to get you all out sight as fast as possible. You have to hide until it's all over. I expect there will be more armed guards here any minute to look for you. There isn't much time. Sarah, do you think you can you lead everyone out of here and down to the old maintenance shack on the edge of the property?"

"Of course I can," Sarah answered reassuringly. "Let's go, everybody," Sarah said, smiling, and started moving more quickly than her age and appearance would imply. For that, Orlando was grateful.

"Okay," Orlando said as the group filed past her. "Everyone stay together, and BE QUIET! Sarah is going to lead the way, and I'll bring up the rear. Let's stay as close to the trees as possible so that no one sees us. And kids," Orlando said, bending down to their level, "hold onto your mothers, and don't make any noise. We don't want those bad men to find us, okay?"

The children looked up to her with wide eyes, nodded, and did as they were told. They headed out of the bunkhouse and away from the main compound. There was an old maintenance shack that was on the edge of the woods. It was stone and wood, and completely overgrown with weeds and vines. Unless you knew the shed was there, it would appear invisible until you were right on top of it. They shoved hard until the ancient door gave way and they crept inside. Once everyone had gone through the door, Orlando helped Sarah secure the door and windows from the inside, and then they passed out the guards' guns and the few knives they'd found in the bunkhouse.

"Use these if you have to," Orlando told the women. "I have to go help Robert, so Sarah, you're in charge. The rest of you, listen to her. She knows what she's doing. Now, whatever you do, don't leave this shed until someone you know comes for you. If you see someone you don't recognize, you know what to do. Oh, and Sarah, keep everyone away from the windows and the door. They've got a helicopter overhead, and there's a patrol out looking for Robert and me."

"We understand," Sarah said.

"Good," she said, smiling with relief. "Okay, Sarah, take care of them. Make sure to barricade the door behind me and I'll be back as soon as I can."

Just then there was another loud explosion and the sound of gunfire. It shattered the peaceful quiet of the wilderness surrounding the maintenance shack, and startled the women and children inside. The children started crying, and there were several loud screams from inside the shack. Trying to quiet the children, Sarah paused just long enough to call after Orlando in a stage whisper: "Be careful!"

Orlando waved to her in acknowledgement and started running in the direction of the explosion. As she neared the house, the sound of semi-automatic weapons and the acrid smell of gun smoke filled the air. From her position behind the wood pile she could hear the shouts of the American ranch hands, as well as the loud orders shrieked by the Russian Mafia. But the screams of men in pain, as fiery bullets penetrated their soft, fleshy targets could be heard above all else. Orlando looked around frantically for Robert but couldn't find him. When bullets started buzzing past her head, Orlando dove for cover. She quickly assessed the situation and figured she wouldn't be of much help to Robert in hand-to-hand combat. But she did know where the explosives were hidden. With them, she could add to the confusion and give Robert and his men the upper hand. Orlando checked the pistol she was carrying to see how much ammunition she had. She'd left one of the two they'd taken off the dead guards at the bunk house with Sarah and had taken the other for her own protection. Orlando ran across the compound to a second wood pile, ducking as she did, and dove behind it just as a bullet intended for her head brushed her shoulder. She screamed at the piercing, burning pain at the spot where the bullet grazed her soft skin. Turning quickly, she checked the wound to see how badly she had been hit. Seeing very little blood, she grimaced and moved her arm slowly in concentric circles, reassuring herself that she would be fine.

Taking a few steadying breaths, Orlando looked under the loose pieces of firewood near the bottom of the wood pile and found the dynamite they had stashed there before. She pulled out several sticks and pushed the rest back into the pile in case her position was compromised. She carefully peered between the loose pieces of wood at the top of the wood pile to determine were Robert and his men were. Orlando reasoned that the ranch hands would assume that a woman would be an American since the Russians hadn't brought any with them.

Thus, the man shooting at her from across the compound would have to be the enemy. Satisfied with her logical approach to the situation, Orlando pulled a match out of her pocket, took a deep breath, and lit the stick of dynamite. She tossed it toward the source of the most recent gunshot fired in her direction, and it hit its mark as the man flew several feet into the air, did a summersault in mid-air and landed on his back. Repeating her assessment of the enemy's position, Orlando sent a half-dozen sticks of dynamite in the direction of the shooters, and most of them hit their marks too. Orlando stopped and peered over the wood pile again to assess the situation. It appeared that Robert had freed all of his men, so she decided to stay put and cause as much confusion as possible to cover their escape. Just as she was about to light yet another stick, a gun was placed at the back of her head, and a heavily accented male voice said menacingly, "I vouldn't do dat if I vas you."

Orlando's hand froze in mid-air, and she allowed the man to take the dynamite from her. Standing at his command, she saw another man leading Robert and Henry into the main house and reluctantly allowed her captor to lead her in the same direction. The other men were rounded up, and led with little ceremony back to the storage shed. They had failed, and from the looks of things, they wouldn't be getting another chance. Orlando was about to give up when she saw the gleam in Robert's eye as he looked at her. He'd allowed himself to be captured! He was up to something!

Orlando was showed into the large living room, with the barrel of the pistol pressed firmly in the small of her back. This was the first time she'd had a chance to see the inside of the house, and she was surprised to see the simple elegance and strong male influence in the architecture and furniture. Any other time, she'd have taken the time to examine it in detail and then enjoy exploring the cavernous rooms. Now, all she could think of was getting out of there. Looking at the man who held her at gunpoint, she also thought about how much she'd like to find a way to wipe the sneer off of his face. He was a short, stout man who was obviously used to getting his own way. Across the room, a tall Russian officer was staring at her as if she wasn't wearing a stitch of clothing. His lustful eyes were steel blue, and his chiseled jaw looked like granite, but his overall appearance couldn't be called handsome because there was too much cruelty in his face. One look at him revealed too much evil pleasure in his humorless eyes as he watched pain being inflicted on others under his command.

He casually sauntered across the room and stood in front of Orlando while the other men restrained Robert. The tall Russian walked around Orlando slowly, assessing her physical attributes as if he were purchasing an expensive racehorse. Orlando felt like she was on the auction block. The Russian finally stopped in front of her and, towering over her, took a step closer. He stood so close to her that all she could see in front of here were the buttons on his shirt. Turning his head and looking directly at Robert, the Russian possessively reached behind her head, took Orlando's long tresses in his hand, and cruelly yanked hard, forcing her head back. Orlando cried out as the sharp stabbing pain followed by burning heat ran from her head down her neck and spine. He was waiting for a reaction from Robert, which would tell him exactly how much the girl meant to him. When Robert showed no reaction, the Russian chuckled and let Orlando go. He walked back over to the guard holding Henry, and ordered the guard to take him to the storage shed with the rest of the men. He did so in English so Orlando and Robert could understand him. Then, turning slightly so that his back was to Robert, he took a step toward Orlando. While he was still facing Orlando, he asked, "How long have you known Miss Corogan, Mr. Taylor?"

"Long enough, Krosky," replied Robert casually.

"Long enough to be able to predict her reaction to interrogation?" he asked, turning to look at Robert.

"I think so," Robert answered calmly.

"I see." Then, turning his attention to Orlando, he continued: "Miss Corogan, you should feel honored. In my circles, it isn't often that a man trusts his life to a woman. You see, that is exactly what he is doing," he said, moving close enough to run his forefinger along her jaw line. "If you don't tell me what I want to know, I will kill him." He looked briefly at Robert and then smugly back at Orlando and continued. "Of course, I will give you the pleasure of witnessing his execution, before you join him."

Orlando stared at him and then at Robert in horror. She realized that if she told this man what she knew, a lot of people would die, and he'd probably kill them both anyway. He couldn't afford to have any witnesses. Looking around the room, she counted at least a dozen armed men, so escape wasn't a possibility. There didn't appear to be any options. Considering the situation, Orlando thought it would be worth trying to buy them both some time.

"You might persuade me to tell you what I know," Orlando said to the Russian suggestively, looking up at him through lowered lashes. She gave him a long, sultry look and continued, "But it won't be by threatening me with killing *him*. He brought me here against my will to begin with, and being free of him wouldn't cause me any heartache," she lied.

The Russian laughed out loud and gave Robert a knowing look. "And what did you have in mind, Miss Corogan?" he replied as he caressed her cheek with the back of his hand.

Orlando was pushing hard to get him where she wanted him. "We could discuss it in private," she said softly. "I don't like an audience when I'm *negotiating,"* she replied, stressing the word "negotiating" and smiling provocatively up at him.

Robert wanted to object, but he was afraid that would throw their hand. Orlando obviously had a plan. She was trying desperately to convince the Russian officer that Robert was unimportant to her, and if he objected to the direction this situation was heading, he could ruin everything.

The Russian smiled hungrily and nodded to the man holding Orlando. The gunman acknowledged his order silently and led her out of the main room and up the stairs. He took her to the master bedroom and shoved her onto the king size bed. The gunman then left the room without a word, locking the door behind him.

Orlando sat up and wiggled off the bed. She walked quietly to the balcony and looked out. She was on the second floor. She considered trying to climb down until she saw the guard patrolling downstairs. There was little chance of her getting out of the room unnoticed. Searching the room for something to use to defend herself, Orlando was beginning to doubt the wisdom of her diversionary measure. She was hoping against hope that Robert would come up with some way for them to get out of there alive.

Back downstairs, the Russian ordered Robert to be taken outside and tied up while a platform was set up in plain sight of the storage shed. When it was complete, he wanted Robert shot in front of his men, as an example of the punishment they could expect for disobedience. The Russian was sure that Orlando and Robert were lovers. Why else would she sacrifice herself to save him? She could provide him with all of the information he needed, so he no longer felt a need to keep Robert alive.

He chuckled to himself when he thought about his plans for the remainder of the day. Once Orlando told him what he wanted to know, he would allow her to watch Robert's execution before facing her own. In the mean time, he would enjoy *interrogating* her. He climbed the stairs to the master bedroom purposefully, his boots making a soft scuffling noise as he mounted each step. Once at the master bedroom door, the man standing guard outside the door unlocked it, and the officer stepped through, closing the door slowly behind him. Orlando heard the loud clicking noise as the officer locked it again. She had been facing the balcony, considering her options, when she heard the door lock being turned.

When Krosky entered the room, Orlando spun around, staring wide-eyed, petrified. Her feet felt like they were frozen in place. Looking directly at Orlando, almost sensing her fear, he smiled and stated simply, "I think the time has come to introduce myself, Miss Corogan. My name is Krosky." He crossed over to the enormous bed that dominated the room. There was little else in the room except a table and two chairs by the fireplace. Sliding the door key into his trouser pocket and taking a step closer to her, he added, "Now, Miss Corogan, why don't we get better acquainted?" When she didn't respond, Krosky looked at Orlando hungrily like a lion eying his prey, and then he moved closer to face a defiant Orlando across the bed.

Chapter 9

AS TIA AND Mel walked to the car outside the diner, she thought about the strange turn of events. Not too long ago, she'd been reading the newspaper and planning a full day shopping with her cousin Orlando. Now it was almost midnight, and her cousin and friends were missing. In addition to that, her once-long-lost lover had reappeared and was almost immediately kidnapped. Then, she was kidnapped and released, and now with the help of a man she'd just met, she was going to try to free Peter and Joe from God knew what. Tia sat in the car while Mel went into the office at the docks and checked on the arrival time for the *Golden Sun.* When he came back, he didn't look too happy. "What's wrong?" Tia asked, unlocking the driver's door so he could get in.

"It's gonna be late. The guy said they were delayed in South Carolina, something about a bad load of fuel, and that they radioed ahead to say they wouldn't be in till about 5:00 a.m."

"Terrific!" Tia said, upset.

"That's not all," Mel said softly.

"What else?" Tia asked, becoming more concerned.

"There's a guy in a Chevy, parked right over there, who's been tailing us since the diner," Mel said quietly.

"That's just great," she said, looking over her

shoulder at the outline of the car across the street. "We can't have him following us down to the boat." Then, almost as an afterthought, she added, "Well, since we have a couple of hours to kill, I'd suggest we get some sleep and think about it. How about we find an inexpensive, clean hotel where we can check into and get some sleep? I saw one not too far from here," Tia said.

"But that won't do any good. That guy will just follow us there," Mel commented.

"That's okay," Tia said, smiling. "I've got a plan," she lied convincingly. "Come on. You drive us there, and I'll take care of the rest." Tia patted his hand reassuringly, while desperately trying to come up with a plan.

The hotel was a small, one-storey building, with all of the rooms in a row. There was a pool on one side of the parking lot and a neon sign across from it flashing VACANCY. The night manager was a kind older man, whose eyebrows shot up when Tia and Mel entered the hotel office together. From the look on his face, it was obvious that this man didn't approve of the two coming in so late at night, and he was suspicious of the difference in their ages.

"Good evening," Mel offered pleasantly. "Could you give us two rooms? We'd sure appreciate it. My daughter and I are very tired and we'd like to get some sleep," he lied easily to the man behind the counter. The manager looked a little less suspicious as he handed over the keys and collected their information. "Oh, and we'll need a 4:30 a.m. wakeup call, please," Mel added.

"I was hoping you could do me a favor," said Tia, smiling sweetly. She took out a $50 bill and handed it to him.

"I'm afraid I don't have change," the manager said quickly, examining the bill closely.

"That's okay," Tia said, smiling. He looked at her, suspicious again. "You see, I was kind of hoping you'd do me a favor."

"What kind of favor?"

"Well, you see, there's this young man, and he's been following me," Tia said, stepping closer as if sharing a secret. "He wants to marry me, and I don't want to marry him. Anyway, I don't want him to know when I leave tomorrow. You see, my dad's not too fond of him either, and I don't want any trouble when we leave tomorrow."

"Okay. What do you want me to do about it?" the man asked, confused.

"I'm sure he's going to come in and ask you to let him know when we're leaving tomorrow. If you could wait 'til, say, six or six-thirty to call him tomorrow, then we'll already be gone when he gets up," she added, patting his hand.

"Why not?" he said, suddenly smiling. "It makes no difference to me who you marry." He looked pointedly at Mel and nodded. "That's room 26 and

27. If you decide to leave before we open the lobby tomorrow at 6:00 a.m., just leave the room keys in your room or put them the night drop box."

"Thank you very much," Tia said as they left the small office.

"Do you think it'll work?" Mel asked her as they walked to their rooms.

"I hope so," she responded. "I don't see the Chevy, but I'm sure he's watching us. He'll probably get a room too, just to avoid attracting attention to himself."

"You're probably right," Mel responded as they opened their side-by-side doors. "The cops around here don't appreciate overnight parkers. They tend to look at them as transients and make them move their cars or run them off." Mel stopped in is open doorway and asked Tia, "Anyway, what'll we do about tomorrow?'

"We'll worry about that later. Right now, we need some sleep. I for one want to be sharp tomorrow. Tomorrow morning, with any kind of luck, we can beat the *Golden Sun* to the dock. I'd like to have a vantage point and be ready and waiting when they arrive." Tia looked up from the door lock before asking Mel, "Do you have any kind of weapon? A gun or pistol, maybe?"

"Just Lucile," Mel said, smiling at her confusion. "Meet Lucile," he said, pulling a sub-nosed revolver out of his jacket. "I never leave home without her."

"Oh, good. I assume you know how to use it," Tia said to Mel as well as to herself. Mel frowned at the implied insult, and Tia quickly apologized. "I'm sorry, Mel. I should've known better. I'm just tired. I'll see you in the morning."

"Okay, no problem," he said, shrugging. "Get some sleep. And listen, if you need me, just bang on the wall or call out. I'll be there before you can call again. Okay?"

"Yes, Mel, and you do the same. I really appreciate you caring so much. She stepped across the short distance between their two doors, stood on tiptoe, and kissed him on the cheek. He blushed and smiled at her, but he didn't say anything as she opened her door and stepped into her room. He waited for her to lock it from the inside before going into his own room.

At 4:30 a.m., the phone in Tia's room rang loudly, breaking the pre-dawn silence. Thirty seconds later, the same sound could be heard in Mel's room. Tia dressed quickly in the semi-dark of the glowing TV in her room, and made sure her .357 was in working order. She'd taken the boxes of ammunition and the gun into the hotel room with her, and now she made sure the gun was loaded and the extra ammunition was stored into a hidden pocket in her belt. Pulling her long hair back, she made one final check to make sure she hadn't left anything behind, and then left her room silently. She knocked softly on

Mel's door, and it opened immediately. Mel was dressed and ready to go.

They nodded at each other, each silently confirming that the other was ready to go, and then they walked silently to his car, looking for any signs of the man who had been following them, or the Chevy. There were none. They drove in silence to the docks, each lost in their own thoughts. When Mel had parked the car in an inconspicuous spot, they quietly made their way down to the dock where the *Golden Sun* would be tied up. They hid behind a stack of empty crates where they would be concealed but where they could still see the water clearly. At exactly 5:00 a.m., the *Golden Sun* came into view.

Peter and Joe had been taken at gunpoint to the yacht the *Golden Sun* in New York, and they were drugged shortly after being brought on board. Once they woke from the sedative, they were brought in for an interview with Grouchev. He was less than pleased with their "screw you" responses, and responded by subjecting them to extensive, brutal, physical persuasion until they agreed to talk. Peter was barely conscious, bleeding from a broken nose and swollen mouth. His back was exposed and bleeding from repeated whippings with a leather strap. Joe was persuaded to talk with multiple burns caused by a white-hot poker, heated in a portable gas oven Grouchev kept aboard the *Golden Sun* just for that purpose. Joe had been burned on his bare chest and upper arms, but it wasn't until Grouchev applied the scorching instrument to the inside of his upper thigh that he collapsed and gave in.

Peter told Grouchev that the information he wanted wasn't in the stone Hartt gave Orlando Corogan, but in an emerald stolen by Joe from the Covington mansion during the robbery. Joe explained that the stone had then been stolen from him, and he was trying to locate it when he and Peter were taken. They were hoping to meet with Orlando and then with Hartt to find out who'd stolen the stone from Joe. "The job was too professionally done to be Hartt's work," explained Joe. "Someone above him had to be responsible for planning and executing the heist. Hartt's just not that smart."

"Then who do you think could've done it, Mr. Cramer?" asked Grouchev, becoming more agitated by the minute.

"I don't know," responded Peter. "I guess I would have to ask who would stand to gain the most from it," Peter stated simply. "That's what we were trying to determine when you grabbed us. Find the person who would benefit from the list and you'll have your thief."

"Your government," Grouchev grounded out between clenched teeth, "is behind this!" Then, he added more slowly, as if to himself, "Or mine. Where's Krosky?" Grouchev shouted angrily at his men in Russian.

"You ordered him to go on ahead to the Taylor ranch in Florida. He was to wait there for the two spies," one of Grouchev's men responded quickly.

Fortunately, Grouchev either didn't know or had forgotten that Peter spoke fluent Russian. Peter had met Grouchev on several occasions in Moscow, and they had had several probing conversations. Grouchev picked up the phone next to him on the coffee table and called the bridge. He ordered the captain to dock the *Golden Sun* at Port Canaveral as quickly as possible, and gave orders to have a helicopter waiting to take him to the ranch upon their arrival at the docks. Next, he made a direct ship-to-shore call to Krosky. The side of the conversation Peter heard didn't sound too good for Orlando and Robert. "You fool!" shouted Grouchev into the phone, his jowls shaking like Jell-O. "You could have killed them! If you kill them, we won't get *FILE 13*. Where are they now? ... Fine. You just keep looking. When you locate them, you call me immediately!"

"Those incompetent fools!" Grouchev said, cursing Krosky and his men under his breath. "How could they have let them slip through their fingers?" Grouchev then turned to Peter and Joe, who'd been forgotten in the corner where they had been left tied to their chairs. "Tell me everything you know about the Taylor ranch!" he demanded.

At this, Joe started laughing, somewhat

hysterically. Peter tried to still him, but was unsuccessful. "We don't know anything about a ranch you fat, old fool," Joe ranted and raved. "We've never been there. And besides, there's nothing you could do to us that you haven't done already to make us talk." Joe was becoming delirious. "You can only kill us, and then who will answer your ridiculous questions?" Joe asked loudly, following the question with a shrill laugh.

"No one laughs at me," Grouchev howled, his jowls puffing in and out. "We will go to the ranch of your friend Robert Taylor, and then, when we have what we want, I will take great pleasure in personally disposing of you, Mr. Cramer. I'd strongly advise you to keep your mouth shut. I can think of at least a half dozen very painful ways to die, and if you insult me again…" Grouchev described, pointing his finger first at Peter and then at Joe. Then, in a lower register, he said very slowly, emphasizing each syllable: "I will try each and every agonizing one until you expire. Is that understood?"

Before Joe could answer him, Peter nodded. He jabbed Joe in the ribs to silence him, but nothing could disguise the hatred Joe had for Grouchev. Joe and Peter would wear the scars of their loyalty for the rest of their lives, and Joe couldn't forgive or forget what Grouchev had done to them. Joe swore vengeance, even if it cost him his life. They were removed from the cabin without any further conversation and taken up onto the yacht's deck by two armed guards. Their guards, like the other crew on the ship, carried automatic weapons. Looking at each other, Peter and Joe realized that escape was going to be impossible. They were handcuffed near the railing, sitting on the hard deck, cold and scared in the clammy grey morning air, until the yacht was finished with its maneuvering and docking procedures. They hadn't had a chance to contact anyone, and they figured that the chances of Tia being able to slip through the net Grouchev's men had put around New York were slim. Peter and Joe resolved themselves to the inevitable end of the road, and they started making peace with their maker. There was really nothing else for them to do.

Tia nudged Mel, pointed, and nodded. There didn't seem to be anyone else on the dock. The sun was rising slowly in the eastern sky, and it silhouetted the yacht. The men on deck were dark, formless shapes, but there were two distinct figures on the fantail of the boat. These two were attached to the railing and didn't appear to have any weapons. The others who were patrolling the deck were obviously holding weapons, some at the ready, some cradled nonchalantly in their arms. Tia knew instinctively that the two kneeling men secured to the fantail of the boat were Peter and Joe. They appeared to be tied up or cuffed, with arms behind them. She said a silent prayer of thanks that they were still alive and that they weren't being held below deck.

The *Golden Sun* finished docking at exactly 5:20 a.m., just as a light fog rolled in off of the ocean. The grey haze made it possible for Tia to make out some of the faces of the men on board. Three crew men had appeared out of nowhere, jumped down onto the dock, and proceeded to tie up the lines. While all eyes were riveted on the docking procedure, Tia slipped around the crates to a spot directly across from the fantail. From this position, she was able to make eye contact with Peter. He had been scanning the docks, against all hope, for a friendly face. He was desperately searching every possible hiding place until he saw Tia. Relief momentarily flooded his face, and then he recovered his composure. He nudged Joe, and he followed Peter's line of vision to where Tia was hiding.

What he saw was so unexpected, he couldn't help grinning.

Then, looking back at Peter, they nodded simultaneously, as if to acknowledge their unspoken plan, and started a diversion to distract Grouchev's men. "Okay, you traitor, that's the last time you squeal on me," Peter said loudly to Joe, as he pulled himself up to a crouching position. "It's all your fault that we're in this mess in the first place."

"That's it!" Joe shouted back, as he followed Peter's lead and also pulled himself up to a crouching position. "I'm not going to take anymore of this abuse!" He attempted to kick Peter and purposely missed, hitting one of the guards nearby in the groin.

"Oh, so that's how you want to play, is it?" Peter asked, shouting equally as viciously. As he pretended to kick at Joe, he missed Joe and hit the second guard, causing him to collapse as he cradled his groin. Hearing the commotion, several other guards had come running to see what the shouting was all about. As they started to level their guns on Peter and Joe, Tia nodded to Mel, and they opened fire on the guards' backs. Two guards fell before the others realized what was happening. Peter and Joe hit the deck and slid their cuffed arms down along the backs of their legs until they could slide them under their feet. Once their hands were in front of him, they took the guns from the fallen guards and succeeded catching the remaining guards in a cross-fire. They used the dead bodies of the fallen guards for protection as they returned fire. When the guards on deck were all down--some dead, some just wounded--Mel ran back to get the car. Tia continued to fire shots to cover Peter and Joe as they jumped from the fantail to the dock and dove behind the crates with Tia. The fallen guards on the deck of the *Golden Sun* were soon replaced by more experienced gunmen, and they were increasingly more accurate with each shot. "Tia," Peter asked loudly, "how are we supposed to get out of here, swim?"

"Nope. No swimming," she replied without looking away from the gunfight. "Just get to the next set of crates. I'll cover you. Mel's already warming up the car for us."

"Okay. Don't be long," Peter replied as he motioned to Joe. Joe nodded and went first, running toward the car, crouched over. Joe handed something small and round to Peter as he ran past him. Peter smiled at Tia's puzzled look and held out his hand so she could see that he was holding a grenade. Joe had obviously taken it from one of the guards on the deck of the yacht. Peter and Tia continued to cover Joe as he headed to the car. Then, once he was safely out of range, Peter pulled the pin out of the grenade he was holding, and lobbed it onto the deck of the *Golden Sun.* A loud explosion followed, and then a loud crash, as Mel plowed through the crates beside Tia and Peter and screeched to a halt. They jumped into the back seat of the car and Mel spun it around and headed away from the dock.

Most of the men on the dock were knocked unconscious, and the few unfortunate armed soldiers who had been on the deck at the time of the explosion were lost. However, Grouchev and his closest aids succeeded in escaping unscathed. Rapid gunfire followed the SUV as it pulled away, but all of the shots fell short. They heard a loud automobile engine and turning around in their seats, and Peter and Tia saw a large, black, powerful SUV pulling up behind them. Two men were leaning out of the car, holding automatic weapons. "Step on it!"

Peter yelled to Mel from the back seat.

"Hold on," Mel answered, as he swerved onto the first side street he found. He was driving the wrong way on a one-way street.

Peter did just that; so did Tia and Joe. Mel drove like a man possessed, dodging the oncoming traffic, swerving left and then right, at increasing speeds. The car was starting to overheat, and Tia realized that they were in real danger. "One of the bullets must of hit the radiator," Joe said, turning around in the seat. "How far do we have to go?"

"Not too far," said Tia, looking ahead anxiously. "The helicopter is in Canaveral Park, but I don't think the car's gonna make it that far."

"Not only that," added Peter, "but that SUV is gaining on us again. I don't think we'll be able to outrun them."

Seconds later, a bullet shattered the back window of their car and whizzed by Tia's head, close enough to her ear for her to feel it. Joe ducked out of reflex, as did Mel. Peter didn't hesitate. He picked up a gun and started shooting back at the SUV. Tia grabbed another gun and started shooting too. Neither of them was shooting at the men inside the car, but at the SUV's radiator and tires. Peter aimed, John Wayne style, and shot the radiator right between the eyes. He looked over at Tia between shots and grinned at her. "Your turn."

Tia smiled back, nodded, and then shot out first one front tire and then the other. The SUV careened off the road into a drainage ditch, rolling several times before landing upright. "One hundred yards to go," Joe said. Just then, the engine sputtered and died. "One hundred yards to go to the helicopter, and this thing has to die!" Joe yelled and cursed the car in several languages. They could've run for it, but the gunmen had climbed clear of the SUV and were shooting as they ran toward the group.

"Get to the helicopter and take Tia with you!" Peter yelled at the group as they scrambled out of their motionless vehicle. "I'll cover you!"

Tia didn't argue. There wasn't time. The only available protection was the car, and one lucky shot into the gas tank could blow it up. Once inside the helicopter, Tia told Mel to hover over Peter, sending a shower of sand into the gunmen's eyes. While he did this, Tia opened fire on the gunmen with her .357 Magnum, covering Peter as he ran toward the building at the side of the park. The building was open, and Peter ran up the stairs to the roof. Tia told Mel where Peter was heading and asked him to fly over the roof of the building, looking for Peter. Tia was sure he would make his way there so they could pick them up.

When they arrived at the rooftop, Peter was there

waiting for them, hidden behind an air conditioning condenser. Just as he reached for the helicopter's pontoon, he carelessly exposed himself to the gunmen below. Grouchev had pulled up behind the battered SUV, and was taking aim with a high-powered rifle. Tia looked on in horror as Peter collapsed in a rumpled heap on the rooftop beneath the helicopter blades. Just then, the echo of the shot reached the helicopter. Tia screamed, and Joe grabbed the gun from her and fired at Grouchev. Grouchev retreated behind the car door, taking cover before climbing into the back of the car. Once he was inside, the car careened past the disabled SUV, spraying dirt and gravel over the man lying motionless in front of it. Mel brought the helicopter down on the roof, and Joe jumped out. Peter was rolling onto his side when Joe reached him, followed by a very anxious Tia.

"How bad is it?" Joe asked as he helped Peter up.

"I'll make it," Peter answered as he tried to stand up. He groaned loudly as he tried to pull himself to a kneeling position.

"Here, let me help you," Tia and Joe said in unison. They all smiled at each other, and then Tia and Joe each took one side of Peter and helped him to the helicopter. Mel made the takeoff as smooth as possible, but Peter seemed to feel every chop of the blades. Tia and Peter stared longingly into each other's eyes as Peter grimaced in pain. Tia continued to reassure him that he would be alright, and that they would get him to the hospital in time.

He held onto Tia as tightly as he could, and then kissed her with all the passion and intensity he'd kept in check since they'd reconnected. No matter how much pain he was in, no matter who else was there, Peter couldn't hide his feelings for Tia any longer. His mouth hungrily searched hers, and her response to him was instantaneous.

"Peter," Tia said against his mouth, breathless. It came out more as a deep moan of pleasure, and was swept away with the wind. As quickly as he'd grabbed her, Peter let her go and groaned in pain as he slipped into unconsciousness. If it weren't for her bruised lips, Tia would've sworn the kiss had never taken place.

The wound in his side was sucking air, a definite sign of a punctured lung. Tia, weeping silently, worked quickly with Joe. They were desperately trying to slow down the bleeding. She cradled Peter's head in her arms while Joe applied pressure to the wound. Peter had fallen unconscious from the pain and sheer exhaustion. Tia whispered, "Darling Peter, I love you. Please don't leave me again. Not now! I don't know what I'd do without you. I love you so much!"

A small smile passed his lips, and he sighed almost inaudibly. *No,* Tia thought to herself. *He couldn't have heard me.*

"Mel, can't this thing go any faster?" Tia asked anxiously as she cradled Peter's head in her arms. "He's lost a lot of blood and I'm afraid he might not make it if we don't hurry."

"I'm going as fast as I can," he replied loudly. "The hospital is only five minutes away, and I've already radioed ahead. They're expecting us, and the trauma team is set and ready to go."

"Tia, don't worry," Joe said, trying to reassure her. "Peter's gonna make it. I've seen him shot worse than this before, and he pulled through just fine. He'll make it this time too, just like he did then."

"I've seen him get hurt before too," she said, close to tears. "Remember? I was there the last time he was shot in the chest. But the bullet is awfully close to his heart this time, and I'm afraid that it might have collapsed a lung from the way he's breathing."

"We're on the final approach," Mel said over the loud swooshing of the chopper blades.

"Thank God," Tia replied. "I can see the trauma team by the helipad, waiting for us. I hope they're good."

"Me too," Joe agreed, looking at Peter's white face. He was getting more and more concerned. The rags he'd used to put pressure on the wound were soaked in blood, as were his hands from holding them. "I just hope we can get him into surgery in time," he said, almost to himself. From the expression on her face, Tia had heard Joe's comment and shared his concern.

"They are," said Mel. "Hold onto him," Mel said over their conversation. "I'm setting her down."

The trauma team took over as soon as the helicopter touched the ground. They quickly helped Joe lift Peter to a stretcher, applied pressure to his wound, and rushed him to the emergency room. Peter moaned in pain as he was moved, but he didn't regain consciousness. Tia and Joe followed the stretcher down the hall into the emergency room, and then the nurse led them to the waiting area. "I'll need some information about the patient," she said efficiently. "Which one of you wants to give it to me?"

"I will," they said in unison.

"Okay," she said, smiling. "Why don't we go sit down over there at that desk, and I'll take down the information?"

She asked for the next of kin information and whether or not he was an organ donor first, which did nothing to relieve Tia's anxiety. The nurse also asked if they knew what blood type Peter was, and if he was allergic to any medications. After she took down all of the information they could tell her, she left them to go give it to the doctor. Tia and Joe paced the floor, and then embraced. "If he doesn't make it, I don't know what I'll do," Tia confessed to Joe tearfully.

"He'll make it," Mel said as he approached the

two. "He seems to be a strong kid," he said, smiling at Tia.

Before either Tia or Joe could reply, the doctor emerged to give them a report on his condition. "He's lost a lot of blood, but it looks like he's going to make it."

"What about the bullet?" Tia asked. "It looked like it punctured his lung."

"It did, but it appears to have lodged in the bone of his third rib. We've inserted a breathing tube to re-inflate his lung, and as soon as he's stable, we'll take him to surgery and remove it. He's a very lucky young man. A fraction of an inch in either direction, and it would've hit his heart and killed him instantly. He can't be moved until we remove the bullet because we can't risk it moving."

"Can we see him?" Joe and Tia asked, relieved.

"Yes, but only one at a time. He's asking for you," the doctor said, looking at Tia. "You are his fiancé, aren't you?" Tia looked at Joe, shocked, and for a moment couldn't speak.

"Yes, she is," Joe answered quickly for her. "You see, doc, they just got engaged, and she's still not used to hearing the words."

The doctor smiled and said, "I understand. Well, if you want to go in, you can, but only for a minute. Make sure he stays calm and doesn't move."

"Thank you, doctor," Tia said, recovering her senses. "I'd like to see him now."

"Okay. I'll take you back to the exam rooms," the doctor replied. "He's in the second room on your right. The nurse will show you where it is."

Without another word, Tia went quickly into the exam room. Evidently a nurse had been told that she would be coming back, and was waiting for her. "This way, please," she said without much formality. Tia entered the room quietly, and Just looked at Peter as he lay on the bed with his eyes closed. He was wearing a white hospital gown with a white sheet over that. There were monitors and tubes attached to him through probes and needles in his arms and chest. The beeping of the heart monitor was the only sound in the room, which was also a stark white.

A pressure bandage had been taped over the spot where the bullet had entered his body, and it was soaked with Peter's blood. The crimson bandage and the bag of equally red blood, which hung beside his bed, provided the only color in the entire room. It was gruesome, and more than a little intimidating, but Tia stood her ground. Her eyes reached his face which was almost as pale as the sheets.

"He's awake," the nurse said suddenly, startling Tia. At the sound of her voice, Peter opened his eyes, and then, upon recognizing Tia, smiled. "Hi," she said softly.

"Hi yourself," he replied in a scratchy, low voice.

The nurse discretely left the room to give them

some privacy, but remained nearby in case he needed anything.

"Are you okay?" Tia asked, taking his hand in hers.

"Oh, I'm great now," he said, grinning.

"Have they given you something for the pain?" Tia asked, smiling. She recognized that glazed look in his eyes.

"Uh-huh," he grunted, smiling again. "I'm feeling pretty good right now."

"I can tell," Tia said, smiling at him. "I knew there had to be a logical explanation for you telling them we were engaged."

"Well, I had to tell them something or they wouldn't have let you in here," he replied.

"Then you didn't mean it?" she asked, smiling at him.

"I didn't say that," he said, smiling back. "You know," he said, suddenly serious, "I never stopped loving you. Even during the time we were separated, I kept hoping against hope that we could work things out, and maybe get back together."

"I think I'd like that," she said, smiling. Tia spent her time with Peter, telling him all the things she'd never told him. She was afraid that if she didn't tell him how she felt now, that she might not get the opportunity again. They made plans, getting to know each other all over again. They planned a future together, and expressed vows to each other that nothing would come between them again.

She left briefly to allow Joe to visit with his friend before he went into surgery, and then they stood together, silently watching as they took Peter into the operating room. She and Joe had taken turns staying with him in the emergency room until the sedative took effect, and the nurse asked them to leave. They paced the floor in the waiting room while Peter fought for his life in surgery. Finally, after three hours, the doctor emerged and told them, "Well, he came through it okay. He'll need a lot of rest, but he should make a complete recovery. He's in post-op now, and it'll be another hour or so before you can see him. Why don't you go get something to eat, and by the time you get back, he should be in the intensive care unit."

"Okay, thanks," Joe said, shaking the doctor's hand. "And thanks. Thanks a lot."

"Yes," Tia added. "We really appreciate all you've done for him."

"I'm glad we could help him. I'll be in to check on him a little bit later," he said, shaking hands with them again before returning to the scrub room. Joe, Tia, and Sam went in search of the cafeteria.

"Joe," Tia said on the way, "I think you need to make a phone call."

"Oh, yes," Joe said, stopping short. "Thanks. I almost forgot. I'll be right there," he said, turning around. "You two go ahead and eat, and I'll join you in a few minutes." Tia and Mel continued onto the cafeteria, and Joe went in search of a phone.

Joe notified the Agency about the day's activities, and suggested that they get a team together to get them to Robert Taylor's ranch in Orlando, Florida. Peter told his contact on the other end of the phone that if they didn't hear from him within the next six hours, they should dispatch the team. Joe then joined Tia and Mel for a bite of hospital cafeteria food, and wished instantly that he'd passed. "God!" he exclaimed after the first mouthful. "No wonder everyone in the hospital is sick! If they give this stuff to the staff too, it's a mystery how they're still on their feet!"

Tia and Mel laughed at him and finished everything on their plates. They were all so hungry, they didn't notice the taste after that first mouthful. When they were finished, they headed back upstairs to the Intensive Care Unit, where the nurse told them that Peter had just arrived and was getting settled. They had to wait ten more minutes before they were allowed in to see him, and then only one at a time, and for only five minutes. Tia was happy to see him, even with all of the tubes and monitors attached to him. "Hi, handsome!" she said, attempting cheerfulness.

"Hi, gorgeous," he said thickly. "I was hoping you'd be the first one I'd see when I woke up, but instead it was the ICU nurse. And believe me, she made me feel like closing my eyes again!"

"Well, don't worry," Tia said, laughing as she ran a soft finger across his stubbled cheek. "When you get out of here, I promise you you'll wake up looking at me every day... that is, if it's what you want," she added coyly.

"You know what I want," he replied, reaching for her hand and smiling weakly.

Before Tia could reply, the nurse came in and told her it was time to let Peter rest. "Okay, but just one more minute, please," she asked sweetly.

"Okay," the nurse said sternly, "but I'll be right back!"

"I thought she'd never leave," Peter said, smiling and squeezing her hand.

"Peter," Tia began slowly, "while we have a chance, there's something I have to tell you."

"Hope it isn't bad news," Peter added before she could continue. "I think I've had about all I can take." He looked pointedly down at the tubes and electric monitors attached to his arms.

"No," she said, smiling weakly back at him. "It's not exactly bad news." She took a deep breath and then continued. "I have to find Orlando. It's been too long already, and I'm afraid if I wait much longer. Something awful may have already happened to her."

"Don't worry," he replied seriously. "I understand completely. I only wish I was in a position to help."

"Just get well," she said sincerely. "That's the greatest help you could be to me right now. I can be at Robert's ranch in about an hour, by helicopter. If I leave now, I can be there before the Agency arrives."

"The Agency!" Peter exclaimed, a little too loudly. His outburst brought the nurse running. "Miss, I'm afraid you really must leave now. You're upsetting the patient!" she said to Tia in her most authoritative tone.

"Okay, I'm going," Tia said agreeably. "Peter, dear, I'll see you when I get back. Don't worry. I know you're in excellent hands," she said, looking pointedly at the anxious nurse. "Get well, and I'll be back before you know it." She kissed him briefly on the lips before walking toward the door.

"But--" he began, only to be silenced by a thermometer being shoved into his open mouth.

"Quiet, Mr. Robinson," the nurse said, acting as if Tia had already left the room.

"Bye, dear," Tia said smiling. She couldn't help but chuckle at the effective way the nurse had shut him up. "See you soon."

With that, Tia met Joe and Mel in the waiting room and told them she'd told Peter of her plan to try to find Orlando. "Mel," Tia began, taking his hands in hers, "I really shouldn't ask this of you, I mean you've done so much already. But, I really need to get to Mr. Taylor's ranch as soon as possible, and you have a helicopter, and..."

"You don't need to say another word," he said, smiling. "I'd be happy to take you and your friend here." He nodded in Joe's direction.

"It could be dangerous," she cautioned him. "I mean even more dangerous than this trip was."

"Don't worry about it, Tia. I've been in danger before, remember?" He smiled and patted her hand. "Besides, I've gotten kinda fond of you. And Harvey wouldn't forgive me for not taking proper care of you."

"Thanks, Mel," Tia said as she gave his hand a squeeze. Then, turning to Joe, she asked, "Is everything set?"

"Yep," he said. "I took care of everything. We have six hours. Then they move in."

"Okay, then," Tia said, taking a deep breath. "Let's go." They took off from the hospital heliport and, after consulting their GPS on board, took the shortest route to Robert's ranch near Buena Vista. They arrived around 2:30 p.m. As they flew over the property, they gave the main compound a wide berth so they would not attract any more attention than absolutely necessary. Some of the armed men walking around the compound looked up when they heard the rotors. At this, Mel made an obvious point of flying off to the horizon, and once out of sight, set the helicopter down near a stand of palms. Tia, Joe, and Mel stepped out of the helicopter and consulted the GPS once more, but this time it wasn't a picture of the state they were looking at. They were studying a detailed diagram of the ranch. "If those men down there were farm hands," Tia said, looking at Joe and Sam, "then I'm Florence Nightingale!"

"I agree," Joe said. "With the part about them not being ranch hands, not the part about you being Florence Nightingale," he added, smiling.

"That means that the Russian Mafia is already here," Tia continued, smirking at Joe's attempt at making a joke.

"The Russian Mafia?" Mel asked, stunned.

"I'm afraid so," Joe said. "If you want to back out, Mel, it's not too late. You can stay here with the chopper. No one will think less of you."

"No thanks," he replied. "I started this thing; I might as well finish it."

"Okay, then," Joe responded, patting Mel on the back. "Let's see what we have to work with," Joe said, leaning over the diagram of the ranch. "We have to assume that Robert and Orlando, if they're here, are being held in the main house. That's over there," he said, pointing on the map. "Krosky, the second-in-command, would be there with his head men. He'll need a place where he can question them and still be close to a phone."

"Right," Tia added. "That means that the people who work for Robert must be locked up somewhere too. How many people do you think that would be?"

"Probably around 50, I would guess, judging from the number of trailers we flew over," added Mel. "And I figure they won't keep the men and their families together. They'll have better leverage over the men if they hold their families in a separate location."

"Mel's right, Tia," Joe agreed as he scanned the diagram. "Those men wouldn't dare get out of line if they're holding their women and children prisoner."

"Okay," Tia said. "Where would be the most logical place to hold that many women and children?"

"Probably either the bunkhouse or a storage shed," Joe answered. "They're the two biggest buildings on the ranch, besides the main house."

"Which one do you think it is?" asked Mel.

"Probably the storage shed," Joe said pointing to it on the map. "There were some men milling around outside it when we flew over, and there was no one around the bunkhouse."

"Okay, so how do we get them out of there?" asked Tia.

"Well," Joe said, looking directly at Tia, "before we figure that out, I think we'd better figure out where the women and children are. If we have problems getting the men out, the gunmen will likely use their families against them."

"Wait a minute," Mel said, hushing them both. "Did you hear that?"

"Hear what?" asked Joe.

"Listen," Mel repeated, listening intently. "There! There it is again!"

"Yes," Tia said. "I heard it too."

"What is it?" Joe said, straining to pick up the direction.

"It sounds like a baby," Tia said.

"You're right!" said Mel. "And it's coming from over there."

They all looked in the direction Mel indicated, and they could just make out a stone shed overgrown with vines and shrubs.

"Let's go see what it is," Tia said as she climbed out of the helicopter.

"Wait!" Joe said putting a restraining hand on her arm. "What?" Tia asked. "It could be a trick. Let me go first," Joe said as he pulled a revolver out of his jacket and stepped out of their position. "Mel, you wait here, and be ready to come running if we need you. Okay? Depending on what we find, we may need to take off quickly."

Mel nodded in agreement and said, "Be careful!"

"Joe, you go to the left and I'll go to the right, and we'll meet at the front door," Tia said, pulling out her gun too. "Okay?"

Joe nodded, and they approached the shed in silence, ready for anything. Once at the front door, Joe hit it twice with his gun and yelled, "Come out with your hands up! You're surrounded, and you don't stand a chance!"

"Don't shoot," yelled a female voice from inside the sheds. "We aren't armed. I'm coming out," she said, opening the door slowly.

Joe and Tia stood up and lowered their guns. "Who are you?" Tia asked.

"I could ask you the same thing," the woman said boldly. She was obviously relieved to see they were Americans.

"My name's Tia, and this is Joe," Tia said, pointing to her companion. "Now who are you?" Tia asked crossly.

"I'm Sarah, and we're hiding here from the men who took over the ranch," the woman replied. "Were they Americans or Russians?" Joe asked.

"Definitely not Americans," Sarah said. "I think they were Russian from their accents," she added.

"Do you know how many there were?" Tia asked.

"I don't know... maybe a dozen," she guessed. "They've got our husbands locked up somewhere else. A young woman came by earlier and told us to hide in here. Then she left. She said she was going to help Mr. Taylor. He's the owner. They were going to get our husbands released. But that was over an hour ago, and I haven't heard anything from her since. I'm getting very worried. She told me to keep the women and children in here, but we don't know what's going on, and some of the women are getting anxious."

"Did this young woman have long hair?" Tia asked anxiously.

"Yes. I think she said her name was Orlando," Sarah replied. "She helped kill two of the men that were holding us prisoner."

"That's Orlando," Tia said, smiling happily. "Which way did she go?"

"I don't know," she answered. "She was headed back to the main compound the last time I saw her. But, like I said, that was quite a while ago."

"Is everyone in here okay?" Joe asked.

"Yes, we're fine," Sarah replied.

"Are there any other women and children hiding in other shacks around the ranch?" Tia asked.

"No," Sarah replied. "Those men rounded us all up and put us in the bunkhouse. That's where Orlando found us."

"Will you excuse us for a minute?" Tia said to Sarah before taking Joe by the arm.

"What is it?" Joe asked as soon as they were alone.

"Do you realize these women could be the answer to our problem?" Tia asked.

"What do you mean?" Joe asked suspiciously.

"We've got a built-in army right here," Tia said, pointing to the shed.

"Tia, are you nuts? Do you know what you're saying?" Joe asked looking shocked. "These women don't know anything about fighting, they've got little kids with them, and they're not even armed!"

"Well, they're all we've got, and the ones who don't want to fight can take care of the kids. We can arm the ones who want to fight," Tia countered. "If they're willing, I don't see why we don't let them help us. After all, it is their husbands' lives, as well as Orlando's and Robert's, that they'll be fighting for." Then Tia added, with a smile at his doubting expression, "Besides, don't underestimate the power of a woman!"

"You've got a point," he said, relenting. "Okay, Tia. We'll do it your way. But we have to see if they want to fight first. No pressure. If they're not interested, then they're not interested."

"Okay," she said, walking back to where Sarah was waiting for them. "Sarah, how would you guys like to help us get your husbands back?"

"We'd love it," she said with a smile. "What do you want us to do?" Joe explained that they'd need weapons. Sarah told him that that would be no problem, as the ammunition shed was unguarded since the sign had been switched and the armed men didn't know it was an ammunitions shed. As Sarah described how it had been done, Joe chuckled. He was starting to feel better about this already. As several women kept the children quiet, the others took turns, two at a time, sneaking into the ammunitions shed and collecting handguns, shotguns, rifles, and boxes of ammunition.

Once the women were armed, they were told to take cover wherever possible, and then, in about 10 minutes, they were to start a commotion. They were to use explosives and pistols, and they were to aim both in the farthest direction from the main house or the storage shed where their husbands were being held.

"The object is to draw the Russians out, not to kill your husbands," Joe said succinctly.

"Listen, Joe," Sarah said in an irritated voice. "We'll take care of the diversion. You just take care of those men. And don't worry about us. We can take care of ourselves. Most of us have been shootin' rifles since before you were born!"

"Sorry," Joe said apologetically. "I didn't mean to offend you."

"Fine, whatever," Sarah said, still irritated, dismissing Joe's apology with a wave of her hand. "Let's get started. The quicker we get things back to normal around here, the better it'll be."

"Right!" Joe said a bit too enthusiastically, smiling at her. He offered his hand in comradeship and, smiling, she shook it. Tia nodded in agreement, and then smiled broadly at Sarah before turning to join Joe on his way back to the helicopter. As they retreated quietly to the helicopter, Joe and Tia formulated a plan to rescue the men and help their friends Robert and Orlando. Sarah had confirmed that they were at the ranch, but no one was sure exactly where they were.

Within minutes, they were back in the air. Mel used the radio aboard the helicopter to notify the local authorities and explain the current situation. Mel wasn't quite sure if the Orange County Sherriff's Department took him seriously or not, but the dispatcher said she was sending officers and a SWAT team. Mel buzzed the main house with the chopper to spook the Russians and hopefully cause confusion. Then, he flew out of range again before the armed men below could take aim. He repeated this stunt from several different directions, causing enough of a distraction that he gave the women the opportunity to arm themselves and get into position virtually unnoticed. Mel circled around the house until he found a secluded spot where there were no guards. He landed briefly to let Joe and Tia out in a position several hundred feet behind the main house. Joe then waved him off, and then he and Tia took cover.

The men held prisoner in the supply shack heard the helicopter too, and they also felt renewed hope. The constant buzzing intimidated the men standing guard, and they were becoming anxious. The women had started bombarding the main house and the main compound area with explosives and shooting bullets into the air. It sounded like an all out assault by a well-trained army. The women were careful not to hit the main house, but much of the farm equipment was damaged, and one of the barns was leveled. Joe took advantage of the confusion to get over to the supply shed where the men were being held.

Tia and several of the women covered the main compound with a crossfire shower of bullets, and the guards trying to cross it fell dead without getting off a shot. Joe silenced the two guards outside the supply shed; one with a bullet to the head, the other with a bullet through the heart. "Stand back," Joe yelled through the thick door and lit the fuse on a stick of dynamite. He ran for cover as the door shattered to pieces with the explosion. When the smoke cleared, the men ran out, ducking for cover as they serpentine across the opening. Tia had the women bring extra guns with them over to the supply shack, and they handed these to each of the men, one by one, as they emerged from the shack.

Tia took two of the women with her and headed for the woodpile at the back side of the house. When they gathered all of the ammunition together, Tia signaled the women to run and then she set off the first explosion. The force of the blast knocked the guard at the rear door off his feet, propelling him into the court yard where he landed heavily on his back, unconscious. Taking advantage of the confusion, Joe ran to the designated rendezvous point, where Mel picked him up and then circled back to the main compound. He flew low while Joe sprayed the area from above with very accurate gunfire, hitting most of the armed guards who were firing from behind the barricade, and holding back the men trying to make their way to the house.

The patrol who had been out searching for Orlando and Robert had returned by this time, and it seemed that there were four Russians for every farmhand. The Russians were experienced soldiers, while the ranch hands were hunters and farmers. Everyone of the men, however, was fighting to free their families and reclaim the ranch, which gave them the advantage. The fighting became more fierce by the minute.

Tia noticed a man tied to a stake in the center of the courtyard, unharmed as yet, but about to be killed. The man who was about to take his life was a Russian, and he had a gun aimed at the restrained main's head. They were both too far away for Tia to make out who they were, and she could only identify the armed gunman by his uniform. She knew that she couldn't hit the man with the gun accurately from this distance, and she didn't want to take the chance of hitting the other man by mistake. Mel also saw what was happening in the courtyard, and brought the helicopter down low over the pair long enough for Joe to get off a couple of shots.

Joe purposely aimed at the ground directly behind the man with the gun, scaring him into moving away from the man tied to the stake. Just as he did, Sarah, a crack shot, hit him in the neck, and then again in the chest as he spun around. His automatic weapon fired harmlessly into the dirt as he turned slowly and then fell down. Tia had made her way to where Sarah was by the time he hit the ground, and she could see that the man tied up was Robert. "I've got to get him out of there," she said to Sarah. "Cover me!"

Tia ran into the center of the courtyard, rolling on the ground several times to miss bullets aimed poorly at her fleeing figure. Sarah, aiming carefully, easily eliminated two of the men shooting at Tia. She reached Robert and started untying his hands and feet, covering his body with her own. "For God's sake, Robert, wake up!" she screamed at him. He was obviously drugged. Tia couldn't get a response, so she finished untying his hands and feet and then dragged him out of the courtyard. Once she had him behind some empty barrels, Tia slapped him several times across the face. "Wake up!" she shouted at him. Then, shaking him, she pleaded, "Robert, you've got to snap out of it!" Tia slapped him again, harder this time, and he started to come around.

"Where... where am I?" he asked groggily. "Tia? Is that you?" he asked again. "What are you hitting me for? And what the hell is going on around here? It sounds like a war out there! What's all the shooting?" he asked, reaching automatically for his gun. Neither the gun nor the holster were under his arm.

"Never mind!" she replied angrily. "We need to get under cover. Now!" she said as she practically dragged his groggy figure to the cover of the porch. Once he was lying on the ground alongside it, Tia calmed down and answered his questions. "They've got Orlando somewhere and I don't know where Peter is," Tia explained. "The wives and children are safe, and some of the women are helping with the rescue." Then, taking a minute to look at him, she asked, "Are you okay? Can you move? Can you get up on your own?"

"Ooh, I think so," he said, shaking his head several times. "I don't know what that stuff was they gave me, but it sure leaves a bad taste in your mouth. And I've got a whopper of a headache!" he added as he sat up slowly. Robert looked around himself anxiously. The gunfire was continuing, but more sporadically now. "Where's Orlando?" he asked Tia, alarmed and grabbing her shoulder with his right arm.

"I don't know!" Tia answered him, looking anxious too. "What time is it?" he asked her.

"About 2:30 or 3:00, I think. Why?"

"I got a message out to the Agency. When you guys got here, I thought it was the Agency's idea of the backup. They should have been here by now."

"That doesn't matter now," Tia said anxiously. "We have to find Orlando and stop Grouchev and his men. If we don't get this thing wrapped up soon, it won't when the Agency shows up. Someone in our civilian army out there is going to get seriously hurt, or worse!"

"Can you handle things out here?" Robert asked hurriedly as he rose into a crouched position.

"Sure. Why?" Tia asked, confused.

"I'm going inside to find Orlando. Krosky must have her upstairs somewhere," Robert said, taking the pistol out of Tia's hands. "I'll need to borrow this."

"Krosky's here?" Tia asked, astonished. "Grouchev mentioned that he thought Krosky was behind this!"

"When did you talk to Grouchev?" Robert asked puzzled.

Tia put a hand on his shoulder and replied, "Don't worry about it now. We'll figure it all out later. But Krosky is definitely behind this, and from what Peter and Joe said, Grouchev would like to have a long talk with him about as much as we would, if you know what I mean."

"I understand," he said.

"Now, you're going to find Orlando, right?" Tia asked. Robert nodded and Tia added, "Be careful, okay?"

"You too," Robert said, giving her a quick kiss on the cheek. "Tell Peter I said to watch his back."

"I will," she said, smiling weakly. She didn't see any sense in telling him about Peter having been shot. "I'll make sure everything is secure here and then meet you inside."

"Okay," Robert said as he stood up again. "Last time I saw Krosky, he was taking Orlando up to the bedroom. I just hope I'm not too late!" From the look on Tia's face, he regretted what he'd said, as soon as he'd said it. "Tia, I didn't mean..."

"I know!" Tia answered him angrily. "Stop talking and just get her away from him!" Without another word, Robert nodded, smiled at Tia, and took off to the back of the house.

He shot his way through the kitchen door and ducked inside. His only thought was a fervent prayer that he would reach Orlando in time. Tia ran, crouched over so that she was the smallest target possible, and joined Joe near a bullet-ridden, old car parked on the side of the main compound. He was reloading when he saw her run up to him. "I just got Robert loose, and he's going after Orlando," she told him.

"Is he okay?" Joe asked as he continued working.

"Yeah, he'll be fine," Tia answered. They drugged him, but he came around. My guess is that they wanted to keep him quiet until they were ready to get rid of him."

"And he's going after Orlando in the house?" Joe asked.

"Uh-huh," Tia answered. "And I told him about Krosky, so he'll be on the lookout for him. How's everything out here?"

"Well," he began, looking up to see where everyone was positioned, and who needed help. "We're doing okay for a group of civilians with guns. I wish the Agency forces would get here. I don't like having to rely on these people. They're inexperienced and they're going to get hurt!"

"I don't know, Joe," Tia answered. "I'm really proud of these women. They're really holding their own."

"Yeah, you're right. They're much better shots than I ever expected," Joe admitted. "Still, I wish we didn't have to put them in danger."

"Speaking of that," Tia said with a smile. "What do you say we stop gabbing and get back at it?" she asked with raised eyebrows.

Just then, a Russian gunman who had been shot in the arm and was bleeding profusely, careened into Joe. He obviously didn't see Joe and Tia behind the car and was seeking shelter there for himself. He raised his good arm, which held his rifle, to aim at Joe and Tia didn't hesitate. She shot him in the heart. The gunman looked stunned for a moment and then started to stagger back. His good arm, holding the rifle started to relax, lowering his aim. His finger reflexively squeezed the trigger, and the gun shot into the hard ground, ricocheting just as Joe, now out of the line of fire, yelled, "Tia! Look out!" Tia didn't t quite move fast enough, and the bullet hit home. She fell back, still.

Chapter 10

KROSKY HAD JUST left the room, slamming and locking the door behind him. Orlando stood still, staring at the closed door, shaking and trying to pull herself together. As she secured what was left of her shirt in an attempt to restore some semblance of modesty, events of the last hour came flooding back with horrifying clarity. When she'd heard the helicopter from the balcony, Orlando had looked out the window to see whose it was. From the reactions of the men below her, she realized it wasn't one of theirs. Help was on its way, and while it didn't stop Krosky from torturing her, it may have bought her the time she needed to escape.

Orlando knew what she had to do now, and there would be no stopping her. When she looked out the window, she had seen Robert bound to the stake in the main compound, and she knew that Krosky had planned to kill him even though he'd promised not to do it. Orlando knew that she had to kill Krosky before he could do any more damage to her, Robert or anyone else. She was surprised to find the idea wasn't as repulsive to her as she'd thought it would be, and without even realizing it, she was formulating a plan in the back of her mind. As objectively as she could, Orlando reviewed the events and conversation with Krosky since he had brought her to the bedroom, trying to find a weakness that she could exploit.

"Come here and sit down," the Russian had ordered her, motioning with the gun. Krosky had seated himself on the bed, occupying more than half of the space between them, and continued to motion with the gun until Orlando complied. He was trying his best to intimidate her. It wasn't working. She could feel her anger growing along with her fear.

"Tell me your name. Your full name," she said, feigning interest in him. "I prefer civilized men," she added, smiling alluringly at him like she had downstairs. "Act civilized, and I will sit down."

"My name is Krosky. That is all you need to know." He smiled at her as if she were Thanksgiving dinner and he hadn't eaten in a month. "You are Orlando. Orlando Corogan."

"Yes, that's right," she said quietly. "Now, isn't this better than making threats?" she added coyly. She was hoping to stall for time until she could figure a way out of the room.

"I am not used to your American directness. We consider it rudeness and respond accordingly," he answered her.

"Apology accepted," she said, feigning calmness as she sat down on the edge of the bed. She kept talking to buy time. "If you know my name, then you must know that I am not part of all of this stuff with the Agency."

"I knew you were Sam Corogan's daughter," he said, ignoring her reference to the Agency. "But I never thought you'd be so... beautiful," he added with lust in his eyes. He reached out and ran his rough fingers through her hair.

Forcing herself not to recoil in disgust, Orlando lowered her eyes and said sweetly, "Thank you, Krosky. You definitely are a flatterer." She looked up at him, staring directly into his eyes, trying to gain the psychological upper hand.

"No woman in my country would dare to be so bold, to stare at a man like you are looking at me now," Krosky said. His expression was one of admiration and irritation, as he looked her over from head to toe as if she were a fine cut of beef. He ran a finger along her arm to where her long auburn tresses hung behind it. He took a handful of her hair and wrapped his fingers in a fist around it, holding her head still, before continuing. "But then, no woman in my country looks like you do. Such magnificent hair, so silky, and such an exquisite color." His hand released her hair and went to her cheek. "And your eyes," he said, running a callused hand along her temple. "I've never seen such fire!" Krosky grabbed her shoulders and pulled Orlando closer, pressing the length of her slender body against his hard lines.

Trying to ignore the pain his fingers caused as they dug into her soft flesh, she responded, saying,

"Why don't you tell me a little about yourself?" She was stalling, trying to buy time. She struggled out of his grip and crossed the room. Krosky's triumphant smile and lustful gaze followed Orlando across the room. "For instance, is Krosky your first or last name?"

"Just Krosky," he repeated, annoyed, as he got off the bed and walked over to where Orlando was standing.

Avoiding his grasp, Orlando slipped past him and continued talking as if her life depended on it. "And just what is it you do?" she asked, turning to face him directly. "Are you the head of this group? Are you really a part of the Russian Mafia?"

"Where did you hear such a foolish idea as that?" he asked, grabbing her shoulders again. He stared down at her with a mixture of amusement and irritation as he tried to physically intimidate her with his sheer size.

Doing her best to ignore his unspoken threat, Orlando replied casually, "Oh, I hear things here and there." Then, she pushed a little harder asking, "So, why are you here, anyway? I mean, why are you in Florida, and what do you want with Robert Taylor?"

Krosky straightened his broad shoulders and his dark brows came together in a deep frown. Orlando knew that she'd hit a nerve, but she wasn't sure why. He ran an anxious hand through his thick, dark, wavy hair before dropping it again by his side. "It is not important," he said in an irritated tone. "What is important is where you have *FILE 13,* the information on our traitorous agents. I believe in your country you call them double agents." He put his finger to her lips to stop her denial before she could voice it. "It's no use your denying that you know what I'm talking about. Your choice of friends alone makes you guilty. Now, why don't you cooperate? It will go easier for you," he added as he grabbed her wrist and twisted it.

Wincing in pain, Orlando replied, "I thought we could discuss it first."

She looked up at him, trying to read the thoughts behind his grimace. Suddenly, his mouth came down hard on hers. She couldn't breathe. His vice-like grip crushed her lips against her teeth, forcing them apart. She whimpered, but not from pleasure. The pain he inflicted on her mouth was searing hot, sending wave after wave of lightning bolts through her head. Her upper arms were losing feeling where his hands held her like vices, and she tried to fight with her arms and hands, but her efforts had no effect. When he heard her moan of pain, he mistook it for one of passion, and his kiss became less violent and more passionate. Although Orlando was repulsed by it, she was grateful that he had let up a bit and she could breathe again. As her head started to clear, she decided that her life and Robert's relied on her ability to act. She had to stall Krosky until help could reach her, or until she could effectively use her knife. He led her over to the bed, still firmly holding onto her arms, and pushed her down onto the satin comforter. "Why are you here?" she repeated, trying to sound more fearless than she felt.

"Why is that important to you?" he asked angrily. "If I tell you, would that really make a difference?"

"Maybe if you tell me the truth," she said, shrugging. She forced herself to smile at him. "Most men would be too afraid of rejection to tell a girl the truth. Besides," she added in what she hoped was a convincingly seductive tone of voice, "power turns a girl on."

"And why is that?" he asked, stroking her hair.

"Because a girl likes to feel in control sometimes," she answered honestly. "And if the guy she controls is powerful… well, then..."

"Oh, please, continue," he said close to her ear. "I am fascinated with your logic."

"I want to know all about you," Orlando said suggestively as she looked past him, over his shoulder to the clock on the wall. Almost an hour had passed since she'd been led to the bedroom by the guard, and almost 20 minutes since she'd heard the helicopter the first time. The minutes were creeping by, and she was no closer to getting free than she was before.

Just as Krosky was about to force his advantage,

ignoring her probing question, a guard hammered on the door. Krosky automatically picked up the gun he had set down and yelled out in Russian that he was not to be disturbed. He got up off the bed and checked the door again, making sure that it was still securely locked. Orlando jumped off the bed and ran to the balcony when Krosky went to the door, but the distance was too great to try to jump. She looked up, and when she saw the helicopter from the balcony, she had renewed hope. Krosky had already stripped her of her dignity, but that wasn't enough. Orlando was afraid that he would shoot her just for the sheer pleasure of watching her suffer.

Orlando spun around when she heard Krosky testing the lock, and turned just in time to see him set aside the gun and pull a long knife out of his belt. Looking up from the blade, Krosky faced Orlando. "We have talked enough!" he said irritably. Orlando moved away from the window to the farthest corner of the room. Every nerve in her body was screaming out in fear. They did a very slow circular dance, as she barely sidestepped his advances. She ran for the door, thinking that she might have a chance of escape if she could get to the discarded gun. But when she attempted to get out of the room, he grabbed her, held the knife to her throat, and brutally twisted her arm until she could feel her bone crack.

Orlando struggled free and running to the other side of the room, turned to face Krosky across the bed. Her gaze was transfixed by the long, sharp blade's reflection of the bright sunlight as he brandished it. He walked slowly, deliberately around the bed toward her, and she started trembling. She willed herself to be strong, not to think about what was going to happen, but to concentrate on Robert and Tia. She knew that she was no physical match for him, and she prayed for some divine intervention.

Krosky walked deliberately to where Orlando was standing terrified but defiant. Without saying a word, he grabbed and held Orlando in a vice grip with one powerful arm, pinning her arms to her sides, while he used the knife to shred the front of her shirt from neck to waist. Taunting her physically and mentally, he ran his rough hands and the sharp blade across her soft skin, sending shivers of fear to her extremities. Krosky pushed her down on the bed under him and pressed his knife to her throat to force her to remain still while he kissed her roughly, biting her lip with his teeth and forcing his tongue into her mouth over and over again, as a prelude to what was next. He smothered her in his vulgar version of amorous kisses for several minutes until she could hardly breathe, she was so filled with fear and revulsion.

Krosky stopped is attack on her mouth long enough to trace the curves of her heaving bosom with the knife, asking her if she could guess how thinly he could strip her skin from her body before she would start to bleed. He mocked her, counting as he pretended to slice her creamy, supple breasts, asking her over and over again if she knew how many cuts it would take before she would bleed to death. Cutting through the thin material that held her bra in place with one swift, upward movement, he moved the point of the knife down to her sensitive areolas, asking her how she thought her nipples would feel against the cold steel.

As he tortured her, the only things she could cling to were the faces she saw when she closed her eyes. Her father's face was smiling warmly at her, giving her strength. Her mother was standing beside her, telling her to be strong. Last of all, Robert was with her. She could see him in her mind, hear his encouragement and feel his strength. She knew they loved her. With that love, came the strength to endure almost anything. She hadn't quite succeeded in blocking out the humiliation and pain Krosky was inflicting on her, but she found, within herself, the strength to endure it.

Krosky moved the blade back to her neck as he uttered a throaty chuckle and used his free hand to explore every inch of her now bare upper body. He pressed his heavy form against her to hold her in place, and she could feel his passion grow. He forced her lips apart again and started attacking her mouth as his hand prodded and pinched her sensitive breasts. He forced his knee between her clenched thighs and pried them open. Krosky was ready to cut Orlando's cheek with the knife to force her to comply with his wishes when he heard the chopper buzz the house again. Krosky swore loudly in Russian and quickly climbed off Orlando. He straightened his clothes, uttered a threat that she should not move because he'd be back, and walked quickly to the door. He pulled the key out of his pants pocket, opened the door, and then left slamming it shut and locking it behind him.

Orlando lay silent for a moment, trying to get a grip on her emotions. She was terrified of what he would do if he did come back, and she was even more angry with herself for putting off the inevitable. She should have killed him when she had the chance. The truth of the matter was, she didn't think she could do it. That was, until he had attacked her. Now she was certain she could kill him, given the chance, without a second thought. Standing up, Orlando reached to the back of her belted pants and confirmed that the blade was still in place. Next, she tried to straighten her blouse, but there was no use. He'd done too good a job of ripping it. She tied it in place, covering herself as much as was possible with the shredded material, and then tried the door. It was still bolted, so she would have to find another way out of the room.

She had stripped the bed and was in the middle of tying the sheets together near the balcony, so that she could climb down, when the door opened and

Krosky stomped in. He slammed the door shut, but not before Orlando noticed that the guard was gone. Krosky didn't bother to lock the door either, in his hurry to reach Orlando. This time she didn't have the bed between her and Krosky.

"Tell me now! Tell me where *FILE 13* is, or I will kill you!" he shouted at her as he stomped across the room, brandishing the knife. He was even more angry than he was when he had left her a few minutes earlier.

"No!" she pleaded. "Don't! I'll tell you what you want to know!"

"Oh, don't worry," he said, grinning at her while he spun the knife in his hand. "You'll tell me what I want to know. Of that I am certain. But first, I will teach you respect the man as your superior. You do not understand. You need to learn your place!"

He took a step forward and shoved her shoulder hard, knocking her down onto the bed. Holding the knife to her throat, he ripped what was left of her shirt from her body, shredding what had remained from their previous encounter, exposing her china white skin. Then, setting the knife aside, Krosky used both hands to pin Orlando beneath him, with her arms folded backward under her buttocks, as if she were cuffed. Orlando wanted to cry for help, to beg him to stop, anything that would end what he was beginning again, but she knew that no one would hear her. She knew that her cries for help, for mercy, would only feed his hatred of her and all that she stood for, so she remained silent.

Krosky wanted to elicit a submissive response from her and was enraged by her defiant silence, so he grabbed her breasts between his rough fingers, squeezing and clutching them brutally, leaving large red bruises where his fingers had been. He ignored her whimpers of pain and the bruises he was creating, and took first one breast in his mouth and then the other, biting down hard. Orlando willed herself not to cry out. Her only thought was how she could access and then use the knife she'd hidden in her belt under her pants. She could feel the cold steel of the flat side of the blade pressing into her flesh, and she found it oddly comforting.

Orlando bit down on her bottom lip, trying to focus on something other than the pain as Krosky's torture increased. She tasted her own blood. Silently fighting Krosky's advances, she tried to shift under his weight in order to reach the knife. When Krosky felt her fighting to get free, he laughed at her feeble struggles. It was a cold, condescending snicker from the deepest part of his evil being. He knew that he could easily dominate her physically, but he wanted to break her spirit too. He wouldn't be happy until he took this brutality to its natural conclusion.

Krosky shifted so that he could reach her and pulled at the waistline of her pants. The belt slowed his progress, but didn't stop him. Orlando knew that

once Krosky had raped her, it wouldn't end there. He
would continue to torture her until she told him
everything he wanted to hear, or she died from the
pain. Once Orlando told him what he wanted to
know, she suspected he'd kill her anyway, just to
avoid any witnesses. If she was ever going to be free
of him, she realized she would have to make her
move now.

Krosky had unwittingly helped Orlando by
ripping the waist of her pants. Now, she could get to
her knife.

With one superhuman push, Orlando used her
legs, hips, and torso to force Krosky onto his back.
He pulled her with him, holding onto her upper arms,
but she managed to get her knife out of the sheath
and hold it flat against her buttocks as he pushed her
over onto her back again. Chuckling, he said, "Don't
struggle so much. You will enjoy it more if you
relax." Then, smirking as he held her shoulders down
on the bed, he gloated, "You have never had any so
good as I am!" Moaning convincingly as Krosky
again lowered his mouth to one of her swollen
breasts, she slipped the knife out from under her
buttocks and pulled it up along her left side. Krosky
had rolled over to her right side so he could more
easily edge her pants down. Orlando had no choice
but to use her left hand to defend herself, which
wouldn't be easy because she was much stronger on
her right side. She took one long, deep breath. It was

now or never. Just as Krosky ripped the zipper and slid his hand between her thighs, inside her pants, Orlando plunged the knife into the side of his heck with all her strength. His head jerked up, and a silent scream of pain and shock emanated from him. He looked at her, eyes wide, bulging, and his mouth gaping. The anger and then the shock Orlando saw in his face, as the last seconds of life slipped away from him, were matched only by her mixed emotions as the reality of what she'd just done set in.

Even unmoving, Krosky appeared to be no less threatening. Orlando didn't know how long she lay there, bare to the waist with his dead corpse on top of her, constricting her breathing. It felt like hours, but in reality, it was only a few minutes. She didn't know if it was the actual weight that was cutting off her air supply and making her limbs feel like lead, or if it was the enormity of the nightmare she was living. Somehow she had to get him off of her and get out of the bedroom before his men came looking for her. Just as she gathered her strength to try to heave him off of her, she heard a commotion in the corridor outside the bedroom.

Orlando froze as she listened for voices. She was desperate to hear who was in the hall and if they were coming into the room. Her heart skipped a beat when she heard Robert's voice calling her. "Orlando! Orlando, where are you?" Robert shouted as he burst into the room.

"Robert!" she cried out weakly from underneath Krosky. "I'm in here! Oh, Robert, please help me! Please hurry!"

Her face wet from tears, Orlando was relieved beyond belief when she saw Robert with her own eyes. She couldn't believe he was still alive, let alone about to free her. The last time she had seen him, he was tied to a stake in the compound, about to be executed. In her struggle with Krosky, Orlando hadn't paid any attention to the amount of gunfire outside, and she assumed that Robert was either dead or very seriously injured.

"Robert!" she exclaimed again. She could feel the wetness on her cheeks, but she didn't realize she was crying. "I can't feel anything! My legs are like lead, and my whole right side hurts. Please, please help me up!"

"It's okay, Orlando, don't worry," Robert said softly, trying to calm her. "I'll get you out of there. Just give me a minute." Robert tried to soothe her as he worked to lift Krosky off of her without causing additional bodily harm. Once he had cleared her body, Robert pushed Krosky's limp body onto the floor so that she wouldn't have to look at him.

"Please," she sobbed. "Please get him off me!"

Robert rolled Krosky off Orlando and then gently laid her right arm across her waist. "Robert, please don't look at me," she cried, hiding her face with her left hand. "I don't want you to see me this way!"

"Orlando, it's okay," he said gently, sitting her up and taking her tenderly into his arms. "I think you're beautiful. Don't worry. I'll take care of you." He gently massaged her right arm and then her legs until she started to get some feeling back in her limbs. "Are you okay? How badly did he hurt you?"

"I'll be alright," she said, still not looking at him.

"Can you sit up by yourself?" he asked, helping her swing her legs to the opposite side of the bed from where Krosky lay face down on the floor.

"Yes, I think so," she said shakily. She rubbed her arms and tried to cover herself.

"Here," Robert said, taking off his shirt. "Let's put this on you." He gently lifted one arm and then the other into the sleeves of his shirt, and then helped her close the front over her bruised and swollen breasts.

"There you go," he said softly, as he helped her into the shirt.

Robert allowed her to button the shirt herself, feeling that she needed at least some semblance of modesty. She cooperated with his ministrations and then buttoned the shirt with shaking hands, all without making eye contact with Robert. "Can you stand up?" he asked, offering a helping hand.

"Yes, I think so," Orlando responded weakly. "My legs are tingling, and a little wobbly, but I think I can make it." She seemed to be regaining more emotional strength as she leaned on him both physically and psychologically. Robert helped Orlando walk around the bed toward the open door, but she stopped short when she saw Krosky face down on the rug beside the bed, the knife still protruding from his neck.

"Don't look at him," Robert said, rotating her head into his shoulder to block the view.

"I'm okay," she said weakly against his chest.

"I know you are," he said softly. Then, tenderly lifting her chin with his finger, he looked deeply into her eyes for the first time. He saw a great emptiness there, as if all life had been drained from her. "I know you probably won't understand what I'm going to tell you," he said, smiling at her. "But I'm very proud of you. It took a lot of guts to do what you did. Especially since you weren't sure if you could do it or not."

Orlando looked at him, shocked. "You understand?" she asked incredulously.

"Yes, I do," he replied with compassion. "I haven't known you long, Orlando, but I think I know you pretty well. You're a survivor. You'll do whatever it takes to protect the people you care about."

"I was so afraid they had killed you. I couldn't let them kill you, Robert," she tried to explain. "Then, when he started attacking me, I... I.."

Something in him snapped when he saw how

unsure of herself she was. He provided the words he knew she couldn't say. "You had to defend yourself," he said softly. "Come on. Let's get out of here."

They walked out of the bedroom and slowly made their way downstairs. Robert looked ahead of them, into the main room for any other gunmen. Orlando hadn't noticed it before, but Robert had his pistol drawn. He must have had it drawn when he came to get her too, she thought. There was a strange quiet in the house, and outside the silence was deafening. She hadn't kept track of how long the gunfire had been going on, but now that it was gone, she missed the constant cacophony of the fighting. It was too quiet.

Cautiously, they walked outside, blinking at the brilliance of the afternoon sun after the darkness of the inside of the house. The glaring sun was still high enough over the trees to make the stagnant heat of the late afternoon and the smell of gun smoke hang in the air. The acrid odor of human blood encircled them as they slowly made their way out onto the porch. Several of the ranch hands moved carefully among the dead gunmen, examining each one, looking for identification and checking to see if there were any survivors.

Mel's helicopter was sitting next to the bunkhouse, isolated, deserted, and Mel was nowhere in sight. Robert looked across the yard and was stunned at the measure of carnage around him.

He saw several men he knew, some on the ground, some nursing others, and the women who had been fighting the Russian soldiers so valiantly just minutes before were now nursing them. The smell of homemade casseroles floated across the courtyard on the breeze, from the direction of the maintenance shack. Evidently, the women who had been watching the children were now fixing them an early dinner. The remainder of the Russian gunmen were being rounded up and placed under guard. They went peaceably to the storage shed where they were being detained for the authorities. Joe walked up to Robert, his arm in a sling. He smiled broadly, slapped Robert on the shoulder with his good hand, and remarked, "Well, I'm glad to see you two are okay."

"How's Tia?" Robert asked when he didn't see her.

"Tia's here?" Orlando asked anxiously. She looked around her, but she didn't see her cousin. "Where is she? Is she okay?"

"You must be Orlando," Joe said, offering her his hand.

"Yes, yes, I am. Where is my cousin?" she asked again, more forcefully this time, ignoring his hand. "Robert, why would Tia be here? What does she have to do with any of this?" she added, looking pointedly at the carnage in the yard. Then, from the expression on his face, everything became suddenly too clear. "Robert, tell me Tia isn't with the Agency again!

Robert?" Orlando was becoming more angry by the minute.

Robert ignored Orlando's probing and said, "Orlando, let me introduce you to Joe Cramer. You may have heard Tia talk about him once or twice." Joe extended his hand again, and this time she shook it, a little shocked, replying, "You're Joe Cramer? I don't know what to say. Tia's told me a lot about you."

"All bad, I'm sure," he said, smiling at her. Then Joe turned to Robert and said, "Quite a girl you've got here. I've heard all kinds of things about her from Sarah." At this, Orlando blushed, rather embarrassed that they should be speaking about her, in front of her, as if she wasn't there.

"Gotta admit though, I don't care much for her tailor."

Orlando looked confused and then looked to Robert for a translation.

"The shirt," Joe clarified, smiling. "Pretty shabby, Robert. Looks like something you'd wear."

Orlando and Robert looked at him incredulously, and then to each other. Of course, Joe couldn't know what had transpired inside the house. Robert immediately took Orlando into his arms as silent tears flowed freely down her cheek. She didn't utter a word, but both men could feel her pain. "Did I say something wrong?" Joe asked quickly.

"You couldn't have known," Robert explained.

"Krosky's inside."

"I'll go take care of him," Joe said as he picked up his gun and started for the front door.

"Wait!" Robert said, putting a restraining hand on his arm. "He's dead. He tried to rape Orlando, and she stabbed him."

"Oh my God!" Joe said, staring at Orlando. "I'm sorry. I... I didn't know."

"Where's Tia?" Orlando asked weakly, ignoring his apology.

"She's fine, Orlando. She's over in the bunkhouse with the nursing staff," Joe said. Then, as she started to leave, he added, "But Orlando, before you go over there, I have to tell you something."

Orlando never heard him. She'd broken away from Robert and was moving as quickly as she could to the bunkhouse. Robert and Joe followed her. "What's the situation over there, Joe?" Robert asked frowning.

"Well, so far there are ten dead, mostly Russian," Joe answered. "One of your ranch hands didn't make it though. Then there was a small boy who got away from the women who were watching the children at the maintenance shed, and he caught a stray bullet. The total number of wounded isn't known yet, but most of them, so far at least, just have flesh wounds. The paramedics are taking care of the seriously wounded, and they are evacuating them to the nearest hospital. The Agency men and the local police are taking statements from everyone. I'm sure they'll get around to you and Orlando sooner or later. Robert, about Tia..."

"What's wrong?" Robert asked frowning.

"Well, after she freed you, she took a bullet," Joe said.

"Joe, she's not..." Robert couldn't bring himself to say it.

"No. She's alive," Joe answered. "The bullet went through the fleshy part of her right side, but it was a clean shot, and the bullet missed any vital organs. They've got a pressure bandage on it right now, and they have her lying down in the bunkhouse until they can get her on the next transport to the hospital. Unfortunately, there are a lot of people with more serious injuries than hers."

"Tia, Tia!" Orlando cried out as he neared the bunkhouse. "Tia! Where are you?"

"Orlando!" Tia replied when she saw her cousin in the doorway. She tried to sit up, but the women tending to her wouldn't hear of it. "I'm over here," she called as she waved with her good arm. "Oh, thank God you're safe!" she said, hugging Orlando for a long time.

"Are you okay?" Orlando asked Tia, frowning at the red bandage covering the side of Tia's abdomen.

"Yeah," she said smiling. "It looks worse than it is. How about you? Are you okay?" At the look on Orlando's face, she quickly regretted the question.

"Never mind," she said, taking Orlando's hand in hers and smiling gently at her cousin. "There's no need to talk about it now. I know I wish this day had never happened."

Inhaling deeply to clear her head, Orlando responded, "I know what you mean." Orlando forced herself to smile weakly. She didn't want her cousin to know what had happened in the house, at least not here, and not yet. "Tia, there's something I have to ask you."

"Yes, Orlando, what is it?" Tia asked.

"Well, Krosky had us held prisoner in the house…" Orlando began.

"Yes," she said slowly.

"When he was telling me what he had in store for me," Orlando began slowly, "he let it slip that Grouchev was on his way here to pick up the information. He said that he was coming in person." Just as Tia was about to answer her, she winced with pain.

"Here, let me look at that," one of the women nearby said.

"It's nothing, really," Tia said, arguing with the woman.

"Tia, just be still and let her take care of you, will you?" Orlando said smiling.

"Alright," she said, sitting back so the woman could attend to her wound. "But I don't want Joe to know about this. He thinks it's only a flesh wound, and I don't want him going back and telling Peter."

"Why? What has Peter got to do with this? Is he here too?" Orlando asked, confused.

"It's a long story, but he is the reason I'm here," Tia said, frowning at what the woman was doing to her side.

"I should've known," Orlando said, making a face.

"Now, don't start," Tia said after thanking the woman who was changing her dressing. "Peter's okay. Really, he is, and he cares for me very much."

"Since when did you start defending him?" Orlando asked, looking suspiciously at her cousin.

"Since we decided to get back together," Tia said, smiling.

"When did that happen?" Orlando asked, shocked.

"It's too long a story to go into now. Just be happy for me, okay, cuz?" Tia smiled and squeezed Orlando's hand.

"I am, Tia, if that's what you want," Orlando said, smiling back. "I always knew you were in love with him. You two have that kind of connection that doesn't just go away. I'm just sorry it took you two so long to realize it!"

"What are you two chatting about?" Joe asked as he walked up behind Orlando.

"Oh, nothing," they denied quickly together, smiling.

"Robert," Orlando interjected quickly, "Krosky mentioned something to me... before... that I think you should know."

"What's that?" he asked seriously. His smile faded as he waited for her to continue. "Krosky told me that Grouchev was going to come here personally for the information, for *FILE 13,"* Orlando said. "He should be here at any time from what Krosky said," she added.

"Don't worry. He wouldn't come here with all the Agency operatives around," Joe assured her.

"That just proves how wrong a person can be," said the corpulent, older man standing behind them. They all turned in unison, and faced the septuagenarian and his three armed men. They had automatic weapons pointed at the small group and were more than ready to shoot the first of them who moved. "Grouchev," Tia whispered in shock.

"Yes, my dear," he said with a heavy accent. "I remember you too. You are a very brave, but very foolish, young lady. I hope your friend," he said, stressing the word *friend,* "is not too badly hurt."

"He'll live," she answered him cautiously.

"Good," he replied before turning his attention to the other beautiful woman, standing beside the bed. "Now, Miss Corogan, if you will kindly give me the information I have so patiently waited for," he said smoothly, extending his hand.

"I... I'm afraid I can't help you," Orlando

answered him nervously. "I don't have it."

"But you can get it, can't you?" he asked slowly. "You do know where it is."

"I... I'd have to call someone," she said slowly, looking at Robert for support. "To... to have them retrieve it... from where it's been hidden," she added hesitantly.

"Good. Then shall we move into the house where you can make that call?" He motioned for them to precede the gunmen by the door.

Tia couldn't move, but she looked terrified for her cousin. "We'll be back soon, Tia," Orlando assured her. "Don't worry about me," she said reassuringly to her frightened cousin. "I'll be okay."

"I suggest," Grouchev began, once they had started walking across the compound, "that you make your phone call from the house as quickly as possible, Miss Corogan. And Miss Corogan, if any ideas of calling out for help, just remember your cousin Tia. Mr. Taylor, you might also want to think about your injured friend, Mr. Cramer."

"We'll remember," Orlando replied angrily.

Grouchev led them all into the house without saying another word. Orlando walked slowly over to the telephone and made the requisite call to Sally at her office. Orlando prayed that Sally would still be there, and that she'd answer the private line.

"Sally?" Orlando asked when the phone was answered. "This is Orlando. Yes, I'm fine. I can't talk long, so please listen carefully." Grouchev and the others could only hear Orlando's side of the call, so she was very careful how she phrased her answers to Sally's questions and comments. "I need you to retrieve that envelope from the safekeeping place. Do you remember where it is? Good. Someone will be by shortly to pick it up. When will I be back?" Orlando repeated the question for the benefit of those standing around her. "I really can't say, for now. Probably when the cat crows," Orlando commented casually. She looked up at Robert and Joe, but they gave no indication that they'd noticed what she'd said. Grouchev was motioning for her to get off the phone. "I have to run now. Make sure you feed my dog for me, okay? Good. Okay, bye-bye."

Orlando knew that Grouchev couldn't know that she didn't have a dog, and he didn't indicate that he'd detected her remark about the cat crowing. These two phrases were a part of a code she'd worked out with Sally many years earlier, which she could use in case she was in trouble.

As soon as Orlando used the phrases, Sally knew that Orlando was in deep trouble. After they hung up, Sally immediately contacted Orlando's attorney and told him to follow Orlando's instructions about the reserved confidential communication to the letter. He was to personally deliver the envelope, unopened, to the person whose name appeared on the front... and to no one else! "We need you to do that immediately!

Can you do that?" Sally asked anxiously.

"I understand. I will take care of it immediately," he assured her.

Robert and Joe exchanged glances. They knew that something was up because Orlando had said some rather bizarre things on the phone, but they didn't mention it. Finally, Robert asked Grouchev, "Now what?"

"Now we wait for my man in New York to call me when he has *FILE 13* in his possession. If you lied to me, you will be killed. If not," he said, shrugging, "I may let you live."

"Just like that?" Robert asked.

"No, Mr. Taylor, not just like that. You, Ms. Johnson, and Mr. Cramer will accompany me back to Moscow where you will be my... guests for an extended visit. When you have told me all I want to know about your Agency and how you acquired *FILE 13* in the first place, you may return home."

"Sure, we could go home, but to where?" Joe asked angrily. "After you get what you want from us, it'll look like we're traitors, and if we don't get thrown into prison by our government, we'll probably be shot by accident on the street."

"Yes, it is a pity, but you are probably correct," he agreed, nodding his head. "If you like," Grouchev said, grinning at him, "you will be welcome to stay in Siberia as long as you like. We can always find need for individuals with your type of skills."

"I think I'll pass," Robert stated emphatically.

"In that case," Grouchev replied, "I regret I will have to have you shot!"

He nodded at the three men who stood behind him, and then motioned to Robert, Joe and Orlando. Grouchev told his men to lead the three away from the house, and to be as quiet about it as possible. They were then to report back to him when the job was finished. The three men nodded and then led them outside the back of the house to a waiting car. Reluctantly, Joe, Robert, and Orlando followed the gunmen's instructions, and climbed into the back seat of the waiting car. Orlando looked at Robert as he fiddled with his watch. She watch him turn the dial on his watch three times counter-clockwise, and then one time back clockwise. He looked up and saw her watching him, and he smiled at her with the same mischievous look he had in his eyes before they were with Krosky. Orlando was praying that he was more successful, regardless of what he was planning.

As they drove down the dirt driveway, past the last of the rescue vehicles, Orlando thought she saw something move at the side of the road, but she wasn't sure. Then, all of a sudden, the driver cursed in Russian, slammed on the brakes, and skidded to a stop. There was what appeared to be several dead bodies in the middle of the road. When the car stopped, all three of the gunmen climbed out of the car, confirming that the doors were locked and that their prisoners couldn't escape. When the three gunman moved in closer to examine the dead bodies, they realized that the corpses weren't corpses at all. There were several mannequins dressed in civilian clothes, and their limbs fell apart and slipped out of the shirts and pants when the gunmen prodded the bodies with their guns. Orlando watched, transfixed. The movement she had thought she'd seen at the side of the road was actually additional agents. There were at least 30 agents who moved simultaneously in their attack on the Russian gunmen, taking them completely by surprise. The agents were able to capture and disarm the gunmen before they had a chance to discharge even one bullet out of their guns.

"God, am I glad to see you!" Robert exclaimed shaking hands with the agent in charge after the three of them were released from the car. "What the hell took you so long?"

"We ran into a few problems," the man said, smiling apologetically. "To begin with, they had blocked the road after you were taken into the house, using a couple of burned out vehicles. I guess they expecting us to try to rescue you. Then, we went into the house to find you, and all we found was Krosky's dead body in the master bedroom." At this, Orlando looked down at the ground. She didn't want to be part of this conversation.

"We asked around, and some of the ranch hands said they saw you three going into the house to discuss business with four men in grey suits, but no one saw you leave. We figured they'd try to sneak you out the back, and so a group of us came down here on foot so we could intercept them on the way out of the ranch." One of the other men joined in the conversation, asking, "Speaking of men in grey suits, I only count three. Where is the fourth?"

Orlando, Robert, and Joe answered, almost in unison. "Grouchev is back at the house." The agent in charge looked stunned, staring at the three with his mouth open.

"Grouchev," explained Joe, "was in the house with us. He must still be there waiting for news of our *termination*."

"Joe, Orlando, would you like to come with me to deliver the news to him personally?" Robert asked, grinning at his companions. "Take care of these guys, will you?" Robert asked the lead man, patting him companionable on the shoulder. Without waiting for an answer, Orlando and Joe followed Robert back into the car and drove back up the driveway to the house. The car screeched to a halt outside the back door and the three jumped out and ran inside. It was dead quiet inside the house. They systematically searched every room, but Grouchev was gone, and there was no one else in the house.

"We were the only ones on the road," said Orlando, trying to figure out where he could've gone. "Do you think he tried to get out of here on foot?"

"Not likely," Joe said. "He suffers from a pretty bad case of gout. Besides, he wouldn't make it a mile in these woods, and he knows it."

"The helicopter!" Robert exclaimed. "That's the only answer! Come on!" he shouted over his shoulder as he headed for the door. When they reached the main compound, they could hear the chopper engine revving up, and they could see the blades starting to turn slowly. Before they could reach it, Mel's helicopter was up in the air.

Robert ran to the closest armed man and grabbed his rifle. But by the time he was able to lock and load it, and then aim it at the helicopter, it was out of range. Grouchev could just barely be seen waving from the passenger seat. "Now what are we going to do?" Joe asked Robert in disgust.

Robert didn't answer Joe right away, but watched to see which direction the helicopter was headed. "Now," Robert began slowly, "we go inside and call the Sherriff's office and report a stolen helicopter. Then we contact the Agency headquarters and tell them to coordinate with the local sheriff so that they can be on the scene when the chopper crashes so that they can retrieve Grouchev," he said, grinning. Joe looked at him confused, so he added, putting an arm around Joe's shoulder as he spoke, "You see, old pal, that helicopter couldn't have much fuel in it after all the time Mel spent in the air, and the direction Grouchev took, takes him over nothing but farmland

and woods. There isn't a decent place to land that thing for a good forty or fifty miles."

They all laughed at that, and walked slowly back into the house. "Orlando," Robert asked slyly, "now could you please explain what all that nonsense was about when you were on the phone with Sally? You don't have a dog, and since when does a cat crow?"

"Well," she replied, smiling meekly. "When I left to meet you Friday night--that seems so long ago now--I didn't know if you were working with Hartt or not. So I worked out a code with Sally just in case. When I told her about the cat crowing, she knew that I was in trouble. When I asked her to feed the dog, that meant she should deliver the *FILE 13* to the proper authorities right away."

"You mean you actually thought I was your father's killer?" Robert asked, looking incredulous and insulted, all at the same time.

"Well, you have to understand," she answered him, blushing. "I didn't know you as well then as I do now."

"Then the Russian Mafia never got ahold of the hard copy of the *FILE 13* information?" Joe asked.

"Right," Orlando confirmed, matter-of-factly. "Unfortunately, I don't think I will ever find my father's killer now."

"That's not exactly right, Orlando," Robert said gently. "What do you mean?" she asked, confused. "You see, I wasn't sure Krosky was your father's killer until I saw him with you today," he explained.

Orlando stared at him wide-eyed, and all the color drained from her face, but Robert continued anyway. "When he saw you for the first time, he looked like he'd seen a ghost. You're so much like your father that Krosky lost it, just for a minute. But that was all I needed to convince me."

Orlando stared straight ahead of her, remembering the scene in the bedroom. Everything faded from her view but Krosky's face. "Krosky!" was all she said. Then she looked at Robert who was watching her closely. There was a silent understanding between them that was beyond words.

"Just out of curiosity," Joe asked, "who did you deliver the *FILE 13* information to?"

"The person who came up with the name," she said, smiling.

"I don't understand," Robert interjected.

Orlando explained, "Back when my dad was with the Agency, even before Tia started working with you guys, there was a security leak pretty high up in the pentagon. The only one everyone knew they could trust was in the White House. They had a list made up of all the double agents in Europe so they could keep track of their movements, and then they put it on microfilm for safe keeping. They couldn't think of a name for it that would confuse the other side, so they had a brainstorming session late one night at the White House. They were all sitting around trying to think of something, and then one of the generals asked my dad to retrieve one of a slips of paper out of the circular file, or *FILE 13*. Everyone on the committee thought it would be a great joke, and a pretty secure name for the list. So, that's how one of the most dangerous pieces of top secret information in the world got its name," she concluded, smiled broadly. Then, she added softly, as if she were speaking to herself, "That was one of my favorite bedtime stories when I was growing up. I never realized it was actually true. Daddy told me so many fascinating, fantastic stories about his work that I never knew what was pretend and what was true."

Just then the telephone rang. Joe picked it up and said, rather surprised, "Hello. Yes, yes, she is. Just a minute please."

"Who is it?" Robert asked.

"It's the White House, and Orlando, they want to talk to you!"

Orlando just stared at Joe. She didn't move to pick up the phone. She just stared at him like he was crazy.

"Orlando," Joe said, holding out the phone. "The president is on the phone, and he's waiting to talk to you!" He motioned to her with his other hand. "Come on! Hurry up!"

Spellbound, Orlando stood up and walked over to the phone. Grasping the receiver in her trembling hands, she spoke in a quivering, hushed tone. "Hello,

Mr. President?"

Chapter 11

THE PRESIDENT SPOKE with Orlando at length, thanking her for all her good work, telling her how proud her father would have been. He invited her to visit him at the White House later that year, and wished her the best of luck in all her endeavors. Then he asked to speak to Joe and Robert. He congratulated them each in turn, and offered them each the same invitation. He asked them to send his regards to Tia and Peter in the hospital, and to please tell them that they would be hearing from him when they were stronger.

The head of the Agency called to congratulate Robert and Joe on a job well done, and to thank Orlando for her courage and assistance in securing *File 13*. "There were a lot of lives riding on what you did, Miss Corogan, and I can't thank you enough on their behalf."

The head of the Agency next offered her an open invitation to join the Agency, whenever she wished to accept. "You've got a good head on your shoulders," he complimented her. "And we could use someone like you." Orlando laughed at that, and said that she'd think about it.

After the phone calls, Robert tried to help his

foreman return things to normal around the ranch, or at least as much as possible, under the circumstances. The agents from the local Agency bureau had returned to their offices, taking with them the surviving Russian Mafia gunmen for interrogation. The ranch hands who hadn't been hurt assisted the paramedics in moving those who had been wounded to the nearby hospital. Tia was taken to Florida Hospital, where she was put on the same floor with Peter. They had asked for a room together, but the doctors felt that their recovery might be delayed if they socialized too much.

Two months passed before Tia and Peter were fully recovered, and returned to their respective positions and put on active duty status with the Agency. In the meantime, Orlando and Robert were inseparable. They flew from the ranch to New York, where they dined every night and ate lunch together every day between meetings. They took long walks in Central Park, and they sailed on the choppy New York Harbor waters around the Statue of Liberty. They flew down to Orlando, Florida several times to visit Tia and Peter as they recovered and they joined them for picnics near Lake Eola, and for a day at Walt Disney World. As the spring wore on, the love between Tia and Peter renewed itself, and the bond between Orlando and Robert blossomed. Robert was very supportive of Orlando when she told him about the attempted rape, and he helped her work through her violent emotions toward men as a result of the experience. Eventually, the pain eased, and the nightmares she had had every night since the incident became less frequent. Orlando returned to her business with unaccustomed vigor, now that her arch-enemy Daniel Hartt was nowhere to be found.

Grouchev had not been seen or heard from since he disappeared in the helicopter that day on Robert's ranch. The police had searched everywhere in a 500 square-mile radius around the ranch, and didn't find any sign of wreckage. Eventually, the search was called off. The Agency sent out probes, and the only information they could retrieve was that he had somehow slipped out of the country. Orlando had to be questioned by the police since she was responsible for Krosky's death, but since it was obviously self-defense, it was treated as a formality, and she wasn't charged.

The first days of summer passed quickly, and two announcements made the society pages. Peter and Tia announced their engagement, and Orlando and Robert decided to make it a double wedding. The second announcement, which also rocked the financial community, came one week later. Orlando Corogan announced that she was moving Investment International corporate headquarters to Florida so that she could be closer to her future husband. The wedding would be coming up quickly, and Orlando busied herself with the move to Florida. They would be married in her their newly remodeled home on Robert Taylor's ranch. The honeymoon, which the couples decided to share, would be a cruise to the Caribbean.

The wedding was over, and the newlyweds spent their wedding night at the ranch. The guests stayed over for breakfast and then a dip in the Olympic-sized pool, still decorated from the festivities of the previous night. The fresh flowers and Japanese lanterns still complimented the gazebo where the marriage ceremony had taken place. Orlando and Robert strolled out to it and were surprised to find that Tia and Peter had already beaten them there.

"What do you say we get an early start on this honeymoon?" Peter asked Tia.

"That sounds good to us," Robert said, surprising the embracing couple. They all laughed, and then headed back to the house and their guests. They ate a leisurely breakfast and then said goodbye to their guests. Once the house was empty, the foursome packed and headed out to the highway. They drove down the Sunshine State Parkway at a leisurely pace to Miami, where they would catch the ship. They made frequent stops to sight-see, as Robert was the only one from Florida. They didn't have to catch the shuttle to the docks until the following morning, so they were in no rush. The foursome reveled in the beauty of the unspoiled countryside and the warmth of the climate and the people. They stopped and bought watermelon and boiled peanuts to munch on in the car. Finally, they arrived in Miami, and the twinkling lights of the big city welcomed them. They passed art deco buildings and palm trees, skimpy bathing suits, and neon signs. But the charm of the South's most famous city didn't pass them by. Robert pulled into the parking lot for the Doral Hotel, one of Miami's best. The valet took the keys to the car and gave the luggage to the concierge. Peter went to the desk, registered the four of them, and picked up their keys, and they followed their luggage to their respective rooms, where they freshened up for a night on the town. They dined at one of Miami's finest restaurants, and then made a round of the nightclubs where they danced and celebrated until the early hours of the morning.

The following morning, after a 6:00 a.m. wakeup call, the two couples dressed hurriedly and caught a quick cup of coffee before boarding the shuttle bus to the dock where they met their ship. The cruise line offered a complimentary breakfast on deck for passengers and guests, and the honeymooners enjoyed the crowd. Walking along the deck, the two couples reveled in the good fortune they'd had, and the happiness to come. With all the adventure and danger behind them, they were prepared to settle back and enjoy the cruise.

The ship blew the horn to signal departure, and crowds of people lined the dock to see the ship off.

Relatives, friends, and even excited onlookers waved frantically as the tugboats guided the cruise ship away from the dock. Among the throngs of people on the dock stood a very quiet, sober man. He stood by himself, apart from the crowd, even though he was surrounded by people. He wore a grey suit and a matching hat, shading most of his face. His clothing was much too heavy for a warm Florida summer, and it was obvious that the heat did not suit him. He was squat and older, and he was hunched over as if he'd lost something and was concentrating on finding it. Someone accidently bumped into him, and he excused himself softly, politely, with a heavy Russian accent. A woman smiled at him, and he tipped his hat to her in a friendly reply. He then turned his attention back to the retreating ship, and the two couples he'd located on the promenade deck, waving from the rail. Quietly, to himself, he said in Russian, "Goodbye. Goodbye to you too, from Krosky, my son!"

The two couples didn't see him, and there was nothing obvious to spoil their planned day of fun. All of the passengers were milling around the decks of the ship now, feasting on the meal the crew had laid out for them. There was cracked crab, shrimp, and several different cuts of meat, including prime rib and freshly smoked ham. There was a breakfast bar with eggs and bacon, kippers, and pastries. There was even a gourmet salad bar for those who were diet-conscious. Waiters walked around with trays of steaming hot coffee, champagne, and fresh Florida orange juice. As the two men ate steadily, the two women joked about having to go on a diet when they returned. A small combo played a light jazz tune, setting the mood for the revelers.

Above deck, everything was peaceful, friendly, and warm. Above deck, everything was romantic and right with the world. There was love, friendship, and companionable friendliness, even among strangers. This was what Robert and Orlando, and Tia and Peter had sought for so long. *Finally!* They had found peace. Below deck, however, below even where the crew slept and the engineers manned the power that propelled the ship, in the cargo hold where it was cool, almost cold and damp, everything was definitely not quiet. The creaking wood of the deck above was audible, and the hum of the smoothly running engines made a staccato rhythm that one could have danced to, if there were room, if one dared.

The cargo hold was full of crates and baggage that had flowed over from the upper holds, things that could be forgotten until the ship reached port. Down there, in the darkness, little red eyes stared blindly, and furry creatures scampered around looking for food. In the cargo hold, the cool dampness lent a strange eeriness to the scene. Down here, in the long-forgotten bowels of the ship, was a small package nestled in with the crates containing all types of paraphernalia. This brightly colored box stood out among the drab, colorless dimness where only emergency lighting provided relief. A small rodent paused in his journey across the crate above it to stare. It was as if he had heard it speaking softly to him. While the party continued above deck, with more food and drinks being brought out for the passengers, the rodent and the brightly colored box below held a conversation. The rodent squeaked at the box. The box, in return said, *"Tick, tick ... tick, tick... tick, tick."*

About the Author

File 13 is the first book in the *Terror by the Numbers* series and we are looking forward to her next book, *Rapture 42*, in 2017.

Elizabeth Leavens is the fictional pen name of Dr. Elizabeth Cruickshank, in honor of her parents. She lives in Virginia with her husband and her two sets of twins.

Be sure to visit her Facebook page **File-13-by-Elizabeth-Leavens** and learn more about the series and the latest news about her upcoming books. She welcomes your feedback on the books and looks forward to connecting with you on Facebook.

63792096R00260

Made in the USA
Middletown, DE
09 February 2018